THE BONE HOUSE

Other Books by Stephen R. Lawhead

King Raven Trilogy:
Hood
Scarlet
Tuck

Patrick, Son of Ireland

Celtic Crusades:
The Iron Lance
The Black Rood
The Mystic Rose

Byzantium

Song of Albion Trilogy:
The Paradise War
The Silver Hand
The Endless Knot

The Pendragon Cycle:
Taliesin
Merlin
Arthur
Pendragon
Grail
Avalon

Empyrion I: The Search for Fierra
Empyrion II: The Siege of Dome

Dream Thief

The Dragon King Trilogy:
In the Hall of the Dragon King
The Warlords of Nin
The Sword and the Flame

BRIGHT EMPIRES **QUEST THE SECOND:**

THE BONE HOUSE

STEPHEN R. LAWHEAD

LION FICTION

What Readers Are Saying about The Bright Empires Series

"**His mastery of the art of description is beyond belief** (I had to stop several times to jump up and down because I loved his style so much, seriously). His level of attention to details like period mindset and speech is a delight to behold (especially for die-hard background-first novelists like me)."

Sir Emeth M.

"This is **a story that has it all**: mystery, history, damsels in distress, and a mind-bending meditation on the nature of reality. It is equal parts *Raiders of the Lost Ark*, *National Treasure*, and *Jumper*. Highly recommended!"

Chad J.

"**Filled with descriptions that beguile all five senses** and all the beauty and charm of the language I have come to expect from Lawhead, this book is **a fascinating blend of fantasy and sci-fi**."

Jenelle S.

"… **a *hold-your-breath* beginning to a new series**. This novel mixes ancient history, time travel, alternate realities, mystery, physics, and fantasy, to create a story so compelling that **I find myself recommending it to any who will listen**."

Sheila P.

"[A] sure winner for eager sci-fi readers... The vivid imagery and witty lines help keep the reader on the edge of their seat."

Jerry P.

"**Time travel and high adventure abound** in this brand new title from veteran author Stephen R. Lawhead."

Ben H.

"**Imagine Narnia merged with *Hitchhiker's Guide***, and you have a starting point for the adventures of Kit Livingstone."

Rick M.

"Lawhead vividly describes the sights, sounds and smells of the markets in Prague, the streets of Restoration England, and even the dry heat of Ancient Egypt... **The premise of ley line travel is fascinating yet mysterious**, with scientific definitions that are detailed without becoming too technical. The characters are personable and complex, and **it's easy to get caught up in their search for that elusive map**."

Malinda D.

"... **an excellent, mysterious storyline** that draws the reader in."

Kieran

To find out more about Stephen R. Lawhead
visit: www.stephenlawhead.com
or: www.facebook.com/StephenRLawhead

Text copyright © Stephen Lawhead 2011
This edition © Lion Hudson 2013

The right of Stephen Lawhead to be identified as the
author of this work has been asserted by him in accordance
with the Copyright, Designs and Patents Act 1988.

Published by Lion Fiction
an imprint of
Lion Hudson plc
Wilkinson House, Jordan Hill Road,
Oxford OX2 8DR, England
www.lionhudson.com/fiction

ISBN 978 1 78264 012 7
e-ISBN 978 1 78264 035 6

Acknowledgments
Cover design © 2011 Thomas Nelson, Inc.

A catalogue record for this book is available from the
British Library

Printed and bound in the UK, February 2013, LH26

For Suzie

"The distinction between past, present, and future is only an illusion – albeit a persistent one."

ALBERT EINSTEIN, PHYSICIST

Contents

Important People

Anen – Friend of *Arthur Flinders-Petrie*, high priest of the temple of Amun in Egypt, Eighteenth dynasty.

Archelaeus Burleigh, Earl of Sutherland – Nemesis of *Flinders-Petrie, Cosimo, Kit,* and all right-thinking people.

Arthur Flinders-Petrie – Also known as *The Man Who Is Map*, patriarch of his line. Begat *Benedict*, who begat *Charles*, who begat *Douglas*.

Balthazar Bazalgette – The Lord High Alchemist at the Court of *Rudolf II* in Prague, friend and confidant of *Wilhelmina*.

Burley Men – *Con, Dex, Mal,* and *Tav.* Lord *Burleigh's* henchmen. They keep a Stone Age cat called *Baby*.

Cosimo Christopher Livingstone, the Elder, aka **Cosimo** – a Victorian gentleman who seeks to reunite the Skin Map and understand the key to the future.

Cosimo Christopher Livingstone, the Younger, aka **Kit** – *Cosimo's* great-grandson.

Emperor Rudolf – King of Bohemia and Hungary, Archduke of Austria and King of the Romans, he is also known as the Holy Roman Emperor and is quite mad.

Engelbert Stifflebeam – A baker from Rosenheim in Germany, affectionately known as **Etzel.**

Giles Standfast – *Sir Henry Fayth's* coachman and *Kit's* ally.

Gustavus Rosenkreuz – The Chief Assistant to the Lord High Alchemist and *Wilhelmina's* ally.

Lady Haven Fayth – *Sir Henry's* headstrong and mercurial niece.

Sir Henry Fayth, Lord Castlemain – member of the Royal Society, staunch friend and ally of *Cosimo*. *Haven's* uncle.

Jakub Arnostovi – *Wilhelmina's* landlord and business partner.

Snipe – Feral child, and malignant aide to *Douglas Flinders-Petrie*.

Wilhelmina Klug, aka **Mina** – In another life, a London baker and *Kit's* girlfriend. In this life, owns Prague's Grand Imperial Kaffeehaus with *Etzel*.

Xian-Li – Wife of *Arthur Flinders-Petrie* and mother of *Benedict*. Daughter of the tattooist *Wu Chen Hu* of Macao.

Previously

Our story thus far concerns an underemployed but agreeable young fellow named Cosimo Christopher Livingstone, who much prefers to go by the name of Kit. He is related by birth to an anachronistic old gentleman named Cosimo, who is in fact his long-lost great-grandfather: long lost in that, owing to circumstances arising from the phenomenon known as ley travel (about which, more later), he disappeared more than a hundred years or so ago while on a routine visit to the local shops.

Cosimo's return was greeted by Kit with disbelief, astonishment, and chagrin. The elder relation's insistence that Kit should accompany him on a quest of great significance was rebuffed and, after a fleeting taste of this heretofore unheard of ley travel, Kit retreated to the arms of his unpleasant girlfriend, Wilhelmina Klug. Due to the time drift involved in ley journeys, he arrived quite late for a long-promised shopping excursion.

When the explanation for his tardiness failed to convince this young woman, Kit endeavoured to provide her with a practical demonstration. Owing to his inexperience, the demo went horribly wrong and poor Wilhelmina was lost in the transition. However, Kit was found once more by Cosimo, who introduced him to a stalwart colleague by the name of Sir Henry Fayth. Together the three of them set out to find Wilhelmina and return her to her proper place and time.

Laudable as their concern may have been, it ultimately proved misplaced. Wilhelmina landed on her feet in seventeenth-century Prague, where she was befriended by a kindly soul named Engelbert "Etzel" Stiffelbeam, a baker from Rosenheim who had travelled to Bohemia to seek his fortune. The two joined forces and opened a bakery, the success of which remained elusive until they introduced an as-yet-unheard-of commodity to the capital: coffee. The Grand Imperial Kaffeehaus was an immediate success, and soon all of Old Prague was abuzz over the latest sensation.

The coffee house brought Wilhelmina into contact with members of the court of Emperor Rudolf II, and among these a coterie of alchemists who were dutifully employed in the pursuit of arcane studies in what is to this day known as the Magick Court.

Now we come to the concept of ley travel, or ley leaping as Lady Fayth, Sir Henry's mercurial niece, is wont to call it. Ley travel consists of utilizing, or manipulating, lines of electromagnetic force that are to be found embedded in the earth, thereby employing these lines of force by methods yet to be described by science to effect great leaps in not only distance but dimensional reality and, consequently, time as well. The reader is asked to bear in mind that *ley* travel is not the same as *time* travel, strictly speaking. Although it must be admitted that, owing to the fact that time is relative to the reality being visited, ley travellers do come unstuck in time, which leads to a sort of chronological dislocation – an unavoidable side effect of ley leaping. It would be pleasant to report that all times everywhere in the universe are the same and that each reality links up perfectly end-to-end, but that is not the case. For reasons described below, each separate reality has its own history and progression in its own time. Thus, travelling to a different dimension involves a sideways slip in time as well as place, but that is not the same as travelling backwards or forwards along a single timeline in a discrete reality.

How many ley lines there are and where they lead, nobody really knows. Nor is it known how they are produced, or why. But one man knew more than most: the explorer Arthur Flinders-Petrie, an intrepid soul who made countless trips to other worlds and meticulously recorded his discoveries on a map. So that he could always find his way home again and so that he could never be separated from his map, he had it tattooed onto his torso in the form of coded symbols – not the most original plan, of course, but highly effective and productive too, in that it allowed him to meet and marry his Chinese tattooist's charming daughter, Xian-Li. Arthur shared with his new wife his passion for exploration, introducing her to the arcane secrets of ley travel. On one such early trip to Egypt, tragedy struck in the form of Nile fever, and the stricken Xian-Li succumbed and died.

At some later time, Arthur died also, and in order that his discoveries should not die with him the map was removed and carefully preserved; for among the many wonders he encountered in his travels there was one that was so amazing, so staggeringly important, that Arthur kept it a close-guarded secret from all but his nearest and dearest kin. Through circumstances yet to be explained, the map was divided into sections, and those sections scattered across the multi-verse. Happily, the Skin Map and its tantalizing secret endure.

Flinders-Petrie has a nemesis – Archelaeus Burleigh, the Earl of Sutherland – an unscrupulous dastard who is wholly obsessed with possessing the map and learning its secrets. He and his nefarious crew will stop at nothing to discover the treasure.

At the end of our first instalment of this tale, Kit and his companion Giles were facing eminent demise in the tomb of Anen at the hands of Lord Burleigh – the same tomb that had already claimed the lives of dear old Cosimo and Sir Henry. Wilhelmina, whose presence in the chase had been understated up to that point, made a sudden and welcome appearance – all the more so because Lady Fayth had proved too fickle. Loyalty, it seems, is a rare and precious commodity in whichever reality one occupies.

With those things remembered, we return to our story, in which some things are best forgotten.

Part **I**

The Book of
Forbidden Secrets

CHAPTER 1

In Which Some Things are Best Forgotten

From a snug in the corner of the Museum Tavern, Douglas Flinders-Petrie dipped a sop of bread into the gravy of his steak and kidney pudding and watched the entrance to the British Museum across the street. The great edifice was dark, the building closed to the public for over three hours. The employees had gone home, the charwomen had finished their cleaning, and the high iron gates were locked behind them. The courtyard was empty and, outside the gates, there were fewer people on the street now than an hour ago. He felt no sense of urgency: only keen anticipation, which he savoured as he took another draught of London Pride. He had spent most of the afternoon in the museum, once more marking the doors and exits, the blind spots, the rooms where a person might hide and remain unseen by the night watchmen, of which there were but three to cover the entire acreage of the sprawling institution.

Douglas knew from his researches that at eleven each night the head watchman retired to his office on the ground floor to make tea. He would be duly joined by his two underling guards, and the three would enter their observations in the logbook and then spend an enjoyable thirty minutes drinking their tea, eating pies, and exchanging gossip.

While they were thus occupied, he would strike.

The pub was quiet tonight, even for a damp Thursday in late November. There were only five other patrons in the place: three

16

at the rail and two at tables. He would have preferred more people – if only so his own presence would not be as noticeable – but he doubted it would make much difference. In any event, there was nothing he could do about it.

"Everything all right, sir?"

Douglas turned from the window and looked up. The landlord, having little to do this evening, was making the rounds and chatting with his customers.

"Never better," replied Douglas in a tone he hoped would dismiss further intrusion. But the man remained hovering over the table.

"Mr Flinders-Petrie, is it not, sir?"

"Indeed so." He offered a bland smile to cover his annoyance at being recognized on this night of all nights. "I fear you have me at a disadvantage. I was not aware that my name would be common knowledge."

The landlord chuckled. "No, I suppose not. But do you not recognize me, sir?"

Douglas looked more closely at him. There was a vague familiarity about the fellow, but… no, he could not place him.

"Cumberbatch, sir," the landlord volunteered. "I worked for your father, I did. Oh, quite a few years ago." At Douglas's dubious expression, he said, "I was his footman – Silas."

"Silas! Certainly, I remember you," Douglas lied. "Do forgive me. Yes, of course, now that you remind me."

" 'Course, I was younger then, and you were away at school and university and whatnot." The landlord wiped his hands on the towel around his waist and smoothed it out as if this put the matter to rest. "Happy days they were."

"Yes, yes," agreed Douglas amiably. He was aware that the other patrons were watching them, and actually relieved now that the place was not more crowded. "Happy times, indeed."

"Pardon my asking, sir," said Cumberbatch, leaning nearer the table. He lowered his voice. "If you don't mind, there's something that I've always wanted to know. I'd be most obliged."

"I'd be happy to help if I can, Silas. What is it?"

"Did they ever find the man who killed your father?"

To buy himself a little space to think, Douglas took a drink of his ale, then, placing the glass carefully on the table, said, "I am sorry to say they never did."

"Oh dear, oh dear." Cumberbatch shook his head. "That's a right pity. Did they never have a suspicion, then?"

"Suspicions, yes," replied Douglas, "but nothing more. The coroner's verdict at the time of the inquest reads 'unlawful killing by person or persons unknown'. At this late date, I fear it is likely to remain a mystery."

"Ah, dear me," sighed Cumberbatch. "That is a shame, that is. He was a good man, your father – a very decent chap, if you don't mind my saying. A solid and upright fellow – always treated me well, and that's a fact, that is."

"Yes, well, as you say it was all a long time ago. Perhaps it is best forgotten."

"No doubt, sir. I'm with you there." Cumberbatch brightened once more. "But it is good to see you, Mr Flinders-Petrie. Here, now, can I get you another pint?"

"Thank you, but no, I –"

"On the house, sir – for old time's sake. It would please me no end."

"Very well, then. Thank you, Silas. I would enjoy that."

"Coming right up, sir."

The landlord beetled off to pull the pint. Douglas drew his pocket-watch from his waistcoat and flipped it open. It was half past nine. In another hour he would make his move. Until then, he had a warm place to wait and watch. The landlord returned with his pint and, after another brief exchange, he was left alone to finish it and his meal in peace.

It was after ten thirty when he finally rose and, promising to return for another visit next time he was in the neighbourhood, retrieved his black cape from the coat-rack and went out into the mist and drizzle. The weather was perfect for his purposes – a miserable night meant fewer folk around to notice any peculiar comings and goings. The gas lamps hissed and fluttered, pale orbs that did little to cut the all-pervading fog. Perfect.

He smiled to himself as he walked to the corner of Montague Street, turned, and proceeded along the side of the museum to where the service alley joined the street at the rear of the building. There he paused to observe the street one last time; a lone hansom cab rattled away in the opposite direction, and two men in top hats staggered along – one in the gutter, the other on the pavement – oblivious to their surroundings, singing their way home from an evening's celebration.

Satisfied, he ducked into the alleyway and hurried quickly and unerringly in the dark to the back of a town house opposite the rear of the museum. There, lying in the lane beside the house, was the wooden ladder. With swift efficiency, he placed it against the high iron railing, climbed to the top of the fence, balanced on the upper bar while he pulled over the ladder, then climbed down. Once on the ground, he hurried to a window near the corner of the enormous building where even the lowest windows were eight feet off the ground. Positioning the ladder, he climbed up and rapped on the glass, counted to ten, and then rapped again.

As he finished the second tap, the window slid open from inside and a pale face, round like a solemn little moon, appeared in the darkness of the opening.

"Well done, Snipe," said Douglas. "Hand me in."

The stocky boy reached out and, with strong arms, pulled his master through the open window.

"Now then," said Douglas, drawing a small tin from his pocket. He flipped open the lid and shook out a few congreves, selected one, and swiped the head against the roughened top of the tin. The slender stick of soft pine erupted with a pop and spluttering red flame. "The lantern, Snipe."

The youth held up a small paraffin lamp; Douglas raised the glass and touched the match to the wick, then lowered the glass and waved the spent stick in the air to cool it before placing it back in the tin. "Let us be about our business."

By lantern's glow they made their way through the darkened stacks of the Smirke Bequest – a small, shelf-lined chamber off the great cavernous hall of the Reading Room. This cosy enclave was given to certain exceptional volumes from the libraries of wealthy patrons who had donated or bequeathed their collections to the national archive for the general benefit of their fellow men. This ever-growing collection housed a particular volume that had long eluded Douglas Flinders-Petrie. It was this book he had come to acquire.

The Rare Books Room, as it was more commonly known, was strictly forbidden to all but the most eminent scholars, and then entry was granted only in the company of the Keeper of Antiquities or one of his assistants, who would unlock the chain at the doorway – there was no door, so that the books could be viewed from a distance even if they could not be perused – and usher the chosen one into the inner sanctum. White cotton gloves were to be worn at all times in the room, and no one was permitted to remain alone in the stacks at any time whatsoever. Douglas, having observed this exacting protocol on his survey trips to the museum, decided to forego the formalities and visit the room outside of public hours.

It had then been a matter of finding a place for Snipe to hide until well after closing: a storage cupboard in Room 55 on the upper floor was adequate to the purpose, and so, during a late-afternoon viewing of the Nineveh alabasters, Douglas had deposited his able servant in the closet with a cold pie and an apple to wait until the clock in Saint Bartholomew's chimed eleven. At the appointed hour, Snipe had crawled out and made his way down to the Rare Books Room to let Douglas in through the window.

So far so good.

"Go to the door and keep watch," Douglas commanded, directing the glow of the lantern towards the nearer stacks. As the servant moved to the doorway, Douglas began scanning the shelves. The books, he quickly discovered, were arranged in a loose chronological order – no doubt owing to their primary interest as artefacts rather than for the value of their contents. He found the proper historical period and started working down the line book by book. What should have been a task of moments, however, dragged on far longer than he planned, owing to the fact that many of the older books had no titles on their spines or covers and had to be drawn out, opened, and thumbed to their title pages before being placed back on the shelf.

He was only partway through the 1500s when he heard a sibilant hiss – like that of gas escaping from a leaky pipe. He stopped, held his breath… waited. The sound came again and was repeated. He quickly turned down the lantern wick and put the lamp on the floor, then hurried to the doorway, where Snipe stood behind the doorpost, peering out into the great hall of the main reading room.

"Someone coming?" Douglas whispered.

Snipe nodded and held up two fingers.

"Two of them. Right." Douglas turned and retreated into the stacks. "Follow me."

They crept off to the furthest corner of the room, placing the main body of stacks between themselves and the door.

"Get down," whispered Douglas.

The two pressed themselves flat to the floor and waited. Voices drifted into the room, and then footsteps could be heard as the watchmen made their rounds of the Reading Room. Shadows leapt from the stacks as one of the guards paused and shone his lantern into the room with a practised sweep. Then the footsteps receded and the voices resumed. The watchmen were moving off.

"That's better," sighed Douglas. "Back to work."

The two returned to their respective places and began again. Midway through the 1500s, Douglas found the book he was looking for – exactly as he had pictured it from his researches. One glimpse of the strange cipher writing and he knew he had it.

"Come to me, my pretty," he whispered, carefully placing the light on the shelf beside him. With trembling fingers, Douglas opened the book to reveal page after page of tightly ordered script in the most fanciful-looking letters he had ever seen. "You little beauty," he mused, brushing his fingertips lightly over the script. He might have spent a happy hour or so paging through the old curiosity – and he would – but now was not the time. He slipped the slim volume into an inner pocket of his cape, retrieved the lantern, and hurried to fetch Snipe.

"I've got it. Come away – time to make good our escape."

They climbed out the window, closing it carefully behind them, and retraced their inward journey, replacing the ladder at the rear of the town house opposite before walking back down the alley to Montague Street. Douglas's mind was so filled with the book and the treasures it was certain to yield that he failed to see the policeman standing in the pool of light under the streetlamp. Emerging from the darkness of the alley like the guilty thieves they were, the pair naturally drew the interest of the policeman, who, raising his truncheon, called out, "Well, well, what have we here?"

"Oh!" gasped Douglas, spinning around to face the officer. "Good evening, constable. You quite gave me a start."

"Did I now!" He looked the pair up and down, his expression suggesting he did not care for what he saw. "Might I ask why you were lurking in that alley at this time of night?"

Douglas's hand went to the gun in his pocket. "Is it that late?" he asked affably. "I hadn't realized. Yes, I suppose it is." He glanced at Snipe beside him. The boy's lip was curled in a ferocious scowl. "It's the lad here," he offered. "He ran away earlier this evening, and I've been looking for him ever since – only just found him a few minutes ago."

The constable, frowning now, stepped closer. "That your son, then?"

"Good heavens, no," replied Douglas. "He's a servant. I'm taking him home with me." As if to underscore this fact, he put his hand to Snipe's collar.

The policeman's brow furrowed as he caught a glare of almost pure hatred playing over the boy's pallid features. Certainly, there was something odd about the youth that meant he could never have been mistaken for anyone's beloved son. "I see," concluded the police officer. "Does he run away often, then?"

"No, no, never before," Douglas hastily assured him. "There was a bit of a kerfuffle with the housekeeper, you see, and the lad took umbrage. A simple misunderstanding. I think I've straightened it out."

"Well," said the policeman, "these things happen, I suppose." He returned the truncheon to the hook on his belt. "You best get yourselves home. It's high time all respectable folk were abed."

"Just what I was thinking, constable. A pot of cocoa and a biscuit wouldn't go amiss either, I daresay." Douglas released his hold on the pistol, but maintained his grip on the boy's collar. "I will wish you good night." Douglas started away, pulling the glaring Snipe with him.

"G'night, sir." The policeman watched them as they moved away. "Mind how you go," he called. "There are thieves and such about. It's weather like this brings 'em out."

"You're not wrong there, matey," murmured Douglas under his breath. "Come away, Snipe. Tonight we let him live."

CHAPTER 2

In Which a Wander in the Wilderness is Good for the Soul

Kit stood staring down the Avenue of Sphinxes feeling very much alone. It was early yet, and there was no one else around. He drew the clean, dry air into his lungs. Deeply relieved to have been rescued from looming death by Wilhelmina's unexpected yet timely intervention, he nevertheless could not help feeling slightly bruised by her brusque manner. In fact, she had socked him on the arm as soon as they were free of the wadi and the tomb that had held them captive to Lord Burleigh's whims.

"Ow!" Kit complained. He had not seen the smack coming. "What was that for?"

"That was for abandoning me in that alley back in London," she told him. "That dark, stinky alley in the rainstorm – remember?"

"I remember, but it wasn't entirely my fault."

She smacked him again. "It wasn't very nice."

"Sorry!" Kit rubbed his upper arm.

"I forgive you." She smiled, then hit him once more for good measure.

"Yikes! Now what?"

"That is so you remember never to do it again."

"Right. Okay. I get it. I'm sorry, and I won't desert you ever again, I promise."

"Good. Now pay attention. We've got some ground to cover, and we don't have much time."

She had then told him about Luxor and what he was to do there. He had been instructed to go to the Winter Palace Hotel and ask for a Mr Suleyman at the front desk. Upon presenting himself, he would be given a parcel and a letter with further instructions. Wilhelmina had been very precise: don't stop to think or look around, hit the ground running, get to the location, secure the parcel. "It is imperative that you retrieve the package and follow the instructions to the letter."

"Why can't I go with you?" Kit had asked.

"We have to split up," she told him. "The Burley Men will soon be on our trail, and they'll follow me. If you peel off now they won't know – they'll think we're all still together."

"What about Giles?"

"He's going with me. If they catch up with us, I'll need someone to help me fight them off."

"I could help," Kit insisted. "I don't think it's a good idea to get separated. Where are you going anyway?"

"It's best if you don't know."

"But if I –"

She had put a hand to his face. "Do you trust me, Kit?"

"Of course I trust you, Mina. It's just that – I mean, we've only just met up. I don't see why –"

"If you trust me, then believe me when I say" – she pinched his cheek between her thumb and finger – "we don't have time for this discussion. The ley is active now, and any minute Burleigh and his goons will learn of your escape. When they do we must be as far away from here as possible."

"But I'm not going very far," Kit pointed out. "You said I was just to go to Luxor – that's only a few miles away."

"If you do exactly what I told you, you'll soon be in a different time zone," she said, pinching his cheek harder. "Now, stop fussing and just do what I say."

"Ow! Okay, okay! I'll do it." He rubbed his cheek. "I don't like it, but I'll do it."

"Good." She released him and gave him a pat. "We can talk about all this once I've given them the slip and done what I have to do." She smiled. "Relax, it's going to be fine."

She started down the broken pavement towards Giles, who was standing guard at the end of the Avenue of Sphinxes. "Just pick up the package and do what you're told," she called, half turning back as she walked. "If all goes well, it'll only be a few days – your time. You'll be busy enough, don't worry."

"A few days," said Kit. "Right."

"No more than a week or two," she hedged.

"Weeks!" objected Kit. "Wait a minute."

"A month at most." Wilhelmina turned and hurried to join Giles. "I've got to go. I'll see you."

Kit had watched her retreating figure, feeling like a child abandoned in a car park. At the end of the paved walkway leading to the ruined temple, she gathered Giles, taking him by the arm. Sir Henry's former footman cast a quick glance behind to Kit, raised his hand in farewell, then fell into step beside Wilhelmina. The two proceeded down the centre of the avenue, passing between the double row of statues at a fair clip. There was a gust of wind, a swirl of dust; both figures turned fuzzy and indistinct – as if viewed through the combined haze of heat and dust – and then they vanished altogether.

Kit drew another breath and held it, listening for sounds of pursuit, but heard only the thin warble of a solitary bird on a distant cliff top. Satisfied that he was alone for the moment, he let out his breath again. Still raw and reeling from the loss of Cosimo and Sir Henry, and the prospect of his own demise narrowly averted, Kit stood contemplating his next leap and thinking that everything was happening way too fast. Off to the east, the sun was just breaching the ragged hill line. If he did not go soon, he would have to wait until evening, and that would very likely be an invitation to disaster. "Might as well get on with it," he muttered to himself.

Mina had told him to start his walk at the fifth sphinx from the end of the row, and to be at full stride by the eighth ram-headed statue – a distance of thirty or so paces. If he had not made the crossing by the time he reached the eighth sphinx, he was to stop dead in his tracks, carefully retrace his steps, and try again. Wilhelmina had been most emphatic about that. Making the leap at the precise spot on the avenue would bring him to the predetermined time period – give or take a few hours, days, or perhaps weeks. Any more than that and he would be wildly off course in time, if not in place as well.

He paced back to the appropriate sphinx at the end of the avenue furthest from the temple, turned, and paused to locate the eighth statue in the long double rank. "Ready or not, here I come," he said, and started walking briskly.

He felt the air quiver around him and sensed a prickling on his skin. The wind gusted sharply as he approached the designated statue. Stepping up his pace, he drew abreast of the eighth ram-headed statue and braced himself for the transition.

Nothing happened.

Against all natural inclination, he forced himself to stop as instructed by Wilhelmina.

"Terrific." He turned, stepped off the ley, and hurried back to the starting place. "Second time lucky," he muttered, and strode off again. Once again he felt the now-familiar tingle on his skin, as when, just before a lightning strike, the air becomes electrically charged. The wind gusted, driving fine grit into his eyes, which instantly started watering so that he had difficulty seeing where he was going. He must have unconsciously slowed a step, because he reached the eighth sphinx and still had not made the leap.

"Bugger!" he muttered. Had he lost the knack?

The thought that he might be stuck in 1920s Egypt with the Burley Men on his tail did not bear thinking about, so he dashed back to the starting point and took his place, putting his toes to an imaginary line. Lowering his head like a sprinter awaiting the gun, he muttered, "Third time lucky!" and shot off.

This time, with a determination absent from the first two attempts, he willed himself to leap. Perhaps it was this heightened resolve that did the trick, for upon approaching the eighth sphinx he felt the air quiver; the ground beneath his feet trembled, and the world around him grew dim and indistinct, but only for the briefest of instants – the merest blink of an eye. He lurched forward and, like a drunk who has misjudged his footing, tottered dizzily for a few steps before righting himself and stopping.

When his head cleared he found himself standing almost exactly where he had been standing before – in the centre of the avenue at the eighth sphinx. The temple at the end of the avenue was still a ruin and empty, the ragged hills just as arid and dusty as before, but the sun was now high overhead and blazing down on him with a ferocity that brought tears to his eyes.

The discomfort of the crossing quickly passed. He noted with satisfaction that with each jump he was a little less nauseated and disoriented. The first had left him dazed and confused and upchucking over his shoes; this last spate of dizziness was nothing compared to that.

Now to get himself to Luxor. Assuming that the leap had been successful, and that he was in the time zone anticipated by Wilhelmina, he knew in general what he had to do: get to the river and follow it downstream until he came to the town, which was ten miles or so as the crow flew – depending, of course, on the crow. Then he was to make his way to the hotel and collect the package. Simple. Mina's letter would tell him what to do next.

He set off. Reaching the river meant working his way up and over the hills – no easy task, as he soon discovered. Following a goat track, he slowly climbed the barren slopes and was soon panting with the exertion. The heat bounced off the pale rock all around, scorching through his clothing. Sweat ran down his face and neck, the fat drops raising little dust puffs with every step. Mina had given him a skin of water for the journey, but as the heat took hold he worried that it would not be enough, so he nursed it carefully, taking only tiny sips of the now-warm, slightly brackish liquid.

To take his mind off his hike, he thought about where he was going and what he might find when he got there. He wondered what year it was, and why he had remained in Egypt when always before when using a ley, the traveller ended up in a startlingly different location. It probably had something to do with the length

28

of distance travelled along the ley, he decided – for lack of any better explanation. Maybe that was why Mina had been so adamant about making the leap between the fifth and eighth sphinxes. If he had missed that mark, where would he have ended up? More to the point, without a map, how would he have found his way back?

That was the question. Finally, if somewhat belatedly, he was beginning to gain a more fundamental appreciation of Arthur Flinders-Petrie's singular courage and the awful importance of his Skin Map. "Don't leave home without it," Kit mused aloud to himself.

Other questions bubbled to the surface: What era had he landed in now? There was no way to judge from his bleak surroundings – the desert had not changed in a few thousand years, as far as he could tell. What epoch was it? Here was another poser: How had Wilhelmina found her way to rescue him and Giles from pretty near certain death at the hands of Burleigh and his goons? She did not seem to have a map – even a paper one – or any other sort of guide. How had she accomplished this feat? More to the point, how had she become such an expert on ley travel? The last time Kit had seen his former girlfriend, she had been bawling in a London alley as a freak storm drenched her head to heel. They had been separated then: he went one place, and she ended up… who knew where? And Kit still didn't know, because she had not had time to tell him.

These and other questions occupied him to such an extent that he was surprised when he looked up and saw, shimmering like a mirage in the near distance, the Nile: a gently undulating line of silver nestled between two verdant strips and cradled by bone-coloured hills and desert highlands on either side. The sight was so arresting that he paused to treat himself to a long drink of water before starting the climb down. In the shade of a rock overhang, he sat and closed his sun-dazzled eyes.

Instantly the image of the corpses in High Priest Anen's tomb came winging back to him: the bodies of his poor dead great-grandfather and Sir Henry Fayth, laid top to tail in the lidless sarcophagus. Shocked by their deaths, and mindful of his own close call, he still felt a little stunned. In their haste to make a clean escape, he had not yet had time to mourn them properly. Instead, what he felt was not grief exactly, but was closer to a churning animosity towards Burleigh at the wicked waste of those good men's lives. As far as Kit was concerned, the earl and his men were vile low-life scum, evil through and through. In his burgeoning fantasies of revenge, Kit concocted inventive and agonizing punishments for them all.

This was the first sign of the new attitude rapidly crystallizing in Kit's character: call it stalwart determination. Perhaps, at last, one could detect the vestiges of a sturdier, more robust backbone. Although it took little more than the form of a swiftly hardening resolve to discover the secret of the Skin Map, still, it was a beginning. Taking up the quest in dead earnest, he decided, would be the best tribute he could offer Cosimo and Sir Henry. They deserved that much, at least.

Whatever else could be said, they did not deserve to die like that: stricken down by the contagion of the tomb, some airborne plague germ or something – wasn't that what killed Howard Carter and those other archaeologists who opened King Tut's tomb? Whatever infested the tomb, dear old Cosimo and Sir Henry had succumbed to it, and if Wilhelmina had not turned up when she did, no doubt he and Giles would have suffered the very same fate. He wondered if he had caught the bug already. Truth to tell, he did not feel too strong just now. *What I need*, he breathed to himself, *is a good meal and a restful night's sleep to see me right. That's all*.

Was that too much to ask? Kit did not think so.

With this thought in mind, Kit roused himself and, fortifying himself with another swig of water, started down the long meandering path into the broad Nile valley. Upon rejoining the rock-strewn way, the heat hit him anew and he considered taking off his shirt and wrapping that around his head turban-style. But that would just be trading a present misery for the future one of sun-fried shoulders. He would get a good hat at the first opportunity.

Picking his way over the shattered landscape, he dropped lower into the valley; the air grew slightly more humid the closer he came to the river. His progress, though steady, was not as swift as he had hoped it would be. Distances could be deceiving in the desert, he knew, and for all Kit's donkey-like progress he seemed to come no nearer his destination.

As the sun drifted lower and ever lower in the western sky, Kit watched his shadow stretch out before him over the rocky waste. Mesmerized by his ever-lengthening silhouette, he was brought once more to his senses when a chorus of barking dogs announced his arrival at a small riverside village.

CHAPTER 3

In Which an Omen is Proved True

Turms the Immortal opened his eyes on the eight thousand and thirty-first day of his reign. Rising from his gilded bed, he bathed in the sacred basin beside the door, his lips moving in silent prayer as he laved perfumed water over his face and limbs. His ablutions finished, he dried himself on clean linen and drew on his crimson robe. A house servant appeared with his golden sash and tall ceremonial hat. Turms allowed the servant to belt the sash, and then put on the hat and went out to greet the crowd that had gathered with gifts and offerings to receive his judgment and blessing. He moved through the marble-tiled rooms of his lodge to the portico, stepped across the threshold, and passed between the sacred blue pillars and quickly down the three clean-swept travertine steps.

As he stepped onto the path, he chanced to see a small black pebble lying precisely in the centre of the path: a stone worn smooth and round by many waters, an almost perfect sphere. Beside the stone lay three long needles from the nearby pine trees; the three formed a neatly placed arrow.

The priest king of Velathri paused to contemplate this small marvel. The pebble, he knew, had come from the seashore a few miles distant. A bird had picked it up – a seagull, perhaps – and then flown inland to drop the stone before his door. The arrow of green needles directed his attention to the west.

It was an omen, a sign to him from the world beyond, the meaning of which became clear to him as he gazed upon the simple beauty of the pebble, for Turms could comprehend all manner of omens. The meaning was this: he would soon receive a visitor – a guest arriving by way of the sea from the west – a foreign visitor, then, whose friendship he would do well to accept.

Turms closed his fist over the pebble and thanked the gods for their continued blessing of his long reign. This little stone would be added to all the others in the jar of his days.

Tucking the omen stone into the wide sleeve of his robe, he continued down the long, sloping ramp of the artificial hill on which the royal lodge was constructed. He walked slowly down the cypress-lined path, enjoying the astringent fragrance of the tall trees. The early-morning sunlight deepened the colour of the soil to a rich rusty red that contrasted nicely with the brilliant blue of the sky. Down below, at the foot of the ramp, his attendants and acolytes waited: two apprentice priests and four temple servants. The latter each held a pole attached to a corner of orange cloth, the canopy beneath which the priest king would receive his faithful subjects. Upon the king's approach the attendants, bare to the waist, stretched out the canopy, and Turms took his place before the small crowd.

Pressing the palms of his hands together, he raised his arms above the heads of the people and said, "May the blessings of this day be yours in abundance."

Then he greeted them, saying, "It pleases me to receive your gifts on this most auspicious morning. Come near to me, for this is the acceptable hour. Who will be first?" He lowered his hands and looked around him at the hopeful faces of his subjects. He saw a young girl with blue cornflowers in her hair, holding a sprig of laurel. "You, little one, what is your desire?"

The girl, nudged forward by her father, stepped timidly closer. She did not dare to meet the gaze of the king, but kept her head bowed, her eyes upon the laurel clasped in her trembling hands.

"Is this for me?" asked Turms, bending near.

The girl nodded.

"I thank you," he said, gently taking the laurel sprig, "and the gods thank you." He placed a hand on her head and felt the gentle heat there. "What do you want me to do for you?" She hesitated, and he said, "Speak, child. All heaven stands ready to do your bidding."

"It is my mother," replied the girl, head low, her voice faint as a whisper.

"Yes? Tell me, what is in your heart?"

"She is very sick."

"Your mother is sick and you would see her made well again – is that your desire?"

The little girl nodded.

Glancing up, Turms addressed the father, who was now standing behind his daughter. "How long?" he asked.

"Two days, my lord king," replied the man.

Turms nodded. He straightened, raised his face to the sky, and covered his face with his hands. He stood in silence for a moment and then, lowering his hands once more, smiled and said, "There is nothing to fear." He reached towards the girl and took her chin between his finger and thumb, lifting her head. "Your mother will be well. This illness will pass. In three days, her strength will be renewed."

"Thank you, lord," said the man, relief visible on his face.

Turning to one of the acolytes, Turms said, "Send one of the court physicians to this man's house with a potion for sleep and the easing of fever." To the man and little girl, he said, "Go in peace. The gods are pleased to grant your petition."

Bowing from the waist, the man backed away through the crowd, drawing his daughter with him, thanking his king as he went.

"Who will be next?" asked Turms.

A man dressed in the short tunic and sandals of a day labourer stepped forward and went down on his knees. He stretched forth his hands, holding a heavy bunch of ripe purple grapes. "My lord and king, hear me. I am in need."

Directing one of the acolytes to take the offered gift, Turms asked, "What is your need, my friend?"

"It is for justice, my king."

"I am listening. Speak freely."

"I have been working for a man who promised to pay me each evening when work was completed. I have worked two days without pay, and last night he dismissed me. When I complained that I was not paid, he set his dogs on me. They tore my clothes." He indicated a ragged rent in the hem of his simple garment. "I seek the promised wages."

Gazing down at the man, who still had not raised his head, Turms asked, "What reason did he give for dismissing you?"

"None whatever, my king."

"Did he have cause to dismiss you without pay?" enquired the priest king gently. "Theft, perhaps, or drunkenness? Or laziness?"

"My king," said the man, bridling at the insinuation that he might have been in some way to blame for his troubles, "I am an honest man and do an honest day's work. I earned my pay and now I am hungry, and my children are hungry."

"How much are you owed?"

"Twenty-five denarii," replied the man readily. Turms looked into the fellow's eyes for a moment, and the man returned his gaze unwaveringly.

"I am satisfied," declared the king. Turning to one of the acolytes, he said, "Give this man fifty denarii out of the treasury. Then send the Master of the Rolls with two soldiers to collect the same from this man's employer."

The acolyte picked up his wax tablet and, with a rosewood stylus, recorded the king's judgment in the soft wax. Other petitioners came forward then – some seeking a judgment, others in search of a decision or knowledge of the most favourable time to begin some undertaking or other, still others for healing of various ailments. Each brought an offering that was added to the growing heap, just as every judgment and decision was dutifully recorded on the tablet.

Then, as the ranks of supplicants thinned, there came a commotion from the rear. Turms, in the middle of a pronouncement, sensed a ripple of excitement pass through the remaining crowd. He finished quickly and then turned to address his people. "What is happening here? Why this unseemly murmuring?"

"Someone has come, lord king," offered a nearby subject. "A stranger. He is asking to see you."

"A stranger has come?" wondered Turms; his fingers felt for the pebble couched in his sleeve. "Make way and let him appear before me."

At the king's command, the gathering parted to allow the newcomer through. Striding towards him was a tall man in strange colourless clothing that bisected his long body – white above and black below – but the face was open and friendly; moreover, it was a face he knew. "Behold!" called King Turms, raising his hands in exclamation. "My foreign visitor has arrived."

The stranger went down on one knee, then rose and was recognized by his friend. "Arturos! Is it you?"

"The sight of you gladdens my heart and makes my spirit soar," replied Arthur Flinders-Petrie, reciting the ancient greeting response. "I have longed to see you, my lord king."

"My people," said the king, "I present to you my friend Arturos. Make him welcome among you during his sojourn with us."

There were murmurs of assent all around, and others called greetings, which Arthur returned in kind.

Turms turned to one of the acolytes and said, "Guide my esteemed visitor to the royal lodge and command my house servants to make him welcome and give him refreshment." To Arthur, he said, "The day's audience is nearly finished. I will join you soon."

"As you must," agreed Arthur. "I have no desire to interrupt your holy offices."

With that, the acolyte led the king's guest away, up the long earthen ramp to the royal lodge where his arrival was announced.

"Arturos! You have returned!" cried the Master of the King's House, rushing out onto the broad porch of the lodge. "On behalf of my king and all the people of Velathri, I bid you peace and welcome."

"It pleases my heart to see you, Pacha," said Arthur, feeling his way back through a long-disused corridor of language. "I had hoped to return sooner, but…" He shrugged.

"Life is a constant turmoil for men in the world," offered the king's housekeeper. "But you are here now, and I trust you will stay long enough to allow Tyrrhenia to soothe your soul." Laying a finger to his lips, he paused, then added, "I think a libation of sweet wine will prove efficacious in this regard." Indicating a low couch covered with red cushions, he said, "If you will please make yourself comfortable, I will return shortly."

"You are too kind, Pacha," replied Arthur. "I am happy to look after myself."

The royal housekeeper bowed and backed away; he disappeared, clapping his hands and calling to the kitchen servants to attend him at once. Arthur sat down on the couch and stretched his long legs before him. He did not feel like relaxing – the opposite, in fact. No doubt he could persuade Turms to take a walk with him in the vineyards and olive groves later. After weeks aboard ship, it was a little light exercise he wanted.

The voyage from England had not been easy. The weather had been against them almost from the start, and the conditions aboard ship were primitive, to say the least. It was not his preferred mode of travel, to be sure, but the other way – ley travel – was out of the question at the moment. The dangers were just too great. Indeed, he had pressed it as far as he dared just to get here.

"Arturos! Stand up and let me see you!"

Arthur glanced up to see Turms in the doorway: a tall, imposing figure, almost gaunt beneath his ceremonial robe, his once-smooth face showing lines of age. His hair, greying at the temples, hung straight to his shoulders, his forehead shaven in the manner of the priestly caste. Turms removed his ceremonial hat and unbelted the golden sash, then turned to receive his friend.

Arthur rose to his feet and was gathered into a firm and friendly embrace. "My heart soars at the sight of you," said the king, kissing him on the cheek.

"Mine too," replied Arthur happily. "Indeed, my soul has been singing since I set foot on Tyrrhenian soil this very morning." He spoke with greater ease and confidence as his former skills, like birds returning from migration, came winging back to him across the years. "How long has it been since I was here?" he wondered. "Five years? Six?"

"Over twenty, I fear," said Turms, shaking his head slightly. "Too long, my friend."

"Ah, me," sighed Arthur. "I had hoped to return much sooner. But events overtook me and it was not possible."

"Still, you are here now." The king turned away suddenly and called, "Pacha! Bring wine and sweetmeats! We must welcome our guest."

He turned back and, taking Arthur by the arm, led him to the couch. "I was made aware of your coming," he said, taking his place beside his guest. "Just this morning I received an omen foretelling your arrival. I did not know it would be you, of course – only that I would receive a foreign visitor before day's end." Turms smiled. "And here you are."

"Indeed, I am," said Arthur. "And I could not be happier."

"I will have a house prepared for you – a new one this time –"

"The old one will be more than satisfactory," said Arthur quickly. "If it is available?"

"No, no, I will not hear it. That house is too far away. I want you close by so that distance will not impede our lessons."

"Your generosity, O King, is as wide as your wisdom," said Arthur, bowing his head in assent. "But you may change your mind when I tell you that I did not come alone this time." He leaned forward. "I have a wife."

"You are married!"

"I am."

"But where is she?"

"Still aboard the ship –"

"What!" exclaimed Turms. "You keep her waiting like a bundle of cargo on the deck of a stinking ship? What a thoughtless, uncaring husband you are!"

"Please, Turms, I meant no disrespect to either yourself or my dear wife. In truth, I was uncertain of my reception."

"I hope you know you can trust our friendship," said Turms. "My regard for you has never altered."

"It was not you or your friendship I doubted," replied Arthur. "Believe me, that thought never entered my mind."

"But?"

"I wanted to see how things stood here."

"Ah!" Turms nodded with appreciation. "Very wise. Yes, I remember now – at the time of your last leaving the Latins were threatening our borders. You might have returned to a very different place than you last visited." He made a laudatory gesture in the air with his hand. "I commend your caution."

Pacha approached, leading a servant bearing a bronze tray with silver goblets and a delicate glass jar of pale, amber-coloured liquid. There were bowls of honeyed almonds as well. The servant placed the tray on a three-legged stand and backed away as the Master of the House poured the wine, sipped from the goblet, then handed it to the king. He repeated the process for the king's guest, then retreated quietly.

"I am glad to see that all appears peaceful now. The realm prospers under your reign."

"For now, yes. The bellicose Latins have been tamed, or at least discouraged. The prime instigators have been caught, judged, and either executed or exiled. The Umbrians – an altogether more reasonable tribe – have taken over administration of Ruma city. At present, you have no need to fear becoming ensnared in a battle between warring nations. Peace, that ever-fragile flower, blossoms in profusion across the land."

"Since that is the way of things," said Arthur, rising once more, "I will inform my wife. She will be most heartily glad to leave the confines of the ship." Arthur's manner became grave. "Xian-Li is the reason I have come. My wife is with child, you see –"

A glance at his visitor's face told Turms that all was not well. "What should be a joyous occasion has been clouded for you in some way. I can see it. What has happened?"

"Xian-Li has had a troubled time," replied Arthur simply. "I have come to you for advice. I have told her of the skill of Etrurian physicians, and she is most eager to meet you. I will go fetch her now."

"You will do no such thing, my friend," said the king. "I will send Pacha to the ship with my bearers and they will bring her in

39

my chair." He raised his hand and summoned his servant. "Arthur's wife is waiting aboard the ship in the harbour. Take my chair to her at once – but see the bearers employ the utmost care. The lady is with child."

"It will be done, my king." Pacha bowed and hurried away; soon his calls urging the bearers to speed could be heard echoing down the hillside.

While awaiting the arrival of Xian-Li, the two sat and talked and drank their wine, renewing old bonds of friendship, casting their memories back across the intervening years to the time when Turms had been but a lowly prince, third in line to the throne, and Arthur his student, assigned by King Velnath to teach the exotic visitor the language and customs of the Tyrrhenian people. The two young men had quickly become fast friends; and though it had been a long time since they had last seen one another, their high regard for one another had not diminished.

"You have not changed at all," remarked Turms, regarding Arthur closely.

"Nor have you, my lord king."

"Careful." He wagged a scolding finger. "It is a dangerous thing to lie to a king. But, see here, for you I put off my crown. When we are together I am only Turms. We will turn back the years and be what we once were."

"As you will," agreed Arthur. "I would like nothing more."

They talked about the time when they had both travelled the country as part of Arthur's schooling. Turms' father had seen in the young foreigner a source of knowledge he was determined to utilize. The old king had died before the summer was out – killed by a Latin assassin's blade. Turms' brother had ascended the throne and, in vengeance, declared war on the Latins, forcing the two young men to abandon their travels and return to Velathri where Turms, under command of his elder brother, had entered the priesthood. With the country deep in preparations for war, Arthur had made his farewells and departed with the promise to return in a year or two when peace had been restored.

"And now you are king," said Arthur, grinning with pleasure to find his old friend in such an exalted position. "You must tell me how that came about. That is a tale I am keen to hear."

"It is nothing," replied Turms, fanning the air as if waving away a fly. Taking up his cup, he said, "Do you remember the last summer we were together?"

"It was in many ways the most glorious summer of my life. How could I ever forget?"

"Two keen and ardent souls without a care in the world. The days we spent in Ruma and Reate." Turms chuckled, shaking his head at the memory. "The *nights*! Sabine girls are the finest in all the world, say the sages. And, from experience – limited as it may be – I can in no way disagree. I should have married one when fortune smiled."

"It is not too late," Arthur pointed out. "Never too late."

Turms smiled. "Perhaps not."

CHAPTER 4

In Which Tea and Sandwiches are Encountered

"Giles?" Sensing that her companion was no longer with her, Wilhelmina spun around to find him on hands and knees, heaving the contents of his stomach into the soft pine matting of the pathway. She returned and knelt beside him. "Take a deep breath and relax. The worst is over." She put her hand on his back. "That's right – a slow, deep breath."

He did as she instructed, and Wilhelmina felt his ribs expand and contract as the breath went in and out of his lungs. "Again," she advised, glancing back the way they had come. "Do you think you can walk? We have to move along. Burleigh's men may catch our trail any moment."

Giles nodded and dragged a sleeve across his mouth.

"Good." She put her hand under his arm and helped him to his feet. "It really does get easier with practice." She smiled. "But you'd better brace yourself. We have two more jumps before we're in the clear. Right now, we have to get off this ley." She turned and started into the trees lining the path.

Giles, on wobbly legs, followed.

They walked a fair distance before Wilhelmina paused to listen. There were no sounds of a chase, so she resumed at a slower pace, allowing her queasy companion to gain a little strength. "The next ley is in the valley beyond that hill," she told him. "It is about an hour's trek. There is a brook in the valley, and we can get a drink before we jump."

Giles nodded again.

"You're not one to wear out a person's eardrums, are you."

"My lady?"

"I mean, you don't talk much."

"No, my lady."

"Please, call me Mina." She smiled and extended her hand to shake his. "Just Mina." She began walking again. "It's this way."

She led and he followed a half-step behind, so that she had to raise her voice to talk to him. "You were Sir Henry Fayth's valet," she said. "Is that right?"

"I was his footman and driver," Giles corrected.

"And I take it you haven't made all that many jumps?"

"My lady?"

At his blank expression, she rephrased her question in the more formal style of address of an earlier age. "Am I to understand that you have but limited experience in ley travel?"

"Yes, my lady. This was only my second time."

"I see. Has anyone explained to you about the time slip – that's what I call it. You know, the way time slips around when you make a jump?"

"No, my lady. But I know Sir Henry made many such leaps. He and Mr Livingstone often travelled together, and I understand that the places they visited were not in the present day and time – if you see what I mean."

"Yes, well, I just want to warn you that we will be returning to Britain – but it will not be the country it was when you left." She cast a quick glance at her sturdy companion. "What year was it when you left England?"

"The year of our Lord sixteen and sixty-six, if I have it right."

"Then it will have changed."

"Are we going back to London?"

"Not just now. We're going to Scotland – Edinburgh, to be exact. You should recognize many things – there is much that remains unchanged from one era to the next. But the Britain we are going

43

to visit lies about a hundred and fifty years into the future – that is, *your* future."

"Is that where you live?"

"No." She smiled. "My home is – or was – three hundred years further still into that particular future. But don't worry, we won't be going there… at least, I don't expect we will."

"Does a body always go to a different place?"

"A different world or dimension, you mean?" Mina considered this. "I think so," she replied. "At least, as far as I know. Even so, it is possible to make a jump and remain in the same geographical area, so to speak. If Kit followed the instructions I gave him, he has made a jump that keeps him in Egypt – only it will be a different Egypt in a different time from the one he left. It took me a long time to work that out, but it is incredibly useful."

Giles accepted this without comment. They proceeded up the long ramping incline of the hill to the top, where they paused to look down into the valley beyond. If there was an old straight track down there, it was well hidden. After taking in the view for a moment, Giles asked, "What is this place?"

"To tell you the truth, I don't know. I have not explored this world. I only use it as a sort of stepping-stone to get from one ley to another. There are many such as these – unknown worlds, I call them." She laughed. "Mostly because I don't know anything about them."

"Are there people hereabouts?"

"A few," replied Mina. "Farmers and the like. I have seen them working in their fields beyond those hills just there. Once or twice I have encountered them herding sheep in the valley as well. I don't know what country this is, or what language is spoken. I hope we won't be here long enough to find out." She pointed to the silver sliver of water coursing along the wide valley bottom. "The ley is just on the other side of that little stream. Once we reach it, we'll be on our way."

Soon their feet were swishing through the bracken that covered the hillside all the way down to the banks of the stream, where they stopped to refresh themselves before moving on.

"There it is," Wilhelmina said, indicating a rough stone shaped like a magician's hat rising from the weeds near the bank. "That marker is where it begins. You will see the line once you are on the path. It is not very long, so we must be in step and up to speed when we reach the stone."

"And this ley will take us to Scotland?"

"I'm sorry, Giles, no. We must make two more jumps after this one to get there from here." She pulled from her pocket a small brass object shaped like a river stone, twisted a tiny dial, and held the thing in the direction of the marker.

Giles watched, and when nothing seemed to happen Mina cast a glance at the sky, observing the clouds and the position of the sun.

"I think we have an hour or two to wait before the ley becomes active," she announced, stuffing the little device back into the pocket of her trousers. "We might as well rest and try to sleep a little. We may not have much chance when we get to Edinburgh."

They rested then, and when Mina again tried the device a tiny blue light flickered on the brass casing. Satisfied, she said, "The ley is not yet at full strength, but it is active." She explained that they must be in step and make the jump on the ninth pace from the marking stone. "This is important," she told him. "If you feel that it is not working, stop at once. Do not take another step. We will hold hands so that we do not become separated."

She saw his worried expression. "Relax, Giles. I won't lose you." She held out her hand. "Ready?"

"Yes, my lady."

"Then here we go." She started for the stone in long, measured strides that, after three or four paces, Giles matched easily. They reached the stone and Wilhelmina counted off the steps. Between the fifth and sixth, the light dimmed as if a cloud had passed before the sun; at the seventh step, the wind whipped up; between the eighth and ninth, there arose a screeching howl and rain lashed out from nowhere. And then the ground dropped from beneath them and they stepped into thin air.

But only for an instant. Their feet touched the ground with a jolt that carried up through the bones of their legs. Giles staggered, but

Mina held him up and they walked on into the sunlight of a crisp autumnal morning beneath scattering grey clouds on a promontory above a wide, sweeping bay. The sea was dotted with whitecaps as the wind blustered out of the west.

The next jump took them to a barren desert in the middle of a storm; biting wind swept over a dune-filled desolation, kicking up gouts of sand and red dust. Thankfully, their sojourn in this inhospitable place was short-lived. The next ley was only a few hundred metres away and, guided by Wilhelmina's homing device, they found it easily and were able to use it at once without waiting.

"Sorry about that, Giles," she said upon completing the jump. "That was a shortcut. It saved us a lot of time."

He coughed dust from his lungs and wiped grit from his eyes. "Where are we now?" he asked. They had arrived in what appeared to be a well-maintained parkland – a long green lane of mown grass between rows of mature elm trees. Rising behind them was the broad shoulder of a steep hillside; the rest of the park was obscured by the trees.

"Welcome to Edinburgh," Mina said cheerily. "Or Midlothian, at least. Look at you," she said, patting his arm. "You forgot to be sick. You'll soon be a master of ley travel."

Giles looked around, taking in his surroundings with a wary expression.

"Have you ever been to Scotland?"

"I have never travelled beyond the Cotswolds," he told her. "Before joining Mr Livingstone, that is." He glanced around warily and confided, "But I have heard that the Scots are barbarians who eat their young."

"Only in the Highlands," she teased, and began walking down the wide grassy lane. "In the capital, folk can be most refined. You'll see. The year is 1819, with any luck, and we have come to see a man called Thomas Young. He is a doctor, a physician with a practice in London – but he's here with his wife, Eliza, visiting his wife's sister and family."

"Dr Young is an important man?" wondered Giles, falling into step beside her.

"Yes, very. Besides medicine, he has gained an international reputation as a leading scientist. He speaks thirteen or fourteen languages and has written on everything from geometry, physics, medicine, and mechanics to philosophy, colour, and music. In short, he will become known as the last man on earth to know everything."

"Is that why we are going to see him?"

"Indeed it is. Among all his other accomplishments, which are considerable in themselves, Dr Young is also the world's leading authority on all things Egyptian."

They left the grassy lane and entered a more public area of the park, walking easily among trees and bushes coming into the full leaf of high summer. "Dr Young is currently conducting expeditions to Egypt. He goes there every autumn to excavate and advance his studies into archaeology and hieroglyphs." She glanced at the taciturn young man beside her. "You know about the Skin Map?"

He nodded.

"What do you know?"

"I know that Sir Henry set great store by it, my lady. And I know he and Mr Livingstone were killed for it."

"Yes, well, Dr Young is going to help Kit find the Skin Map."

"He knows where it is?"

Wilhelmina shook her head. "No, he doesn't. But if the map is to be found in Egypt, he is the man to find it."

The park run ended in a wide expanse of lawn behind a brooding baronial-style edifice – the house of a wealthy shipping magnate.

"This way," said Mina, turning away from the stately house. "They are a bit touchy about trespassers. We'd best stay out of sight." She led them to a low iron fence, swung easily over it, and started down a rutted road. "We're still a few miles from the city, but with any luck there will be a coach along and we can catch a ride."

The expected carriage did not appear, however, and they reached Edinburgh through its grubby suburbs of low, mean houses, their whitewashed walls darkened by the smoke and soot of Auld Reeky – which in no way prepared Giles for the impact of the sprawling city itself. By the time they reached the city centre the effect was complete; Giles took in the grand red stone buildings lining the streets and the citizens going about their business. A sprawling castle soared high above them on a sheer rock cliff right in the heart of the town, and Giles could only stand and gape in mute wonder.

"What do you think?" asked Wilhelmina.

"It is a fine and handsome place," Giles concluded, looking around. "Greater even than London – more buildings of stone, and the carriages are bigger."

"That's just the beginning." Just then a clock high up in the tower of a church at the far end of the street began striking the hour: three o'clock. "We best hurry along. We don't want to disturb them at home over tea."

Again the puzzled expression played over the young man's broad features. "Do they not go to the tea house?"

Mina sensed the cause of his confusion. "Oh, sure. There are still tea shops around – loads of them. But increasingly, people take their tea at home. Also, they take a light afternoon meal along with it."

Giles accepted this explanation with his customary nod.

She turned and began walking at a ready pace along the street.

"Speaking of meals – are you hungry? We have just time enough to grab a sandwich –" She regarded the blank look on her companion's face and guessed its source. "Sorry, I forgot you won't know about those yet. But don't worry. You'll like them."

Three ham, cheese, and mustard baps, two mugs of milky tea, and a carriage ride later – the tea was drunk at a cab stand, and the sandwiches devoured in the back of the carriage by a ravenous Giles who pronounced the experience a very marvel – they arrived on the steps of a large stone house on Charlotte Street. Wilhelmina yanked the bellpull, and in a moment the black enamelled door was opened by a young woman in a serving maid's blue uniform. She gazed at them impassively, but said nothing.

"We have come to see Dr Thomas Young," Mina announced. "I believe he is staying here."

"I am to say that Dr Young is with his family. He is not seeing patients today."

"We are not patients," replied Mina crisply. "We are fellow explorers. Rest assured, we would not disturb him unless it was of the highest importance and interest to him. Please inform Dr Young that we have come from Egypt with important information about his forthcoming expedition."

"If you please to wait here" – the girl turned away – "I will tell him."

A minute later the door was opened again – this time by a bewhiskered man wearing round steel-rimmed glasses and a black frock coat. "Good day to you, friends. How can I be of service?"

"Good day, Dr Young. Thank you for agreeing to see us. We will try not to take up too much of your time."

"Am I to understand that you have information regarding my expedition to Egypt?"

"Information, yes," affirmed Wilhelmina. "And a proposition for you to consider."

The doctor made no move to open the door, nor admit them. "A proposition," he said flatly, taking in her curious garb. "Am I to know the nature of this proposition?"

"It concerns the discovery of the tomb of Anen, High Priest of Amun, and the recovery of a wealth of treasures, many of which have never before been seen."

The kindly doctor smiled knowingly. "I'm sorry, but you are mistaken, dear lady. There is no such tomb."

"I must beg to differ, Doctor. The tomb exists, but has not yet been discovered. However, I can assure you that it will be." Mina leaned forward and imparted her secret. "And you are the man who will discover it."

He gazed at her benignly from behind his glasses, his professional manner firmly in place. Clearly, he was accustomed to dealing with people in all manner of debilitating mental and physical states. "May I presume to ask how you can possibly know this?"

"Because," replied Wilhelmina, offering her most sincere and confident smile, "I am from your future."

CHAPTER 5

In Which a Guest is Honoured

Kit strolled into the village: a small farming hamlet consisting of low mud-brick houses strung along the banks of the slow, silent Nile and surrounded by darkly fertile fields of beans and squash, onions, leeks, melons, sesame, and the like – all of it guarded by a noisy greeting party of mongrel dogs. The houses, he noted, were mostly unadorned mud brick, though some featured the occasional wall daubed blue or green. The buildings were uniformly doorless, windowless, and most had small beehive-shaped ovens in their bare back gardens. The more prosperous-looking dwellings had small cloth-covered, palm-lined pavilions on the roof – to make use, no doubt, of any errant cooling breeze – but the roofs of the more humble dwellings were topped with heaps of sun-blasted rubbish; any discarded, used-up household items ended their useful lives roofside, along with the accumulated garbage and detritus of daily life.

He glimpsed the first dog as he passed the third house on the edge of the hamlet; the animal was quickly joined by two more, which were in turn trailed by a pack of curious children. They all stared at him, dogs and kids, with wide dark eyes. Kit smiled and waved, which sent the youngsters racing off to find their elders, setting off a general commotion of greeting for a stranger who had wandered out of the desert.

Kit was mightily relieved to discover that his first attempts at communication were met with success. Whatever time he had landed in, Westerners were apparently a common enough sight among the locals that it did not provoke instant alarm; at least his appearance did not send them reaching for weapons or running for cover. Instead, as the small crowd of villagers gathered around, a dark-skinned older fellow with stubbly grey hair stepped forward and handed Kit a clay cup full of water, which Kit accepted with a smile and nod. Kit tipped the cup to his lips and guzzled it down. The man watched him, then said, "*Deutsch? Français?*"

"English," replied Kit, wiping his mouth. "*Parlez vous* English?"

"*Non*," said the man. He laid hold of a nearby boy and spoke a quick command that sent the lad racing away. Turning back to Kit, he said, "*Français?*"

"No," replied Kit, passing back the empty cup.

The man sighed with weary resignation, and then everyone stood looking at each other and at Kit until a slender young man in a white kaftan appeared.

"Hello, sir," he said, pushing his way through the throng. "I am Khefri."

"You speak English."

The young man nodded gravely. "What is your name, sir?"

"Call me Kit," he said. "Kit Livingstone."

"How can we help you, Kit Livingstone?"

"I am travelling hereabouts," replied Kit. "I am on my way to Luxor. Do you know of anyplace where –"

"You are on foot?"

"Yes."

"You have been in the desert?"

"Yes, that's right. I –"

"You have been in the desert on foot?"

"Yes, you see, I am looking for someone."

"You are looking for someone," repeated Khefri, his large dark eyes narrowing in disbelief, "in the desert on foot?"

"As it happens, yes," said Kit, feeling that this line of questioning could go on for quite some time. "But now I am on my way to Luxor –"

"You have money?" wondered Khefri.

"A little," replied Kit. Wilhelmina had given him a handful of coins. "Not much."

"This is my father," said the youth, indicating the older man, who was now smiling and nodding in welcome. "He is head man of this village. You will stay with us tonight, and I will take you to Luxor in the morning."

"Great," said Kit. "Terrific. I mean, thank you very much."

"It is pleasure. The cost will be six dinar." Khefri exchanged a few words with his father, then said, "You are invited to come now and share a meal with us. My father would speak to you of your England."

"I would be delighted," said Kit, trying on his most charming manner. "But I do not wish to put you to any trouble."

"It is not trouble for us," replied Khefri. "Hospitality is a duty. If you will please to follow me, I will take you now."

The dark-eyed young man turned and pushed his way through the onlookers, crying for them to make way. Kit followed in his wake, in a procession that displayed all the qualities of a two-man parade.

"You speak very good English," Kit pointed out from his place a few steps behind his guide. "Where did you learn?"

"In my school. I went to a mission school in Al-Qahira," he explained. "The brothers there, they teach me good."

"I'll say."

"I finish school two years ago. Now I work in Luxor."

"What do you do?"

"I am guide sometimes," he replied. "Sometimes I help my cousin with his boat. My cousin, he speaks French. We help each other."

"I see," nodded Kit appreciatively. "So together you cover the waterfront."

"Here is our house."

Kit looked up to see that they were standing outside of the largest house in the village. Oil lanterns were alight along the rooftop, illuminating a sizeable cloth marquee.

Khefri led him to the front door. "Please to come in," he said, kicking off his shoes. "You are guest."

"My thanks," said Kit, removing his shoes. "If you don't mind my asking, what year is it?"

Khefri regarded him quizzically. "You wish to know the year?"

"If possible."

"It is the year twelve hundred and thirty-five," replied the young man with a shrug.

"Ah," said Kit, his heart sinking at the thought that he had seriously overshot the mark and wound up in medieval Egypt. But that erroneous assumption was swiftly overturned by the bald facts: the mission school, the oil lamps, the guide business, and all the rest.

"By the calendar of England," Khefri continued, "it is the year one thousand eight hundred and twenty-two."

"That's more like it," said Kit, not at all certain what conditions might greet him in 1822. Whatever they were, they would have to be more amenable than those that existed in the Middle Ages.

"Please to enter now."

The interior of the house was dark and the air thick with the oily scent of heavily spiced cooking. His mouth watered and his empty stomach rumbled. Whatever they were making, Kit was certain he could eat his weight of it. He padded after his young host, who led him through the lower floor, which featured a single large room divided by a woven curtain. Rugs covered the floor, and cushions of various sizes were strewn about the perimeter; in the centre of the room stood a low table with a large round top of hammered brass. Khefri led him out to the back of the house where two women and two young girls were tending a charcoal fire over which a very large and very black cauldron was bubbling.

One of the women was spreading a thin layer of dough over the bottom of a round cast-iron vessel to make flat bread. She looked up as Khefri approached, concern visible on her round face. A word from him and she lowered her head; then, taking up a newly cooked round of wafer-thin bread, she tore it in half, rose, and, stepping around the fire, presented it to Kit.

"This is my mother," Khefri informed him. "Her name is Mariam."

Kit accepted the warm bread with a smile and nod. "How do you say thank you in Egyptian?"

"*Shukran*," replied his young guide. "Just say *shukran*."

Kit repeated the word and added her name, saying, "*Shukran, Mariam*." The young man's mother hid her mouth and laughed, then made a comment to her son before returning to her cooking. "What did she say?" wondered Kit.

"My mother says you are very tall and not too ugly," answered Khefri. "She thinks you would make a good husband for Bet – that is my oldest sister."

"Please tell her that when I decide to find a wife, I will come here first," Kit said.

This remark, when translated, was the cause of much sniggering among the women around the fire. The two younger girls stole glances at their visitor and laughed behind their hands.

Khefri's father arrived just then and, with a show of pride, laid a hand to his chest and said, "I am Ramesses. Pleased to meet you."

"And I am very pleased to meet you, Ramesses," replied Kit, extending his hand. "You have the name of a very famous pharaoh."

The elder man smiled and nodded.

"He does not speak English," Khefri told him. "That is all he knows."

"Tell him that Ramesses is a very famous pharaoh. Everyone in England has heard of him."

"He knows that. Ramesses is not his real name," the young man explained. "His real name is Copt. Very old fashioned – too difficult to pronounce. Everyone knows him as Ramesses."

"Copt?" wondered Kit.

"We are Copts, yes," Khefri explained. "Christians."

"Ah." Kit nodded. "Please thank your father for allowing me into his home. I am honoured."

This was done under Ramesses' benevolent smile. He spoke to his son, who translated, "May the peace of God be with you while you sojourn in our land."

"*Shukran*," replied Kit.

The village patriarch beckoned his son and guest to follow him up to the rooftop, where Kit was given a prime place in the little pavilion – a simple structure of cloth and boards on three sides and covered with palm fronds to keep off the sun. Rugs had been spread and cushions arranged for reclining.

While the elder man busied himself with lighting a small charcoal fire in a brass bowl, Kit leaned back and watched the stars come out. In a little while, when the coals in the bowl were glowing, one of the daughters brought out a hookah or, as Kit knew it, a hubble-bubble pipe, and a small packet of some unidentified substance that would be smoked. The father prepared the pipe and, giving it a few draughts to get it going, passed the hose and nozzle to Kit, indicating that he should have a puff.

Not wishing to offend his host, Kit took an exploratory draw on the tube and was rewarded with a mouthful of cool, curiously menthol-flavoured smoke, on which he promptly choked – to the roaring delight of his host. "Thanks," gasped Kit. "That was… nice."

Khefri took a draught and passed the hose back to his father, who then proceeded to puff away happily while plying his guest with questions as interpreted by his son. How was the health of the king? Did Kit think the king would come to Egypt? How many horses did Kit own? Did he live in a castle? Was it true that it rained in England every day? Had he ever met the king?

To these and many more, Kit gave simple, good-natured answers, albeit some of his replies were decidedly vague since he was not certain which king was on the throne. Nevertheless, his forthright responses seemed to satisfy his inquisitive host, who smoked away like a happy sultan. All the same, Kit was grateful when the meal arrived in big brass bowls – a spicy stew of mutton and aubergines with lentils, apricots, and pine nuts. This was served alongside fine, yellow couscous and eaten with the fingers. The men dipped into a communal dish, while the women and girls flitted around filling drinking cups with the local beer – a watery, sour brew that went down astonishingly well. They continually replaced the torn bread with new warm loaves.

When the men had finished, the women made their meal of the remains. Kit was yawning and thinking seriously about bunching up a few cushions and closing his eyes when the entertainment for the evening arrived: four men, two with drums, one with a lute-like instrument, and one with a rattle. The musicians had been engaged solely for Kit's benefit – an honour befitting the guest of the head man of the village – and there proceeded a lively, thumping ruckus that drove all thoughts of sleep from Kit's weary head. A few of the neighbours showed up to lend a hand, and dancing broke out. Much to Kit's chagrin, he was pulled into the festivities and forced to stomp about with the men while the women clapped in time to the music and laughed.

It was late – much later than he wished – when the musicians finally laid aside their instruments. They were all treated to jars of beer and then, paying their respects to their host, departed. Ramesses rose and with the pomp of a proper pharaoh wished his guest a good night.

Kit thanked him for a wonderful evening. "I don't know when I have had a more enjoyable time," he said, meaning every word.

"*Sala'am*," said Ramesses as he disappeared down the steps, still humming a tune the musicians had played.

"You will sleep here tonight," Khefri told him. "There is a cloth if you get cold."

"I am sure I will be just fine."

"I will come for you in the morning. We will leave at sunrise."

"I'll be ready," declared Kit. "Good night – and, Khefri, thanks. Thanks for everything. It was just what I needed."

"Pleasure," replied the young Egyptian. "Good night."

Khefri slipped away quietly, and Kit dragged some of the cushions together and shook out the blanket. In the space of one day – was it really only a single day? – he had been imprisoned and in fear for his life, then hot and thirsty and alone in the desert. Now here he was, full of good food and song and the unstinting hospitality of people that before this night he had never imagined might exist.

Just as he stretched himself out and pulled the blanket over him, the dog-and-donkey chorus began – each setting the others off until the entire Nile valley reverberated with the barking and baying cacophony.

Since sleep seemed to be the last activity any creature was allowed to pursue in this place, Kit lay on his back and stared up at a sky ablaze with far more stars than he had ever seen in any one sky. The Milky Way, never so much as glimpsed in his London, and most often seen elsewhere as a thin dusting of stars, was in the arid atmosphere of Egypt a bright band of luminous cloud. He watched in wonder as the dazzling show slowly wheeled across the gleaming dome of the sky, spinning majestically around the fixed bright point of the Nail of Heaven. And although the moon was late rising, the fulgent starlight radiating from the cloudless heavens cast hard shadows on the earthly landscape below.

How very bright this empire of stars, he mused. Which poet had said that?

The illimitable star field stretched away in every possible direction, everywhere alive with constellations he had never seen before with names he did not know. Here and there he picked out familiar conjunctions of stars, but the glowing firmament was largely unknown to him, easily outstripping the smattering of astronomy he had learned as an eleven-year-old member of his school's Stargazer Club. He had attended all of three meetings before tumbling to the most basic fact that the pursuit of this hobby took place mostly at night in the cold when winter skies were brightest. He remembered but little of the various stellar arrangements. Mostly, he recalled hopping from one foot to the other and blowing on his hands in a futile effort to keep warm while awaiting his too-brief glimpse through Mr Henderson's six-inch telescope.

In this – as in everything else of late – he wished he had paid more attention to his studies.

Still, he considered, it was not too late to learn. And he *would* learn. He would find someone to teach him. Failing that, he would find some way to teach himself. Because, in all likelihood, his life depended on it. If even a portion of what Cosimo and Sir Henry had believed was true about whatever it was that lay beyond those glittering stars, the future of the world might just depend on it.

His last thought, as sleep overtook him, was that it was true what Cosimo had said: the universe was far stranger than anyone imagined, or *could* imagine.

CHAPTER 6

In Which the Pregnant Question is Asked

Though she felt obliged to protest at being carried in a chair like the Empress of China, Xian-Li actually enjoyed the attention being lavished on her by the bearers and their overseer. After weeks aboard a fetid ship, lurching about on uncertain seas, the slow swaying of the chair was a pleasant change. Arthur had explained that the ruler of this land on the Italian peninsula had once been a good friend to him in younger days. "But that was many years ago," he said. "Things can change. Just to be safe, I will go ashore and assess the situation. If all is well, I will return for you."

Thus the arrival of the chair, though unexpected, was a sign that the situation at court was as good or better than Arthur's hope. She lay back on feather-stuffed pillows, surveying a land whose gentle hills above a silver sweep of sea made her feel as if she were coming home. As the bearers made the climb up from the harbour and into the town, she felt a sense of peace and calm overtaking her: a sensation of warmth and relaxation she had not known for many weeks now. After the initial jump, Arthur had insisted that further ley travel was simply too dangerous in her delicate condition; Xian-Li had her doubts. Another leap or two seemed far preferable to the voyage she had begun to think would never end.

By the time the bearers and their officious little overseer reached the long, sloping path leading to the royal lodge on the hill, she was already firmly under the spell of Etruria. Meeting the king, whose easy charm and welcoming manner so delighted her, she completely forgave the hardships she had endured getting there.

"Xian-Li, my love," said Arthur, upon presenting her to the king, "I would have you greet Turms. He is lord and king of Velathri, and a very old and dear friend of mine."

"I am your servant, my lord," replied Xian-Li, beginning a curtsey. The movement, made awkward by her advanced pregnancy, unbalanced her, and she swayed dangerously.

The king reached out, took her elbow in a firm grasp, steadied her, and helped her to her feet. "We will not suffer any more ceremony in this house," he told her.

"You are most kind," she said when Arthur had translated the king's words.

Turms, still holding her arm, led her to his place on the red couch. "I think you will be more comfortable here," he said, helping her to sit. "I commend you on your choice of bride, my friend," he told Arthur. "She is exceedingly beautiful. You are a lucky man."

At Xian-Li's questioning glance, Arthur said, "He says you are very beautiful and that I am a fortunate fellow."

"Tell the king that I fear for his eyesight. I am a hideous bloated whale."

Turms laughed when he heard this. "May all whales be as ugly to behold," he said. "Come, let us share a drink together and begin a season of gladness in one another's company." The king called for wine to be brought at once. "And, Pacha, bring the silver cups."

"Sire? Those cups are only ever used on holy days," the servant pointed out in a terse whisper.

"Indeed!" cried the king. "So you are right to remind me. What occasion, I ask you, can be more holy than this welcoming of friends new and long absent? In honour of this glad day, we shall drink the best wine and sup on the finest festal dishes. I, Turms the Immortal, declare this a day of celebration in this house."

"It shall be done, O Great King." Pacha bowed and scurried away.

Turms winked at Xian-Li. "He is a most capable housekeeper,

but he does forget his place and must be reminded more often than is seemly." He laughed. "Another king would have had his head on a stake long ago. But I like him."

As the wine was served, they talked of Xian-Li's homeland. Turms listened with great interest, having heard that traders had begun calling on Chinese ports. But he had never known anyone who had been there, much less seen a native of that far-off realm. He wanted to know how the rulers of her country comported themselves, how they governed, what they wore and ate, and how they directed their affairs. He listened closely as Arthur translated, nodding now and then, storing away the knowledge he obtained.

When Arthur announced that he would like to walk around the grounds of the lodge and see some of the countryside, they moved their discussion out into the groves and vineyards of the royal estate. Gradually their talk came around to the reason for their visit.

"Arturos has told me that this journey has been provoked by a matter of some importance."

"What else has my husband said?" wondered Xian-Li, with a glance of mild disapproval at Arthur as he delivered her words to the king.

"Only that what should have been a time of joy and anticipation for you has been troubled in some way. He said that he has come to seek my counsel." Turms stopped walking, turned to her, and smiled. "It is my hope that I may repay that confidence."

Xian-Li looked to Arthur when he explained what Turms had said. "Go on," Arthur urged her. "Tell him."

"It is as my husband has said," began Xian-Li, licking her lips. "I have had some difficulty. Twice I have narrowly averted miscarrying the baby. But then it seemed that all was well and everything was proceeding as it should. I have felt strong, and my health has been very good."

"And now?" wondered Turms at Arthur's translation.

"It has been a month since I felt the baby move," Xian-Li replied, her voice quivering slightly as she spoke. "I fear the child may be… in difficulty."

"Ah," sighed Turms, as Arthur finished relating what his wife had said. "I understand. You want me to tell you if this is true. You wish to know if the infant will be born alive" – his voice softened – "or dead."

"I would not have presumed on our friendship for anything less," Arthur told him. "But I could think of none better to advise us on the correct course."

Turms turned and began walking down the row of neatly tended vines. He stopped at one vine and lifted a heavy bunch of blue-black fruit in his hand and, with his finger, rubbed away some of the waxy white coating on the nearest grapes.

"I am sorry if we have –" began Xian-Li.

Arthur touched her shoulder and shook his head to silence her.

In a moment, Turms turned and walked back to where the worried couple stood. "Of course I will advise you. I only wished to see if this request lay within the realm of foreseeable knowledge. I have been asked many things in my time as king, but never this."

"And it is something you can foresee?"

"So I believe," Turms replied. "In any case, the answer is within my power to seek."

They resumed their stroll among the vines, taking in the warmth and beauty of the day. Xian-Li soon became tired, and they returned to the lodge where rooms had been made up for the use of the king's guests. Then, when they had been settled to his satisfaction, Turms put on his robe of state and went down to the temple at the base of the sacred hill to speak to some of the priests about organizing the necessary items for the divination.

The chief priest, a venerable old man with a slight hump in his back, shuffled into the audience room just as the king was taking his leave. "May peace abound in your company, my lord and king," said Sethre. "I only just learned you were here, or I would have come sooner."

"Greetings, Sethre. I did not wish to intrude on your meditations," replied Turms. "I came only to prepare for a divination this evening. All is in order; there was no need to disturb you."

"Your presence is never a disturbance, O King," replied the aged priest with polished deference. "I have good news for you. Your tomb is almost finished."

"That *is* good news," said Turms, nodding with approval. The building of a tomb was the priest king's first, highest, and most sacred duty. His own plans, modest in comparison to some few of his predecessors, had nevertheless been fraught with complications of many kinds. The delays resulting from these difficulties had pushed the completion further and further into his reign.

"The artists assure me the tomb will be ready before the equinox," said the old priest. "The inauguration can take place in the spring."

"Well done, Sethre. Your experience and service have been invaluable." It was true, the old man had guided the construction with an unflagging determination. What Turms did not say was that it was an error on Sethre's part that had resulted in the first setback; the site chosen along the Sacred Way had proven wholly unsuitable owing to an unseen fault in the tufa stone – a fault that should have been detected in the divination ceremony long before construction ever began.

"I knew you would be pleased." He gave a bow, then turned to go, hesitated, and asked, "The rite you are planning tonight, my king. Would you like me to assist?"

"There is no need," replied Turms. "It involves the birth of a child."

"A simple matter, then. I have a dove that will serve."

"Not as simple as we could wish," said the king, who went on to describe the fear that the child might be dead inside the mother. "Have you ever encountered such a request?"

"Only once, my king. It was many years ago." He put a finger to his pursed lips. "I used a ram, then, as I recall. I don't think I would use a ram now."

"No?"

"A lamb would be better," he said. "Or even a kid. With an older animal you risk too many complicating factors. It could cloud the issue unnecessarily. You want a young beast, and a healthy one."

"Wise counsel, Sethre. I yield to your judgment," said Turms. "Yes, as I think about it now, I *would* like you to assist me this evening. See that an unblemished lamb or kid is prepared."

"As you will, my king."

Satisfied that all was in order for the ceremony, Turms returned to the lodge and, after informing Pacha that no one was to disturb him, he helped himself to a plum from a bowl on the table outside his chamber. He removed his robe, hung it on the stand beside the door, then lay down on his bed and closed his eyes. But he did not sleep.

Instead, he turned the events of the day over in his mind and was instantly overcome with a sense of the rightness of all things. Everything that happened in life happened for a reason. His long acquaintance with Arturos, for example: the happy years they had spent together in one another's company and, later, his own troubled ascendancy to the kingship and the years of intense study and preparation that followed – perhaps it had all been leading to this day, a day when that friendship could be called upon in a time of need. Turms was impressed once again, as he often was, how even the most seemingly insignificant and trivial actions and associations could, in the fullness of time, command great import.

Despise not the day of small things... Was that how it went? It was a saying he had learned in Alexandria from a bearded eastern sage – a wise man of the cult of Yahweh – the god, it was claimed, who reigned above all others, who ordained and sustained all things for his creation, and who was worshipped by Hebrews to the exclusion of all others.

Turms the Immortal thought about this, and his heart soared anew on the knowledge that in the eyes of the wise there were no small things.

In a little while, when the sun had begun descending into a sea like molten bronze, he rose, stripped, and made his ablutions from the bronze bowl, performing each action three times. Then, dressed in his crimson robe and seer's hat, he departed, leaving orders for Pacha to bring Arturos and his wife at the appropriate time for the ceremony.

The king walked slowly down to the temple with deliberate, measured steps, his mind already searching the myriad pathways of the future for the sake of his friend.

CHAPTER 7

In Which December Proves the Cruellest Month

Two lonely figures, muffled and wrapped against the cold, shuffled through the snow-covered streets of the unfamiliar spa town of Harrogate. A mother and her young son, they were newly arrived, having travelled by night coach from London. "Stand up straight and tall," the mother advised. "Mind your manners as I showed you." She glanced down at him doubtfully. "Will you do that? Promise me."

The boy nodded, his small face pinched tight against the cold.

"You will be a gentleman soon," she added, softening her tone. "Think of that."

"What if I don't like him?" the little boy wanted to know.

"Of course you will like him," she chided. "Anyway, he is your father. It doesn't matter if you like him or not."

"Why?"

"Because he's your father, that's why," she told him in a tone that let him know there were to be no more questions about it.

They walked on. The early-morning streets were still dark. In the frozen depths of December, light came late to northern towns. Beneath a flickering streetlamp, they paused to rest a little and warm themselves by stamping their feet and blowing on their bare hands. A few paces up from where they stood, a baker unlocked his door, stepped out in his flour-dusted apron, and proceeded to take down the shutters covering the windows of his shop. The aroma of fresh bread wafted out into the street on a gush of warm air.

"I'm hungry," piped the little boy, his eyes wide as he gazed at the bakery.

"We will eat soon," advised his mother. "Your father will give us a nice meal. I expect he has all kinds of good things to eat, for he is a fine gentleman and lives in a great house with butlers and maids and footmen and a carriage and horses." Taking his small cold hand in hers, she pulled him along past the bakery. "Come along, Archie. We'd best move on before we get too cold."

They slogged on through the slush-filled streets of the town. It had been a long and sleepless journey in a cold and uncomfortable coach, and she had used almost all of her meagre funds to purchase the tickets that had brought them this far. There was nothing left over for niceties like a cab or necessities like hot rolls. To keep her young son's mind off the hunger and cold, his mother told him stories about his father and the mansion he would soon enjoy as part of his birthright.

Eventually they left the High Street and entered a broad avenue lined with large redbrick houses. Here they stopped to rest again. "I'm tired," complained the boy.

"It is just a little further," said his mother. "We are almost there."

She pointed to a large, grey stone house at the far end of the street; three storeys tall, sprawling with out-flung wings to the right and left, and surrounded by a high iron fence, it stood in impressive solitude amidst an expanse of gardens at the end of a grand, sweeping drive. "See, Archie? That is his house. It is called Kettering House, and it is very fine indeed."

She had been there only twice, but knew the place well. The first time she had come was as an uninvited guest to a summer party on the lawn. The occasion had been the birthday of a prominent minor royal and peer of the realm, and she, newly arrived from London to visit her best friend, had simply tagged along. "Do come, Gem," her friend had urged. "It will be such fun. There will be ever so many people – no one will even know you're there, and Vernon Ashmole is the most handsome man you've ever seen."

Egged on, she overcame her innate reluctance, and the two young women went along together. And while it did seem that half the town had turned out to help celebrate this illustrious citizen's birthday, someone did notice that she was there: only a few minutes after slipping into a garden festooned with Chinese lanterns and red silk bunting, the pretty young women attracted the intense interest of His Lordship's son.

A glass of wine in his hand and a knowing smirk on his well-featured face, he stared at the two young ladies with the predatory gaze of a lean and hungry wolf, and then, downing his wine in a gulp, tossed aside the glass and strode to where they stood half-hidden inside a rose trellis. "How is it," he began, looking directly at Gem, "that I know everyone here, but I don't know you?"

"Oh, Vernon! I didn't see you sneaking up on us," gasped her friend.

"Nonsense, Juliana," replied the heir apparent, never taking his eyes off the strange interloper. "Now tell me, who is this ravishing creature?"

"This is my dearest friend, Gemma Burley," said Juliana, somewhat taken aback by the young man's interest in her friend. "She's come up from London for a few weeks, visiting. I asked her to join me, as I didn't want to come alone. I hope you don't mind."

"Oh, but I'm afraid I *do* mind – terribly," he protested. "It is a very grave infraction of the fearfully strict Ashmolean Code of Social Conduct, my dears. You simply cannot come barging into one of Lord Ashmole's festive celebrations unbidden. There are dire consequences, you see."

Juliana laughed. "Pay him no mind, Gem," she said, putting her flame-red head near Gemma's own dark curls. "He's joking."

"I never joke about such things," he insisted. "There are penalties."

"What, pray tell, are the penalties," laughed Juliana with forced gaiety, "for such a *grave* social infraction?"

Gemma smiled nervously, uncertain how to take this bold fellow. Whatever else he was, Juliana was right: Vernon Ashmole was a most handsome young man.

"You must dance *every* dance with me," said Vernon with a wink. "A punishment out of all proportion to the crime, but there you are." Reaching for Gemma's hand, he coaxed her from the flimsy shelter of the arbour and out onto the lawn where tables had been set up with food and drink, and a wooden floor had been laid over the grass. A string ensemble was playing a Strauss waltz, and Gemma was pulled into the gracefully spinning wheel of dancers.

The rest of the night passed in a giddy whirl of music, wine, and laughter. Vernon proved an engaging and attentive companion, and before the long summer evening was over, Gemma Burley was well and truly smitten. The blossoming love affair was too much for Juliana, who ended their friendship that very night. Even so, four years later, Gemma's most cherished memory was of that one magical evening when His Lordship's son had danced with only her.

The second time she had been inside the door of Kettering House she preferred not to think about. It was after she had been driven from the family home by her father, who could not face the ignominy of an unmarried pregnant daughter. Vernon had brought her home to announce their matrimonial intentions to his own father. The resulting scene was so harrowing Gemma refused to dwell on it – relegating the unhappy memory to the outer darkness, along with the regret, recrimination, and disappointment of the last four years.

But now, this day, a new future lay before them. The misery and unhappiness of their plight was over. When Vernon saw them standing there on his doorstep he would instantly realize the difficulty his tardiness had caused; he would embrace them and welcome them into his home – *their* home – and they would assume their rightful place in his affections. For there was no question that Vernon loved her. There had never been any question of that – she had letters, bundles of letters, to prove it: letters in which he vowed his undying adoration and devotion to her. She had other letters he had written promising that they would be married as soon as it became possible; and whenever he came to London on business, Vernon made time to visit her – at first in the Magdalene Home, and then at the flat he rented for them in Bethnal Green. He sent them money too.

They would have been married long since, but for the angry objection of Vernon's father, the old Lord Archibald Ashmole, who took violent exception to what he considered his wastrel son's illicit dalliance and threatened to disinherit Vernon if he so much as looked at Gemma again. Nothing would do for the old lord but that his son should marry a woman from an aristocratic northern tribe – especially one whose family held extensive industrial assets in mining, say, or shipping – definitely not some southern slattern from the wrong side of the Thames. Needless to say, the old lord knew nothing about the letters, the visits, or the flat.

And then, against any such expectation, the elder Ashmole had dropped dead – hustled off the world's stage by a virulent case of the Spanish influenza that had scourged the nation last year. It had taken a few months for the dust to settle, but Vernon had come into his full inheritance and was now firmly installed as Lord Ashmole, taking his place in the family pantheon of patriarchs. Moreover, he was free to marry as he wished. There was nothing now to prevent Gemma and her son – their son – from joining him at last and becoming the family they were always meant to be.

She had waited, thinking that any day he would come for them. A month went by, and then another. The money stopped. Gemma wrote letters. They were unanswered. Two more months passed and finally, at the end of her resources, she had decided to come to him.

Stepping boldly to the door, she passed a motherly eye over the small boy beside her, licked her thumb and rubbed a smudge from his little chin. "There, that's better. Stand up straight and tall. Be a big boy now," she told him. Then, her hand shaking, Gemma took a deep breath and knocked on the door.

She waited a moment and knocked again. There came a click from the other side, and the great mahogany door swung open. A servant in a black coat gazed imperiously at them. "Yes?" he said, his manner implying the opposite.

"If you please, Melton," she said. "It's me, Gemma Burley. I've come to see Vernon."

"Forgive me, madam," intoned the servant. "I did not recognize you." He opened the door to allow them entry. "If you don't mind waiting here," he said, "I will see if His Lordship is receiving."

"We're expected," Gemma declared.

"Of course, madam."

The two were left to stand in the vestibule. "Was that my papa?" asked the boy when the servant had gone.

"No, my sweet, that was one of your father's servants. He has many servants. You'll have to learn all their names, I expect."

"I'm tired," said the boy. "I want to sit down."

"Not just yet," said his mother. "In a little bit, we'll all sit down together. Won't that be fine?"

"I'm hungry."

"We'll have something good to eat very, very soon. I promise."

They waited, the little boy fidgeting until they heard the sound of quick footsteps approaching. "Here he comes, Archie. Smile and shake hands as I showed you."

"Gemma!" Vernon cried, almost bounding towards them. "What in heaven's name are you doing here?"

"Hello, Vernon," she said, trying to keep her voice steady as relief coursed through her like a rare tonic. They had surprised him, to be sure. He was still in his silk dressing gown with his shirt collar open. "I wrote to tell you we were coming. Didn't you get my letter?"

"No, my dear. I received no such communication."

She studied his face and did not like what she saw there. "Aren't you glad to see us?"

"Us?" he said distractedly.

"Archie and me," she told him. "We simply could not wait any longer."

The dark-haired handsome man glanced down at the small round face peeking out from behind his mother's skirts.

"How do you do?" said Archie, extending a small hand.

"Hello, Archibald; you *have* grown a bit," replied Vernon, bending to grasp the hand. He held it for a moment, then released

71

it. "You should not have come," he said, rising once more to address the mother.

"What do you mean?"

"It's awkward. I can explain."

"But I thought — that is, now that your father has passed — you said —"

"I know what I said," he growled. "I said a lot of things. We all say things, you know, that… Well, never mind. What is to be done about it now?" Glancing down, he gave the boy a thin smile. "We must find a way to get you home again."

"Vernon," gasped Gemma, "what are you saying? We've left London for good. We've come here to be with you, to live with you."

"I'm afraid that is not possible," replied the lord stiffly. "Things have changed. My circumstances have changed. I think it would be best if you were to take a room at the hotel near the station, and I will come to you later and explain."

"A hotel!" Gemma could not help shrieking the word. "What has happened? What has changed? You said we would be married. You promised."

Lord Ashmole became stiffly officious. "Now, listen to me. Take a room. I will come to you later, and we'll talk this over." He turned and summoned Melton to attend him. "The lady and her son are leaving," he informed the valet. "Send for a cab to take them to the hotel."

"Of course, sir."

"Don't bother," snapped Gemma Burley. "We'll find our own way."

She spun on her heel and marched to the door, almost yanking the little boy with her. Outside, she paused to gather her wits, and little Archie, bewildered and frightened about what had just taken place, began to cry. His mother picked him up and, holding him close for comfort and warmth, murmured to him, "There, now. It's going to be all right. There has been some mistake, is all. I'm sure everything is going to be all right."

She was still standing there when the door opened again. Vernon, in slippers, stepped out, his dressing gown billowing behind him as he ran. At first she imagined he had come to confess that it was all

72

a dreadful misunderstanding, that he had repented of his folly and would now make it right. Then she saw the wallet in his hand.

"I simply cannot bear to see you leave like this," he said. "Here, take this." He shoved the leather pouch at her. "Please."

"Vernon," she said, her voice trembling, "why?"

"I can't… I'm sorry, Gem," he replied. "I meant to tell you. I tried…" He thrust the wallet into the crook of her arm where she held their whimpering child. "It is all I have at the moment. Take it."

"I don't want your money."

"I can't give you anything else. I'm sorry." He took a step backwards, already distancing himself from them.

"But why, Vernon? You loved me once. We could have been happy. We can *still* be happy together."

"It's over, Gem. We come from such different worlds." He spoke as if the words had been rehearsed until all meaning had leached from them. "My father was right. It would never have worked out between us. Surely you can see that."

There was no reply she could make to that rejection. He turned and, without another word, stepped back inside and closed the door on them. Gemma, stunned, simply stood in the cold and gazed at the tightly shut door. As she turned to leave, she caught a reflection in the bay window overlooking the porch and realized she could see into the room – the morning room. Inside, seated at a table spread for breakfast, was a young lady she recognized. "Juliana!" she gasped, her empty stomach turning over.

As she watched, Vernon entered the room and, pausing to kiss his new bride, resumed his seat at the table. Gemma felt the earth shift beneath her feet as her world crumbled around her. Juliana, in a silk dressing gown, buttered her toast as if nothing had happened.

Gemma had seen enough. Struggling to keep her head high, she started down the long drive, placing one foot in front of the other as if it somehow mattered now that her life was over. Stunned and confused, her mind numb with shock, she paused at the great iron gates at the entrance and glanced back over her shoulder for one last glimpse of what might have been.

A little later, she came to herself once more. They were in the town and people were passing them in the street. "I'm hungry," whined Archie, tugging on her sleeve. "Mummy, I'm hungry."

"We'll get something to eat now," she said, gathering her thin coat around her. She looked at Vernon's wallet in her hand and opened it. Inside were three ten-pound notes. "Thirty pieces of silver," she said absently, staring at the money.

"Mum?"

She stirred herself then, taking the young boy's hand. "Come along, my sweet one. Let's go find that bakery."

Part **2**

Suspicious Meetings

CHAPTER 8

In Which the Aid of a Good Doctor is Sought

"Keep your mouth shut and your eyes open," said Douglas, casting a critical eye over his accomplice. The soup-bowl haircut was good, if a little lopsided – Snipe refused to sit still beneath the shears – but seemed all the more convincing for that. And Snipe's sullen demeanour seemed especially well-suited for the portrayal of a grudging medieval lackey.

"I'm giving you a knife, and I want you to keep it hidden, right?" He slapped the youth on the cheek to centre his attention. "Look me in the eye and listen – the knife is only to be used in an extreme emergency. I do not want a repeat of last time, hear?"

The lad ran his thumb along the blade, drawing a bead of blood, which he licked off.

"Yes, it's sharp enough," Douglas continued. "Keep it out of sight. I do not expect trouble, but you never know."

He released his servant to finish preparing for the leap and turned to his own disguise. He pulled the coarse-woven robe over his head, adjusted it on his shoulders, and knotted the simple corded belt. His enquiries into the dress and manners of his hoped-for time and place had led him to believe that impersonating a travelling priest accompanied by a junior brother would be unlikely to raise comment or suspicion from the locals.

Douglas felt, as he always did, a rising sense of anticipation, and wondered if all the Flinders-Petrie men experienced the same sensation when thinking about their impending interdimensional expeditions; certainly his father and grandfather had intimated as much. For him it was like the turning of a tide, a feeling that events were no longer stagnant but beginning to move in a single, inexorable direction towards an inevitable destination, a surge that in this particular instance would carry him to a long-forgotten time and place: Oxford in the year 1260. If he had marked the positions along the ley correctly on previous fact-finding trips, he reckoned they had a decent chance of turning up a month or two either side of October when the university would be active and the object of their quest easiest to locate.

This journey was the most ambitious he had made to date, necessitating a lengthy and elaborate research process including, among other things, the rental of a town house on Holywell Street to serve as a staging area while he studied, prepared Snipe, and gathered the sundry materials they would need for their assault on early medieval academia.

He had hired theatrical seamstresses and outfitters to provide him and his assistant with the necessary costumes; he told them he was auditioning for a performance of one of Shakespeare's lesser known plays – *Cymbeline* – and wanted sturdy, serviceable clothing that not only looked authentic but could stand up to hard wear, as he anticipated many performances. He also demanded hidden pockets concealed in the voluminous sleeves and ample hem of the garments. He engaged a medievalist from King's College, London, for a series of private coaching sessions to perfect the forms of address and chief customs of the day. Diligent practice and unstinting repetition had led to a flirting familiarity if not a complete mastery of the conventions of that far-off time – at least, as far as could be determined with any accuracy at a remove of six hundred years or so.

The clothes and manners were the easy parts; an outward appearance could always be made to correspond, however roughly, to an acceptable norm and modified as necessary. Communication, however, would be much more difficult in that it unerringly revealed the thought processes of the individual and the society of which any man is part, and these change over time. A nineteenth-century businessman does not think or speak like a seventeenth-century farmer, much less like a thirteenth-century priest. Thus, communicating with a living person from a distant era would be most taxing. To that end, Douglas had spent three years steeped in the study of early medieval Latin.

Happily, experts in that arcane subject were thick on the ground in the university just now, and he had no difficulty pursuing the rigours of the language as far as his own considerable intellect could carry him.

He had also taken great care to assemble an unassailable cover story to explain any glaring discrepancies or oversights on his part – mistakes in his preparations which could not be foreseen, but were sure to crop up – and in this he schooled himself and Snipe until both could recite it in their sleep: they were visiting monks from Clonfert in Eire, and had come to Oxford to consult with scholars regarding some of the finer points of various doctrinal issues such as transubstantiation and angelic hierarchy. Such rustic monks, while steeped in learning, eschewed the ways of the world and were, on the whole, ignorant of current fashions and opinions, maintaining, as they did, lives of semi-seclusion and freedom from financial necessity.

On the other side of the equation, Douglas placed much hope in the assumption that the average Englishman of the early medieval period was sufficiently uninformed of the world beyond the shores of England that any anomalies, discrepancies, or irregularities perceived in either himself or Snipe would simply be attributed to the fact that they were strangers in a strange land.

Snipe, of course, was the weak link in the close-forged chain Douglas had so painstakingly constructed; the young man could not read or write simple English, let alone Latin, and it was always an open question whether the youth fully comprehended even the most basic points of human interaction, or whether he just did not care to accommodate any manner of civilized discourse. This was the reality of working with Snipe, and Douglas had taken it fully into account. Accordingly, he proceeded on the premise that if anyone should happen to overhear them speaking to one another, the eavesdropper would simply conclude he was hearing some dialect of thirteenth-century Irish, and not modern English. Should the need arise, Douglas stood ready to assist this false impression in sundry ways.

As for the various creature comforts, he had provided himself with a small personal cache of silver and gold – cast in tiny ingots or sticks as described in old manuscripts – which he kept in a kidskin bag in the satchel. But, as common priests were not expected to carry much in the way of worldly wealth, he would keep that out of sight and resort to it only as needed. For most things, he would depend on the kindness of strangers and the largesse of Mother Church.

The last, but by no means least, item to be secured was the location of the ley that they would employ to make the leap into medieval Oxford. Initially this had posed an intractable difficulty. Try as he might, Douglas could not find any reference to a ley that had Oxford as its destination, or even south-central England in the early Middle Ages. None of his father's papers or books, none of the usual sources upon which he relied, had so much as a mention of where such a ley might be found.

To be sure, he did possess that portion of the Skin Map he had liberated from Sir Henry's trunk in the Christ Church crypt. This was, at present, virtually worthless to him because the map was in his great-grandfather's peculiar code, which he could not read: the very reason he aspired to 1260 in the first place.

Douglas had begun to suspect the problem was insoluble when he remembered Alfred Watkins' book, *The Old Straight Track*. In the pages of that book he found not only a reference to an Oxford ley but a simple hand-drawn map of it as well. Ordinarily he would not have looked twice at this. For, after all, ley lines always led to other places and times… did they not? The idea that there could be a ley in a certain place linking that same place to its other-dimensional counterpart had never occurred to him.

Could there be self-connecting leys?

He did not know. Yet it was a very simple theory to test. All he had to do was find the Oxford ley and try it. And this he did.

One morning before dawn – and before the traffic virtually consumed the road – Douglas, armed with a diagram he had copied from Watkins' book, walked out onto the High Street. A few false tries, a lot of pacing, retracing, and sidestepping, but he eventually sensed the tingle on his skin that told him he had located a ley. After another attempt or two, he achieved a successful crossing – a fact not completely realized until he reached the crossroads and saw torches burning outside Saint Martin's Church.

Douglas hurried to the crossroads he knew as Carfax and paused to search for any clue that might establish the date of this particular iteration of Oxford. The buildings were mostly the same ones he recognized, but of more recent age; the streets were not paved with tarmac, but with cobblestones; heaps of dung mouldered at the street corner. There was no one else around, so he could not derive a guess from clothing. He might have been able to delve a little deeper into this mystery, but the sun was just rising and he knew that he must either depart again at once or spend at least one day and maybe more in this place. He was not prepared for that, so he ran back to the ley and made the jump back to the home world – albeit three days later by the calendar.

Over the next few weeks Douglas made many more excursions, calibrating by trial and error the distance coordinates along the ley that corresponded with what he thought of as the Otherworld time-scale. In the end, he succeeded in locating the era that formed the centre of his search, as confirmed by the Roll of Vicars plaque on the wall of Saint Mary the Virgin Church.

Satisfied that he had done all he could to prepare, Douglas pulled the hood over his robe, settled it on his shoulders, and stepped to the mirror. The image reflected there was of a healthy and well-nourished man of middle height and weight dressed in a good, serviceable robe of a country priest. The newly shaved tonsure on his head completed the effect. He smiled at his reflection.

"Come along, Snipe," he said, stepping quickly to the door. "It is time to go."

They walked out from the town house and proceeded towards the centre of Oxford. It was just before daybreak, but being a busy modern city, there were already a few people about. They passed a milkman and his mule and some black-gowned students asleep in doorways. At Broad Street, a rag and bone man with his pushcart trundled along, and on Turl Street the lamplighter with his pole was putting out the last lights. If anyone marked the strange apparition of a pair of medieval monks flapping towards the city centre, they did not show it. In a place like Oxford, where students still wore the vestiges of medieval robes to tutorials and their professors still addressed formal assemblies in Latin, things that might have been considered an oddity to be remarked upon anywhere else were merely too common to be afforded attention.

They followed Turl Street to the end and turned onto the High, joining the ley line as it ran towards Carfax. Here Douglas paused. "Ready, Snipe?" he asked. "Do not be afraid, and do not make a fuss. You have done this before. Remember?" When this brought no response, Douglas gave him a light slap on the cheek. "Remember?"

The surly youth shook his head.

"Good. Then hold on." He extended his hand to the lad, who gripped it tight. "Here we go!"

They began walking very quickly along the street, and Douglas counted off the steps. As he fell into the optimum stride, he looked for the marker he had chalked on the base of Gill the Ironmonger's shop a few metres from the corner. As they approached the crossroads, a gaggle of students – either hastening to their studies or returning from the night's revels – straggled by. Douglas's first instinct was to turn and flee – to have his sudden and inexplicable dematerialization publicly witnessed seemed far too risky. He wavered on the brink of abandoning the attempt.

That impulse was swiftly jostled aside by another: What did he care if a clutch of bleary-eyed scholastics got an eyeful? What did it matter if they talked? What difference would it make?

He saw the chalk mark and stepped up his pace. A sound like a banshee howl reached them, falling through the upper atmosphere.

In the same instant, a stiff wind gusted out of nowhere, driving a sudden rain shower. The street and buildings, the bus and its passengers, all the world around them grew misty and indistinct. Then they were falling through darkness – but only for a moment, the fractional interval between one heartbeat and the next – before striking solid earth again.

Snipe stumbled upon landing and went down on hands and knees; his lips curled in a curse that was interrupted by a gagging sound as his stomach heaved. Douglas, too, felt the incipient nausea. Bile surged up his throat, but he swallowed it back down. Resisting the urge to shut his eyes, he tried to maintain contact with some physical object, fixing his gaze on the steeple of Saint Martin's Church rising like a dagger blade pointing towards the heart of heaven.

The queasy sensation passed, and he drew fresh air into his lungs. "Breathe, Snipe," he advised the heaving boy beside him. "Don't fight. It will pass."

He glanced quickly around. A pair of figures moved among the shadows a short distance away – too far to have seen them arrive, he thought. Indeed, the only living thing to have seen the translocation was a scrawny dog standing in the road a little way off, its head lowered and hackles raised. Douglas kicked a dirt clod in its direction, and the animal scurried off.

The light was dim – but was it early morning or evening? He looked to the east and saw only darkness, yet the western sky still held a glimmer of light. Nightfall, then. "Stand up, Snipe," he commanded. "Wipe your mouth. We made it. We are here."

The youth climbed to his feet, and the two moved slowly on towards the church. Douglas paused at the crossroads to look both ways up and down each street, getting his bearings. Much of the town that he knew was here – in a general sense, as old Oxford of the medieval period remained in the outlines of the modern city – and he recognized it. He knew where he was; now to find out *when*. That was the first item of business – to find out the exact date and time.

As the two travellers hurried across the road, a monk carrying a large candle appeared in the doorway of the church. The fellow proceeded to light the torches in the sconces either side of the door. He turned, saw the strangers, and called to them in a language Douglas assumed was some local dialect. He had his reply ready. "*Pax vobiscum,*" he said, folding his hands before him and offering a small bow from the waist. Summoning his practised Latin, he said, "May grace attend you this night, brother."

The monk responded likewise. "Peace, brothers." He made to retreat into the church once more. "May God be good to you."

"A moment, brother," called Douglas, striding forward. "We have just arrived in this place and have need of information."

The monk turned back and waited for them to come nearer. "Have you travelled far?" he said, his Latin tinged by his broad, oddly flattened accent.

"Far enough," replied Douglas. "I am charged with a duty to find one known as Dr Mirabilis – a fellow priest, I have it, whose writings have reached us in Eire."

The monk rolled his eyes. "You and all the rest of the world!"

"Am I right in thinking that he resides hereabouts?"

"He does," replied the monk without enthusiasm. "He has rooms in one of the university inns – I cannot say which one." He turned and started into the church.

"Perhaps you can tell me how best to find him?" Douglas called after him; he put on an expectant expression in the hope of coaxing more information from the reluctant fellow.

"I must beg your pardon, brother, but no," replied the monk over his shoulder. "However, that is no hardship, for unless you are supremely blessed, you cannot safely avoid him."

CHAPTER 9

In Which Full Disclosure Takes a Drubbing

The rumbling growl of the young cave cat announced the arrival of the new day, waking the sleepers. The Burley Men roused themselves and set about their allotted daily chores: one to feed Baby, one to make breakfast, one to see to the prisoners. Dex had drawn that last straw. So, slipping his feet into sandals and pulling on his desert kaftan, he shuffled out of the tent. The sun was up, though still so low that the early-morning light did little to penetrate the shadows of the wadi. He drew a deep breath of clean morning air and, yawning, started for the tomb entrance.

Since Burleigh had ordered that no more food or water was to be given to the captives until they agreed to talk, he did not bother filling the water can or food pan. Nor did he bother firing up the generator for the lights. What he needed to learn could be discovered in the semi-darkness of High Priest Anen's tomb.

Pressing a hand to the stairwell stone, he descended the narrow steps into the tomb's vestibule, paused a moment to allow his eyes to adjust, then proceeded into the first chamber. He crossed the empty room to the door of the smaller second room, wherein lay the remains of the great granite sarcophagus that had once contained the coffin of the high priest. This room was secured by an iron grate. All was quiet in the darkened chamber.

He approached. No one stirred at his arrival.

Dex stood listening for a moment, but heard nothing – neither the brush and rustle of men moving about, nor even the intake and exhalation of sleeping men breathing. The tomb was silent.

"Wakey! Wakey!" he called, his voice loud in the emptiness. "You're wasting the best of the day!" He smiled at his little jest.

There was no response.

"Are you dead in there?" he called and considered that this was only too likely to be the case, and that the captives had succumbed in the night, following Cosimo and Sir Henry – two right royal pains in the arse if ever there were – into the grave.

Splendid. Now he would have to go and fire up the generator, turn on the lights, and then get the key and come back and deal with the bodies. *Bloody bother*, muttered Dex inwardly. But before he went to all that trouble, he decided to make sure the two remaining captives were not merely sleeping after all. Thinking to rattle the iron with a sound loud enough to rouse them, he put his hand to the grate and gave it a shake.

The door swung open at his touch.

The Burley Man pushed it open and stepped inside. He could dimly make out the great bulk of the stone sarcophagus in the centre of the room, but the rest of the chamber remained steeped in darkness. He could not see into the corners, but a heavy stillness lay all about and the air reeked with the sickly pungent sweet stench of death.

Pressing the back of his hand to his nose, Dex turned and fled the room. *What are we doing in this awful place anyway?* he wondered. *What's the point?*

Back outside, he sucked in clean air, then went to the equipment room to crank the generator to life and switch on the lights. He paused at the mess tent to dip the hem of his kaftan in some vinegar, then returned to the tomb. This time, with the lights on and the vinegar-soaked material over his mouth and nose, he confirmed what he feared: the captives were gone.

Spinning on his heel, he ran back up the stairs and out into the wadi, shouting, "The prisoners have escaped!"

Con and Mal were still in the bunk tent and seemed unimpressed with this news. "Pipe down, will you?" muttered Mal, a hand to his head. "It's too early to be yelling like that."

"What're you on about?" asked Con.

"The prisoners aren't in the cell. They're gone. They must have escaped somehow."

"You sure?" Mal regarded him with suspicion.

"Of course I'm sure. Idiot!"

"Okay, okay, keep your shirt on."

"What about the other two?" asked Con. "They still there?"

"Which other two?"

"The dead ones. Who do you think?"

"Yeah, they're still there."

"They still dead?" wondered Mal.

"Shut up," snarled Dex. "I'm warning you."

"They can't have got far," Con said. "We'll find 'em."

"You better hope so – and before Tav gets back. He won't like this."

The three trooped out into the canyon.

"I'll get Baby," said Con. "Maybe she can track them down."

"I doubt it," said Dex. "Leave her. Go get the guns instead. Those two yobs don't know their way around the wadi, so we should still be able to catch them before they work out how to get out of here."

Armed and keen to recover their charges, the three Burley Men set off to work their way along the two main branches of the dry ravine. "Mal, you check out the back way," ordered Dex. "And Con – you come with me. We'll take the big wadi." The other stood looking at him. "Well? Let's get cracking."

Mal turned and soon disappeared along the winding path that was the canyon bottom. Dex and Con made their way towards its mouth, moving quickly, senses alert to any stray sight or sound. They passed the burial niches of a former age and civilization, quickly searching those large enough to hide a fugitive or two.

After walking at least halfway to the end, they stopped to reassess the chase. "Maybe they went up over the top," suggested Con. "If they'd have come this way, we would have picked up some trace of them by now."

"Could be you're right," agreed Dex. "And we would have heard Mal's signal if he'd found anything. Let's go back. There's a cutting back there at the bend. We can climb up that way and have a good look 'round."

The two retraced their steps, following the undulating gorge back towards the camp. At the bend – a great curving bank of mottled sandstone – the wadi made a lazy quarter-circle from south-west to a more northerly direction. A deep natural crevice in the rock face had been widened by the tomb builders at some time in the past, and shallow steps were cut in the stone to form a crude staircase leading up out of the wadi to the plateau above. The two scrambled up the crease, eventually gaining the top. Whatever they hoped to glimpse from that high vantage, they did not see.

A quick scan of the surrounding area revealed only the drearily unchanging landscape: sun-blasted rocks and shattered hills stretching into the heat-dazzled distance in every direction. Of the fugitives there was neither sign nor trace. Still, they waited awhile, shielding their eyes from the sun, surveying the empty, dun-coloured landscape for any sign of movement – any sign of life at all.

There was nothing.

"Now what?" Con wanted to know. He wiped the sweat from his face. "If they were anywhere around we'd have seen 'em from up here."

"We should get back to camp," Dex said. "Tav will return soon. We'll have to give him the bad news."

"Burleigh ain't going to be happy," Con observed.

"No. He won't be happy."

"It ain't our fault."

Dex shrugged.

"It ain't," Con insisted.

"You tell him that. You get on so well with him. He listens to you, right? You can tell him how it wasn't our fault the prisoners let themselves out while we were asleep."

Con muttered an oath under his breath.

"Let's get back." Dex started for the rock-cut staircase leading down to the wadi floor.

"What's so almighty important about those two anyway?" Con asked, growing sullen. "They didn't look like no threat to me. Pretty near hopeless, in fact."

Dex shrugged again. "I guess that's another thing you can discuss with the boss. Me? I keep my mouth shut and do as I'm told. The boss has his ways. I stopped trying to figure it all out years ago."

By the time they reached the camp, Mal was waiting for them. His search had been no more successful, and he had nothing to report. "Looks like they got clean away," Dex concluded.

"Looks like," agreed Mal. "I'm starving. I'm going to get something to eat."

"Good idea," agreed Con.

The two started for the mess tent. Dex, with nothing better to do, followed.

The sun had long since passed midday by the time Tav returned. The men heard the rattling sputter of the truck echoing down the canyon long before it came into view. They instinctively assembled themselves before their tent, weapons at their sides, to await his arrival. The clapped-out vehicle came to a dry, scrunching halt in a cloud of dust. The door swung open, and Burleigh's right-hand man stepped out. One glance at the others standing at loose attention roused his suspicions. "What is it?" he asked. "What have you done?"

"It's the captives," replied Dex.

"Are they dead, then?"

"They're gone."

"Gone…" His glance took in the others, who hung back, waiting to see how he would greet this news. Tav frowned.

"Escaped."

"I see." Tav's eyes narrowed; his frown grew fierce.

"We searched both ways up and down the wadi," volunteered Con. "We even went up top. We searched half the morning, but we couldn't raise so much as a footprint."

"You looked everywhere? You're sure?"

"Everywhere," confirmed Dex. "I swear it."

"Then there's nothing to be done about it now," concluded Tav. "Strike the camp. Load it up – everything. Boss wants it all cleared out. We're done here. We've got until sunset, so jump to it."

"What do we tell the boss?" asked Con.

"The truth," replied Tav.

"He won't like it." Con had an uncanny ability to grasp the obvious. And of all the implications of the situation, this was the one that had taken firm root in his mind. "He won't like it at all."

"I don't expect he will," confirmed Tav.

"Then I say we don't tell him."

"We *have* to tell him," countered Mal.

"Why?" demanded Con.

"He'll find out eventually," suggested Dex.

"So? If he ever does find out, we just say they were still alive when we left here. They must have got out somehow after we packed up."

"That might work," agreed Dex. "I'm with Con. Telling Burleigh they escaped will only get us in trouble, and it won't make a bean's worth of difference anyway."

"What about you, Mal? Are you with the other two?"

Mal shrugged. "I guess."

Tav was quiet for a long moment. He raised his eyes to the sky and seemed to contemplate the faint horsetail wisp of high cloud he saw drifting there. The silence became an oppressive force, and the Burley Men were already wincing with anticipated pain when Tav drew a deep breath, as if preparing himself to deal out desolation in heavy doses, and said, "That's it, then: don't breathe a word of this to the boss. If he finds out, we know nothing about it. Which isn't far from the truth anyway."

Just then a roar that resounded down the wadi walls announced that a very hungry cave cat had not yet been fed and was growing exceedingly peeved at the situation. "Con, see to Baby. It won't do to have that creature scrapping at everyone along the way."

"What about the generator?" wondered Mal. "What are we supposed to do with that?"

"I don't care what you do with it. Just get rid of it. Wipe out any trace that we were ever here. Got it?"

When no one moved, Tav added, "What are you waiting for? Move!"

As if startled into life, the Burley Men jolted away, each hurrying off on his own separate errand. It was not the first time they had decamped at a moment's notice, and it would not be the last.

"Where are we going?" called Dex, backing off a step at a time.

"Never you mind," Tav answered. "We're done here – that's all you need to know."

CHAPTER 10

In Which an Identity is Mistaken

A fortnight of rain and indecent weather had left the horses lethargic and indifferent to the commands of the rider. What they wanted was a good fast chase across the downs to get their pure blood racing again and remind them what sort of creatures nature intended them to be. At least, that was Lady Fayth's assessment – a view upheld by her father.

"Capital!" cried Lord Fayth when informed of his daughter's wish to ride across the estate to the next village. "Tell her that I will accompany her. We will take tea on our return."

"Of course, my lord," replied Chalmers, Sir Edward's butler. "Shall I notify the stables of His Lordship's intentions?"

"No need. I shall do it myself. I will be going out as soon as I finish reviewing the accounts."

"As you will, sir."

After a light lunch of kippers and toast, Sir Edward went to the stables where Lady Fayth was checking the straps and harness on her mount. "Hello, my darling." He bussed her cheek, then noticed the saddle. "I hope you are not thinking to ride with… *that*," he said, distaste tugging down the edges of his mouth.

"Hello, Father," she replied sweetly. "Why? Whatever do you mean?" She glanced around at the saddle. "Is there something wrong with the tack I have chosen?"

"In all honesty, Haven, if you insist on riding like a man, I do believe you deserve whatever fate befalls you."

"The only thing likely to befall me today is a splash of mud on my new boots." She lifted the hem of her dress and extended one shapely, booted foot for his inspection. "Do you like them?"

"Yes, very nice. But see here –"

"No, you see here. Do you really expect me to ride side-saddle in a samite gown and wimple?"

"You think this a cause for levity, do you?"

"Perish the thought, my lord. I assure you, I give this matter all the seriousness it deserves."

Seeing there was no arguing with her – there was never any way to gain the upper hand with the headstrong girl – Lord Fayth relented. "Have it your way, my dear," he said. "But do not come crying to me when you find yourself a wizened spinster of twenty-five because all the eligible young men have shunned you as a pariah."

"Is that likely to happen?" She seemed to consider this, and then smiled. "No." she laughed. "I cannot foresee that at all. In any event, it is years away, and by then the shocking indiscretion of this day will be long forgotten – if not overshadowed by some other, ever greater transgression. So, come, Father dearest." She looped her arm through his. "Let us ride while the sun is shining and we still have our good name. I will race you to the village green."

The ride over the open hills and uplands of the western portion of Clarivaux's vast acreage was an exercise in exhilaration. Lady Fayth, whose regard for her mount was suspect at the best of times, gave herself to the race and easily outdistanced her father – which was not entirely surprising for a man with both weight and age against him. She was strolling on the village green when he joined her.

"You ride like a hellion," he told her bluntly. "It will be a miracle if you do not break your pretty neck one day."

"Thank you, Father," she replied. "But I thought you were constitutionally unable to believe in miracles. Your brother Henry believes enough for both of you – is that not what you always say?"

"Hmph!"

Lord Fayth patted the neck of his mount and looked around. "I fancy a tot of ale. Let us have a drink."

"None of that," his daughter chided. "It is much too early in the day, and besides, we will have tea waiting for us at home, remember."

He gave another snort and dismounted. Lady Fayth strolled to her father and took his hand. "Someone has to keep an eye on your well-being, my lord. What will you do without me?"

"Do without you?" he wondered. "It is what to do *with* you that keeps me awake nights."

"I am in earnest, sir." She pressed her father's hand for emphasis. "You know I only have your best interests at heart. Who will look after you while I am away?"

"I daresay I shall survive the ordeal, my dear, onerous as it may be. I only hope Henry can say the same when the year is out. All being well, I shall come up to London for Christmas." Across the green, His Lordship's eye caught the sign of the village bakery. "If we are not to imbibe a stirrup cup, let us at least bring home something tasty to have with our tea."

They tethered their horses on the green and strolled to the bakery, where Lord Fayth selected an assortment of sweetmeats and fruited breads to be boxed and taken back to the manor as an accompaniment to afternoon tea. Owing to his seat on the board of the East India Trading Company, Lord Fayth, like his father before him, enjoyed a ready supply of the new commodity and saw it as his sworn duty to propagate the use of the substance in every way possible.

Upon their return, they saw that another horse had joined theirs on the green. The rider was nowhere to be seen. "There is a splendid animal," Sir Edward said approvingly. "The man who owns that knows something of horses, I daresay."

Lady Fayth regarded the creature with its shiny black coat, white fetlocks, and white star in the middle of its broad forehead. She did not share her father's passion for all things four-legged, but knew a good nag when she saw one. "It is a fine specimen," she agreed. "I wonder whom it belongs to."

As if in answer to her question, they heard a voice calling to them and turned to see a man just then emerging from the inn. "I say, hello there!" he called again.

They stopped and waited for him to approach. "Is this your horse, sir?" asked Lord Fayth.

"Indeed it is, sir," replied the stranger. Lady Fayth cast an appraising glance over the tall man striding quickly across the green towards them. He carried himself with a bold confidence that seemed well-suited to his dark good looks. "This is Aquilo," he said, indicating the horse.

Lady Fayth regarded the man instead: with his long black hair, proud moustaches, and flamboyant sideburns, the stranger gave every appearance of one who was part horse himself.

"I hope you do not mind sharing a bit of the green?" Before either of them could answer, the fellow bent his long torso in a crisp bow. "Archelaeus Burleigh, Earl of Sutherland, at your service. Whom do I have the pleasure of addressing?"

"I am Sir Edward Fayth, and this is my daughter, Haven," answered her father.

Lady Fayth smiled and offered her hand, which the man who called himself Burleigh accepted and, after the briefest hesitation, raised to his lips. His eyes, however, never left her face. "Charmed," he said, as she pulled her hand from his grasp.

"You are a long way from home, Sutherland," observed Lord Fayth mildly. "What brings you to our patch – if I may be so bold?"

"Not at all, sir. It is a long story – which I shall not presume to inflict on you – but suffice to say that I am thinking of buying a property hereabouts. It is so very cold and dreary in the north. I have reached the time in life where I believe one must have a southern redoubt if one is to survive from one winter to the next."

"Indeed, sir," barked Sir Edward, all amiability and smiles. "I could not agree more."

"If not for the tenants, I would consider a more permanent southern sojourn," Burleigh explained, almost apologetically. "But with such a great many of them, what with seven towns and villages within the Glen Ardvreck boundaries…" He paused. "Forgive me, I am wool-gathering. Northern habit, I fear. I am sorry."

"Think nothing of it, sir," offered Lord Fayth grandly. "I quite understand. This is a beautiful corner of the world, I say." He brightened with a sudden thought. "If you are at a loose end this evening, would you like to come to dinner? Nothing fancy, mind, just an informal private supper. Bring Lady Burleigh, of course, and anyone else in your party."

Lord Burleigh glanced at Lady Fayth and hesitated. "Well, I –"

"Ah, I have sprung it on you. Thoughtless of me. I suspect you have another engagement."

"No, no, nothing like that," Burleigh countered hastily. "I am so newly arrived I have no other engagements at present. And as for 'Lady Burleigh', well – I am entirely on my own. My dear wife died several years ago, and I have never remarried." He offered a wistful smile. "I am entirely without encumbrance at present, and I would be delighted to accept your kind offer."

"Capital!" replied Lord Fayth, moving towards his horse. "We will expect you around half seven."

"I will be there."

They left the Earl of Sutherland on the village green. Lady Fayth made a point not to look at him again; there was something about the man she did not trust entirely – a touch of ruthlessness around the mouth, a coldness in his dark eyes… something she could not name but which put her on her guard.

Later, when they had returned their horses to the stables and were walking back to the house, Lord Fayth observed, "Good man, that Burleigh."

"Oh? Really?" She stopped walking. "You had heard of him, then?"

"How should I have heard of him? He said himself he's only just come south."

"Indeed!"

"He is an earl, my dear," asserted His Lordship. "Sits a peg or two above our station, I daresay. A fine gentleman – as anyone can plainly see." He glanced sideways at his daughter. "Do you disagree?"

"I do not profess to know the man. I fail to see how anyone can form a cogent opinion based on a few pleasantries muttered in passing."

"Ha!" Her father continued striding across the gravelled yard. "Obviously, you are no judge of character, my dear. Breeding always tells."

These words were still echoing in her mind when, after their cosy meal of cold mutton and turnip mash, talk turned to families and mutual connections the men might share. The three were sitting in her father's study where a fire had been laid; the men were sipping brandy and Haven was pretending to occupy herself with a swatch of needlepoint, the same piece she had been working on for over a year to no appreciable effect. She was listening to their talk and trying to decide where to place Burleigh precisely in her estimation – an ordinarily simple matter for a young woman of strong opinion and quick judgment. But for some reason, the earl was proving extremely elusive in this regard. Every time she felt she had gained an understanding, he would say something – a turn of phrase, an observation, a single word even – that confused her and put her usually reliable feminine intuition out of joint.

"Of course," Burleigh was saying as he swilled his brandy around the rim of the bowl, "as a student of the natural sciences myself, I am sure I would find your work fascinating. I hazard a surmise that we might even share some of the same interests."

"My work?" Lord Fayth frowned. "I must confess that I do not dabble in the sciences, sir. These modern men of inquiry," he sniffed, and took a sip of brandy. "Not worth a boot rag the lot of them, if you ask me."

For the first time that evening, Burleigh's expression betrayed confusion and something else. Shock? Whatever it was, Haven thought she had glimpsed something of the real man beneath the veneer of aristocratic indifference. "Perhaps I misunderstand you, sir," he suggested delicately, and his manner resumed its easy bonhomie.

"I do not think I could be any clearer on the subject. This science will be the death of us all."

"Father," said Lady Fayth, speaking up, "I think our guest has confused you with Sir Henry."

"Oh? Is that so?" Lord Fayth turned to Burleigh once more. "Ah, yes, I see. Of course."

"Sir Henry?" wondered Burleigh.

"My lunatic brother, Henry Fayth – he's completely taken in by all this natural science tosh. A wicked waste of a man's time, if you want my opinion."

Before Burleigh could respond to this provocative sentiment, Lady Fayth challenged her father's assertion. "He is *not* a lunatic, dear Father. Far from it. Uncle Henry is one of the wisest men I know." She smiled at Burleigh, adding, "My uncle is a charming and gracious man – and one of the leading lights of the new sciences."

"Mad as a March hare," put in Edward. "Always has been. Lives alone in London like a monk in a cell – a miserable hermit. Never married. Claims it would interfere with his valuable work. Though what that is, God knows. Can't make head nor tail of his gibberish."

"Father, really," chided Haven. "You give our guest entirely the wrong impression."

"Please, I assure you I have formed no impression whatsoever," offered Burleigh. "I prefer to take things as I find them – a practice that has served me well all my life."

"Good for you, sir," affirmed Lord Fayth. He reached for the decanter. "More brandy, my lord earl?"

Conversation moved on to local matters – chiefly farming, horses, and hounds – and Lady Fayth, having endured enough of what she considered boorish blather, announced that it was time for her to retire. "I will leave you two to set the world to rights," she said lightly. "Lord Burleigh, it was very nice making your acquaintance. I pray your stay in the southlands is entirely to your edification and profit."

"I thank you, my lady," he said. "Even in my short acquaintance I have found the folk hereabouts very much to my liking. Edification will surely follow in its course." He rose from his chair and took her offered hand. "I wish you a good night and pleasant dreams." He patted her hand, then kissed it. "Until we meet again."

"I very much doubt that we shall," replied Lady Fayth. "I am away to London in the morning and plan to be there for some time. But inasmuch as I expect you and my father will find all sorts of pursuits with which to occupy yourselves, you shan't miss me in the least."

CHAPTER 11

In Which Wilhelmina Learns the Ropes

Before Egypt, long before travelling to that time and place – or any other – became even a remote possibility, Mina had paid her dues. Haltingly, painstakingly, maddeningly. Transplanted entirely on her own and completely unexpectedly from her twenty-first-century London home to seventeenth-century Bohemia, and having no Cosimo or Sir Henry to guide her, she had acquired her knowledge and skill through hard graft and a long and exhausting process of trial and error. It was an exacting apprenticeship, and it began back in the Grand Imperial Kaffeehaus in Prague on the day she took delivery of the device her friend Gustavus Rosenkreuz had made for her using the plans given him by Lord Burleigh. It began the moment the young alchemist placed the curious object in her hand.

Now, as she stood alone on a hilltop north of her adopted city, Wilhelmina studied the odd device, neatly rounded like a stone and of a similar size, shape, and heft. It reminded her of just that: a surf-tumbled cobble whose edges have been blunted and streamlined by the endless wash and worry of the waves. That, however, was where the similarities ended. Stones were not made of burnished brass; their surfaces were not chased with a lacy arabesque of filigreed lines; wave-tumbled rocks did not feature a curved row of tiny holes along one side, nor sport a knurled dial. Moreover, beach stones did not possess a central aperture that resembled a squinting eye from which radiated a gently pulsating indigo light – at least, not in Mina's experience.

This last she had not seen herself, but had it on Gustavus's authority that it was so. "The substance inside gives off light when it comes into contact with certain ethers," the young alchemist had told her. Mina had no idea what these *ethers* were, but how the device was to be used was another matter.

As she pored over the peculiar instrument, she mustered the scant facts she possessed and tried to imagine how they might be applied to the task at hand. The instrument had been made according to a design supplied by Lord Burleigh to be employed by him for what the alchemists called astral exploration. If her hunch was right, the earl's explorations were connected in some way to ley travel: the peculiar phenomenon that had plucked her from the twenty-first century and dropped her so rudely into the seventeenth. From what she could recall of the information Kit had imparted – fractured and confused as it was – and her own limited experience, ley travel was a thoroughly unpleasant and wholly unpredictable exercise that nevertheless could yield serendipitous results, and she was determined to repeat the procedure and, if possible, master it.

Although she no longer wished to return home to London – a lack of desire that she could not explain, even to herself – as an unwitting transplant in an alien world she felt it something of a duty to learn more about the means and mechanisms by which she had come to take up residence in another time and place. Burleigh's device, she supposed, had something to do with facilitating such leaps, or calibrating them in some way, and this was where she would start.

She had decided that her experiments should take place in solitude, reasoning that whatever happened, it would be best if it happened out of sight so as not to alarm any casual passers-by. So, after thoughtful deliberation on how to safely embark on the venture at hand, she had told Etzel that she wanted to go breathe some country air and perhaps collect some wild flowers. It was, after all, in the country that she had landed following her first and only ley jump. Leaving the coffee shop, she took the wagon out of the city and up into the surrounding hills. The day was bright and fine; an unseasonably warm spring was swiftly melding into summer – as good a day as any for an experiment in ley travel.

Holding the device in her hand, she puzzled over how to start. As she recalled, her first leap had been made simply by walking with purpose, so Mina began striding along the hilltop, holding the device before her as if it were a flashlight and she was trying to find a darkly hidden path. She stepped off fifty paces, turned, and walked back. When the expected result failed to materialize, she did the same thing in another direction and obtained the same disappointing result. The mechanism remained happily inert and uninvolved in her efforts. Undeterred, she took herself to a new spot further away and tried again.

This went on for some time, and with no different result. After a while, Mina began to feel discouraged – not that she had expected to conquer the device easily, but she felt her efforts entitled her to some small reward for her determination, if not for the considerable effort she had made to obtain it in the first place.

In the end, she slipped Burleigh's gismo into the pocket of her smock, collected a large bouquet of wild flowers, and bundled them into the wagon for the drive back to town. Over the next few weeks, she would try her experiments again in various locations around the outskirts of the city. Each time she returned better for the exercise, but no closer to unravelling the mystery of ley jumping.

Then one day it happened. Quite by accident, and on another errand entirely, she was walking along a sunny open stretch of the Moldau, the river dividing the city. She strolled through the lower town and out into the fields and farming hamlets of the countryside and, as always, had thoughts of the coffee house percolating away on the back burner of her mind. She had an eye peeled for a new source of honey for the bakery; her city purveyors all bought theirs in bulk from rural sources and offered it to her at a price that included a tidy profit for themselves. Well and good, but Engelbert's recipes were using more and more sweetening as their patrons demanded pastries to complement the natural bitterness of the coffee. Honey was the costliest ingredient, and Mina had begun thinking about contracting directly with country beekeepers to supply the commodity fresh from the source. By cutting out the middleman, both she and the beekeeper would get a better price, and she could guarantee a constant ready market.

She walked along beneath a sky of bird's-egg blue, past fields of ripening barley, beets, turnips, and beans; small herds of cattle, flocks of sheep, and geese. The river rolled away to her right, its long, slow currents barely ruffling the quiet jade-green surface. Mother ducks surrounded by a flotilla of half-grown ducklings paddled among the weeds growing long at the banks, the little ones dibbling for insects and bits of edible flotsam.

A dairyman walking beside his donkey cart approached on the lane that ran along the bank; he tipped his hat as he passed. The air was momentarily filled with the slightly sour, milky scent of the dairy, and Wilhelmina was instantly plunged back into a time and place she scarcely remembered ever having been: a farm in Kent when she was barely six years old. It was a school trip, and her class had visited a farm that produced the milk she and her classmates drank every day from little bottles. The farmer had shown them into the separating room to see the huge machines at work dividing the raw milk from the cream; the smell of the room – strongly pungent and steeped in the sharp rancid odour of fermenting cheese – had so overwhelmed her young senses that it remained with her ever after.

She greeted the farmer and then paused to watch him on his way, breathing in the scent as he passed. Mina was still thinking about that school trip, so long forgotten but vividly revived, when the lane turned to follow a bend in the river and passed into a beech wood copse. The sunlight through the trees threw dappled shadows on the path, and she was looking at the pattern as she walked. She happened to slip her hand into her pocket and brushed Burleigh's device. To her surprise, it was warm to the touch.

She looked down and saw a deep blue light burning through the fabric of her smock. The thing was glowing.

She stopped and with trembling fingers drew out the brass-encased device. A strong blue light streamed through the little holes that lined the curve of one side, and through the central half-moon aperture as well. Something had stirred the instrument to life, but what?

Mina gazed around her. She noted the trees, the leaf-shadowed lane, the wide sweep of the river, and even the cloud-spotted sky above and the birds soaring there. She regarded everything, yet saw nothing she supposed might trigger the sudden awakening of the curious little gismo that was even now filling her hand with an appreciable warmth.

Slowly, keeping her eyes on the object, she began walking again. The lane curved as it followed the river, and gradually the light in Burleigh's object faded. She kept walking until the last little glimmer of blue light died. She turned and retraced her steps. As she half expected, after a few steps the glow rekindled… a few more steps, and the glow grew brighter.

She marched a dozen swift paces along the lane, moving out from the shelter of the copse. The softly glowing blue light slowly faded once more, and the device cooled in her palm.

She stopped and, certain that she stood on the brink of discovery, made a slow about-face and moved once more into the copse. The deep indigo light returned, and this time she imagined she heard a small squeaking sound – almost like the chirp of a baby bird. Still walking slowly, she held the device to her ear and confirmed that yes, indeed, the thing was speaking to her. Instinctively, she put her finger to the tiny knurled nub on the surface of the device and gave it a twist: the peeping sound grew louder.

"Hello!" she muttered to herself. "It's a volume knob."

Still walking slowly, she noted when the blue glow began to fade once more, then instead of waiting until it went out altogether, she spun on her heel and headed back the opposite way, still holding the instrument out in front of her. At the exact place where the light was brightest and the sound loudest, she stopped.

Burleigh's mechanism was obviously marking the place, but try as she might she could not see why. She stood perfectly still and gazed at the little woodland glade around her. What was different or special about this place? What was the gismo trying to tell her?

She cast her mind back to the first time she had made a leap. Something that Kit had said about lines etched on the landscape came drifting back into her consciousness, and she looked for anything that might resemble a line. Although it took a few moments, the realization finally dawned on her that she was, in fact, staring right at it: a perfectly straight course through the beech copse, a thin trail with trees on either side and the merest trace of a path on the ground like that wild animals made – a fox run, perhaps – but straight as an arrow until losing itself in the deep shade of the little wood.

Wilhelmina swallowed and found that not only had her mouth gone dry, but her heart was beating very fast. "This is it," she said to herself. "This is one of those leys."

Her feet were already on the path before she had even decided what to do. Walking steadily into the grove, her eyes fixed on the stone-shaped instrument, she noted that the glowing light began to pulse gently with every step. The faint chirping sound did not grow louder, but the squeaks came faster; she stepped up her pace and the chirps came more quickly.

A breeze stirred the nearby leaves; the branches overhead moved with a sudden gust, and darkness descended over her – as if she had moved into the deep shade of a large tree. Just that. Nothing else. Three more steps carried her out from the shadow of the tree and into… a broad sunlit glade.

The beechy copse was gone. The curving riverbank was gone too, along with the surrounding fields and hills. Instead, she stood in a pool of bright sunlight at the bottom of a deep canyon. Behind her stretched a long incline etched into the cliff face leading to the grassy sward on which she stood. Towering over her on every side were high limestone cliffs, and directly below her a shallow river sloshed around the huge stones and boulders littering the valley floor. She heard a ragged screech and glanced up to see a hawk soaring through the cool, bright air.

"Mina, you're not in Bohemia any more," she whispered, her voice falling softly in the silence of the glade.

The device in her hand still glowed softly but was no longer sounding. *What a clever little thing*, she thought; and then, *What shall I call you?* Ley lamp, she decided on a whim, and the name seemed to fit.

Curious about where she had landed, Wilhelmina proceeded to look around, taking care not to wander too far lest she lose her bearings. She tucked the ley lamp into her pocket and continued down the path to the bottom of the canyon. Around the next bend, the valley widened; the limestone walls receded. Someone had planted fields of corn on the rich flat ground either side of the river. A short distance ahead she could see a few stone and timber buildings, but there was no one about.

As Mina approached the buildings, the riverside trail became a twin-track road that ran through the tiny settlement and on, through the little farmyard and around another bend. Since no one seemed to be about, she paused to look inside one of the buildings as she passed; it was a simple animal shed with straw covering the floor and an empty manger below a squared hole in the wall, which served as a window. She moved on, following the road as it wound round the bend. In the heights above her another hawk had joined the first, and both soared in slow wheeling circles.

Just around the bend she saw that someone had made a dam of river rocks – a primitive construction of stones heaped one atop another across a narrow part of the river. The water pooled nicely behind this simple barrier, forming a wide, placid pond. On a rock ledge just above the pond stood a stout stone building, which on closer inspection turned out to be a ruin. The roof was gone, and two of the four walls had tumbled into rubble, but the remains of a great wooden wheel and several grindstones lay among the jumble of wreckage.

"A mill," Mina surmised. The thing had long been derelict; weeds grew in the rubble, and grass had seeded itself on the upper courses of stone and the ledges of what had been windowsills. But someone still used the pond, for she saw a rope tied to an iron ring in the wall overlooking the water, and on the end of the rope a wooden bucket.

She stood for a moment wondering where she was, and when. As far as she could tell, she could be anywhere at nearly any time; the things she saw around her certainly had an antique air about them, but little more than that. The surrounding landscape gave almost no clue to her whereabouts; it was nowhere she had ever been, but it could have been in any number of countries. Still, something about the construction, rude as it was, seemed European rather than, say, South American. Definitely not Asian.

What to do now?

She raised her eyes to the sky. The light had taken on the golden sheen of late afternoon, and the already faint warmth in the air was fading. The shadows of the canyon walls were lengthening and deepening towards evening. She did not care to be caught wandering around in the dark, so she turned and hurried back the way she had come.

Upon reaching the spot where she had entered the valley, Mina pulled the ley lamp from her smock and, holding it as before, started walking quickly up the long ramp-like trail angled towards the top of the canyon walls. After half a dozen steps, the bronze-cased instrument began to glow with its eerie indigo light… a few more steps and she heard the faint chirping sound. She kept walking. The path rose between two rock stacks, which stood as pillars on either hand. Wilhelmina passed through this crude gateway and into a shadow. For an instant, all was darkness and an absence of air. Her breath caught in her throat, and she stumbled forward and into the little beech wood with its narrow fox run of a trail.

She stood blinking as her eyes adjusted to the light. The air was soft and warm, and sunlight streamed through the leaves in shafts, which dappled the grove around her.

She was home.

Halfway back to the city, it occurred to her to wonder if she had returned to the same time she had left. Was it still the seventeenth century? Was Rudolf still on the throne? Was the bakery still there? Would Etzel be waiting for her?

Her heart sank, and for a good few minutes she entertained a wild variety of frightening thoughts about all the things that could have gone wrong; she kicked herself for how stupid she had been. What, after all, did she really know about this ley line business?

But then she heard church bells. The sound rang out, filling the streets and echoing across the river and beyond. The familiar sound called her back to her senses, and somehow she knew that all was well. She quickened her steps as she passed through the city gates and hastened to the old town square. When she saw the good green-and-white facade of the Grand Imperial Kaffeehaus, she smiled.

Etzel was there in his flour-dusted apron, just as she had left him. He looked up as she came in, his round face beaming as she bustled into the shop. Although there were several patrons lingering over their afternoon coffees, she went up and gave the big baker a fat kiss on his smooth cheek. "Mina!" he exclaimed, cupping a floury hand to her face. "I thought you were going for a walk."

"I did."

He regarded her askance. "But you only left a moment ago."

Mina shrugged. "I changed my mind. I would rather be here with you."

"But you are with me all the time," he pointed out.

"I know." She kissed him again and went upstairs to her room. There, with the door closed, she removed the ley lamp from her pocket and crossed to the large chest where she kept her clothes and the few valuable things she owned. She unlocked the chest and wrapped the brass instrument in a stocking.

I wonder, she thought as she tucked the bundle under her spare nightdress at the bottom of the chest, *what else it can do?*

CHAPTER 12

In Which Sheer, Bloody-Minded Persistence is Rewarded

It would be a happier world where each child enjoyed the love and care of two devoted parents to supply a firm foundation on which to build a solid and productive adult life. But, sadly, that is not our world. And it is not the world into which Archibald Burley was born. Little Archie's story is darker, more desperate, and yet drearily familiar. How not? We have heard it all before: a story as old as time and repeated daily the world over; we can recite it by heart. For the plight of unwed mothers is too, too predictable, and Gemma Burley's descent from prim and respectable Kensington to noisome, crowded Bethnal Green is almost too banal to report in detail. Still, that is the task before us if we are to understand all that flowed from that initial rejection of her and her son by the boy's father, and all that was to come after…

* * *

"Archie!" moaned Gemma, her voice ragged and low. "Archie, come here, my darling, I need you."

The boy crept to the doorway, slender shoulders hunching, already dreading the request he knew was coming.

"I'm out of medicine. You must run and get me some more." She held out her hand. "Here is some money."

"Aw, Mum," he whined. "Do I have to?"

"Look at me, Archie!"

He raised his eyes to her ravaged face. Hair filthy and matted, her dress soiled, missing buttons, she no longer looked like the woman he knew.

"I'm sick and I *need* my medicine," she insisted, strength coming to her voice. "Now. You come here and take this money."

Moving slowly to the side of her bed, he regarded his mother. Her face haggard, dark circles under her dull eyes, her forehead pale, there was sweat on her upper lip and her flesh looked waxy. He had seen her this way before, and knew with a sinking heart that there would be no supper for him tonight. He held out his hand for the few coins she gave him.

"Now, you be a good boy and run along."

Head down, the slender body turned and, feet dragging, the lad started away.

"Don't dawdle, Archie. Promise me."

"I won't."

"There's a good boy. Off with you now, and hurry back. We'll have bread and cheese for your tea. The sooner you come back, the sooner you can have your bread and cheese – we'll toast it too. You like that, don't you, Archie? You like your bread and cheese toasted, I know you do. That's what we'll have as soon as you get back. You run along now." She sank back, exhausted. "There's a good boy."

Outside, Archie flitted down the cinder path behind the house he and his mother shared with other itinerant lodgers, his fist closed tight on the three coins she had given him – two farthings and a six-pence piece. Tucking the coins into his pocket, he darted down the alley, dodging puddles of standing water and fresh slops emptied from kitchen buckets and chamber pots. At the end of the alley, he picked up his speed – he'd have to hurry now to still have time enough once he'd got the medicine to make it back to the greengrocer and buy or steal another apple or two to sell on the bridge before the bakery closed. Then again, if luck smiled on him, there would be day-old bread out back and he could get that for free. And besides, stale bread was better for toasting anyway.

Once on the street, Archie ran to the nearest chemist and, knowing better than to go in, hurried round to the back. He pounded on the door until it rattled.

"Keep yer shirt on, mate," growled a voice from the other side. A chain was unlatched and a bearded face pressed itself into the space between doorpost and door. "Oh," said the man with undisguised disappointment. "It's you. What is it this time? No, let me guess – you want more laudanum."

"Please, sir, it's for me mum. She's terrible sick."

"You got money?"

The boy held up the silver sixpence.

"Wait here," said the chemist.

The door closed. Archie stood in the backyard, shifting from one foot to the other, aware that the sun was lowering, the daylight soon fading. It would be late before he could reach the bridge with an apple or two to sell. In a moment, the door opened once more. "Let me have it," said the man, shoving out his hand.

Archie dropped the coin into the extended palm, which was withdrawn and replaced by a small brown jar. "Tell yer mam she still owes me for last time, hear?"

"I'll tell her." Archie was already running back to the lodgings, the jar safely in his pocket. His mother was up, waiting for him at the door when he returned, berating him for being slow. He handed over the jar and dashed away again before she could detain him further. He heard her call something after him, but ignored it and ran on. Once on the street, he flew pell-mell down the beaten dirt road, dodging the carts and pedestrians until he reached the shops at the wide intersection.

The greengrocer was already closing up for the day, and the boy had a hard decision to make – wait until the shop was closed and try to find something in the refuse heap in the alley behind… or bargain with the grocer using the two farthings he had left. The evening lull was coming on; the time between the day's traffic and the night's was no time to be selling fruit. If he did not hurry, he might not get another sale today, and night was no time to be abroad. Though only eight years old, Archie already knew that nothing good happened on the streets of Bethnal Green after dark.

Digging in his pocket, he snatched up the two farthings and ran to the shop. The greengrocer was just doing up the last shutter. "Three apples," he gasped breathless.

"I'm closed up, boy."

"Please, sir."

"No. Come back tomorrow."

"Please, sir, they's fer me mum," he whined, putting on his best street urchin accent. It was the one he'd learned since arriving in the neighbourhood a year or so ago, and most useful for wheedling and begging. "She's full sick, she is, an' asked me to fetch her some apples to help get her well, like."

"Can't you see I've closed up?"

"I got money – I can pay yers."

The shopkeeper straightened, turned, and looked at the boy for the first time. "You're the brat 'as been thieving my stock of late."

"No, sir," lied Archie. "I ent nivver stole nuffin'."

"You look like the one."

Archie extended a grubby hand with the two small coins. "It's just three apples." He offered a forlorn smile. "Fer me sick mum, see?"

"God help us," sighed the greengrocer. "I must be going soft in the head." He turned back to the door of his shop. "Wait here."

Archie stood on the pavement at the door while the shopkeeper rustled about inside. The fellow reappeared a moment later with three good-sized apples. "There," he said, holding them out. The boy reached for them. "The money first," he said.

Archie delivered the coins and received the apples. He stuffed two of them in his trouser pockets and ran away again.

"A word of thanks would be in order," shouted the greengrocer after him.

"Thanks!" called Archie without breaking his stride.

He ran until he reached the bridge, taking up his customary spot. As he suspected, the traffic passing from one side of the city to the other had already begun to dwindle. There were few foot travellers and carts, and even fewer horse-drawn carriages. Yet there were still some making their way from the city to the suburbs. He polished up an apple until it shone, and then went to work, approaching each carriage as it passed and calling loudly, "Buy an apple from an orphan! Buy an apple! Help an orphan!"

With the better prospects – carriages containing well-dressed ladies and gentlemen – he often ran beside the vehicle a little way; sometimes, when they saw his determination, they stopped and he made a good sale. He did not bother approaching pedestrians or any of the hundreds of handcart pushers – he never got anything from them but blunt abuse.

He tried each coach that came his way, but the passengers of the first two did not even look out to see him. The third and fourth vehicles, likewise, rolled on without stopping – as did the next three. He had to wait for the next carriage to come by, but when it did, he managed to make three pence – this from a white-bearded gentleman in a tall silk hat.

After that, there were no more carriages to be seen in either direction. Archie waited for a while, watching the shadows deepen around him and listening to the wash of the river beneath the bridge. There were still a few handcart pushers coming his way, and some workers and others on foot, but no carriages. He wondered if it might be a good idea to run along the embankment to the next bridge. Maybe the traffic there was better and he might still make a sale.

Just as he was about to abandon his post, a lone coach bumped onto the bridge from the opposite end. Archie polished the apple on his shirt once more and put on his most abjectly hopeful expression. One more sale would mean supper for tonight, with maybe a little left over for breakfast. As soon as the horses came abreast of him, the boy leapt to the side of the carriage with his plaintive song: "Help an orphan! Buy an apple!"

The vehicle rattled on, so he began to jog alongside, holding up the apple and calling to those inside. After the third plea, he heard someone call out to the driver, who brought the horses to a halt. Archie stood at the carriage door as the window slid down. "Please, sir," he called, "buy an apple. Help a poor orphan."

A face appeared in the window: a youngish, long-nosed fellow with a shock of fair hair falling over a high forehead; he wore a knotted silk cravat with a gold stud. "Let me see the merchandise," commanded the young gentleman, reaching a gloved hand through the window.

Archie dutifully handed over the apple, saying, "It's a fresh one, sir. Very good fer yer appetite, sir."

"Ha!" sneered the young gentleman. "I'll be the judge of that." He took a big bite from the middle of the apple, chewed it, swallowed it, then took another. Fully half the apple was gone in two bites. "This apple is bloody rotten!" cried the gentleman, flinging the apple into the gutter. He gave a rude guffaw. "Ta, you little blighter!"

Archie heard the twitter of female laughter from inside the coach. "Driver," shouted the man, "drive on!"

The coachman, laughing at Archie, snapped the reins, and the horses jolted away.

"Oi! That's not fair," shouted Archie. "You ate my apple! You owe me!"

"Yah-boo!" The young toff waved his arm out the window, offering Archie the vee sign with upturned fingers as the carriage rumbled on. The boy scooped the apple from the gutter, drew back his arm, and let fly. The apple struck the broad back of the carriage, but missed the window.

"Thief!" shouted Archie. "You stinking bloody thief!"

Shaking with anger, he watched the back of the retreating carriage, and the thought came to him of running to catch it, jumping on the back. He had heard the older boys talking about this. Once a wealthy occupant had been identified, the boys hitched a ride and rode it to its destination – most often a great house or large town house – where they disembarked before anyone was any the wiser, and waited for an opportunity to enter the house and steal whatever valuables they might find to carry off.

In this instance, Archie felt the thievery justified: the young aristocrat had stolen from him first. Archie gathered himself. He was just drawing breath to start his run and scramble up onto the footman's stand of the coach when he heard someone call from the pavement a few paces away. "They're gone, lad. The damage is done.

Let them go."

Archie glanced around to see that he was being watched by a man in a long black coat and old-fashioned beaver-skin top hat. The man had dark, full moustaches and a little pointed beard shaped like a heart. He appeared to be of middle age and stood with his back to the bridge rail, holding a cane upright over one shoulder.

Embarrassed that his humiliation had been observed and his attempt at retaliation so nearly discovered, Archie felt the colour rising to his cheeks. He turned aside quickly and started to run away. He still had an apple left. If he hurried he could get to the next bridge and maybe still make a sale before dark.

"A moment!" called the man in the black coat. "A moment more of your time."

Archie looked over his shoulder to see that the man was following him. Ignoring the man, he ran on.

"Wait, I say," insisted the man. "Come back. I want to talk to you."

"Can't stop now," called Archie.

"I shall definitely make it worth your while," offered the man.

Although Archie did not fully understand what was being said to him, something about the man's dry, clipped tones suggested an aristocratic bearing that compelled him to pause and turn back – if only to try selling his last remaining apple. He hurried back, fishing out the apple as he ran.

"I saw what happened," called the man. "A most deplorable cad, that fellow. He should be publicly horsewhipped."

"Would you like to buy an apple, sir?" asked the boy, rubbing the red skin of the fruit on his filthy shirt. He held it up to be admired.

"Are you really an orphan?"

"Yes, sir. Orphaned these four years." He pushed the apple higher. "You like this apple, sir? Very good for you."

"Tell me the truth, lad. Are you an orphan? I have a particular reason for asking." When the boy hesitated, the man insisted. "The truth now."

Archie shook his head. "No, sir. But it's just me and me mum. I'm not really a orphan."

114

"As I thought," replied the man crisply. "And not a street rascal either, though no doubt well on your way. Here now –" Dipping his fingers into a waistcoat pocket, he withdrew a coin and flipped it to the ragged boy. "That is for telling the truth."

Archie saw the glint of yellow metal in the fading light and caught the coin in mid-air. He opened his hand, and his eyes nearly started from his head. On his palm was a solid gold sovereign – a coin he had never seen before, but dreamed about often.

Clutching the coin, Archie extended the apple. "It's too much, sir," he said, his throat going dry. In truth, he knew there had to be a mistake, and when the man realized what had happened, he would cry thief and Archie would face a beating or worse – he'd be taken by the bailiff and thrown into gaol. "Please, sir, it's too much. You made a mistake."

"No mistake," said the man, regarding him keenly. "Keep it."

"Thank you, sir." Archie whipped the coin out of sight.

The man still held him with a fierce attention. The boy squirmed, growing uncomfortable beneath such unwonted scrutiny. "How would you like a job?"

"I don't understand, sir," replied Archie, still holding out the apple.

"A job, lad – work and wages." The man smiled suddenly. "There are more gold sovereigns to be had."

Archie said nothing.

"Well? Come now! I could use a persistent, resourceful lad like you. How about it?"

"I don't know how to do nuffin' – I mean, anything."

"Do you know Marlborough House? Do you know where to find it?"

Archie shook his head. "No, sir."

"Well, you'll have to ask someone. Come to me there first thing tomorrow morning, and we will discuss your future." He gave the boy a stern look. "Hear me, lad. This could be the most important decision you are ever likely to make. Do you understand me?"

Archie understood the part about more gold sovereigns, so nodded slowly.

"And you will come to me at Marlborough House?"

"I will, sir."

"Good. I will take you at your word. When you come, ask to see Granville Gower," said the man, taking the apple at last. "Until tomorrow, then."

CHAPTER 13

In Which an Impossible Birth is Celebrated

Serenity seemed to flow over Etruria in wave after wave, like the gentle surf of an endless ocean of blissful calm. Never had Xian-Li felt more at peace. Although she still had not felt the baby move, she no longer feared the worst.

Turms' continued assurance that all would be well served as a restorative tonic. It was as if the ceremony performed by the king to learn the likely fate of the unborn child had driven off the clouds of doom and disaster that had gathered so thickly about her, and dispelled any lingering doubt. Since that night, everything had changed; she held the memory of the strange ceremony as a rare and precious gift.

They had stood in the temple portico before a small stone altar. The king was attended by a fellow priest and one identified as the *netsvis*; dressed in a blue robe with a tall conical hat similar to the king's, he would conduct the augury. A few curious onlookers had also come to observe the ceremony.

In the last rays of the day's sun, a young lamb had been brought to the temple, its legs bound with a golden cord, and laid upon the altar. After a brief incantation, Turms, splendid in a crimson robe and tall hat trimmed in gold, stooped low and thanked the animal for the sacrifice of its life. With a nod to Arthur and Xian-Li, he beckoned them to the altar and instructed them to place their hands upon the lamb. He then drew a knife made from black volcanic glass across its throat. The small creature lay still and expired without a sound. Then, while attendants eviscerated the carcass, a golden bowl in which some of the blood had been collected was passed to Turms.

He lifted the bowl and drank, then offered the bowl to both Arthur and Xian-Li. After she had taken a sip, he pointed to her stomach and said, "Open your gown just there." She did as instructed and bared a section of her rounded belly. The priest king dipped a finger in the still-warm blood and, with the tip of his finger, drew a small circle on her stomach; he dipped again and added a cross inside the circle of blood. As he did so, he breathed a single word, "*Imantua.*"

The netsvis approached and, with a bow of deference to the king, offered up a golden dish bearing several of the animal's internal organs. The two exchanged a few private words, whereupon the king announced: "As you have seen, the animal died at peace and without distress. This is a good omen. The liver and entrails were pristine and perfectly formed – this, too, bodes well for our inquiry. We will now conduct the augury."

He passed the dish to the seer, who carried it back to the altar where he began to examine the contents, standing with one foot on a block of uncut stone that had been placed beneath the altar. Other attendants gathered around, and all leaned near to study the organs and determine from the signs what could be told of the unborn child's future.

Twilight overtook the ceremony, so torches were lit. Arthur and Xian-Li stood waiting while the priests continued their deliberations amid much mumbled discussion. This continued far longer than Xian-Li might have expected. She watched with dread fascination as one of the priests took up the obsidian knife and began to divide the liver into sections, subjecting each section to minute examination.

The first stars were shining in the east when the netsvis finally turned and offered his judgment. Turms listened, his head bowed, nodding now and then as the blue-robed seer spoke. The king thanked him for his counsel, then summoned an attendant, who brought forth a censer on a chain. The attendant blew on the coals in the bowl, then dropped a pinch of something onto the glowing charcoal. Fragrant smoke billowed from the bowl. Turms bowed at the waist as the censer was swung before his face. He closed his eyes and breathed in the smoke... once... twice... three times; he made a gesture as if he were washing his hands in it, then placed his hands over his face. Palms pressed to his eyes, he grew very still.

Xian-Li had begun to think he had fallen asleep on his feet when Turms opened his eyes and gazed at her. With the glint of a rising moon shining in his dark eyes, he said, "I have seen the life light of the child stretching far into the future like a radiant silver cord. The end of this cord cannot be seen. It is lost to view in the unformed darkness of the distant future." He smiled. "I believe this signifies a long and meaningful life for the child soon to make his appearance in the land of the living."

Arthur squeezed his wife's hand. "The child will be born alive," he said, more a question seeking confirmation than a statement.

"The birth will be blessed with success, and the resulting infant will thrive," the king assured them in a tone that allowed no room for doubt. "I, Turms the Immortal, have seen this."

"Thank you, O King," breathed Xian-Li. Then the tears began to flow as the fear that had held her these last weeks released its unforgiving grip. "Thank you."

"I have seen something else," Turms continued. "After this child, your womb will be closed. There will be no more children for you."

Arthur darted a glance at his wife to see how she would receive this blow, but her smile did not alter. "I understand," she murmured, resting her hand on her belly. "I will cherish this one the more."

The ceremony moved to its conclusion, but Xian-Li remembered little of what happened after the pronouncement. That night she slept better than she could remember and rose the next morning at perfect peace. The house was still asleep when she slipped out. Unseen, she walked down the path to the temple and there, as the first rays of the sun touched the temple steps, she knelt and gave thanks for the life of her unborn child.

Now, as the first pangs of birth came upon her, Xian-Li recalled the serenity of that sacred moment. Her heart rose, and she pressed a hand to her swollen belly. Soon – before another day had dawned – she would hold her babe in her arms. When the next quiver of pain came upon her, she reached over to her sleeping husband and let her hand fall upon his shoulder. She did not shake him, but let the warmth of her body gently awaken him.

"It is time," she said when he raised his head from the pillow beside her.

He sat up with a jerk. "Now?"

She smiled. "Soon. In a little while. Lie down beside me." He put his head down again and closed his eyes; she closed hers too, remembering that day a few weeks after the ceremony when, over a dinner of roast quail and greens, Turms had announced, "It would please me to have the child to be born here in the royal palace." Before either she or Arthur could reply, the king had quickly added, "It is a long time since this house heard the sound of a baby's cry. I would consider it an honour if you agreed to this request."

"After all you have done for us, the honour would be mine," she had said, picking out the words in his language – the first time she had spoken to him on her own. This surprised and delighted their noble host. "We accept."

"She has been learning," Arthur told him.

"I am impressed."

"You have done so much for us already," said Arthur. "We are in your debt."

"How can friends ever be indebted to one another?"

Thus, Xian-Li had completed her time in the best place she could have imagined – luxuriating in the sun and warmth, the food and company, and all the accoutrements of the palace. Had she been a queen, she could not have been treated more royally. And the knowledge that she would be delivered of a living child made it all that much more to be cherished. The final weeks had passed, and now it was time for the child to be born. She was ready.

When, later in the day, she was in the throes of birthing the baby and surrounded by skilled Etruscan physicians, she knew that all was as it should be. There was a rightness to things that surpassed understanding, but she knew beyond all doubt that in each and every circumstance her feet had been guided along this path and to this place. A favourite saying in China – which she had heard on occasion from her own grandmother – was that the threads of life are easy to weave, but difficult to untangle. Xian-Li knew, for Arthur had shown her, that the threads of her life were being woven by a master of the loom.

Arthur, having spent the better part of an anxious day sitting outside the birthing house, appeared at her bedside to receive his first glimpse of the newborn. "Well done, Xian-Li," he said, beaming with pride. "We have a son."

"Yes, a son," she whispered, somewhat dizzy with exhaustion. "Is he not the most beautiful child?" Xian-Li pulled back the edge of her robe, which swaddled her baby, to reveal a small, pinched red face with a mass of spiky black hair resembling the glistening pelt of a bear. The infant's eyes were shut tight and its tiny lips pressed firm as if the child was determined to sleep through any efforts that might be made to introduce him to this strange new world.

"He is perfect," murmured his father. Arthur leaned close and gave his wife a kiss. "Thank you," he said.

She reached for his hand and squeezed it.

"What shall we call him?" he asked, perching on the edge of the bed, his hand resting on the tiny lump beneath her robe.

They had been so preoccupied with the troubled pregnancy – and, truth be told, in some part of their deepest hearts they had not fully believed Turms' prediction of a successful birth – that they had utterly neglected the important task of selecting a name. Whatever the reason, they now realized this oversight.

"He is your son," said Xian-Li, brushing the infant's forehead with her lips. "You should choose, husband."

"Very well," agreed Arthur. "Do you have any suggestions?"

She shook her head. "The son of an Englishman must have an English name. Whatever pleases you will please me also."

He gazed at his newborn son, hoping for inspiration, but nothing came to him. "I don't know," he confessed. "There are so many."

She laughed. "He needs only one."

He rubbed his hand along his unshaved jaw. "This is going to take some thought."

The Etruscans had a custom that a newborn infant should not be named until seven days had passed. "On the eighth day," Turms told Arthur, "the child receives his name. This is a very old tradition. The eighth day − it is the most propitious day for naming, beginning a new venture, or undertaking a journey."

Arthur liked that idea, since it allowed him plenty of time to think. It did not, however, make the thinking any easier. In his search, he conjured before him the faces of all his male ancestors − all those he could remember, alive or dead − to see if any of them had qualities he admired and whose names he might borrow and commemorate. This proved a useful exercise, but all the time devoted to the project failed to bring him any closer to a final decision.

When, after four days had passed, Xian-Li asked him what he was thinking, he was forced to admit that while he had begun drawing up a list, he had not yet chosen a name. He told her what Turms had said about refraining from conferring a name until seven days had passed. She accepted this, but warned, "Ponder as much as you like, but you have only four more days."

His ruminations carried him to the final hour of the final day.

"The king has asked me to inform you that tomorrow morning at sunrise we will hold the naming ceremony," the king's chief housekeeper told him. "I am to come and wake you at the appropriate time."

"Ah," replied Arthur, wondering where the days had flown. "Thank you, Pacha. Please, tell the king we will be ready."

So, as the night ended and the moon began to set over the Tyrrhenian Sea, Arthur and Xian-Li walked down the moonlit path to the little temple at the bottom of the hill. Xian-Li carried the infant asleep in her arms. It was the first time she had been out since the baby was born, and it felt good to move and feel the soft night air on her face, and to see the world once again. Turms had come to see her several times since the birth, and she wanted to thank him for his thoughtfulness.

When they reached the temple, however, he was not there. In fact, no one was about except a young acolyte, who had been charged with the task of informing them that the naming ceremony would not take place in the temple. "I am to ask you to follow me," he said. "It is not far. But there is a donkey ready if you would like to ride."

"It feels good to walk," Xian-Li said when Arthur had relayed the offer.

"Thank you, but we will walk," Arthur told the youth. "Lead the way."

They continued along the path towards the town and soon came to a small pillar standing to one side. The acolyte paused here and, turning to them, said, "They are gathered at the king's tomb. It is on the sacred road." Indicating the little pillar, he said, "You are to wash before you enter the sacred way."

The top of the pillar had been hollowed into a shallow depression, and this was filled with water. The young man demonstrated how to make the symbolic gesture by dipping his hands and then passing them over his head and face. "Also the child," he said when they had done as instructed. Xian-Li dipped her fingertips in the water and, pushing away the unruly shock of hair, dampened the child's forehead and wet his curled little hands.

The young acolyte led them off the path towards what appeared to be nothing more than the edge of a small defile – a place where the ground had crumbled away, or where a stream had cut through the soft earth over time. They quickly discovered, however, that it was not a natural feature at all, but man-made. Steps had been cut in the soft tufa stone that lay beneath the ground.

This hewn staircase led down and down, passing between narrow walls until they could no longer see the surface they had left behind. At the bottom, the steps joined a passage wide enough for two horses to pass abreast; the passage stretched away on either hand. Torches had been lit and set in simple sconces carved into the towering stone walls.

"This is the sacred road," the young man informed them.

"Where does it lead?" asked Arthur.

"It joins other sacred ways in other places," replied the acolyte. "There are many such throughout the land."

They walked along, the passageway cast in deepest gloom though the sky above held the faint glimmer of the rising sun. They passed an elaborate doorway that had been carved into the tufa; columns, also carved, supported a triangular pediment that bore the sculpted image of a man in long robes lying on a low couch. There was an inscription, which seemed to be a name carved into the architrave. The doors were of stone and sealed.

"What is this?" asked Arthur.

"It is the tomb of Lars Volsina," answered the youth. "He was a king of our people many years ago."

They passed another doorway set in a niche on the opposite side of the sunken road, then two more; as they continued along, there were more of these elaborate facades: some larger, grandly decorated porticoes with steps and columns; others simple posts and lintels framing a stone door. "Are they all tombs?" wondered Arthur. "All these doorways?"

"Yes, all are tombs of kings and noblemen."

The deep-carved passageway wound gently down, curving as it went. As it straightened again they saw a short distance ahead a group of people standing before another of the rock-cut tombs, this one somewhat larger than the others and more elaborate, with stone steps leading up to a covered porch. A fire had been lit in an iron bowl supported by a tripod, and torches attached to the columns and walls of the sunken roadway gave the tufa a warm, ruddy glow. There was a stone plinth covered with an orange cloth in front of the steps. King Turms stood before it, flanked on either side by women in long white linen gowns. Both had their hair braided in such a way as to fall over each shoulder; one of them held a golden bowl, the other a knife with a blade of black glass.

"Welcome, friends," called Turms as they came to stand before the plinth. "This rite is best observed on the sacred way in the presence of venerable ancestors," he explained. "This is a most auspicious place."

At Arthur's sceptical expression, he said, "I suppose it will seem strange to you that the celebration of new life should take place among the tombs. Even so, this, like the road you have taken to come here, represents the journey of life itself. We are travellers, and each of us, body and soul together, is a companion for life's journey. One day we will part company, as we must. The body, grown weary, will take its rest at last." Turms lifted a hand to the surrounding tombs.

"But for those whose spirits are alive to the purposes of creation," he continued, "there is no final destination. For such as these, death is merely a pause, an interlude where one can gather strength for new and greater journeys. Friends, we are created travellers. I ask you, what true traveller ever arrived in a new place who did not wish to explore it, and in exploring did not continue his travels, seeing new sights, learning new ways, breathing the air of a new land under new skies, and rejoicing in new discoveries?"

Turms the Immortal, priest king of the Velathri, turned and motioned to the woman with the bowl. She stepped forward, placing the bowl on the orange-draped plinth. "Though the body you bring before me in this most favourable hour will one day grow weary and die, the new spirit which has entered the world in this body is immortal and will never die. Know this, my friends: we are – all of us – immortal."

He held out his hands. "Give me the child."

Xian-Li, who had been following Turms' explanation with Arthur's whispered translation, extended her arms and gently placed her newborn son in the king's hands. Turms raised the infant above his head, then passed him to the woman who had held the bowl. She unwrapped the baby and presented him naked to the king, who cradled him in his arms. "As the last stars of the night fade into the dawn, so begins a new day in the dying of the old. This is as it must be."

Turms dipped a little water from the bowl and wet the baby's head. "We welcome you, little soul, into the life we all share in this

125

world," he said, his voice growing as soft as a mother's. Extending his hand to the woman with the knife, he said, "Yours is not a solitary life, little one." With a quick deft stroke he pricked the sole of the infant's foot with the point of the knife.

Xian-Li stifled a gasp, and the child gave a squeak of surprise at the sudden, fleeting pain. A big drop of bright red blood welled up on the little heel. Turms dabbed the blood with a forefinger and made a spot on the baby's forehead, then repeated the gesture three times, placing a spot first on Xian-Li's forehead, then on Arthur's, and finally on his own. "This sign is to remind you that your life is not yours alone – it is mingled with your parents, and with all those who came before you and will come after. But it is mingled with others, too, just as their lives are mingled with still others. In this way, we are all part of one another."

The baby, growing cold and uncomfortable in the morning air, squirmed and gave out a growl like that of a kitten or a cub. The king smiled and returned the child to the woman holding the swaddling cloth; she gathered the infant once more into the soft folds and returned him to the king. Turms placed his hand on the infant's head and said, "Our hope for you is that you will grow to be strong and virtuous in spirit and deed, and that whether the length of your journey through this world is short or long, it will be a boon to you and all those around you. Learn well, little soul, so that the knowledge and wisdom you gather on your way can strengthen and sustain you in the life to come."

Turms raised his eyes and asked Arthur, "By what name will this child be known?"

Arthur's mouth framed the word *Benjamin* – a name he had decided on that held some resonance for him. Curiously, his tongue uttered, "Benedict."

The king nodded. Taking the infant's curled fist in his, he dipped the tiny hand into the water, and then pressed that little fist to the baby's chest. "From henceforth you will be called Benedict."

Xian-Li glanced at her husband and mouthed the question, *"Benedict?"*

The ceremony was completed, and Turms handed the child back to his mother. The two women attendants took up the bowl and knife once more.

"Wait," said Arthur. "I meant to say *Benjamin*."

Turms' smile grew broad, and he put back his head and laughed. "And yet you did not."

"But –" Arthur started to object.

"It is done, my friend," the king told him. "And it is right. The name you have given is what was chosen for him. All is as it must be."

Arthur gave in to the decision with rueful acceptance. They all walked back to the palace to eat a celebratory meal in honour of the newly named infant, retracing their steps along the sacred way, passing the silent tombs. They mounted the steps and, upon reaching the top, the rising sun broke above the horizon, for a moment dazzling them. Arthur felt as if, having spent the night in the tomb, he was rising to new life.

On the way back up the hill, Xian-Li leaned close to her husband. "Why Benedict?" she wondered. "What does it mean?"

"I'm not exactly sure," confessed Arthur. "Blessing or blessed one, I think – something like that."

Xian-Li smiled and held the infant up before her to look at him. "He is our blessing," she decided, and the awkwardness of the mistake dissolved. In that moment, the world settled into place once more.

CHAPTER 14

In Which the Truth Cannot Be Ignored

A few scrawny cats and a beggar scrabbled among gently smouldering heaps of rubbish. A swirl of black vultures circled overhead in lazy loops, keen-eyed for anything dead or dying. The naked sun slammed down like a hammer upon the poor anvil that was Kit's throbbing head, smiting through the thin cloth of his sweat-soaked turban. "My kingdom for a straw hat," he muttered, blinking in sunlight so hot it dried his eyeballs in their sockets.

An endless avenue of pale, human-headed sphinxes stretched before him, its end lost in the shimmering heat haze. Somewhere in that wavering mirage lay the ruins of one of the ancient world's wonders: the Great Temple of Amun. It was somewhere in the temple complex at the end of the avenue, Kit had been informed, that he would find the man he had come upriver to meet. Squinting his eyes against the glare bouncing up from the white-paved street, he started walking. After only a minute, he was wishing he had not been quite so hasty in rejecting Khefri's suggestion that he hire a donkey for the journey. "It's a straight shot to the temple, right?" he had said. "How bad can it be?"

To take his mind off the heat, he tried to imagine why Wilhelmina had been so insistent that he meet this man. What did Young know that could help them? He also wondered how much Wilhelmina had told this fellow about the quest they were conducting, and consequently how much he might risk saying. That, Kit decided, would be the first thing he must discover.

After a leisurely boat ride down the Nile, and a brief stop to haggle for the turban, Kit and Khefri had shaken hands and parted company at the steps of the Winter Palace Hotel. "*Shukran*, my friend," Kit had said. "If I have need of a boat, I will come looking for you."

"May God be good to you, Kit Livingstone," replied the young man. "Farewell." The last Kit had seen of him, the young man was hurrying back to join his cousin in the boat.

Following Wilhelmina's instructions, he had presented himself to the concierge at the reception desk and asked for the parcel that, all being well, was waiting for him. The concierge, a robust Egyptian in a black frock coat and fez, disappeared into an office, returning a moment later with a package. He held it in his hand and regarded Kit dubiously. "Could this be the parcel, sir?"

"Why, yes, I believe so."

The fellow hefted it in his hand, but made no attempt to deliver it.

"May I have it, please?"

"Do you have anything for me?"

"Ah, no," answered Kit slowly. "I don't think so."

"Nothing at all?" wondered the fellow.

"No. Nothing at all. Why? Was I supposed to have something for you? I was not given anything –"

"A small gift, perhaps?" He regarded the parcel in his hand.

"Oh!" said Kit, as understanding broke upon him. "Yes, I see."

The concierge smiled.

"But I am terribly sorry," Kit offered. "I don't have any money. I've been in the desert, you see." He turned out an empty pocket. "Nada. Nothing. Sorry."

With a shrug, the fellow handed over the small packet, and Kit wandered into the lobby to open it. About the size and thickness of an old-school exercise book, it was wrapped in brown paper and tied with string; a small handwritten note had been stuck in where the ends of the string were tied in a neat bow, and it was addressed to him. It read: *Kit: Do not open this package. Take it – unopened – to Dr Thomas Young at the Karnak temple dig just outside Luxor. You will find him there from late spring to early autumn. The parcel will serve as your letter of introduction. He will know what is to be done. Remember, DO NOT open this package. Not even a little!*

He turned the parcel over. The folded flaps were sealed with a blob of old-fashioned sealing wax. Beside the seal was a message: *Do not even THINK about opening this package!*

"Okay! Got it," muttered Kit. "Sheesh, what a nag. I won't open the stupid package."

Tucking the packet under his shirt, he had then made his way to the old temple. When he finally arrived at the shattered remains of the temple gate, he was perspiring from every pore, the sweat drying almost instantly as it hit the dry desert air. The huge blocks of the fabled pylons – the great slant-backed walls flanking the temple entrance – lay tumbled on the ground, though the parts of the wall extant rose to the height of several storeys. Many of the courses still bore their original paint, and the colours glowed in the fierce light. Through the now-empty gate he could see collapsed pillars and more jumbled heaps of rubble across a very lumpy landscape, most of which was covered with low acacia bushes, stunted palms of various sorts, and coarse, scrubby saw grass. More beggars reclined idly in the broken doorways, while in the shadows he could see the furtive shapes of feral cats.

Kit wiped beaded sweat from his face, put his hand to the cargo he carried beneath his shirt, and started into the temple courtyard, climbing over a heap of rubble and into what had once been an immense expanse of gargantuan columns shaped like bundles of papyrus; some of these stood upright, proudly supporting their connecting lintels as if bearing the weight of the clear blue sky above. His presence was quickly seized upon by the more enterprising beggars, who hobbled to greet him with toothless whines and filthy palms outstretched. "*La, shukran,*" he told them as firmly and politely as he could.

"Sir! Sir!" one of the beggars called in English. "You need a guide, sir?"

"No, thank you. I'm fine." Kit did not even look up, since to do so would only encourage the fellow. "Thanks all the same."

"You are looking for someone, maybe?"

At this, Kit glanced around to see a wizened Egyptian in a very dirty kaftan and skin like creased leather standing perfectly still, a little apart from the importuning gaggle of his comrades in rags. "You are looking for someone," the man repeated. "I think so."

"Yes," admitted Kit, instantly regretting his lapse. "I am looking for someone – an Englishman, actually."

"You are looking for Dr Thomas Young, perhaps," suggested the bold fellow.

"The very man," confirmed Kit, pulling up short. "Do you know him?"

"I know him, sir." The Egyptian raised his voice and shouted a single word of command, and the others promptly ceased their mewling and silently drifted away. To Kit, he said, "Your friend is not far."

"Thanks," said Kit, much relieved. "But I don't want to put you to any trouble. If you could point me in the right direction, I'd be much obliged."

The man smiled, his teeth a flash of white in the tangle of his matted beard. "It is no trouble. Please, follow me."

Despite his obviously much reduced state, the man held himself with great dignity, walking through the crumbling ruins – shattered monuments on every side – as through a palace entire, treading lightly on the stones beneath his feet. Kit trailed along behind him, stumbling now and then over the rough, uneven surface, mindful of the treasures buried only a few feet underground. He had a vague memory of having seen photos of what in his day was – or would be – called the temple complex of Karnak – a vast acreage of honey-coloured buildings inscribed with every manner of hieroglyph imaginable. The tumbled remains of the once-great temple now trampled underfoot would one day rise again. The acres of broken blocks would be set one atop another once more, the carvings would be lovingly restored, the walls and lintels, obelisks, and innumerable statues of gods and men would be reclaimed from the waste and wilderness of uncaring eons, and the whole made accessible to the tourists who would fill the hotel boats that would

131

be built to ply the Nile and spill their human cargo over the ancient sites in a living flood.

But this – *this* mouldering ruin was how the place looked before excavation became a big business in the land of the pharaohs. Considering what the sprawling temple complex would eventually become – yet another heritage site swarming with short-shorts and baseball caps – Kit much preferred seeing it like this: a forest of half-fallen columns and collapsed structures, many still bearing their original paintwork, with here and there a smaller temple or storeroom completely intact, standing firm against the ravages of time. Aside from the beggars and stray dogs – did the two always go together? – there was no one. Not a single T-shirt shop or Coca-Cola sign in sight. And Kit was the only foreigner.

The beggar guide led him through the haphazard maze of devastation, past primitive campsites of squatters and mounds of garbage – the locals dumped here, obviously – and over fallen remnants of mighty Ramesses' imperious statues, at last reaching a small, square building, the front of which was obscured by a toppled obelisk. Around the back of this structure Kit glimpsed a white flap of canvas; a ramshackle lean-to of timber and canvas had been set up over a sizeable hole. Six or eight men in dirty blue kaftans and black turbans stood around the edge of the hole, ready to receive baskets full of sand and rock that were being lifted up to them.

"Here is the man you are looking for," said his guide.

Kit regarded the ring of workers and thought there must be some mistake, and was about to say as much when a voice called up from the hole. "*Shukran! Shukran!* That will be all for now!"

A white straw hat appeared at the edge of the hole, followed by a round, whiskered face, flushed red by the man's recent exertions. The fellow took one look at Kit and put out a hand. "Greetings, friend! I am Thomas Young. How do you do?"

Stepping to the edge of the hole, Kit bent and extended his hand to receive a hearty handshake. "Kit Livingstone, sir. I am well, thank you."

"Would you mind terribly?" asked Dr Young, still gripping Kit's hand. "A small assist would be most useful."

"Not at all," replied Kit, who gave a solid tug.

The fellow scrambled out of the pit and patted the dust from his beige linen suit. "That is better."

He straightened and, hands on hips, stood regarding Kit, his grey eyes keen behind small round steel-rimmed glasses. A compact, tightly knit man, he gave the impression of barely contained energy, like a coiled spring. Beneath his tropical linen he wore a white shirt and a waistcoat of yellow silk. The boots on his feet were of the heavy, serviceable type a military man might favour. "So!" he cried at last. "Here you are!"

"Here I am indeed," confirmed Kit. The physician stood gazing at him as at a prize exhibit in a zoo until Kit, growing uncomfortable under the man's scrutiny, blurted, "I believe we have a mutual friend."

"Yes," agreed Thomas Young amiably, "I rather believe we do."

"Wilhelmina —"

"Striking girl," said Thomas, stirring himself. "Most remarkable young woman. Possessed of a strength of will one encounters only rarely. A genuinely unique individual."

"She's all that," conceded Kit.

"Come, sir, it is the heat of the day. We must not stand out here jawing like a pair of yahoos. I have a jug of lemon water standing by. Splendidly refreshing. Will you share a drink with me in my tent?"

"I would be delighted," replied Kit, falling into the more formal rhythms of nineteenth-century speech. "I am positively parched."

"Khalid!" shouted Thomas. "We are retiring to my tent. Rest the workers now and give them something to eat and drink. Tell them we will resume at the usual time. When you have done that, join us, please."

The servant made a slight bow and then, turning, clapped his hands for attention. As the workers moved off, Kit observed, "You sent him to look for me."

"I did," replied the doctor, leading the way to a large tent that had been erected in the scant shade of twin palm trees. "Every day at this time he went to look for you. I thought if you came at all, it would be in the morning. It is just too hot later. It is still early in the season," he said, "and already it is beastly – much too warm for this time of year." He stepped to the entrance of the tent and held aside the opening flap. "I fear I shall soon be forced to suspend excavations. Pity."

Kit ducked under the flap and into a commodious, well-ventilated space that was less tent than open-sided marquee. Two sides were hung with gauzy material; periodically, a servant would come by to sprinkle it with water using an olive branch and a wooden pail – a primitive but surprisingly effective form of air-conditioning. The reprieve from the heat and hammering sun was instant and welcome, and Kit could not help offering up a sigh of relief.

The interior was divided into two distinct areas: a working place with a desk and lamp, three folding chairs, and a wicker settee, and a sleeping place with a cot shrouded by insect netting; the two were divided by a standing screen of woven palm fronds. The slightly uneven floor was covered by heavy Egyptian carpets laid one atop another. It was, Kit decided, the temporary abode of a well-seasoned traveller, one who knew and understood his surroundings. This was further demonstrated when the doctor removed the lid of a covered bowl and drew out a roll of wet cloth. "Put this around your neck," he said, passing the roll to Kit. He took one for himself and draped it around the nape of his neck. Kit did likewise and instantly felt the better for it.

Beside the desk stood a small tripod bearing a large oval tray of brass; on the tray were a painted pottery jug and several upside-down glasses. A shallow bowl of almonds sat beside the jug, and it was to this that Thomas Young was first drawn. "Here, my good fellow, get some of these into you," he said, offering the bowl.

Kit took a few of the heavily salted almonds and popped them into his mouth; his host did the same.

"You need the salt in this heat. It's good for you. Prevents heat prostration." Returning the bowl to the tray, he waved Kit to a chair. "Please, sit down, Mr Livingstone. We will rest awhile and chat."

Kit lowered himself into the canvas chair and accepted a glass of the pale yellow liquid. It was tepid, but the sharp tang of the lemon made it palatable. Thomas settled into his chair behind the desk and sat gazing at his guest from behind an untidy mass of papers and various drawing utensils. Kit sipped his water and waited for his host to begin.

"Do I dare ask if you have brought something for me?" wondered Thomas at last.

"As it happens," replied Kit. He placed his half-empty glass on the tray and, fumbling at the buttons on the front of his shirt, produced the brown paper package he had retrieved from the hotel. "I was instructed to deliver this to you unopened. As you can see, I have obeyed these instructions." He rose and, holding it in both hands, ceremoniously placed the paper-wrapped bundle on the desk before his host. "I am happy to pass this to your care."

Thomas made no move to pick it up, but sat with his hands folded before him, regarding it quizzically. "Do you know what is inside the wrapping?"

"No, sir, I do not," replied Kit. "I was not told. Do you?"

"In part." Thomas raised his eyes to Kit and then returned to his survey of the parcel. "If it is what I think it is…"

Kit waited. The archaeologist neither altered his gaze nor made any move to pick up the packet. He simply sat staring at the string-bound rectangle.

"Dr Young?" said Kit after a moment. "Is anything the matter?"

"If this is what has been promised, history will change." He raised his eyes once more, his round glasses glinting in the soft light of the tent. "You know that, do you not? The world will change."

"Right." Kit nodded. He could wait a little longer for that.

Outside, the braying of a donkey echoed across the ruins. As if in response to the sound, the doctor drew a sharp intake of breath and pulled the package closer. He lifted it, diffidently balanced between his hands – the very picture of a man trying to delay an action he might well regret. Kit could sympathize. Who could guess what Wilhelmina had put in that parcel?

"The thing must be done, I suppose," Thomas said and, with trembling fingers, untied the string and peeled open the paper wrapping to reveal a curious assortment of objects: an old shilling coin, a letter, a newspaper clipping, and several printed pages that appeared to have been torn from a book – more or less what might be found in the average scrapbook – nothing that appeared likely to be of much importance, let alone world-shattering consequence.

Kit watched as his host examined the coin, then put it aside and lifted the letter, scrutinizing it front and back. The letter was in Mina's hand and addressed to Christopher "Kit" Livingstone in the care of Dr Thomas Young. The white envelope was sealed and stamped, but the stamp had not been cancelled. Thomas placed the letter before him on the desk. "This alone would have been enough," he murmured.

"Sir?" wondered Kit.

"See here," Thomas said, pointing to the stamp – a simple black postage stamp with an engraved silhouette of a young Queen Victoria with the words *one penny* beneath – a fairly unremarkable example, to Kit's eye.

"The stamp, yes?"

"This *stamp* as you call it" – Thomas touched it lightly with a fingertip – "has never been seen before – at least not by me."

"May I?" said Kit, picking up the letter. "I see the letter is addressed to me."

"By all means," said the doctor. "You must open it at once."

Kit slid his finger under the flap and drew out a single piece of plain white paper that read: *Kit – If you are reading this, you have met Dr Thomas Young – the last man in the world who knows everything. Trust him with your life. Ever yours, Mina.* And that was all.

Thomas, in the meantime, had picked up the coin and now held it between his thumb and forefinger, turning it over and over with a look of bewilderment on his face – an expression Kit guessed was highly unusual for the man. He passed the shilling piece to Kit for examination. The silver coin bore the profile of Victoria on one side and, on the other, a crown with the simple words *one shilling* beneath. Below Victoria's disembodied head was the date: 1835.

"Have you ever seen the like?" asked Thomas.

"Yes, I have," replied Kit, handing it back. "Many times."

The English gentleman simply nodded and laid the coin beside the letter. He picked up the newspaper clipping, glanced at it, and then looked at Kit. "Have you ever been to Kew Gardens?" he asked.

"Once or twice," replied Kit. "It is a well-known attraction. People go there for picnics and a pleasant day out."

The doctor set aside the clipping and, placing his hands flat on the printed pages torn from the book, he said, "This, I believe, will be the ultimate test."

Kit could not think how to respond to this, so remained silent.

"Unless I am very much mistaken, our mutual friend will have provided me with undeniable proof that what she has claimed, outrageous though it seems, is in fact the naked truth."

He then lifted the pages and, with a slightly trembling hand, offered them to Kit. "Would you read it to me, please?"

Taking the loose sheets, Kit scanned the top one quickly on both sides. It was merely the title page – torn hastily from the spine, it would seem, judging from the ragged edge; the reverse contained part of an acknowledgement by the author. "You want me to read this?"

"Please," replied Thomas Young, removing his glasses and closing his eyes.

Kit cleared his throat and began: "A Course of Lectures on Natural Philosophy and the Mechanical Arts, by Thomas Young, MD. A new edition with references and notes by the Rev. P. Kelland, MA, FRS. London and Edinburgh. Printed for Taylor and Walton, Upper Gower Street. 1845."

Kit glanced up at his audience. Young was sitting very still, his eyes closed. Kit turned the page over and continued reading: "Having undertaken to prepare a course of lectures on natural philosophy to be delivered in the theatre of the Royal Institution, I thought that the plan of the institution required something more than a mere compilation from the elementary works at present existing, and that it was my duty to digest into one system everything relating to the principles of the mechanical sciences that could tend to the improvement of the arts subservient to the conveniences of life."

He paused for breath and waited. In a moment Thomas nodded, and Kit resumed: "I found also, in delivering the lectures, that it was most eligible to commit to writing, as nearly as possible, the whole that was required to be said on each subject, and that even when an experiment was to be performed it was best to describe that experiment uninterruptedly and to repeat the explanation during its exhibition. Hence it became necessary that the written lectures should be as clearly and copiously expressed and in a language as much adapted to the comprehension of a mixed audience as the nature of the investigations would allow…"

The doctor gave out a groan, and Kit broke off. Thomas Young sat as still as a sphinx, eyes closed, outwardly composed. The only sign of an internal struggle was to be seen in his hands, which were clasped so tightly together the knuckles were white.

"Would you like me to continue?" asked Kit, his voice breaking into the intense reverie of the man behind the desk. "Is everything all right?"

"No," breathed the physician. "Nothing is right." He opened his eyes and looked at Kit with an expression of wonder and despair. "It is from a book – *my* book. That is what your Wilhelmina has brought me as proof of her assertions."

"Yes, so I gather, but –"

"That is the trouble." Thomas stretched a finger towards the page in Kit's hand and gestured mutely at it as if at the certificate of his own death. "This book is not yet published. In fact, it is not even finished."

Kit could imagine how that might be a problem. "Oh," he said, trying to sound sympathetic. "I see."

Thomas's glance became sharp. "Do you?" he demanded. "I submit that you do not see the half, sir! This –" He snatched the page from Kit's grasp. "This scrap of paper comes to me from another world and a future not my own, a world where all I have thought and done is already past – where I am dead and buried and the things I see before me, now worn with age, are yet to be." The doctor shook his head again. "Do you see it yet? Time is out of joint, and reality merely a delusion. All I have believed about the world is a mirage, a chimera, a fantasy. My work, my science… worthless. How," he asked, his voice falling to a lament, "how am I to live in light of that?"

Part 3

Coming Forth by Day

CHAPTER 15

In Which an Apprenticeship is Begun

Xian-Li thrust her hand into the bowl cradled on her hip. She smelled the dry, sweet, floury scent of the cracked corn as she filled her palm, then flung the handful in a wide, generous arc around her. The chickens, already flocking to her, squawked and fluttered as they scurried to snatch up the kernels she had scattered. She watched their sleek heads bobbing as they pecked at the corn. A simple chore, feeding chickens, yet she took great pleasure in it – knowing that it was something her mother and grandmother had done all their lives. The uncomplicated act linked her to generations past and present and yet to come, and that gave her a comfortable feeling.

"I thought I would find you here," said Arthur, a slight reproof in his tone.

She turned and smiled as he came to stand beside her.

"We have servants to do this, you know," he said. "You are the lady of the house. You don't have to feed chickens."

"I enjoy it." She flung another handful to her circle of plump brown hens. "And they like it."

He caught her wrist as she returned it to the bowl. "Your hands, my love," he said, lifting her palm. "They are getting rough. You do too much."

"I do what pleases me, husband," she countered. "Would you deny me that?"

He kissed her palm and released it. "It will be tomorrow," he said after a moment. He felt her stiffen beside him. "I cannot put it off any longer."

"But he is only six years old," Xian-Li declared. Her face clouded, and her lips pursed in objection.

"He is old enough." Arthur waited, watching the chickens scratching for errant kernels they had missed in the first flurry of feeding. "We've always known this day was coming. It is time he began his apprenticeship."

"But he is only a child," she complained, resisting what she knew to be true.

"The boy must learn." Arthur was adamant. "He must be taught."

Xian-Li turned and flung another handful of grain to her flock.

"He won't be going alone," said Arthur, pointing out the obvious. "Do you imagine for a moment I would let any harm come near him?"

She frowned, her normally smooth brow furrowed now.

"Xian-Li," he said softly. "It *is* time."

She sighed, lowering her head in submission.

To assuage her anxiety, he added, "Besides, he must have some experience of it if we are to consider taking him to see your father and sister in Macau."

"You are right, husband. I worry too much. But if anything happened to –"

Arthur interrupted before she could finish the thought. "I know."

Since coming back to England, Xian-Li had taken charge of the smallholding that had been in Arthur's family for over a hundred years. Tucked away in the Cotswold countryside, she had devoted herself to her family and made a good life for herself and Arthur and little Benedict – away from the judgmental stares of city sophisticates who considered her a member of an inferior race. To the country folk of Oxfordshire, Xian-Li was a curious and somewhat exotic novelty whose presence among them provided interest in what was often a drearily mundane existence. As people in the neighbouring holdings and settlements had grown to know her, they accepted her, according the family a higher rank and status in respect of Arthur's learning and manners. Arthur became known as "the squire" and Benedict, affectionately rechristened Ben by the locals, became "the young squire". The boy was their sole pride and joy – all the more so because both Xian-Li and Arthur knew there would not be another child.

Later, Arthur took his turn at tucking little Benedict into bed so he could deliver the good news. "Tomorrow," he said, "we are going on a journey."

Ben looked up, excited. "Are we going to town?"

"No." His father shook his head. "We are not going to Banbury, or Whitney, or even Oxford. We're going somewhere far away from England."

"China!" The little black-haired boy rose up in bed.

"No, not China. Not this time. That is a difficult journey, and you must be older for that."

"Where are we going?"

"We are going to Egypt."

"Egypt?"

"That's right. Remember I told you about my friend Anen who lives in Egypt?"

The boy nodded.

"We are going to pay him a visit."

"And I can go too?"

"Yes," his father assured him. "You will come with me this time. There is much to learn, and it is time your lessons were begun."

The boy sat up in bed again and clapped his hands. His father pressed him back down. "We must leave very early in the morning, and you must get your rest. Now, say your prayers and blow out the candle. Morning will be here soon enough."

When Arthur came to wake him the next morning, he found his son already awake and dressed, shirt laced, shoes buckled. "You look a fine traveller," Arthur told him. "Did you sleep at all last night?"

Ben nodded. "Are we leaving now?"

"Right this very minute," replied his father. "The carriage is ready. We can eat our breakfast while Timothy drives." He tucked in the boy's shirt tails and tightened his belt. "Now, run and kiss your mother goodbye. Then put on your coat. I will be waiting for you in the yard outside."

Ben ran downstairs, his feet clumping heavily on the wooden floorboards as he ran. Arthur followed, retrieving his own coat and hat on the way. Xian-Li was waiting for them in the yard, a bag of provisions in her hand. Arthur gave her a farewell kiss and pressed both her hands in his. "Never fear, I *will* take good care of him."

"Of course you will," she said, forcing a smile.

Daybreak was still some time off when the coach rolled out from their farm and into the gently folded hills and valleys of the Cotswolds. Their farm, on the edge of the village of Much Milford, was only a little way off the main thoroughfare linking the nearby towns and hamlets. Timothy, the farm manager, drove along the deep-rutted road, letting the horses trot along easily while keeping a sharp eye for any holes likely to break a wheel or an axle. Arthur opened the bag Xian-Li had prepared for them and passed his son a barley cake, which had been split and buttered. He took one for himself and leaned back in his seat.

"Papa," said little Benedict thoughtfully, "will we see God?"

"Why do you ask?"

"You said we will jump up beyond the clouds and stars to a new place," he said, picking off a bit of his barley cake. He chewed for a moment and observed, "That is where God lives. Can we see him?"

Arthur recalled the previous conversation with his son when he had just returned from one of his trips. Benedict, only four years old at the time, had asked where he had been, and Arthur had told him, in a light-hearted way, that he had been to a place beyond the clouds and stars. In his childish way, the boy considered this just one more way people travelled whenever they went on long trips to distant places.

"Would it surprise you," Arthur replied, "to know that God cannot be seen – even up among the stars?"

"Why not?"

"Because he is a spirit, and spirits are invisible. No one can see God."

"Vicar de Gifftley does," Ben pointed out. "He talks to God all the time."

"I do not doubt it," allowed his father. "But even the vicar does not see God with his eyes."

"Vicar says that if you see Jesus, then you see God," countered Ben. "Lots of people have seen Jesus."

"Well, yes, but that was a long time ago." Arthur enjoyed these little talks, challenging, as they so often did, his own assumptions of the universe and its exceedingly odd mechanisms. "When we take a journey using the force lines we *will* see people from other times. The man we are going to visit – Anen, remember me telling you about him? – he lived a very long time ago."

"Will we see him?"

"Anen?"

"No – I mean *Jesus*. Will we see Jesus?"

"No, we won't see him."

"Why not?"

"Well, because Jesus lived in another place and time from the one we are going to visit."

He watched his son puzzling over this and resisted the urge to say more. It had long been an ambition to find the line of force that might lead to the Holy Land in the time of Christ. He had yet to find it, but knew it was out there somewhere. The search went on, and Arthur contented himself with the thought that his relentless mapping of the cosmos would eventually yield the location. To this end, Arthur still faithfully recorded the coordinates of his travels on his skin through the tattoos he gathered and meticulously refined with every journey into the ether. He watched his son eating the barley cake. One day soon, he would share with Benedict the meaning of the strange runes that covered his torso, and how to read them – a secret known only to one other: his own dear wife, Xian-Li.

"How long will it take?"

"To go to Egypt?" guessed Arthur. "Not long. As I told you, it happens in the blink of an eye. It is travelling to the jumping-off place that takes all the time. The jumping-off place for this journey is very close to our farm."

"Black Mixen Tump," offered Ben, stuffing the remainder of his barley cake into his mouth.

"That is right." Arthur scrutinized his son closely. "How do you know about that?"

"I heard you and Mother talking," Ben told him. "Can I have another barley cake?"

"Later. Have a little cheese or an egg instead." Arthur dug into the bag and brought out a lump of cheese wrapped in muslin and a clutch of eggs boiled in the shell. He offered an egg to his son and took one for himself. He tapped it on the window ledge of the carriage and began to peel it, tossing the shards out the window.

They talked of what they would see in Egypt and how ley travellers were expected to comport themselves on their journeys. "We must always be respectful of the people we meet. It is their world, and we are guests. We never do anything to call unwanted attention to ourselves. We try to be good guests. We mind our manners." He regarded the boy, willing him to understand. "Promise me you'll always mind your manners, son."

"I promise, Papa."

"Good," said Arthur. "Now look outside. You can see Black Mixen Tump from here."

The great hulking eminence of the Stone Age mound stood out as an ominous dark shadow. A hill in a landscape of hills, it was a place apart, sacred to the ancients who had built it. Early morning mist wreathed the broad base and swirled along the winding trail leading up the steep slope to the strangely flattened top. The Three Trolls – the trio of great old oak trees guarding the top – stood out against the greying dawn sky. Black Mixen still kindled in Arthur a singular dread, in spite of his long familiarity with the place. What power the site contained, he hardly knew; but he suspected he had only skimmed the surface of its manifold energies.

Timothy brought the coach to a halt on the west side of the mound and waited while his passengers climbed out. Then, handing down the leather satchel his employer always carried, he said, "I will wait until you have gone, sir. Just to make certain no one comes by – if you know what I mean."

"Thank you, Timothy," replied Arthur. He reached out for Benedict's hand. "Ready, son?"

The boy pulled his hand away. "No."

"Now, son."

"I don't want to go." He crossed his arms over his chest, staring balefully at the great conical hump of Black Mixen rising before them.

"Why?" said Arthur. "We've come all this way."

"I don't *want* to."

"Nothing bad is going to happen," Arthur assured him.

"I'm afraid."

"There is nothing to be afraid of."

"I don't like the Trolls."

"The Trolls are trees – just ordinary trees. Now come along, and stop this foolishness at once."

"Excuse me interrupting, sir," said Timothy, speaking up. He indicated the sky with a tilt of his head. "The sun is coming."

"We must go. It is time to be a brave boy," Arthur said firmly. "Now, take my hand and come along. I will be right here beside you. There is nothing to fear."

The two travellers followed the serpentine trail to the summit, and Arthur quickly located the stone he had planted a few years ago to mark the location of the prime energy field. Taking his customary stance on the stone, he placed his son before him and said, "Put one hand to my belt." The boy did as he was told and snaked his fingers around his father's wide leather belt; with the other hand he held tight to his father's free hand. "That's right. Now, whatever happens, do not let go. Remember what I told you about the wind and rain?"

"I remember – the wind will scream and the rain will sting. And I will feel a bump."

"A bump, yes. Who told you that?"

"Mum said."

"She is right. You will probably feel a bump – like a little jump – but do not worry. You won't fall. I will be there with you to catch you."

"And I won't throw up."

"You might," his father advised, slinging the satchel strap over his shoulder. "But if you do, it is nothing to worry about. Just go ahead and throw up, and you will feel better."

Clasping his son's hand tightly, Arthur raised his arm in the air above his head. He felt the familiar shimmer of the force field on his skin; the hair on his arms and on the back of his neck stood up. The air crackled with the presage of lightning, and a heavy mist descended around them. The wind howled down as if descending from distant, blizzard-scoured heights. "Hold on!" he cried, shouting into the whirling maelstrom of forces writhing around them. He tightened his grip on the boy's hand. "Ready! Here we go!"

The familiar English hilltop dimmed, and the rain flew sideways in stinging torrents. Arthur felt his feet leave the marking stone, but only for an instant – the lurch between steps on uneven ground – and the solid ground of a new land rose beneath them.

It was done.

The wail of the wind died away, and the rain ceased abruptly. The mist cleared. The hill was gone, the Trolls, the grey English sky – all replaced by the soft warmth and gleaming bright blues and golds of a desert morning. They were standing in the centre of an avenue lined with crouching sphinxes. Benedict, his eyes wide, stared at the long double row of statues and the empty white desert and rock-bare hills beyond.

He gave a cry of delight and darted forward, remembered himself, and halted. Far from being made sick by the experience, the boy positively enjoyed the wild, disorienting leap across the dimensional divide. Here was something new in Arthur's experience; perhaps the very young did not experience the effects of what was for older folks a most uncomfortable transition. It had taken him a fair few journeys before he finally became inured to the more unpleasant sensations; the minor inconveniences of extreme temporal dislocation no longer bothered him.

"Let's do it again," Ben chirped, his earlier anxiety entirely forgotten.

"We *will* do it again, yes," replied Arthur. "When it is time to go home. Just now we are going to visit Anen."

"Is this Egypt? It's hot!"

"It is very hot." Arthur opened the satchel and pulled out two lightweight linen cloths. He wrapped one around his son's head, and then fashioned a turban for himself. "There. That's better." He held out his hand. "Come along. We should be on our way before it gets even hotter. When we get there Anen will have a cool drink for us."

CHAPTER 16

In Which Ruffled Feathers
are Smoothed

Engelbert folded the edge of his apron over the hot baking tray
and lifted a fresh batch of muffins from the oven. He turned and
closed the oven door with the heel of his shoe – a move both
deft and quaint, and which never failed to amuse Wilhelmina. He
removed his soft hat and wiped his face with the back of his hand
and, glancing up, noticed her watching him.

Etzel smiled, his plump cherubic face flushed from the heat.
"These are the best yet, *Liebste*," he said, placing the tray on the
table. "Our people are going to love them." He rarely called them
customers any more; he spoke of the Grand Imperial clientele as *our
people* – as if they were tribesmen or family members.

"The muffins smell wonderful," she assured him. "You have
mastered the recipe in no time at all."

"*Jawhohl!*" he agreed, his broad, good-natured face alight. "You
have good ideas, Mina."

Introducing muffins to seventeenth-century Prague was
Wilhelmina's idea, that was true; but the design of the baking trays
and the execution of the recipe were all due to Engelbert's singular
expertise. Since opening the coffee house, the German baker had
gone from strength to strength as his confidence rose, and his skill was
rewarded by the success. The shop enjoyed a steady and lucrative trade
– enough to keep eight helpers busy: three servers dressed in green
livery; two additional bakers to help with roasting the beans, mixing

149

dough, and preparing pastry fillings; a general helper to prepare fuel, feed the ovens, and run errands; a dishwasher; and a cleaner. From the moment the shutters opened at dawn until they closed again at dusk, the Grand Imperial Kaffeehaus was heaving with activity.

Wilhelmina had taken the position of chief overseer of the enterprise, maintaining a gentle but firm control over the business. But she also indulged her latest, and necessarily secret, passion: ley exploring. Since making that first successful journey, she had attempted three more using her copy of Burleigh's device, discovering two new leys in the process: one leading to an arid desert of red earth and towering rocks and cacti, and one to a bleak steppe, treeless and windswept beneath low grey skies. She had also made a second trip using the ley she had discovered previously, which led to that massive limestone gorge. Though she still could not yet fit a name to that destination, nor a time, she had nevertheless begun to nurture a growing insight into ley travel in general, as well as finer points such as how individual lines might be manipulated. For, while she was content with merely mapping the leys and trying to determine how to calibrate her crossings, Wilhelmina had begun to wonder about the incredible possibilities of her new avocation – as well as the inherent implications and problems. For example, what would happen if she attempted a "double cross" – using two ley lines in two separate dimensions to travel to a third? She had no idea, but was intrigued by the possibility nonetheless. Once she felt secure in using the leys she knew, she would push the boat out a little, so to speak, with her experiments.

Very occasionally she thought about returning to her home in London – if only to reassure anyone who might be concerned about her disappearance, and to wrap up her affairs. However, that would obviously mean returning to the ley that had brought her to this dimension, and that was several long days' journey away from Prague. When it came down to it, the prospect always seemed like a huge bother for such a piddling payoff. Then, too, she was not at all certain she could return to the same London she had left. What if she got the time horribly wrong? There was no guarantee she could even get back to the twenty-first century anyway.

The plain truth was she missed nothing about London or her mundane, drudging life there – not when set against the possibility of roaming a multidimensional universe with its offer of infinite worlds awaiting her discovery. That being the case, she could effortlessly think up a thousand more exciting things than returning to her flat to examine the mound of junk mail piling up on the doormat.

Chocolate, for one.

Wilhelmina was ever mindful of the fact that she had, quite unwittingly, introduced coffee to Prague, and was now reaping enormous benefit from that happy accident. Not only was she half owner of the first coffee shop in Bohemia, she was also a partner in an increasingly successful shipping company that supplied her coffee beans. Lately she had begun to think of importing beans of another sort: cocoa. It was only a matter of persuading Herr Arnostovi, her principal partner, to expand their import business to other commodities – specifically sugar and cocoa beans – and if that likewise proved successful, her future would be secured. For if she could secure sufficient quantities of those two items, she could make chocolate, a luxury as yet unknown in this Europe. The main problem with the scheme was getting her hands on a ready supply of the raw materials, which meant forging a partnership with a Spanish shipping company. Tricky, but not impossible, and well worth attempting. When she considered the rewards that would flow from that revelatory introduction, even her most modestly placed estimate was well nigh astronomical.

There was simply no telling how rich she could become from a venture like that. And once loosed from the constraints of having to work to earn a living, she would be free to travel and explore. Plus, of course, she would have chocolate.

These thoughts were in her mind as she placed the fresh baked muffins on a cooling rack. As she finished, she turned just at the moment that her accomplice entered the shop. The emperor's assistant chief alchemist was wearing his customary green robe with purple stole and fox trim, and his hat shaped like a collapsed bag with a brim. He took a seat in his usual place – the furthest corner of the room near the *Kachelofen* – and folded his hands on the table. In a moment one of the serving girls hurried to take his order, and Wilhelmina, placing a fresh muffin on a plate, went to greet her friend.

"Greetings, *mein Herr*," she said, perching on the edge of the chair next to him. "Here, I want you to try something." She pushed the plate in front of him. "It is a new kind of pastry we are thinking of introducing – one that has never been seen before in Prague."

"*Grüss Gott*, Fräulein Wilhelmina." He smiled wanly at her, swiped off his hat, and dipped his head in a polite bow. "Very interesting," he said, peering at the speckled little cake. He prodded one of the tiny black specks with a fingertip.

"Those are poppy seeds," she informed him. "They're good. You'll like them."

"I have no doubt whatsoever that it is very nice," he said, looking at the plate doubtfully.

"What is wrong, *mein Freund*? Is something the matter at the palace?"

"Oh, nothing of consequence," he answered quickly. "I am very busy just now, and –" He hesitated.

"And?" she prodded. "Go on. We are friends – you can tell me. What's wrong?"

"It is that man – that *Engländer!*" he blurted, as if releasing a pressure valve.

It took a moment for Wilhelmina to think who he was talking about. "Lord Burleigh, you mean?" she guessed.

"The English earl, *ja*. He is insufferable!"

"No doubt," conceded Wilhelmina mildly. "But why do you trouble about him?"

"He has returned!"

"Has he, indeed?"

"*Ja*, he has returned with even greater demands – impossible demands! That is bad enough, but he treats us with utmost disdain – as if we were mere slaves bound to do his bidding. The man is a tyrant and a bully. If he were to fall down a well I would not lift one finger to fling him a rope."

Wilhelmina gazed at her companion. Clearly, he was frustrated and angry. It was probably good to allow him to vent a little steam, and she was more than happy to assist the process. Anything she could learn about Burleigh and his dealings with the imperial court, she counted to her advantage.

"Well, have some of this muffin," she urged in a soothing voice, nudging the plate nearer. "Taste it, and tell me what you think. If enough people like them, we will begin selling them in the shop very soon."

Gustavus broke off an edge and lifted a bit of the freckled yellow cake to his mouth. He chewed it thoughtfully and announced, "It is very good. Moist and sweet. What are you going to call this *kleiner Kuchen*?"

"We have not decided yet – but we are open to suggestions."

He nodded and ate some more. The maid appeared with his coffee, put down the little pot and cup and, at a nod from Mina, retreated again. "Here," said Mina, pouring his coffee, "taste it with this and tell me what Burleigh has done to upset you so."

Gustavus sipped his coffee and recovered some of his usually placid demeanour. "It is not seemly to take on as I have," he said, gazing into his cup. "Forgive me, *Fräulein*. I did not mean to inflict my personal concerns on you. I am sorry."

"Nonsense," she said, reaching across to pat his hand. "What are friends for? Come, now. Eat some more of this cake and tell Wilhelmina what is bothering you."

The young alchemist did as he was told, and in a moment began to relate how early that morning the mysterious earl had appeared at the palace. The visitor had spent a long time in close consultation with the Lord High Alchemist while Gustavus continued with his work in the laboratory.

"Then," he said, "all of a sudden, I am summoned and told to abandon my present work in order to undertake a new commission from Herr Burleigh. But I am deeply engaged in a most delicate experiment, I tell them. I will be finished in a day or two – and I must not lose all the work I have already completed. But no! It is not to be. Nothing will do but that I must sweep everything aside and begin at once on this new project – and they will not even tell me why it is so important that it cannot wait another day!" He puffed out his cheeks in exasperation. "Months of the most exacting labour gone up in smoke – poof! Just like that!"

"Most upsetting," sympathized Wilhelmina. "What do they want you to do?"

"It is to be another device," answered Gustavus. "Like the one I made before – to aid in His Lordship's astral investigations, *ja*? But this one is a little bigger, and more powerful and more complex in every way."

"I see." Wilhelmina feigned a mild interest. Inside, her pulse quickened at the news. She let him enjoy some more of the muffin and drink some more coffee, then said, "Did they tell you the purpose of this new device?"

"No." He shrugged, then gave her a sly smile. "But I overheard them talking about it when they thought I had gone." He sucked in his breath with an audible clutch. "They treat me like a child."

"Tch!" Mina gave her head a derisive shake. "That is a great shame. But I hope you know that I have the utmost respect for your intelligence and skill. I am grateful for your expertise." She paused, then offered, "I suppose they hope to keep such important work a secret."

"It is to be similar to the first device in many respects," offered Gustavus. "But this one, I believe, is to be used to locate people as well."

"People?" wondered Wilhelmina. "Which people?"

"Fellow travellers – if I overheard them correctly – those who likewise journey on the astral paths. The earl says he wishes to meet those who share his explorations." The chief under-alchemist leaned forward. "But I do not trust him. I think this Lord Burleigh is not what he appears."

"You could be right." Wilhelmina frowned. There was no question about it: she had to get her hands on a copy of Burleigh's latest mechanism, whatever it was, and add it to her collection. At the same time, she thought it best not to let on how badly she wanted the new gismo.

She was thinking how best to phrase the request when the young alchemist asked, "Would you like me to make one of these new instruments for you?"

"Well, I don't know –" Wilhelmina began, not wanting to sound overeager. "I appreciate you are in a very precarious position. I would not like you to put yourself at risk in any way."

"I will do it." Gustavus slapped the table with determination. "I will make a copy for you." He saw her hesitation and offered, "You will not have to pay me anything. It will be my gift to you."

"I am not worried about the cost, *mein Freund*," she told him. "It is *you* I am worried about, Gustavus. It is such a big risk. If the earl discovered what you were doing, he could cause a great deal of trouble for you. I would not like to see you come to any harm."

"Do not worry, *Fräulein*. No one will ever know. Of this I am quite certain." He took another drink of coffee. "I am a scientist. I have devoted myself to years of study. I have mastered the arts of my profession, and I refuse to be treated like an ignorant stable hand to be commanded at every idle whim." He smiled ruefully. "Excuse me, I seem to be forgetting myself."

"It is nothing," Wilhelmina assured him. "Drink your *Kaffee* and I will bring another pot. We have a few more things to discuss."

CHAPTER 17

In Which a Burden Shared is a Burden Halved

The dig at Karnak was abandoned for the rest of the day in favour of other, more pressing investigations. Dr Young, having recovered from the shock of Kit's revelations, was now in the grip of scholarly excitement and, in a fit of exuberance, treated Kit to a meal at Luxor's newest sensation, the Golden Ibex Hotel, recently erected to cater to the city's nascent tourist trade. There on a table spread with clean linen, he fed his new friend on substantial Egyptian fare and began a preliminary examination of the nature and mechanisms of his latest discovery: ley travel.

Unfortunately, the scientist's enthusiastic queries very soon outstripped Kit's own very limited experience and understanding. "I honestly wish I could tell you more," Kit finally confessed as they sat staring at the remains of the meal. "The real expert was Cosimo, my great-grandfather. He is the one who got me involved in this, and the one who knew the most about it. I'm sure he could have told you far more than I can."

"He sounds like a man after my own heart," said Thomas. "I should have liked to meet him."

"If only that were possible," replied Kit gloomily. "Sadly, Cosimo is no longer with us."

Thomas, catching the note of grief in his companion's voice, raised his eyebrows. "Am I to understand that his passing was quite recent, then?"

Kit, suddenly unable to speak, merely nodded.

Thomas sat back, regarding Kit across the table. "Forgive me, but I am puzzled. I had assumed —"

"That he must have passed many years ago?"

The doctor nodded.

"Cosimo and Sir Henry died only a couple of days ago."

"My dear fellow," said Thomas, his physician's manner coming to the fore; he reached across to pat Kit on the arm. "I am truly sorry. Please, accept my sincerest condolences."

Kit thanked the doctor for his sympathy and proceeded to tell his host about the untimely demise of Cosimo and Sir Henry. Thomas listened to the sorry tale, hands folded beneath his chin as Kit unburdened himself of the weight he had shouldered since landing in Burleigh's clutches. "It is up to us — Wilhelmina, myself, and Giles, that is — to carry on the work of those two good men."

"A most noble ambition," affirmed Thomas. "I salute you, sir. Moreover, I stand ready to aid the enterprise in any way I can."

"Thanks. You don't know what a relief it is to hear you say that."

A white-coated waiter in a blue turban came to remove the dishes. Dr Young spoke a few words of Arabic to him, and then rose. "Come, we will continue our discussion in the garden. The walk will do us good."

They crossed the dining room to a pair of French doors that opened onto a canopied terrace. A pebbled path led into a palm-shaded garden, lush with tropical vegetation. They strolled among lime-green tree ferns and dwarf figs. Peace returned to Kit's soul. After a moment, he asked, "What did Wilhelmina tell you — about all this, I mean — however did she explain it?"

"Well!" sighed Thomas. "She said the most outrageous thing I have ever heard uttered from a rational human being. She told me in no uncertain terms that she was a traveller from another dimension who had come to enlist my aid in helping her locate a very valuable artefact which was believed to be buried somewhere in Egypt."

"Wilhelmina can be very… forceful."

"I thought her demented, of course," replied the physician. "In my professional practice, I occasionally encounter people suffering from various forms of delusion and insanity. However, those were merely her introductory remarks. I offered her refreshment and sought to keep her talking so that I might observe her better and improve my diagnosis of her particular hysteria." He smiled suddenly. "That was where she captured me, the dear girl."

"Literally?"

"The more she talked – lucidly, calmly, with animation, intelligence, and fervour, but entirely lacking any of the more explicit signs of mental aberration – the more fascinated I became. In short, I allowed her to spin me such a splendidly impossible tale that I confess I was wholly taken in by the audacity of her creative invention."

Thomas raised a finger in his own defence. "Not that I did not argue – I put forth numerous and vigorous objections, which she could not entirely answer. Neither did she back down from her assertions. In the end we made a bargain. In exchange for my help, she would provide me with undeniable proof that her claims were genuine."

Thomas Young glanced at Kit, and his voice softened with awe. "I thought it all a splendid lark. I never dreamed what she said might have even the slightest smidgen of veracity in it. Just think – the ability to travel at will through time and space." His gaze lost focus for a moment as he contemplated anew the enormity of the implications of the new reality that had broken in upon him. "You must excuse me," he said. "I still find it all but impossible to credit."

"So do I," Kit assured him, "and I've made the leap a few times."

"You must teach me this skill at the earliest opportunity. I do insist upon it."

"Well, why not?" said Kit. "But getting back to Wilhelmina and the bargain you made with her, why did you go along with it if you believed it was some sort of mental illness?"

"Because, my dear fellow, Miss Wilhelmina made me give her my word as a gentleman that, providing her assertions proved true, I would help you." He chuckled to himself. "She can be a most persuasive and determined young lady."

"The proof – the coin, the clipping, and the pages from the book – that convinced you," observed Kit.

"Not forgetting the postage stamp," added Thomas. "Yes, I am convinced. You see, King George sits on the throne of England at the moment. Princess Victoria is a mere child, and not even in the direct line of succession. Yet, apparently, she is to become queen with her image on every coin. Extraordinary!

"But the book is the thing that removes all doubt. That book has been in my mind for quite some time. As president of the Royal Society, I've been collecting my papers and organizing them, of course, for the last several years. But I have not submitted them to be published, as they are nowhere near ready yet, and more remains to be done."

They reached the end of the path, turned around, and started back the other way. The afternoon had dwindled, and the heat of the day was fading somewhat. As they walked together, Kit felt he had found a true friend, a person of integrity, one whom he could trust. He was still uncertain as to how much to reveal about the problem of Burleigh and his thugs, but that was more out of a genuine concern than any wish to obfuscate or deceive. Having just secured a new and trustworthy ally, he did not want to risk scaring him away.

So they strolled in companionable silence, watching the shadows lengthen on the path as evening hastened on.

Thomas, pensive and brooding over the earth-shaking revelations of the day, at last confessed, "Just when I begin to imagine I have achieved some pinnacle of understanding, reached the summit of the highest climb... I scramble the last few feet to the top only to see that I have merely gained a foothold on a narrow plateau and that entire new mountain ranges rise before me, serried ranks of peaks, each one higher than the last." He laughed softly to himself. "I feel that way now."

Kit nodded in commiseration. "I feel that way all the time."

"Time... strange stuff," mused Thomas. "Time is the central mystery of our existence. It confines and defines us in many ways. We are obedient to its inexorable mechanism throughout our lives, and yet we know almost nothing about it. Why does it flow in only one direction? What is it made of? How is it regulated? Is it everywhere the same for everyone? Or might its substance or speed be altered by mechanisms as yet undiscovered?"

"I think Albert Einstein had something to say about it," put in Kit.

"Who? I do not believe I know the gentleman."

"No," said Kit. "I don't suppose you would. But he caused quite a stir in my world."

"Tell me about your world. What is it like – is it very different, the future?"

"Well, where to begin?" wondered Kit. "I guess things are –"

Young stopped on the path. "No! Wait. Do not say another word."

"No?"

"Whatever you tell me could have unforeseen implications. There could be disastrous repercussions." He pulled on the corner of his moustache. "I must think about this. I must consider it most carefully."

"Okay," agreed Kit. "You know best."

"Where were we?"

"You were talking about the mystery of time."

"Indeed. Sometimes I think that if we could only gain a knowledge of the working of time at its most fundamental level, we might at last begin to understand something of the mind and purposes of God."

"I'm not so sure," Kit replied. "It seems pretty random to me – but I'm no expert."

Thomas regarded his companion for a moment, then turned his gaze up into the clear blue sky. "Do you know why I am here in Luxor?"

"To dig up history, study the past – that sort of thing?"

"Partly," said Thomas. "But only in that all this digging and study serves a far greater ambition."

"Which is?"

"To unravel the mystery of tombs."

"The pharaohs' tombs?"

"*All* tombs." At Kit's quizzical expression, he said, "Since the human creature became a conscious being, we have made tombs and graves for our dead. Is this not so?"

"I suppose."

"It is a fact. From one end of the world to the other, and in every successive age from the dawn of human consciousness until now, and from the simplest societies to the most sophisticated, we have made graves and tombs for our dead. Have you ever stopped to consider why?" Thomas peered at him expectantly. "Why engage in such an expensive and ultimately pointless activity, if death is the final, irrefutable answer to all of life's questions?"

"Maybe," Kit ventured, thinking of how he rued leaving Cosimo and Sir Henry unburied and unmourned, "we don't do it for them, but we do it for ourselves."

Thomas commended this response. "Very good! Yet, if we do it for ourselves alone, what do we hope to gain by such taxing endeavour? For if annihilation is all there is at the end of life, then tombs ultimately make no sense whatsoever."

"True," Kit allowed.

"True – *unless*," countered Thomas quickly, "there is something more than mere physical existence, something that lies beyond the grave, something even our most primitive ancestors knew that we moderns seem to have forgotten."

"What did our ancestors know?"

"That is the riddle of the tombs," declared Thomas. "And *that* is what I am trying to discover."

Kit considered this for a moment. "After all your work, you must have some theories."

"Oh, I do," Thomas assured him with a laugh. "In my avocation as a scientist, there is no shortage of theories. Indeed, it is the one commodity we have in admirable abundance."

"So, what's your theory about the tomb-building?"

"It is all of a piece with the very plain and simple fact that we are immortal."

"I don't feel very immortal," admitted Kit, a little unsettled by the turn the conversation had taken.

"But you are – and so am I!" Thomas declared. "All human beings, by virtue of having been born into this world, are immortal beings – not our material bodies; those are sadly quite fragile, inasmuch as they are bound by the laws of matter and time. The spirit, however, is indestructible. It obeys different laws."

Dr Young turned on the path and started back to the restaurant. "Do you have a place to stay?" he asked.

"Not as such."

"Then you will be my guest." He glanced at Kit. "Unless you have any objection?"

"None whatsoever," Kit replied. "Thanks." He looked at the hotel facade rising above the palms. "You have rooms here?"

"My dear friend," chided Thomas lightly. "I am but a simple London doctor. I cannot afford to stay in such luxurious accommodation. Besides, it is not convivial to my work. Instead, I have a *dahabiya*."

"I'm sorry?"

Thomas chuckled. "It is a kind of sailing boat. You will have seen them on the river. As it will soon be dark, I suggest we go there now, if you have no objection."

"Lead on, Doctor."

They mounted the steps and made their way through the hotel lobby and out onto the street where three lonely mule-drawn carriages waited for passengers. Thomas called a few words to one of the drivers, they climbed into the carriage, and they were soon clip-clopping along the road fronting the river. The sun was low, turning the hazy sky a warm golden orange and the Nile to molten bronze. They passed through a market – a chaos of shops no bigger than broom cupboards; flimsy kiosks constructed of cloth and palm branches and held together with, as far as Kit could see, bits of raffia twine; and street sellers whose place of business was merely a hand's breadth of cloth spread out on the ground to showcase their meagre wares.

The press and confusion of people was daunting, the cacophony of voices alarming. The carriage slowed to a crawl. Thomas bought a bag of dates from one of the sellers and some onions from another; the carriage did not stop for these transactions, but squeezed through the heaving throng of merchants and customers at a pace slower than walking.

Dr Young's boat was moored a little distance downriver, away from the noisy centre of the town. Once away from the crush, the coach rolled briskly past a row of large and very ornate colonial-style buildings that housed government administration offices.

"It isn't time travel," said Kit, repeating to himself what Cosimo had told him. Why was that so hard to keep in mind? "Ley travel is not the same as time travel. We have to keep remembering that – at least, I do."

"You are right, of course," agreed Thomas.

"What you said this morning about being dead and buried and everything being worthless and all – that's not exactly true."

"I suppose not. Forgive me, I was not thinking very clearly and spoke in haste."

"You *were* right about time being out of joint. The different worlds overlap somehow, and history gets a little slippery. But just because Wilhelmina found your book already published in one world doesn't mean that what you've done in this one is worthless. None of us ever knows what impact we have on the world around us." He shrugged. "We can only live the life we've been given, and we have to do the best we can with it – no matter what is happening in any other world or universe. Just do the next thing – that's all we can do. Anyway, I expect the work you've done here is just as valuable to this world as it was in the world where Mina picked up your book."

"That is a gladsome thought," observed the doctor. "I shall accept it in that generous spirit." He thought for a moment, then asked, "Do you suppose that if I were to visit that world – where our Wilhelmina retrieved my book – I should meet myself composing it?"

Kit frowned. "Is it possible to meet yourself in another world?" The thought had crossed his mind, but he had never asked Cosimo for clarification on this precise point. There was still so much to learn. "Maybe," he conceded. "Cosimo never told me one way or another. I don't know."

"Well," allowed Thomas, "we shall add that to the growing list of questions to be investigated when we are more at leisure to do so."

They talked on, and soon the carriage rolled to a stop at a large mooring. "It is called *The Blue Lotus*," said Thomas, gazing down the line of low feluccas and stately *dahabiyas* tied up along the riverbank. "It is just here."

He charged off along the riverbank. Kit followed, falling into step beside him. "There is still one thing you haven't told me – why Wilhelmina wanted us to get together."

"I thought you knew."

"Things got a little rushed. She didn't exactly have time to fill me in on everything," reflected Kit. "In fact, she didn't tell me very much."

"Then allow me to enlighten you."

"Please."

"The young lady was, as I say, most intent on recovering a certain artefact." He peered at Kit with a hopeful expression. "Am I right in assuming you know the object in question?"

"I have a pretty good idea."

"This artefact, she believed, was to be found in a particular tomb of which she had a certain knowledge. She wanted me to organize the excavation of said tomb – an experience, she suggested, that would prove invaluable to my ongoing work." He glanced at Kit for confirmation. "She also said you would be my guide. Am I to take it you know the location of the tomb of which she spoke?"

"I'm pretty sure I could find it again." Kit felt his stomach squirm, and a clammy feeling washed over him.

"And you will show me?"

Kit nodded. The thought of returning to the scene of his recent ordeal – and the decaying corpses of Cosimo and Sir Henry – filled him with dread, but he did not see that he had any choice in the matter just now. And then he saw it: the sheer beauty of Wilhelmina's plan, and it brought him up short.

Dr Young saw him stop and turned to ask, "Is anything the matter?"

"Call me a slow coach, but I've just realized that Wilhelmina is some kind of genius." Now that he saw it, her plan was as obvious as the nose on his face. How many times did he have to remind himself: this was not the same world he had left behind. Mina had sent him to an alternate Egypt where, in the year 1822, the tomb of Anen had not yet been discovered, much less excavated. The notion of snatching the map from the tomb *before* it could be found by anyone else was a shrewd bit of guile. The girl was canny, give her that. "I think we're in for a real treat," Kit said. "We can leave whenever you like."

"Is it far, this tomb?"

"Not too far. With transportation, less than a day."

"Splendid!" The physician rubbed his hands together, his steel-rimmed glasses glinting in the pale evening light. "Ah, here we are! *The Blue Lotus*." Dr Young stopped beside a low-slung, rather boxy-looking boat with a broad open deck and twin red sails, which were furled to the masts for the night. A gangplank extended from the bow, at the foot of which three sailors in pale blue kaftans squatted around a hookah pipe, which gurgled as the smoke bubbled up. A most acrid smoke drifted on the soft evening breeze.

"*Salaam!*" called Thomas. He greeted the captain and crew of his vessel by name, and then climbed the gangplank. "This way. Watch your step!"

A servant appeared bearing a tray with a jug and glasses.

"Welcome aboard, my friend," said Thomas, pouring fresh lemonade into the glasses and passing one to his guest. "Please, make yourself at home. Mehmet here will show you to your quarters. I have only the one guest cabin. All the others are filled with the accoutrements of my work."

Kit gulped down his lemonade and followed the servant to the companionway below deck, and to the guest quarters. "Please to refresh yourself, sir," said Mehmet, ushering Kit inside. "I will sound the gong for dinner."

The cabin was snug and contained two narrow beds at one end and a small water closet at the other. There was a round porthole window and, between the beds, a bedside table with two candles. The beds were laid with clean white sheets, and there was a lace curtain at the porthole. The floors and walls were teak with brass fittings – all in all, a trim and tidy little stateroom.

"Well, Kit, old son," said Kit, gazing around with approval, "it looks like we've landed on our feet." A basin of fresh water sat on a stand. Stepping to the porcelain bowl, he dipped his hands and washed his face, then wet the linen towel and, kicking off his shoes, stretched out on the bed with the damp cloth over his eyes.

"Thank you, Wilhelmina," he sighed. At the invocation of her name, he mused, "What was it she called Dr Young?" The phrase from her letter came back to him: *The last man in the world to know everything.*

CHAPTER 18

In Which a Visit to Prague is Wangled

Lady Haven Fayth sat on the edge of the bed and laced up her shoes – good sturdy high-tops to protect her feet from the hazards of unfamiliar roads in lands and times unknown. Burleigh had promised to teach her the intricacies of what she called ley leaping, and so far the Black Earl – as she thought of him – had been as good as his word. He had taken her on several of his journeys to various worlds and shown her how to recognize some of the more subtle elements of ley lines. Under his somewhat haphazard tutelage she had begun to master a few of the basic skills necessary not only for making such leaps but for finding her way around strange new places.

If not exactly a fount of valuable wisdom, at least the earl was reliable in that the things he chose to show her worked. Even so, it was clear to her that there was much more to be learned, and that he was withholding far more than he was telling. For example, she knew from her long association with her uncle that there was a prize of inestimable value associated with the cause, and which Burleigh and his men were determined to find. The earl was careful never to make mention of this fact directly, and Haven thought best to pretend ignorance of it too. She let on that, as far as she knew, it was only ever about the exploration of the other worlds connected by the leys – about discovering and mapping.

She also knew Burleigh was desperate to get his hands on the Skin Map, but that he had not yet achieved even so much as a glimpse of the genuine article – a fact that surprised her, given his enormous expenditure of money, time, and energy. Then again, the only two people she knew who had ever possessed a piece of the fabled map were now lying in an Egyptian tomb – dead at the Black Earl's hand.

And for that, Haven Fayth would loathe him to the end of time.

As for the rest – abandoning Kit and Giles… well, regrettable as that might be, it had been simple expediency and could not be helped. In that dreadful, tragic situation – made prisoners and entombed with poor dead Cosimo and her dying Uncle Henry…

To remain locked up with the others would have been death. To stay alive gave her a fighting chance. It was as simple as that. And if she were able to stay alive long enough to master the technique of ley leaping, and gain the necessary knowledge, there was every chance that she could return to the tomb in time to rescue her friends.

As far as Haven was concerned, there had been only one choice. She did not regret making it, but she hated Burleigh for forcing the issue. The man was a dastard and a brute.

Outwardly she pretended to be a compliant accomplice – a willing ward to his stern and watchful warden. She feigned a friendly regard for him and, in a mildly coquettish way, led him down the primrose path towards a belief that, given time and the right incentives, she could become something more – a paramour, perhaps. She appealed to her darkly handsome companion's ego and vanity, allowing him the impression that he as the older and wiser master was winning her admiration. She used her beauty and her feminine wiles to appeal to his innate masculine pride. And Haven Fayth, as she had learned long ago, could be very, very appealing.

Just now was a case in point, for Burleigh, against his initial reluctance, was allowing her to accompany him to Bohemia. This was not the first time he had gone there, and he much preferred going alone. The precise destination, Haven had yet to learn. That was no matter. The bare fact that Burleigh wanted her to stay home made her all the more determined to go. And through charm alone she had got her way.

"This will not be a simple journey," he told her as they climbed into the carriage later that morning. "Three leys are employed. The first is some miles from here, and the second and third require a strenuous march. In point of fact, we'll have to walk a fair distance before we get there. Are you certain you want to put yourself to all that? It is not too late to change your mind."

"And miss the wonder that is Prague?" she said, smiling sweetly as she handed him her rucksack.

"Who told you we were going to Prague?"

"No one," she snipped. "I deduced it on my own. Am I correct?"

"Get up there," Burleigh said, opening the carriage door.

"Are we to expect any of your hirelings to attend us as well?" she asked as she settled in the seat facing him.

"Not now. They will meet us there later." He knocked the top of the carriage, the driver cracked the whip, and the coach lurched into motion. Burleigh regarded her doubtfully. "I only allow the men to come when they can be of use. In fact, I should not have let you talk me into allowing *you* to come."

"Oh" – she pulled a pretty pout – "where would be the fun in that? It is so stultifyingly tedious when you are away. And you are forgetting that you promised to teach me everything there is to know about ley leaping. I intend to hold you to that promise."

"Well," he huffed, "see that you make the most of the trip. We will not be there very long."

"Then why go at all?" she challenged. "If it is putting you to as much bother as all that, what, pray, is the point?"

"Because," he said, growing irritable, "it is an errand of some importance. If you must know, I have commissioned a special instrument to be made, and I am going to pick it up. Straight in and straight out again."

She had pushed him far enough; it was time to retreat and leave him the field. "The merest possibility of seeing such a fabulous city is satisfying enough for me," she said, favouring him with a smile. "I am certain that it will be worthwhile – however much time we have to spend."

"We shall see," he said, softening somewhat. Beguiled by her winsome and innocent smile, he added, "Perhaps we can do better than that. The palace is impressive, and the Rathaus. Then there is the emperor himself, of course – Rudolf is an enthusiast of the first order, very grand, extremely generous, and also a complete ninny. You will enjoy meeting him if the chance should come your way. And, would you know it? There is now a coffee house in the old square. The first one in Europe, I believe."

"I believe we have coffee houses in London. Yes, I am sure of it. Of course, I have never visited such an establishment myself, but I would dearly love to see such a place, and taste some of this coffee for myself."

"We shall see," he allowed. "We shall see. Did you bring a change of clothing as I told you? We cannot have you traipsing around Prague dressed as you are." He meant in her travelling clothes, which consisted of a simple drab linen dress and high-topped boots. "You cannot be presented at court looking like a milkmaid."

"To be sure," she agreed blithely. "As instructed, I have packed silk and lace suitable for just such an occasion."

A short while later they reached the first ley, and Burleigh sent the carriage away. The first leap took place in the usual way and, as usual, Haven experienced the acute disorientation and nausea resulting from such sudden and violent dislocation. They landed in a rural landscape that seemed to be a wooded river valley in some remote place devoid of any sign of human habitation.

"Where are we?" she asked when she could speak again.

"I have no idea whatever," Burleigh replied impatiently. "Are you quite finished? We have a fair way to walk."

"I am truly sorry if my discommodious behaviour has inconvenienced you, my lord," she replied tartly. She dabbed her mouth with her sleeve. "I assure you it cannot be helped."

Although she was growing more used to what she thought of as the seasickness accompanying the leaps, it still had the ability to momentarily immobilize her, and Burleigh had little patience for such weakness.

"Come along when you are ready," he said, striding off.

"Are there people about?" she asked when she had caught up with him.

"None that I have ever seen."

"How odd."

"Not at all. If you care to think about it rationally for a moment, there is nothing remotely unusual about it. See here," he said, stumping along, "our world has not always been as populous as it is at present. Indeed, the reverse is more the rule, since for long epochs of human history vast areas of landscape – whole continents – were devoid of human presence. Thus, I suspect that we have arrived in this world at a particular time in its history where this place is still virgin territory. In short, there may be people in this world – I should be surprised if there were not – but there are none around here."

"And you have never undertaken to explore this world at all?"

"A bloody waste of time," he sneered, waving a hand at the empty plains. "There is nothing of interest here."

"So it is only a connecting place, then – a station on the way."

"A way station, yes. In my experience, there are many such places," he told her. "While they may have other uses, to me they merely serve as a means of getting from one ley to another." He walked on a little further, then continued, "The next ley is a few miles distant, and between the one we have just used and the next one there are no towns or villages, farms, or what-have-you that I have ever seen."

"How did you know to come here?"

"My dear," he said, offering her a sardonic smile, "I am not without resource, you know. I have been about this business for some considerable time. The parts I know, I know very well."

"Such as those in Egypt."

"Yes," he agreed. "Egypt in several of its epochs – at least, the ones that interest me." He walked on a few steps, then added, "So far."

Although Lord Burleigh did not use any external references for travelling to places he knew, Haven was making her own map. Using Sir Henry's green book as an inspiration, she had begun writing down descriptions of the places she had visited, the locations of the

171

leys, and any salient features she deemed important to remember. As yet it was a fairly wordy affair with directions and orientations for setting and location and such, but she was working on a way of coding the information in a more compact and precise form.

It was a good mental exercise, and she had the distinct feeling that it would prove useful in days to come. If nothing else, it filled the idle hours when she was alone – which happened more frequently than she liked. Burleigh did not take her everywhere; most of his journeys were made without her and for reasons he kept to himself. For despite whatever he might say to the contrary, the earl maintained a fierce secrecy around his plans and doings. Far from discouraging her, it only made her the more determined to discover what he knew that he did not care for her to know, or was not prepared to share.

What Burleigh hoped to gain from their liaison was also something of a mystery. As yet, he had not made any untoward demands or advances on her; he seemed content to allow their rapport to develop in its own good time – an expectation Haven was happy to encourage as long as it proved a useful ploy.

They walked along beneath a low grey sky into a freshening wind. The air was clean and cool and laden with the scent of rain. At the edge of the wood they came to a rise, which led up and out of the shallow river valley and onto a grassy plain. Far in the distance a range of low hills rose in a ragged line, but on the plain itself there was nothing to be seen save the grass undulating in waves like a wide green ocean.

Haven took one look at the formless expanse and asked, "However did you find a ley out there?"

"I have my ways, my dear." He put his head down and started out into the prairie.

By that she thought he meant a map, though she had never seen him use one. She followed in his wake, listening to the swish of their feet through the tall grass. After a time, they came to a narrow crevice – a vee-shaped cleft in the ground like a miniature fault line running west and east, cutting through the plain in an unwavering line.

"Here it is," Burleigh said, holding out his hand. "Hold on. This won't take long."

She took his hand, and they walked half a dozen steps. While physical contact was not strictly necessary, she had learned that it made for more accurate leaps. Or at least lessened the chance that they might become separated. Why this should be, she had yet to discover.

In the space of those first steps, the sky seemed to dim and the prairie grew hazy around them. The wind gusted, flattening the grass, driving down along the fault line. Rain spattered, sharp and heavy. There came a shriek from a great height – as if the sky were being torn – and then all turned black.

She landed with a jolt that sent a tremor up through her bones. Bile rose in her throat, but since she had nothing to throw up, she gagged it back, swallowing hard. She wiped the rain from her eyes and looked around. The landscape was dark, the evening stars bright in the east. They seemed to have arrived on a promontory above a crescent bay. There were boats lined up on the beach below, and at the point of the cove some distance ahead she could see the lights of a village kindled against the gathering evening gloom.

"Time is against us today," Burleigh said. "We'll have to stay there tonight and get an early start in the morning. The ley is a few miles the other side of that headland."

"The village," said Haven as they started towards the lights, "does it have a name?"

"Trondheim, I think."

"We're in Norway?"

"They speak Danish – or some dialect of it, as far as I can tell – but we're not in Norway… too far south. I suspect it is a trading colony established by Danish settlers – something like that. Fishing boats call in here for supplies and water. There are two inns and several taverns. The people are friendly enough, for all you can understand them."

"What will they make of us?"

"Who knows? I pay in good silver; that is all they care about."

True to form, they were welcomed at the inn and enjoyed a hearty supper of fish paté on brown bread, followed by stewed mutton and greens. They were given rooms at the top of the house, which was quiet enough, though Haven, alone in her lumpy bed, was kept awake by raucous singing late into the night. The two travellers slipped out of the inn and were back on the trail again before sunrise. Burleigh located the ley and, as the first rays of the new morning broke over the hilltop to the east, they made the leap to Bohemia.

Burleigh had marked the ley using small white stones in a line beside the trail, which was delineated by a standing stone, a burial mound, a notch in a distant hilltop, and, of all things, a gallows beside a lonely crossroads. The earl had calibrated the leap precisely – Haven heard him counting off the steps under his breath as they walked briskly along the line. There was a blur of cold mist and a screech of wind, and they landed on a quiet, sunny hillside a few miles from the city of Prague. They walked through a countryside of young green fields and arrived at the city just as the gates were being opened for the day.

Once on the road, they fell in with the ordinary traffic of merchants and travellers arriving for the day's business; they passed through the city walls, down some narrow streets, and across a wide and handsome bridge, where Burleigh stopped at last.

"It is very like London," observed Haven, gazing around approvingly. "Smaller, and better paved. Cleaner, to be sure. But not without similarities."

"The palace is up on the hilltop," he said, indicating the brooding eminence commanding the high point of the town. "Who is the emperor?"

"Rudolf the second," replied Haven crisply. "Everyone knows that. I am astonished you should ask."

"I was just making sure *you* knew." He started off again just as the bells in the cathedral tower began to ring. Within moments, every other church bell throughout the city began chiming as well, urging the faithful to attend Mass.

"Will we see His Majesty?" asked Haven after a moment. "I should very much like to."

"It is possible," Burleigh allowed. "If he happens to hear that I have come for a visit, he may demand an audience. He fancies himself leading a renaissance of science and likes to keep a finger in every pie."

"Is that why you have chosen Prague to have this instrument made?"

Burleigh cast a quick sideways glance at his companion. She was a quick-witted lass; beneath those russet curls was a mind as quick and supple as any he had ever met. "Very good, my dear. Yes, the science here is in its infancy, but their craftsmanship is more than adequate for my purpose. They are amenable and do not ask many questions." He paused, then added, "Unlike yourself."

"You flatter me, sir," she replied brightly.

The street rose steeply before them and began winding its way up the hill to the palace precinct, passing rows of tidy houses and shops.

The people going about their business seemed reasonably well-dressed and prosperous and, above all, clean. The front steps of the dwellings were washed, the windows too – even the streets were swept, and the rubbish left in neat little piles for the refuse cart to collect.

As they walked along, Haven kept an eye out for the coffee shop, hoping to inveigle Burleigh into stopping for a cup of the fashionable elixir. But she did not see it, and they climbed higher into the city, very soon arriving at the palace gate, which was open to allow visitors to pass through unimpeded. They crossed the yard and were met by two guardsmen in gleaming silver breastplates and helmets. They crossed their long pikes in a ceremonial barring of the way until Burleigh, speaking in rough German, stated his name, title, and business.

Whatever he told them, the guards raised their weapons and allowed the two visitors to continue; they passed beneath the statue of Saint George slaying the dragon and into the great vestibule of the palace. There they were intercepted by one of the imperial ushers – youths whose duty it was to conduct the emperor's guests to their desired destinations.

Again Burleigh spoke a few words, and they were escorted deeper into the warren of rooms and buildings that was the imperial residence. "How is your German?" asked Burleigh as they progressed along a seemingly endless gallery.

"Why, sir, I have no knowledge of the language at all," confessed Haven readily.

"You know more than you think you do," the earl informed her. "Since you speak English, you already know a thousand words or more. However, you will not be required to speak. Just pay attention and you can pick up most of what you need to know by way of gesture and situation. Just remember, the Bohemians are very formal people."

They arrived at a large panelled door and stopped. The usher knocked on the door for them and a voice from inside answered, whereupon the usher bowed and stepped away, indicating that they should enter.

"After you, my dear," said Burleigh.

CHAPTER 19

In Which a Three-Cup Problem is Expounded

Kit woke from the first deep and restful sleep he had known in weeks. He lay for a while listening to the sound of water slapping gently against the hull of the *dahabiya* – such a serenely peaceful sound. Rousing himself, he sat up and realized that the boat was moving. Wearing the nightshirt the doctor had given him, he crept from his room and up the companionway to the deck above. It was almost dawn, and the captain was taking the boat upriver. Luxor was behind them already, and ahead only the green banks of the Nile with date palms and fields of flowering sesame on either side.

"Good morning, my friend!" called a voice from the raised quarterdeck at the stern of the boat. "Fancy a drop of tea?"

"Don't mind if I do," Kit answered. Moving to the steps leading to the higher deck, he saw Thomas, in a silk dressing gown, enthroned in a large rattan chair with a gently steaming mug between his hands. On a low table beside his chair was Wilhelmina's letter. Kit joined him, drawing up another of the rattan chairs from its place at the rail.

"I do my best thinking this time of day," Thomas told him. "Cooler, more conducive to clear thoughts." He removed the cosy from a painted ceramic pot, poured another mug, and passed it to Kit. "Whenever I am faced with an intractable problem, I find tea helps concentrate my mind."

"Nothing like the first cup in the morning," agreed Kit. "Is there milk?"

"In the jug. Please, help yourself." As Kit poured, he added, "It's camel milk, by the way."

Kit took an exploratory sip – sweet and mildly nutty, he decided, but wholly acceptable. The two men drank in silence for a moment, watching the riverbank slowly slide by beneath a sky the colour of rose petals. After a while the doctor said, "I have been awake half the night thinking about your problem."

Mehmet the steward came with a fresh pot of tea and took away the old one. The doctor refreshed their cups, settled back in his chair, and said, "What are you prepared to tell me about this artefact we hope to find in the tomb?"

Kit thought for a moment. "You know about ley travel – as described by Wilhelmina."

"Interdimensional transportation, yes." Young became keen. His steel glasses flashed in the early-morning light. "That is an area I intend delving into in far greater depth, but for the purposes of this present discussion we will consider it amply demonstrated." He took a sip of tea. "Continue."

"Well, the phenomenon was discovered, or at least actively pursued, by a man named Arthur Flinders-Petrie, who roamed around exploring the various ley connections and their destinations. He recorded his findings on a map."

"A very prudent fellow," approved the doctor. "I like him already."

"In order to preserve the map and, I suppose, have it ready in any circumstance, he had it tattooed on his body." Kit ran a hand over his chest and torso. "That way, the map was permanent and could never be lost."

"Ingenious."

"They call it the Skin Map, and it takes the form of a very sophisticated symbol code. I have seen some of the symbols, but I don't know how to read them yet."

"You have seen this map of skin?"

"Not exactly – I mean, I have seen an imitation of it. My great-grandfather, Cosimo – he had found a portion of the map and kept it under lock and key. But when we went to look at it, we found someone had stolen the original and substituted a poor copy instead. The copy was worthless."

"You said it was only a piece," Thomas pointed out. "Do you mean that the map has been apportioned in some way?"

"It has," confirmed Kit. "Cosimo thought the original map had been divided into at least four pieces. Why it was divided, and who divided it, we have no idea. There was a suggestion that it was cut up to protect the original secret of the map in some way, but I don't think anybody really knows. Nevertheless, in the years Cosimo spent in the chase, he succeeded in finding one piece. I never learned how."

"A pity." Thomas drained his tea and reached to pour another. "I can see this is going to require at least one more cup."

Kit held out his cup for a refill. "But the map is only the beginning."

"I daresay."

"Thing is" – Kit grew earnest – "Flinders-Petrie found something – something incredibly, unimaginably valuable – a treasure of some sort he kept hidden from the rest of the world."

"Truly," breathed the doctor, wholly caught up in the tale. "As if the secret of ley travel were not enough!"

Kit nodded solemnly. "Cosimo pledged himself to discovering that treasure, and it killed him in the end. As I've explained, we're not the only ones looking for the map." He went on to tell more about Lord Burleigh, Earl of Sutherland, and his men, describing how they always showed up at just the wrong time, what they were like, and what he knew about them. He ended his account, saying, "Unfortunately, bad as they are, they aren't the only ones in competition for the map. After all, *someone* stole Cosimo's portion of the map, and it wasn't the Burley Men."

The doctor was silent for a long moment, then said, "Am I to take it that the object we hope to find in the tomb is, in fact, a piece of the map?"

"Nothing less," confirmed Kit. "Cosimo and Sir Henry gave their lives to the quest. The map is part of it, and I have pledged myself to carry on their work. It's as simple as that."

Thomas Young pondered what had been said for a moment, then replied, "The scientist in me is begging for confirmation. Can any of this tale of the map be proven factually?"

"I think," ventured Kit, "that when we excavate the tomb, we'll find the factual confirmation you need – providing the map exists in this present reality, of course. We won't know that until we look."

Thomas considered this. "Please, do not misunderstand. I believe you implicitly. The proofs already in evidence are enough to swing the balance in your favour…" He waved a hand at the letter on the table. "That, along with the stamp, the coin, the pages from my book of essays which has yet to be published… these have more than satisfied me." Thomas leaned forward, his voice rising with excitement. "But see here, the implications of what you have shown me – and what we hope to learn from the tomb – are nothing short of world-shattering. If confirmed, this discovery leads directly to a radical new understanding of the universe."

"You're telling me," said Kit quietly, but the scientist was not finished enthusing about the connotations of a universe full of multiple alternative worlds.

"This is perhaps the greatest scientific discovery of all time. We must begin a systematic study of ley travel and determine its driving mechanisms." He raised a finger in the air as if lecturing. "That is of utmost importance, for when we have gained a thorough mastery of that, we will have gone a very long way towards unravelling the mysteries of the universe – time, space, reality…" He smiled as a new thought occurred to him. "Perhaps even the very nature of existence itself."

Kit was all for advancing scientific knowledge, but allowed himself a slight frown. "It starts with getting our hands on the map."

"To that end, I will underwrite the venture with funds I have at my discretion. All I ask is to plot and catalogue the find, and to requisition any objects of special interest for further study."

"Be my guest," said Kit. "Just as long as we secure the map, I'll be happy."

While the two continued their discussion, Mehmet appeared on the quarterdeck to say that the captain required Kit's direction in locating the village.

"There are five settlements on the west bank of the river," Mehmet said. "The captain wishes to know which is the one you seek."

Kit thought for a moment. "The third, I think. I remember passing two as we came downriver. But I'll know it when I see it."

"We are coming to the first one now," said the steward.

Kit rose and went to the rail. He saw tall date palms, their spindly trunks high above a collection of low mud-brick hovels. Women were washing at the water's edge, their children playing in the shallows. Atop the bank, two men loaded a donkey to twice its height with new green rushes, and another led a buffalo along the path to pasture while dogs barked at his heels.

"This isn't the place," Kit announced after a quick survey.

Mehmet relayed the message to the captain, and then announced that breakfast would be served. Kit and the doctor returned to the main deck where, beneath a striped canopy, a table had been set up and places laid. "I hope you are as hungry as I am," called Thomas. "We must eat a hearty breakfast if we are going into the desert today. It will be too hot to eat until after sundown."

They enjoyed a good breakfast of fruit and sweet breads, tiny red sausages spiced with paprika and onions, yoghurt, and coffee. While they were eating, the boat approached another riverside settlement, which after a cursory inspection Kit decided was not the right village. "Third time's a charm," he said, returning to the table.

They finished their meal as the boat rounded a slight bend and the next hamlet hove into view. He saw the well and the stone steps leading down to the river's edge. He saw the boat that had taken him downriver to Luxor. "This is the one!" declared Kit from the rail. He pointed to the tallest structure in the village. "There is Khefri's house."

The captain brought the boat to moor, and the crew put out the gangplank. "Ready?" asked Thomas, donning his white straw hat.

181

"Ready as I'll ever be," replied Kit.

"Then lead the way."

Down the gangplank, up the bank, and into the village where, thanks to Khefri and his father, Ramesses, the requisite negotiations for labourers and animals were begun. By the time the sun was standing directly overhead, the expedition had swelled to respectable proportions with the acquisition of four donkeys, two mules, and six additional workers to undertake the excavations. They then set about assembling the necessary provisions for the men and animals. Khefri had wangled himself a job as overseer and interpreter for the workers, and took his new role with a seriousness that Thomas admired. While Kit and Thomas stood in the shade of a date palm, the young Egyptian organized the party and supervised the packing.

By the time all was ready, the sun had long since begun its descent into the west. Ramesses, who had done quite well out of the negotiations, invited Kit and Thomas to supper. They spent another night aboard the boat, and set off the next morning with Kit and Khefri leading the way.

"All I know," Kit confided to his new colleague a few minutes after setting off, "is that the tomb is in a wadi to the west of here – beyond the ruined temple." He glanced at Khefri. "You know the temple?"

"Of course. But there are many wadis," Khefri told him. "It is not possible to know which one you mean."

"I was afraid you'd say that." Kit thought for a moment. "This particular wadi is very large and splits into two branches after a few hundred metres or so. Also, there are small tombs and burial niches carved in the walls all along the way."

"Why did you not say this at the beginning, Kit Livingstone?"

"You know the place?"

"Of course. Everyone knows this place."

"If you can get us there, I can find the tomb."

They spent the night in the desert camped outside the ruined temple. Kit showed his new benefactor the avenue of sphinxes and the ley line it contained. "The leys seem to be time sensitive," he explained as the two stood looking down the straight path between the paws of the crouching lions. "Early morning and evening seem to be the best times to attempt a leap. I can sometimes feel when it is active."

"Extraordinary." The scientist squatted down and put a hand to the broken pavement. "Do you feel anything now?"

Kit shook his head. "Not at the moment, no." He cast a glance to the sky. The sun was well down, the night stars rising in the east. "It may be too late. Maybe, when we have found what we are after, I can show you how it works."

"I will look forward to a demonstration with keenest anticipation."

The next morning Khefri led them to the wadi entrance, and the expeditionary party proceeded down the long, winding stone corridor of the gorge. They reached the divide, and a little further along began seeing the burial niches; they came to the steep cutting where Kit and Giles and Lady Fayth had climbed up to await their assault on the tomb in the ill-fated attempt at rescuing Cosimo and Sir Henry. Shortly after that, they arrived at the place where the main channel split into east and west tributaries.

"This is the place," said Kit, gazing around. "Here is where we make camp." The bowl-shaped gulley was much the same as he remembered it, with only slight variations – so slight, in fact, that Kit had difficulty remembering that this was not the place he had been before. In this world, it was 1822 and there were neither tents nor Burley Men, and no excavated tomb either: just the sheer dust-coloured rock walls and the dry and empty wadi floor winding away on either hand. The great empty temple was there and still empty – though the interior, when inspected later, bore signs of scavenger activity. Indeed, there was no guarantee that Anen had even lived in this world, much less that he had been buried in the wadi.

"Are you certain this is the place?" Thomas, sweating beneath his big white straw hat, patted his brow with a handkerchief and looked around doubtfully. "I have to say, I have never heard of a tomb located in such a remote and inaccessible location. I would never have thought of digging here."

"If the tomb is here at all, it will be in this wadi," Kit assured him. "Somewhere…" He paced along the eastern branch a few dozen steps and stopped at a bend in the rock that looked faintly familiar. "Just about here, I'd say."

He pointed to the base of the curtain wall. "Somewhere along here is the entrance. There are steps leading down to the burial chambers below." He looked along the seamless wall for any sign of the tomb but saw nothing to betray a hidden entrance. "At least, that's the way I remember it from the other place."

"Then that is where we will begin." The doctor told Khefri to have the men unload the animals, unpack the equipment, and set up camp.

Soon the area resembled a bedouin village, complete with low, wing-shaped tents and a tiny campfire of twigs and dried dung over which flat bread baked on the bottom of an upturned pot. Sweet acacia smoke drifted on silvery threads into the air, and as the sun sank below the surrounding hills, an air of peace and calm descended over the ancient burial ground.

While the evening meal was cooking, the doctor took a long, thin iron rod and began probing the sandy floor of the wadi where Kit had indicated, thrusting the tip of the rod deep and waggling it around, searching for any fissure or other anomaly that might betray a man-made structure. "This is how we begin," Thomas explained. "You would be surprised what can be learned by literally poking around."

Working methodically, he applied the rod along the base of the wadi wall; when he had finished, he had identified half a dozen places where exploratory trenches would be dug. Kit was satisfied that at least one of them would turn out to be the sealed entrance of the tomb.

Darkness claimed the day, and after their simple meal the men rolled in their cloaks to sleep, and soon the camp was at rest in the silence of the desert. Kit himself spent a restless night troubled by dreams of finding the bones of Cosimo and Sir Henry, or worse: being locked in the tomb with their rotting corpses.

Those unhappy thoughts cast a dark cloud over his soul that lingered through the next day until, at the third trench, the diggers uncovered a large capstone set in the wadi floor. Khefri came running with the news. "Sir! Sir, come quickly. Dr Young is calling for you."

"What is it?" Kit was lying on his grass mat in the shade of the tent, having completed a tiring stint at the second trench. "Have they found something?"

"It is the entrance of the tomb." Khefri dashed away again. "Hurry!"

Kit jumped to his feet and rushed after the swift Egyptian. "That's what I'm talking about! Now the fun begins."

CHAPTER 20

In Which the Infant Science of Archaeology is Radically Advanced

It took two days to clear the rubble from the tomb entrance and the small forechamber, filled as both were with sand and rocks and bits of shattered pottery. On the morning of the third day of the dig, Thomas and Kit stood together and viewed the main chamber of High Priest Anen's tomb. "Someone was in a terrible hurry," Thomas pronounced upon seeing the extent of the wreckage.

A new worry snaked through Kit. "You mean the tomb has been robbed?"

"Oh, no. That is not my meaning at all – quite the reverse, if I am not mistaken."

"Then…" Kit puzzled over this, but the sense eluded him. "What?"

"The burial crew would seem to have been in some haste to discharge their duties and seal the tomb before it could be discovered. See here" – he gestured at the box-like room filled chockablock with debris – "in a funeral of state, the priests would have taken care to preserve the sanctity of the tomb. Egyptians loved ostentation – have you noticed how they decorated every inch of every available surface in a temple with all manner of paintings and carvings?"

"I have, yes." It was true, thought Kit. Egyptian temple art was nothing if not spectacularly busy.

"It is the same with their tombs. Ordinarily, the chambers are filled floor to ceiling with objects the deceased required for his journey through eternity. A high priest would have anticipated a sumptuous afterlife surrounded by the objects he valued and all that was most needful for his eternal existence."

"But they didn't do that here," said Kit, grasping for the meaning, "because they didn't have time?"

"Precisely," affirmed Thomas. He gestured towards the great heap of broken stone, the remains of building rubble. "We may learn the reason for their unseemly hurry when we have cleared all the chambers. There are two more, I believe?"

"That's right." Kit pointed across the room to a barely visible wall. He tried to visualize the chamber as he last saw it. "The room we're interested in is somewhere back there. At least, it was the last time I was here."

"Correct me if I am wrong," suggested Thomas, his steel-rimmed glasses glinting in the faint light as he turned to address Kit directly, "but strictly speaking, you have never been in this tomb."

"Strictly speaking, you're right." The tomb Kit remembered was in a different dimension – a fundamental fact, but one he had trouble remembering.

"We will begin clearing this chamber today," Thomas said, rubbing his hands in anticipation. "But we want more workers. I think I shall send Khefri back to fetch Khalid and his crew from Luxor. Have you any objection?"

"None whatsoever. You're the doctor."

Three days later Khefri returned with the new workers – seven expert excavators, including Khalid – and three donkeys and five pack mules laden with additional tents, tools, water, and provisions for an extended stay in the desert. After half a day's rest from the journey, the dig shifted into a higher gear, and Kit was glad to see the work progressing by leaps and bounds. At the end of the second day, the main chamber was cleared of rubble and the back wall fully exposed to reveal an expanse of white plaster with vertical bands of hieroglyphs in black and yellow.

"There is a door to a smaller chamber," Kit explained, stepping to the wall. He ran his hands along the surface, turning his palms white from the plaster. "It should be right about here." He brushed his hands on his trousers and turned to Dr Young. "But you have to remember, none of this was here when I saw it before."

"The plaster will be removed – starting in the area you have indicated," Thomas told him. "That will be tomorrow's exercise."

The labourers were sent out to sift the rubble for any fragments of interest, while the doctor assembled his drawing instruments and drew up a scaled representation of the wall. Then Thomas, Kit, and Khefri set about painstakingly recording the hieroglyphic bands covering the area of the hidden doorway, a task that occupied them far into the night – and would have taken far longer but for Khefri's native facility with rendering the old symbols.

The next day they were back at work before sunrise. The more skilled workers were detailed to chisel away the plasterwork covering the doorway to the hidden chamber – but only *after* Thomas was satisfied he had matched every symbol against the rendering copied the night before. "I will save these to decipher at my leisure," he explained, rolling up the last long scroll of paper. He gave a nod to Khalid, who commanded the workmen to ply the hammer and chisel to the wall.

"Do you know how to read them?" wondered Kit, watching as the first blow of the hammer erased a line or two of ancient pictorial text.

"It is devilishly difficult at best," allowed Young, "but we are making progress. Each new discovery adds to our store of words, and the knowledge of the ancient text increases. There are some here I have never seen before, but I can foresee the day when we will be able to read the old script as easily as the daily newspaper."

"The ones you have deciphered," prompted Kit, "what do they say?"

"They seem to be prayers of a sort, addressed to various gods – invocations of protection for the tomb and for the *Ka*; that is, the soul of the deceased. Others seem to be petitions for guidance on the journey to the afterlife. Some of the writings I have seen undoubtedly show incidents from the life of the deceased – lists of properties and assets, descriptions of family members, notable events, and that sort of thing. Because we are beginning to see certain collections of symbols repeated in the tombs and on sarcophagi we surmise that the prayers seem to follow what we believe is a rote formula."

Kit nodded. What little he knew about Egypt, he had learned in school visits to the British Museum. "From the *Book of the Dead*, perhaps," he volunteered. A large chunk of plaster tumbled to the floor and smashed into pieces, disclosing bare stonework behind.

"Ah! You have heard of it. But of course you would. In your time, it must be very well known. Tell me, is Egyptology a well-studied discipline in your world?"

"It is very popular," Kit allowed, thinking primarily of mummies and movies about mummies. "Archaeology is big business in the home world."

"And do its practitioners solve the many riddles posed by hieroglyphic writing?"

"Well, I would say –" began Kit.

"No! Do not tell me. I should not know. It was wrong of me to ask. I have already pressed you far enough." He smiled nervously. "Please, excuse my impetuosity. I sometimes forget myself."

"No harm done," replied Kit amiably. "What's a little professional curiosity between friends?"

"All the same, professional curiosity could lead to some very unfortunate consequences. A single word might put time out of joint – if you see what I mean."

"I might say something that would reveal too much of the future," Kit surmised.

"And that could cause irreparable harm," the doctor concluded.

"Or good."

"I am not prepared to take that risk. Are you?" His gaze became intense.

"I suppose not," replied Kit, realizing he had been revealing whole reams of knowledge about the future from the moment he showed up. "Getting back to the *Book of the Dead*," he suggested by way of changing the subject.

"In actual fact, its title is *The Book of Coming Forth by Day*. As I was about to say, we have yet to recover the whole text, but we have retrieved many portions and fragments." The doctor paused a moment and collected his thoughts, then recited a verse from memory:

I wake in the dark to the stirring of birds,
a murmur in the trees, a flutter of wings.
It is the morning of my birth, the first of many.
The past lies knotted in its sheets asleep.
Winds blow, making flags above the temple ripple.
Out of darkness the earth spins towards light.
I feel a change coming.
My thoughts flicker, glow a moment and catch fire.
I come forth by day singing.

"That's very good," said Kit appreciatively. "I like that."

"It is not about death, you see, but about rising to eternal life. For the ancients, death was simply an emergence – a coming forth – from darkness into the glorious light of a new and better day. They were fascinated by immortality – obsessed with it. As a civilization, they turned vast resources to furthering their understanding of the afterlife in the hope of eradicating death entirely."

Whole sections of plaster were tumbling to the floor now, raising clouds of thick white dust. Khefri, a damp *keffiyeh* over his nose and mouth, was given the task of supervising the demolition work; Thomas and Kit retreated outside to wait until the dust-making destruction was finished.

Kit tumbled up the steps and into the bright morning light. He stood blinking up at the sky, clean blue and high above, and it did seem as if he had stumbled from darkness into the all-pervading radiance of a better world. Stepping free of the tomb, he felt compelled to ask, "Why were the ancients so in love with death?"

"Who told you they were in love with death?" wondered Dr Young, pulling a soft cloth from a rear trouser pocket. He removed his glasses and began wiping off the dust-covered lenses.

"Is that not why they perfected mummification – to preserve the body as long as possible? Isn't that why they went to such great lengths with all their elaborate tombs and mortuary temples and such?"

"On the contrary, dear fellow. They were in love with *life!*" corrected Thomas, replacing his spectacles. "And such life – life in great abundance, life in all its glorious splendour. Death was anathema to them. Death, though natural and common, was unacceptable. Death was seen as nothing short of tragic disaster – at the very least an unfortunate accident along the happy road of existence, and one which, in time, they hoped to learn to avoid altogether. They were searching for immortality precisely because they wished life to continue forever without end."

"Don't we all."

"We do!" cried the doctor. "Of course we do. We were made for it, after all. I know not what it is like in your time – perhaps your world enjoys a more enlightened view – but in this current mechanistic age such thoughts are increasingly considered backwards and unscientific." He shook his head sadly. "Too many of my brother scientists are succumbing to a view that holds all religion as outdated nonsense – nursery tales from mankind's infancy, dogmas to be outgrown and swept aside by scientific progress."

"I'm familiar with the view," confirmed Kit.

"But see here," continued Thomas, brightening once more. "Contrary to what many may think, immortality is not a fairy tale invented to compensate for an unhappy life. Rather, it is the perception shared by nearly all sentient beings that our conscious lives are not bounded by this time and space. We are not merely lumps of animate matter. We are living spirits – we all feel this innately. And in our deepest hearts, we know that we can only find ultimate fulfilment in union with the supreme spiritual reality – a reality that appears, even during this earthly life, to take us beyond the narrow limits of time."

Kit pondered this. Although somewhat alien to his thoughts, he heard in the words, as from a far country, the distant but undeniable ring of truth. At last, he said, "Do you think we live forever?"

"Oh, I do. I most certainly do. We are all immortal, as I said."

"That's right, you did." Kit savoured the idea for a moment, thinking of Cosimo, Sir Henry, his own parents, and all he had known who had gone before. "It's a good thought."

"Yet I perceive you remain unconvinced." The doctor pursed his lips and regarded Kit doubtfully. "Could it be as I fear? Has the concept fallen out of favour in the age to come?" Before Kit could reply, he rushed on, "I challenge you to clear thinking, Mr Livingstone. Consider! Consciousness is who we are – we interact with the material world as conscious beings and in no other way. Is that not so?"

"That is so."

"Consciousness, then, is the most evident brand of existence there is. You might call it self-evident, and it is not necessarily bound to matter at all. That much is easily demonstrated. Can you not bring images to mind of far-off places, friends and relations fondly remembered, or of things that made you happy in the past? Can you not imagine acts of kindness, or cruelty? Do you not recognize the truth of something when you hear it, or know beauty when you see it?" He glanced at Kit for confirmation, then pressed towards his conclusion. "All these, and more, are expressions of consciousness, and they are not bound by matter or space or time in the least. Since this is the case, it will be most natural for our more limited human consciousnesses to recognize and yearn for an affinity with the One Great Consciousness that made us – the spiritual consciousness of the Creator. Sharing in this divine awareness is the most natural form of existence." He leaned forward and planted a finger on Kit's chest. "See here, if we can establish an affinity with the eternal, ever-living Creator, then is it not likely that this affinity, this relationship if you like, will endure beyond the death of the material body?"

The doctor did not wait for an answer. "I tell you it is," he declared triumphantly. "And it is because we can establish an affinity with the eternal Creator that immortality becomes more than a fairy tale. At the very least, you must allow, it becomes a most reasonable hope."

Just then they heard raised voices echoing up from the open stairwell behind them, and Khalid's head and shoulders appeared in the excavation hole. "Come quick, sirs!" he called, waving them towards him. "The doorway is revealed."

Once inside, Thomas inspected the work and approved it. "Well done, Khalid. Have this rubble cleared away, and then we shall dismantle the sealing blocks."

The Egyptian overseer bowed his head to show he understood, and then turned to command his crew. "*Yboud!*" he ordered, and the workers began scooping rubble into baskets of woven hemp.

"It is of utmost importance not to rush at this stage," the doctor explained when they returned to the wadi. "Everyone is always curious to see what lies beyond the door, what treasures may appear. In haste, irreparable harm often results – injury to artefacts and grave furnishings that can easily be avoided allowed sufficient patience and care."

"That sounds like the voice of experience," Kit observed.

"Oh, aye," agreed Thomas ruefully. "It has been my misfortune to have arrived on the scene of several digs too late to prevent the stampede, and I have witnessed what can happen when excavators contract gold fever. In the race to get their hands on the treasure, they will trample valuables still more precious to the scholar and scientist. Some of these items are in an utterly fragile and delicate condition." Thomas turned to gaze at the dark rectangular hole as the first workman appeared, bearing a heaped basket on his shoulder. "We will be having none of that on my digs!"

"Glad to hear it," remarked Kit. "I expect the map is especially fragile. It's just an old piece of skin, after all."

"And, if you are right, Mr Livingstone," added Thomas, "that old piece of skin is one of the most uniquely valuable artefacts the world has ever seen."

Once the room had been cleared and swept clean, more oil lamps were lit and placed all around the area to be excavated, and under Dr Young's eagle eye, the sealed doorway was opened, block by carefully chiselled block. As the hole grew bigger, Kit's pulse quickened. When the hole was big enough to reach through,

Thomas took up a lamp and, standing on some of the blocks, passed the lamp through the breach.

"See anything?" asked Kit, edging forward.

"Objects," replied Thomas, stepping down once more. "The room is filled with grave goods." He nodded to Khalid. "Take it down."

The bricks came thick and fast now, and soon the last of the sealing blocks was removed; Thomas ordered more lamps to be lit. He passed one to Kit, and one each to Khefri and Khalid.

"After you, Dr Young," said Kit, indicating the darkened doorway with his lamp.

The archaeologist hesitated.

"Seeing as you're the leader of this excavation and its benefactor, I insist."

The doctor gave a nod and stepped to the threshold and, holding his lamp high, peered into the darkened room. He stood motionless – as if frozen in an attitude of searching expectation.

"Doctor?" said Kit. "What do you see?" He glanced at Khefri, who held his hands clasped beneath his chin, his dark eyes aglint in the flickering lamplight.

"Indescribable," breathed the doctor, edging further into the doorway. Turning slowly, he beckoned Kit and Khefri to join him. "You had better come and see for yourselves."

The two stepped through the darkened doorway. In the faint illumination of the single lamp, he saw a confused and jumbled wall of objects and furniture crammed floor to ceiling and jammed into every available space: boxes large and small; chests of cedar, lime wood, and acacia; latticework room screens; collapsed bed frames; stools and footrests and headrests; chairs both simple and ornately carved; bronze-rimmed chariot wheels and disassembled harness trees; innumerable jars of all shapes and sizes; weapons – spears, swords, daggers, throwing sticks – both functional and ceremonial; a collection of painted rods and flails of office; and a host of small clay models of everything from cows and hippos to women making beer and men planting barley, bald-headed scribes, half-naked slaves, kohl-eyed goddesses in form-fitting gowns, and enough servants to populate a village, and more. It was as if the entire contents of an antique dealer's showroom had been stuffed higgledy-piggledy into a receptacle no larger than the living room in Kit's old flat, and then locked away for several hundred eons. Moreover, everything was shrouded with a heavy layer of powdery ochre dust.

He did not know what he had expected, but the sight left him speechless all the same. Somewhere in the midst of a small museum's worth of antiquities, awaiting discovery, lay the Skin Map – perhaps in one piece. It was all he could do to keep from tearing into the heap.

Sensing something of the frustrated expectation, Thomas offered, "We will find your treasure, my friend. Never fear. If it is in there, we will soon have it in hand."

* * *

Over the next two days, the contents of the main chamber were cleared piece by piece, and each item was numbered by Thomas and recorded in a book along with a brief description of the item and its condition. In order to speed the process along, Kit set up a relay system and convinced the fastidious doctor to go along with it. He had a canopy erected in front of the elaborately carved doorway across the wadi from the tomb; there, in the great empty chamber Kit called the temple, he established Dr Young at a table beneath the canopy. Then, with Kit directing the excavation work inside the tomb, each object was carefully pulled from the tomb and either carried or relayed hand to hand by workmen to the table, where Thomas first inscribed a small number on it in sepia ink, then recorded the find in his ledger; the artefacts were then conveyed to the empty chamber, where Khefri supervised their storage. There they would remain under guard until Thomas could arrange for their transportation to London and, ultimately, the British Museum.

Each box, chest, and jar was personally examined by Kit as it came from the burial chamber. Hands, clothes, hair, and every inch of exposed flesh became pale with dust; he looked like a powdered ghost.

With a damp handkerchief tied around the lower half of his face, he doggedly kept at his work, always expecting that the next ancient container he put his hand to must contain the map. In this he trusted to Thomas's simple dictum that by process of elimination they must, sooner or later, find his treasure. While all this cataloguing and recording might have been a logical and reasonable and properly scientific way to proceed, it did nothing to assuage Kit's continual urge to just rush in and start prying open the various containers until he found it. And although there were no end of interesting objects issuing from the tomb, they found neither gold – in the form of rings, bracelets, belts, or other items of jewellery – nor the prized roll of human parchment they sought.

This exacting activity continued each of the four days it took to unpack the burial chamber. On the morning of the fifth day, the workmen finally removed the folding room screens of carved acacia wood that had stood along the back wall of the tomb – the wall of painted panels depicting various events in High Priest Anen's life, all impressively rendered, vivid and lifelike.

"More lamps!" called Kit, and sent Khalid to invite Thomas and Khefri to come and see the masterpieces. "These are the paintings I was telling you about," said Kit. The three stood together holding their lamps high to admire the exquisite rendering.

"I must bring an artist as soon as it can possibly be arranged," Thomas said. "Though I doubt any mere copy could do justice to the original." His expression, alive with pleasure in the glow of the lamp, was that of a boy at Christmas. "They are wonderful."

"That one looks like my father," observed Khefri quietly. He pointed to one of Anen's priestly attendants. "And there – that is the very image of my cousin Hosni."

"Over here, gentlemen," said Kit, directing their attention to the panel where a shaven-headed priest stood next to a Caucasian man in a colourful striped robe, open at the chest to reveal a cluster of tiny blue symbols on his skin. "I give you the man himself."

"Upon my word!" gasped Thomas. "Here he is." He searched among the hieroglyphs beneath the painting, found the one he was looking for, and traced it lightly with a fingertip. "The Man Who Is Map."

"Arthur Flinders-Petrie," said Kit.

"He was here," said Khefri. "High Priest Anen knew him."

"Yes, he did." Kit stepped to the last panel. "And now," he said, with a gallery owner's flair, "the *pièce de résistance*." He directed their attention to the figure of the shaven-headed priest, a little older and heavier, standing with what looked like a scrap of leather in his hand. "That," declared Kit, "is the Skin Map as it once existed. And see, Anen is pointing with his other hand to that big star behind him. What is that?"

"Hmmm." Thomas held his lamp closer. "It appears to be the constellation Canus Major. I take it to be Sirius – a star especially revered by the ancients, no doubt due to its prominence and seasonal qualities."

"That is more or less what Cosimo and Sir Henry thought," confirmed Kit. "And the object Anen is holding," he continued, "that is the Flinders-Petrie map – you can tell from all the little blue symbols on it. And, based on Cosimo's assessment, it appears to be all in one piece."

"Extraordinary," breathed Thomas. "It is very much as you described." He turned a grinning face to Kit. "As it has not been discovered in any of the boxes or chests yet examined, it must be in one of the few left."

Kit cast a glance around the room at the several dozen or so remaining containers. "We live in hope."

The work resumed. Kit returned to removing and, with Thomas, opening the last boxes and chests, his hopes soaring and crashing with each one until Khalid appeared at the table beneath the canopy to say, "This is the last." He placed a small black lacquered box on the table. Inlaid with ivory and lapis in a geometric design, it did seem the kind of box to hold a treasure.

"Open it," instructed Thomas. With a trembling hand, Kit lifted the lid upon an elaborate beaded necklace of lapis, carnelian, and amber… a priceless object in anyone's estimation. There was also a matching ring and brooch.

But no map.

"Well, that's it," muttered Kit. "All this for nothing."

"Not for nothing!" tutted Thomas. "We have excavated a very important tomb and have made considerable archaeological finds. The hieroglyphics alone will prove invaluable to our understanding. This is a major discovery. It will advance the science of archaeology by leaps and bounds. You should be proud."

"Sure," allowed Kit, "but you know what I mean. We came here to find the map." He gestured forlornly in the direction of the storage chamber cut in the sandstone of the wadi wall behind them. "We've got a whole truckload of treasures – everything except the one we came to get."

"And yet," suggested Thomas, his steel-rimmed glasses glinting in the sun, "there is one container we have not searched."

"I looked in every blessed box and jar myself," blurted Kit, disappointment making him raw. "It wasn't there."

"Oh, ye of little wit," admonished the doctor. "Use that brain of yours, sir. Think!"

"I *am* thinking," Kit muttered. "I am thinking we've been on a wild goose chase."

"My impetuous friend," chided Thomas, shaking his head, "we have not looked in the sarcophagus."

"The sarcophagus…" Hope, instantly renewed, flared in Kit's despairing soul. He started back to the tomb on the run. "All hands on deck! We're going to need all the help we can get."

"Khalid, bring the heavy-lifting equipment," called the doctor. He paused and shouted towards the temple. "Khefri, fetch the cook and bring a team of mules – we may need them."

Carved from a single block of red granite, the hulking mass of stone sat in the centre of the chamber, as yet untouched. Kit swept away the dust with a handful of rags to expose the smooth, stylized visage of a man, features impassive, staring with blank eyes into the darkness of eternity. Below the face, the rest of the stone lid was engraved with row upon row of hieroglyphs.

"This won't be easy," observed Kit. "The thing must weigh twenty tons. How are we going to lift it?"

"Give me a lever and a place to stand, and I shall move the earth!" Thomas told him. "Archimedes." He squatted down beside the massive granite case and ran his fingers along the seam joining the lid to the bottom. "We will also use wedges and ropes."

Setting the lamps in a perimeter around the great stone case, the labourers set to with levers and wooden wedges; working in tandem – two levers a few inches apart – they eased up an edge of the lid and held it while another workman hammered in a wedge. The process was repeated time and again all along the right-hand side of the huge stone top. When they had finished, they started over again, raising the lid a little more and driving in the wedges that much further.

After the third round of prying and hammering, they had succeeded in raising the weighty red granite a few inches. Ropes were passed around the centre of the lid and these sent up to be secured to the mule team. The levers were applied, nudging the carved top a little higher – enough to drive even larger wedges into the gap and tilt the lid to one side. Little by little the top rose and tilted until, with a low grinding sound like the rumble of distant thunder, it began to slide off. The ropes grew taut as the mules took the strain. Khalid dashed to the chamber doorway and called instructions for Khefri to relay to the mule drivers. Slowly, slowly, with a creaking complaint of ropes and wood, the massive stone lid tilted and slid. All at once, one of the ropes gave way. The stone slewed to one side, teetered, then crashed to the floor with a thud that shook the ground beneath their feet.

The dust was still rising in the air as Kit, Thomas, Khalid, and the nearest labourers rushed forward to catch the first glimpse of the interior of the sarcophagus. Any hope for jewelled treasure or golden ornaments was swiftly dashed. For inside was a second sarcophagus of limestone, richly painted to resemble the deceased high priest in his ceremonial robes. The lid of this second sarcophagus was lighter and was raised with little difficulty by the workmen to uncover a third coffin of wood, also painted.

The third lid was prised off in a moment to reveal the mummified body of Anen, tightly bound in linen bands to withstand the ravages of time. Over the chest had been placed not jewelled ornaments or ceremonial trinkets, as in the case of others of high-born caste, but only a simple olive wood ankh, the ubiquitous cross with a loop, symbol for life. Nothing more.

Kit, leaning over the mummy, scanned the interior of the coffin, but saw no boxes, chests, or bundles of any kind. He felt the heat of discovery begin to fade into the gloom of disappointment once more. "Well, what do you think? Should we unwrap him?" he asked doubtfully.

"We do not have the proper equipment," said Thomas. "But I doubt we would find anything. I am sorry. I fear we have been grossly misinformed."

"I guess." Kit, miserable with frustration, moved to the painting of the priest holding the map and pointing to the star. What was the old boy trying to tell them?

"Kit Livingstone!" said Khefri suddenly. "Look here. The headrest!"

The doctor returned to the sarcophagus. "What sharp eyes you have, my boy," breathed Thomas. "I do believe you're right..."

Kit turned to see the doctor and Khefri leaning over the mummy once more. Crossing the distance in three bounds, he watched as Thomas reached down beside the linen-wrapped corpse. "Here, give me a hand. Lift the mummy – gently, carefully... there. Got it!" He straightened, and in his hand was a square of something wrapped in linen; it looked like a mummified sofa cushion. "Our friend Anen was using it as a pillow."

"Here – let's get it out into the light where we can see it better," suggested Kit, already heading for the door.

Out in the daylight, the carefully wrapped packet was examined for any external markings. There were none; the linen bindings were the same as those used to swathe the mummy. "I will enter this find in the ledger," said Thomas, moving towards his station beneath the canopy. "Then we shall open it."

If Kit had had his way, he would have torn off the bandages then and there, but he agreed and followed the doctor to the table and watched with mounting impatience as Thomas made his entry.

Then, handing Kit a thin-bladed knife, he passed the parcel to Kit along with the admonition to be very careful and take his time so as not to damage the delicate artefact within.

With trembling fingers, Kit slit open the top layer of bands and began unwinding the long narrow strips.

One after another, the layers were removed – seven in all – and as each fell away, excitement grew until Kit was almost hopping from foot to foot. The last layer of binding strips was unwound and there, on the table before them, lay a pair of wooden plaques tied with a cord of braided hemp that had been dyed red. The plaques were olive wood, raw and unvarnished, but covered with columns of black writing – not hieroglyphics, nor any language Kit had ever seen before.

He licked his lips. "Do you recognize the script?"

The doctor raised his glasses and bent down to scrutinize the writing, so close his nose almost touched the ancient wood. "I cannot say that I have ever encountered it." He clucked his tongue. "Alas, I don't know what it might be."

The cord was tied with a simple knot, and the doctor reached for it, then hesitated. "I think," he said, pushing the bound wooden plaques towards Kit once more, "that you should have this honour."

Kit, his mouth dry, tugged at the woven cord, which parted as the ancient fibres shredded beneath his fingers. He brushed aside the disintegrating fragments and, holding his breath, lifted the top wooden plate. There, covered with a thin square of gossamer-fine linen, pressed like a rare leaf between the preserving sheets of a scrapbook, lay an irregular scrap of parchment almost translucent with age. The fine-grained leather, as thin as gossamer and as brittle as a scarab shell, was covered with a wild scattering of the most superbly etched symbols in dark blue.

Like a shadow shrivelled by the noonday sun, doubt vanished at the sight, and Kit knew that he had found the Skin Map.

Part 4

The Language of
Angels

CHAPTER 21

In Which the Scholarly Inquiry Bears Strange Fruit

Douglas Flinders-Petrie stood beneath the dripping eaves marvelling at the pageant. There were maids with pails of milk on yokes across their shoulders, ferrying their wares to the college inns; ironmongers selling skewers and sconces; bakers with trays of fresh bread on their heads hurrying across the square; vendors in ramshackle booths selling candles, ribbon, cloth, cheese, and spices. A butcher working from the back of an open wagon, carving up the carcass as required by his customers; a pie seller with a handcart, shouting for business; a farmer with braces of trussed and squawking chickens strolling through the milling throng; and on and on, like a live action study for a Brueghel painting.

How any of the students could concentrate on their professor, who was holding forth a few dozen paces away, Douglas could not fathom. But the lecturer, tall and gaunt upon his wooden crate, lifted his voice above the general din and declaimed in precise Latin on the subject of the day while the students, dressed in scholars' robes of green and blue, faces earnest beneath the level brims of their square hats, sat or lounged on bales of straw that had been dragged together to form a loose semicircle around him. Not a few of the townsfolk stood listening as well, sometimes calling out facetious answers to the rhetorical questions posed by the renowned teacher.

It was the professor Douglas had come to see, the sole reason he had so painstakingly polished his Latin and assembled the wardrobe, studied the history, manners, and customs in order to make this trip to the mid-1200s. Therefore, Douglas studied him intently. A trim, solemn-faced fellow of middle years with a strong nose and high-domed head, Roger Bacon – doctor, professor, scientist, and theologian – had established himself as a prime moving force in the fields of academia that were his domain: anatomy, medicine, science, alchemy, philosophy, and theology. He wore his dark hair short and tonsured like any other priest of his stripe, and his simple brown Franciscan robe, though threadbare and frayed at hem and sleeve, was clean, his belt of braided cord neatly tied.

At one point in the lecture, some local youths muscled their way to the fore and began talking loudly and making rude imitations of the professor standing on his wooden box. From this Douglas grasped another fact of his research: the petty jealousy of some of the townsfolk of what was increasingly considered the educational elite in their midst. Some, like the crude yokels Douglas observed, felt themselves hard done by a system that seemed to favour those they considered transient interlopers and effete snobs. Indeed, owing to his propensity for unorthodox notions and the inexplicable behaviour that often accompanied his various experiments, the esteemed man of science was steadily establishing himself as a leading eccentric, if not a cap-and-bell fool, in the court of public opinion.

The troublemakers pursued a rather half-hearted attempt to interrupt the proceedings, until two bulky bailiffs with long pikes appeared and moved them along. Order restored, the open-air symposium continued. Douglas turned his attention to the lecture and tried to follow it as best he could. The Latin was accomplished – fluent and fluid, eloquent, and elegant in expression – and so highly polished by years of scholastic application that even when Douglas knew the words being spoken it was difficult to ascertain what sense was being conveyed. The students, and a smattering of townspeople, seemed to grasp the meaning of what Douglas eventually concluded was a discourse on the nature of the universe and the place of reason in framing the human conception of reality.

It might well have been riveting stuff, but it took all of Douglas's newly acquired expertise in the ancient language just to identify the subject; actually following the subtle nuances of the argument were well beyond his nascent abilities. Still, he had a basic general idea of the flow if not the particulars, and anyway he had not come to sit at the feet of the learned professor. He was on a far more important mission.

"Snipe!" Douglas hissed under his breath. "Do *not* throw that." He had seen his pugnacious assistant fingering a rotten pear he had picked up from the gutter on their way to the lecture. "Drop it now."

The youth turned a baleful gaze upon his master, but still clutched the overripe fruit, juice oozing from his fingers.

"Drop it!" said Douglas. "Obey."

With a sneer of defiance, the pale youth released the fruit. The pear hit the ground with a dull splat; Snipe stomped on it with his foot and ground the soft fruit into the dirt. He then stood, rigid with rage, and glowered at the rabble around them.

"Good boy," Douglas commended him, and offered him a sop. "We will find a cat for you later."

The lecture eventually came to an end and the students began drifting off in twos and threes, melting into the general bustle of the busy town square. A few lingered to ask questions, and Douglas waited for these to finish. When all had gone away, he approached. "*Pax vobiscum, Magister Bacon,*" he said, removing his round monk's cap and making a nicely practised bow of deference. "*Deus vobis.*"

"*Quis est?*" said the professor, as he turned. Taking in Douglas's robes, he said, "God with you, brother."

Douglas introduced himself as a visiting priest who had come seeking enlightenment on a scholarly matter. "I wonder if I may call on you in your lodgings to discuss it?"

"It would be a sublime pleasure for a certainty," replied Master Bacon. "Alas, my duties are many, and I have not found a way to expand time to accommodate them all. Therefore, I must sadly decline your offer to attend me – attractive as it may be."

"To be sure," replied Douglas, who had anticipated a similar response and was ready with a reply. "I would not presume to add to your burdens in any way, God knows. Yet it may interest you to know that I come from the abbey at Tyndyrn, where an exceedingly peculiar manuscript has come into our hands, we know not how." He saw the glint of curiosity spark in the professor's dark eyes. "Some of my brothers believe you may be the only person alive who can read it."

"This manuscript of which you speak," said Roger Bacon, rubbing the back of his hand, "what can you tell me about it?"

"Very little, sir. You see, it is written in no language ever seen before. At least, not one that our best scholars can identify."

"Congratulations, my friend," declared the august professor with a bow of his tonsured head. "You have succeeded in intriguing me – an eventuality that grows more difficult with each year that Christ tarries. Will you come to me tonight at the Bear? We will have supper together." He indicated the inn behind them. "I take my meals within, and my table is always ready. I shall keep a place for you." His eyes shifted to Douglas's companion. "And your acolyte, of course. God's greeting, my son." Upon regarding the youth more closely, his smile wilted.

"He is mute and does not speak," Douglas informed the master with a pat of Snipe's overlarge head. "My thanks, Master Bacon. Until this evening, then."

"God with you, friend," replied the professor, stepping away.

Douglas waited a moment, then crossed the square and proceeded to the Star Inn, where he had taken rooms. He spoke to the matron and requested food and drink to be brought to him. He and Snipe returned to their upstairs lodgings, Douglas to study some more Latin in preparation for the evening's conversation – an activity he expected to tax his linguistic powers to their utmost – and Snipe to sleep in preparation for tonight's vigil.

Then, just after sunset, the two ley travellers donned their outer robes once more and went out to meet Master Bacon at the Bear. They crossed an all-but-deserted square – now occupied only by a few old women gleaning morsels from the detritus and garbage heaped at the street corners, and some mongrel dogs snuffling through the refuse in the gutters. Ignoring their beggarly imprecations, Douglas hurried to the inn, paused beneath the torch above the door, and with a last warning to Snipe to be on his best behaviour, lowered the hood of his cowl and went inside. The interior was a fog of smoke and steam and the scent of the beeswax candles that lit the room, casting everything in a warm amber glow. He stepped to the serving hatch and procured a pie, then turned to get the measure of the place. There were tables of assorted sizes scattered about the large central dining area served by a wide, deep, and glowing hearth where spitted meat roasted, cauldrons gurgled, and bread baked; three smaller rooms opened off the main room, each containing a single long table and benches. In one of these snugs they found Roger Bacon, surrounded by a bevy of students – sallow-faced striplings with straggly beards and long tousled hair, some wearing their scholars' robes, others dressed more informally in dark satin jerkins and tunics. All clutched jars of ale, and they rose as one to greet the newcomers.

"Pray you, do not stand on our account," Douglas told them. "Please, sit and take your ease." Posting Snipe at the door with a pie, he took the seat offered him at the end of the table.

"Our friend is visiting from Tyndyrn Abbey," the professor informed his audience. He poured another jar and pushed it along the table to Douglas. "He comes seeking enlightenment. Is this not so?"

"Verily, that is the purpose of my visit," replied Douglas. He noticed the twitch of the students' eyes as they darted glances to one another when he spoke. He guessed the cause and swiftly moved to disarm any mistrust, adding, "Before we converse further, I will apologize for my lack of learning and the crudeness of my speech. I was not brought up to the Latin of my betters. I was born and raised on the Isle of Man. Whatever learning I possess, I acquired late in life and through the instruction of those but little better informed than myself." He gazed steadily around the table and concluded, "I am sorry if my speech offends you, brothers. I humbly beg your indulgence."

"Nonsense!" cried Roger Bacon. "All scholars are pilgrims on the same journey. Some may have set foot on the path the sooner, and so have advanced a little further." He, too, passed his gaze around the gathering. "As a pilgrim people, we do not presume to hold judgment over one another, but accept all like-minded travellers in our company as friends for the journey."

The students, subtly chastised, ratified this sentiment with hearty cheers and thirsty quaffs of beer, hailing the newcomer in their midst.

"My thanks," said Douglas, wiping his mouth on his sleeve in imitation of his companions. "I am your servant."

"Since our company is complete," said the master, "let us break bread together and commend our converse to the Almighty; may our erudition bring him glory."

"Amen!" cried the students. "To supper!"

Three of the more junior members were dispatched to the kitchen to collect the food and bring it to the table. They trooped off noisily, returning shortly with a collection of crockery filled with roast meats, small loaves of bread, and a variety of vegetable porridges. Wooden spoons were passed around, and they all fell to with a will. Douglas was glad he had remembered to bring along a knife of his own since, in an age where everyone was expected to furnish his own cutlery, the hospitality of the inn did not extend past the communal wooden spoons.

The meal soon settled into a convivial hum presided over by Master Bacon, and Douglas observed the manners and culture of his fellow diners. The camaraderie was genuine and seemed deep, as was the esteem in which they held their renowned professor. When Friar Bacon spoke, all eyes turned to him, as all thoughts yielded to his guidance.

His was the last word in all discussions. As might have been expected of academics, the talk around the table was a heady stew: chemistry, mechanics, mathematics, astronomy, all mixed together with heavy dollops of philosophy and theology – much of it beyond Douglas's ability to digest. However rich, the master was always able to elucidate any matter further, or expound in greater or finer degree. Douglas sensed that the scope and sophistication of the man's thoughts were staggering, and though he could not follow the intricacies of expression, he could marvel at the suppleness of mind that produced them.

When, long after the dishes had been cleared and the ale jars filled once and again and again, the students were dismissed to their evening prayers and the master at last turned to his newest guest. "Now, my friend, we have some time to ourselves. Will you accompany me to my laboratory, where we can speak more privately?"

"Of course, I would be honoured."

Leaving the inn, they went out into the night, passing through the city only intermittently illumined by torches and braziers set up at the street corners and tended by the town's bailiffs – the local militia who acted as peacekeepers and enforcers of the king's law. Tonight the old town was quiet, and the two men – accompanied by a truculent shadow in the form of Snipe – walked easily and unmolested down the wide street leading to the bridge and its imposing tower. Upon reaching the base of the tower, Master Bacon produced a large iron key and proceeded to unlock his laboratory, which occupied the ground floor.

While the professor worked his key in the lock, Douglas turned to Snipe. "Stay here and guard this door," he told him, bending near. "I do not wish to be disturbed. Understand?"

By means Douglas did not perceive, the professor lit candles with a mere snap of his fingers. As soon as it was light enough to see the interior, Douglas observed that it was a single large square room, its stone walls unadorned, its floors bare. Two long board tables set up on trestles side by side ran the length of the room, their surfaces covered with books and parchments at one end and bottles, vials, jars, and mixing bowls at the other. In a nearby corner stood a brick oven something like a small blacksmith forge; smouldering coals sent a thin tendril of smoke rising towards a hole in the ceiling. Surrounded by arcane tools and vessels of copper, iron, tin, and bronze, it gave that corner of the room the appearance of a combination foundry and chemist's laboratory.

Near to the oven was a large wooden chair piled high with fleeces and coverings. A large iron candle tree stood to one side of the chair, and a contraption resembling a cantilevered drafting table stood on the other. From this Douglas surmised that it was the place where the eminent professor did his reading and thinking and writing.

"Welcome, my friend," said Master Bacon, waving out the reed he had used to light the candles. "Every creature has its true home. This is mine. Here I have everything I need for the sustenance of the inner life."

"A most commodious dwelling," agreed Douglas. Indicating the collection of bottles and jars on the table, he said, "Am I right in thinking that you are engaged in alchemical investigations?"

"You are perceptive," replied the master. "For some years, I have been pursuing the promise of alchemy. Alas, it is proving a very elusive prize. It is with no small regret that I confess I seem no closer to achieving the goal I have set for myself – although I have made many discoveries and enjoyed some small success along the way."

"Nothing is wasted," said Douglas.

"Verily." Roger Bacon smiled indulgently. "For the scholar no effort is ever wasted." He moved to the end of the table covered by his manuscripts. "I believe," he said, rolling up one of the parchments to clear a space, "you have brought something for me to examine. Let us be about our business."

"I am your servant," said Douglas. Reaching into the inner pocket of his robe, he brought out the small, linen-wrapped parcel; he removed the cloth and placed the book on the board. "I would be most grateful, sir, to receive your erudite opinion, for I confess its contents are wholly mysterious to me."

"Not *sir*," corrected Bacon, "but brother only. We are fellow priests, are we not?"

Douglas merely smiled and pushed the book nearer. Roger Bacon's gaze fell onto the volume, his dark eyes suddenly agleam with the excitement of the chase. "Let us see what we have." Taking up the book, he carefully opened the leather cover and stared for a long moment at the first page, then turned it, glanced at another, and then three more in quick succession.

"How did this come into your possession?" he asked, his voice trembling. His gaze turned fierce. He stabbed a finger at the text.

211

"This… this book – how was it obtained?"

"Is there some difficulty?" replied Douglas slowly. Unable to read the meaning behind Bacon's words, he stalled for time to think.

"Do not be offended, I pray thee," Bacon said. "But I must know. It is of utmost importance to me."

"It belonged to the previous abbot, I believe. As I have it, the book was found among his things when he died last spring," Douglas lied. He had practised the story so often, he almost believed it himself. "How it came into the dear man's possession, I cannot say. The present abbot could no doubt tell you more, but as he is too old and infirm to make the journey here, I was deputed to the task." Douglas offered a smile of wan sincerity. "Beyond that, I can offer nothing. I am sorry."

"A great pity." The eminent scholar shook his head gently. "It may be that certain questions must remain unanswered until another day. In the meantime, we shall proceed with the task before us."

Roger Bacon opened the book again, and Douglas breathed an inward sigh of relief as he watched the scholar brushing his fingers lightly over the close-written lines of abstruse symbols, his lips moving all the while.

"Can you read it?" Douglas asked, trying to affect a scholarly disinterest.

"For a truth, I can," confirmed the master. "You see, my friend, I am the one who devised it."

"Devised?" wondered Douglas, uncertain he had heard correctly. "Do you mean that you *wrote* this?"

"Oh, no," Bacon replied with a quick shake of his head. "I did not compose this book, but I transcribed the script in which it is written."

"Pray, what language is represented here? I confess neither I nor anyone else I know has ever seen the like."

Here the master scholar allowed himself a bemused smile. "That does not surprise me in the least," he said gently. "Few mortals will have ever seen it." He lowered his gaze to the text once more, brushing a line of the flowing script with his long fingers. "It is the language of the angels."

CHAPTER 22

In Which Blood Tells

"Pay strict attention now, Archibald," instructed Lord Gower. "Use that clever brain of yours. Think!" He turned to the table behind him, which was covered by a sheet. "We will try this test again. Are you ready?"

Archie, dark brow furrowed with concentration, nodded. "Ready, my lord."

The earl whipped away the cloth. "Now, tell me – which among these items are the genuine articles, and which are the imitations?" He indicated a spread of small objects arranged on a rectangle of blue velvet. "Take your time," he urged. "And concentrate. Remember all I've told you."

Hands folded beneath his chin, the young man stepped forward and gazed at the array of objects on display: a brooch with a cameo surrounded by a ring of tiny sapphires, a cat carved of ebony, a silver owl with jet eyes, a golden ring in the shape of a scarab with a shell inset with lapis and carnelian, an alabaster statue of a crocodile fighting a hippopotamus, and a pair of pendant earrings of blue, green, red, and yellow glass beads. These objects had been pulled from the Earl of Sutherland's extensive collection of antiquities, and all were fine specimens of their kind.

"You may look, but do not touch," cautioned the earl. "An expert must be able to tell from the very first glance. Concentrate. Which are the fakes, and which the authentic creations?"

Archie Burley reached a tentative finger towards the cat figurine, then pulled back his hand. He went on to the ring, and then, after havering between the owl and the crocodile statuette, chose the gold

214

ring and earrings instead. "The scarab and the pendant earrings," he announced. "These are genuine."

Lord Gower raised his eyebrows questioningly. "The little scarab and the earrings? Are you absolutely certain?"

Archie gave a curt nod.

"Not the owl? Not the brooch?" His Lordship tapped the cameo, making the sapphires sparkle. "This is a valuable piece." He indicated the alabaster statuette. "Why not the crocodile? It is very beautiful."

"The question was not which is the most beautiful or costly," declared Archie. "You asked which were the genuine artefacts and which the fakes. I choose the scarab and the earrings."

"Well done, Archibald!" The earl began clapping his hands very slowly. "You are correct. Those are genuine Egyptian antiques. You have the talent, lad. You will get on."

"Thank you, sir."

"But tell me," continued Lord Gower, picking up the brooch. "Why did you not choose this pretty bauble, or the hippo and crocodile?"

"The brooch is too…" Archie hesitated, then offered a shrug. "Too shiny. Real gemstones are more subtle. I think the setting is real, but the stones must be imitation. And the hippo is wrong."

"What do you mean, *wrong*? Explain."

"The hippo is too small, and it looks like a pig. I suspect the object was made by someone who had never seen the real animal. Or perhaps the craftsman simply copied this piece from another figurine." He waved a hand at the cat and owl. "The cat is of good design and workmanship, but the material is not authentic. An Egyptian artist would have used stone. Likewise the owl."

"What is wrong with the owl?"

"The figure is cast in silver – again, not a material an Egyptian artist of the classical period would have used." He glanced at his instructor for approval. "Am I right?"

"You are entirely correct." Gower beamed at his pupil. "My boy, you have learned your lessons well. I think you are ready to accompany me to the sales room."

"I am honoured, sir." Archie felt a quiver of excitement at the thought. Although inwardly spinning cartwheels of joy, he maintained a calm and disinterested manner – the way His Lordship had taught him: a shrewd trader never revealed his true emotions. An unguarded gush of enthusiasm could easily drive up the price of a bargain, or worse, ruin an acquisition altogether. "I will do my best not to betray the trust you have placed in me."

"I am certain you will acquit yourself in a right worthy manner." The earl began picking up the valuables to return them to their respective cases in the hall. "Tomorrow," he said, fingering the brooch, "we will begin your education on the floor of Sotheby's Auction House."

The next day they rode by carriage along the Strand, disembarking at the end of Wellington Street and proceeding on foot the last few hundred yards so that the earl might view some of his London properties. His holdings in the city were by some measures modest, but provided a steady income that to Archie seemed positively astronomical. Not that the young man was in any position to complain; Lord Gower provided him with a weekly allowance as well as a yearly stipend, a fair portion of which he passed along to his mother.

During his time in Lord Gower's employ, Archie had risen from the humblest of beginnings as menial dogsbody, ascending rung by rung in the earl's estimation as greater trust and responsibility were conferred upon him. From odd job and errand boy, Archie had become, in turn, scullion help, groom, assistant footman, footman, second under-butler, assistant valet, and so on, to arrive at what amounted to the role of personal private secretary. When the earl went upcountry, Archie went with him; when the earl travelled on the Continent, Archie was there to help with all and sundry arrangements; when the earl and his entourage decamped for the earl's northern estate, Archie was sent on ahead to make ready the house and grounds for His Lordship's arrival. And nowadays, whenever the earl was summoned to Windsor, or attended the House of Lords, Archie went too.

All the while the young man was learning the manners and

customs of the elite, biding his time until he could strike out on his own to make his fortune. "A man must have an occupation," the earl had advised him years ago. "What will be yours, I wonder?"

"Can I not remain in your service, sir?" he had asked. Archie was twelve years old at the time and could conceive of nothing better than being a member of the earl's household staff.

"As long as you like," answered Lord Gower. "But, my dear boy, I shall not live forever. Much as I might regret it, when I go, my lands and titles will pass to a cousin whom I have not seen in twenty years. That is a fact of law. In any case, I do not wish to leave you without a way to make a living in the world. You cannot be a servant forever. You are made of finer stuff."

"I do not care to leave you, sir."

"Nor I you. But blood tells, Archibald." The earl smiled and put a fatherly hand on the young boy's shoulder. "There is aristocratic blood in you, and that cannot be denied."

The earl had long since discovered the circumstances of Archie's birth and ancestry. Moreover, through his various connections he had succeeded in orchestrating a reconciliation of sorts between Lord Ashmole and Gemma Burley, extracting a tidy settlement for Archie's mother. Yet, with a steady eye on the future, Lord Gower was determined to provide Archie with an occupation he could take up in years to come. To this end, he had decided to teach his fosterling the ins and outs of the burgeoning trade in antiques and ancient artefacts that had taken the British aristocracy by storm, and in which vast sums of money were to be made by one who knew the business well.

Gower knew his business. For a man in the earl's position, his interest in antiquities was merely a glorified hobby; he did not need the swathes of cash that came his way in the trade. Nevertheless, he saw a substantial livelihood in it for a young man, especially one as promising as his protégé. By the time his tutelage was finished, His Lordship was in no doubt that Archie Burley would make his way in the world quite well.

Now, as they approached the auction house, Lord Gower rehearsed his pupil on what to expect inside – how the auctions were conducted and the bidding progressed. He concluded, saying, "We will observe today – although if something of interest comes up, I may enter the fray. In any case, I want you to pay attention to those who place bids. One can tell a great deal of their interest or means from the way they hold themselves as the bidding reaches the upper limits. It can be most instructive."

Archie nodded.

"In days to come, we will select an object to acquire, and I will have you place the bid. I want you to become accustomed to the feelings associated with the game, as I see it, and learn to control them. In this, as in everything, your best advantage is a cool head and an unclouded mind."

"I will do my best, sir."

"I know you will, Archibald." They came to a halt before the large Regency building that was home to Sotheby's Auctioners. "Ah! Here we are. Shall we go in?"

The earl led the way through the brass-encrusted doors into the red-carpeted lobby, where he was met by liveried staff who greeted him and conducted him straightaway to the manager who, with much bowing and scraping, made His Lordship welcome.

"Your Lordship, we are honoured. Please make yourself comfortable while I arrange chairs to be placed for you on the floor."

"Good day to you, Mumphrey," replied the earl. "There is no need to trouble yourself. We only just called out of idleness and curiosity."

"Would you care for a soothing libation, my lord? I have some excellent sherry wine just in from Portugal. I would value your opinion, sir. The partners are thinking of taking a consignment to let out at auction."

"Certainly, Mumphrey, it would be my pleasure," replied the earl. While the manager scuttled away to fetch the sherry, Lord Gower allowed his attention to roam the room. "There is no one here at present," he declared, although the grand entrance was, in fact, quite full, and more people were entering. "Let us see what we have on offer today."

They joined the mingling crowd gathered around the presentation tables lining the lobby. There were also easels set up with broadsheet announcements and descriptions of the various items that would be offered during the day's session.

"As I expected," observed the earl after a brief perusal. "There is nothing here of interest to us. Still, that is not our chief concern. We are not here to acquire; we are here to learn. It will be instructive."

And instructive it certainly was… though not perhaps in the way His Lordship intended, much less approved. For in this first visit, as well as those that were to follow over the next months, what Archie learned first and foremost was: the enormous leverage of an aristocratic title. Allied to this, keen student that he was, Archie also gained an appreciation of the immense usefulness of an auction house as a disinterested purveyor of goods.

As he observed the ebb and flow of the auction's ritual dance, the young man quickly formed the opinion that while it was all well and good to acquire pieces from places like Sotheby's to sell at a profit to rich clients, it was a slow and inefficient way to amass a fortune. It seemed to Archie that the best position was that of the originator of the sale. The greater profits were realized by the seller, not the middleman buyer. Rather than being a broker for others – for that, in essence, was the role Lord Gower played – a man with taste, good judgment, and a sense of the market, and who also possessed the means and inclination to travel, could easily acquire the same objects in their native countries, so to speak, and sell them directly to private clients, or simply put them onto the market through the auction houses.

Furthermore, if that man also possessed an aristocratic title, then his future was assured. Archie had seen how doors opened to the earl that were barred to lesser mortals, how men deferred to him, how women fawned over him – and all due to his title, which preceded him wherever he went, smoothing his way through the world. If Archie were to own a title, others, both clients and vendors, would trust him for that reason alone.

Little by little, as his understanding of the antique trade increased, his resolve hardened; a vision of his future began to crystallize in his mind. In the meantime, he was content to add to his store of knowledge. A greedy sponge, he would soak up all Lord Gower had to offer. When the day came for him to part company with the earl, Archie knew what he would do and how he would go about doing it.

CHAPTER 23

In Which Patience and Practice Pay Off

"Are you certain you won't come with us?" asked Kit. They were standing once again at the end of the sphinx avenue in the early-morning light. Both Thomas and Khefri gazed apprehensively down the long row of statuary towards the temple set in the face of the sheer rock cliff.

"I have made my decision," replied the doctor somewhat wistfully. "Someone must remain behind to take care of all the treasures we have liberated from Anen's tomb." He put a hand on the young Egyptian's shoulder. "My young friend and I have several years' worth of work to do, thanks to you. This experience has been most enlightening. I am in your debt."

"Not a bit of it," Kit countered. "If anything, it is the other way 'round."

"You will come back?" asked Khefri. "When you have found what you are looking for – you will return to Egypt?"

"I will," promised Kit. "If at all possible, I'll be back before you know it."

Wilhelmina fished the brass ley lamp from the pocket of her jumpsuit. A tiny glint of blue winked in the early-morning light. "We should be going," she said, replacing the odd instrument. Moving to Dr Young, she extended her hand. When he took it, she pulled him into a hug. "Thank you for everything, Thomas. I knew I could trust you. And Kit's right – we will return as soon as possible."

"Rest assured that in your absence I will endeavour to further my inquiries into the philosophical implications of ley travel," said Thomas, gently extricating himself from her embrace. He patted the copy of the Skin Map he had carefully sketched and now wore beneath his shirt next to his own skin. "God willing, I may even be able to translate the cypher."

"Then we'll leave you to it," said Kit.

"On your return, I will happily accompany you wherever your further journeys take you," added the doctor. "On that you have my word."

"Until then," said Kit, clasping his hand.

Mina touched Kit's arm. "It's time."

Wilhelmina and Giles had shown up the previous evening in the midst of the excavators' celebration at having found the Skin Map. Kit, in an expansive mood, took them down into the tomb and showed them the wall paintings. "See here," he said, indicating the third panel. "We didn't have time before, but here is the man himself – Arthur Flinders-Petrie, dressed in a striped robe, open at the chest to reveal the tattoos."

"Extraordinary," agreed Wilhelmina. "Probably the first – if not the only – portrait of the man and his map."

Giles, who had last seen the room as a prisoner locked up with the corpse of his master and condemned to die of thirst, turned his gaze slowly towards the sarcophagus where he and Kit had put the bodies of Sir Henry and Cosimo.

Kit saw the glance and involuntary grimace that followed and recognized the reaction. "I know, Giles," he said. "It takes a little effort to put it behind you. But it might help to remember that this is *not* the same tomb where Sir Henry and Cosimo died. That tomb – the one we were in – is in another place and time, in another world."

Giles nodded, but said nothing.

"Now," said Kit, moving on to the fourth panel of the giant wall painting, "take a look at this last one. There is High Priest Anen holding the map – the whole thing – as he points to the star."

"But ours is only a piece," commented Wilhelmina. "Isn't that what you said?"

"Possibly a fourth or fifth of the whole – just as Cosimo believed, and which more or less corresponds to the portion I saw in the Christ Church crypt."

"But you said that was a fake," Mina pointed out.

"It was," confirmed Kit, "although someone had gone to the trouble of making it roughly the same size and shape as the original he had stolen."

"What will you do with the map?" wondered Thomas. "Now that you have found it, what will you do?"

"First," Kit considered, "we must learn to read it. And then we'll use it to carry on Cosimo and Sir Henry's quest to find Flinders-Petrie's treasure."

Wilhelmina put her face close to the painting. She held her lamp nearer and studied the map in the high priest's hand. "Are these in any way accurate, do you think?"

"I wish they were," said Kit. "They're just the artist's representations. I don't think the people who drew those symbols had any interest in rendering them in exact detail. My guess is they probably never saw the real map at all." He shrugged. "Who knows?"

"Let me see it," said Wilhelmina.

Kit turned to Thomas, who produced a bundle wrapped in fresh linen. The doctor untied the cord and unrolled the nearly translucent patch of human parchment. In the gentle lambent glow of the lamps, the indigo symbols etched on the skin seemed to pulsate with strange power.

"May I?" said Wilhelmina. Thomas passed the map to her, and she held it up to the painting. Though the symbols in the painting were crude squiggles next to the real thing, the basic shapes seemed more or less correct. The piece Mina was holding did match up with the upper right quadrant of the map in High Priest Anen's hand. "Whoever cut up the map was very careful," she observed. "Look at the ruffled edges." She pointed out the lower portion and left side of the map. "See how irregular the line is?"

"Whoever did it was at pains not to cut into other symbols," replied Kit. "So they cut around them, producing this deckle edge."

"The adjoining pieces will match precisely," offered Thomas. "By that you will know they are genuine."

Wilhelmina carefully re-rolled the human parchment and passed it to Thomas, who returned it to its cover. The four had then returned to the wadi camp, where Khefri had organized a special dinner of roast goat to celebrate the successful completion of the dig. They had eaten and talked late into the night, and now, as the sun was rising in the east, it was time to depart.

Wilhelmina started down the avenue towards the spot where Giles was waiting. Kit lifted a hand and called, "Farewell!"

"Go with God, my friends," shouted Thomas, waving them away. "Grace and peace attend you."

But his words were lost in the shriek of the wind that suddenly gusted along the ancient pavement. The world grew hazy in a mixture of dust and grit… and the next thing Kit knew, a fierce rain was beating on his face. His clothing whipped about his limbs in a gale-force wind that, unlike his other experiences, did not summarily die away upon their arrival.

"I think we've landed in the middle of a hurricane!" he shouted, trying to be heard above the crash and roar.

"What?" came Wilhelmina's voice from a distance that sounded like miles, but must have been only a few feet away.

"This storm," he cried. "We're in the thick of it."

"It's always stormy here," she shouted, emerging out of the lashing wind. "It never stops."

"Never?"

"Not ever." She pressed her wet face closer. "Not in my experience."

"You've been here before?"

"Lots of times."

He felt her hand grip his arm.

"This way. Stay with me." She turned her head and shouted over her shoulder. "Giles! Are you with us?"

"Here, my lady," came the reply from somewhere close behind.

"Take hold of my hand. I'm going to count to three, and we run straight ahead. Ready? Here we go… one… two… three… Go!"

Kit did as instructed, sprinting blindly into the teeth of the storm. For an instant it felt as if his flesh would be ripped from his bones, and then… darkness and silence. He was tumbling through an emptiness, through an airless void so absolute he thought he was suffocating. He gagged, but could not draw oxygen into his lungs.

He felt a sharp sting on his cheek.

"Breathe, Kit!"

He opened his eyes to see Wilhelmina standing before him with her hand poised to strike again. "Hah!" he gasped, staggering backwards. "Stop that! I'm okay."

Mina turned to Giles, who was kneeling on a broad, leaf-strewn path a few paces away. "You okay?" Upon receiving his grunted reply, she said, "Sorry, guys. That one was the worst – but it saved us four more jumps and maybe two days of overland travel."

"Anything for the cause," said Kit, woozily shaking water from his clothes. "I'm soaked to the skin."

"You'll dry." Wilhelmina started away. "Have you still got the map?"

Kit patted his stomach, where the bundle resided under his shirt. He nodded.

"Good." She started away. "You'll feel better once we're moving again. It's best to walk it off. Come on."

"Where are we?" Kit glanced around. They seemed to be standing in a lightly wooded countryside; the air was cool and redolent of fallen leaves. He could hear insects buzzing in the branches of the nearby trees.

"We're about three miles north of Prague," she said, stepping off the path. "There's a road a little further along. It runs beside the river. It'll take us into the city. If we're lucky, we might be able to hitchhike the rest of the way."

"*When* are we?" Kit asked.

"Well, we're somewhere in the autumn of 1607 during the reign of Emperor Rudolf. If we hit it right, we're in early October." She started towards a blackberry bush growing beside the path. "Or possibly September."

"And we've come here why?" wondered Kit.

"I live here," she said. "We need a good safe place to lay up for a few days to study the map and figure out what to do next. Wait here," she said, stepping behind the bush. "I have to change."

"You stashed a change of clothes?" said Kit. "Nice."

"I dare not be seen dressed like this in the city. Too many people know me."

Kit looked down at himself. "What about Giles and me?"

"Giles is fine the way he is," came the reply from behind the bush. "As for you, take off that dumb turban and wrap it around your waist. Tie it like a sash; it will help disguise your flouncy shirt."

"Flouncy shirt," muttered Kit. "It's a *jalabiya*, I'll have you know."

"I'm sure it is. With a sash, people will just think it's a labourer's smock. They wear those around here."

Kit obeyed as instructed, much to the amusement of the watching Giles. "Where did you go, you and Giles, when we left the wadi the first time? While I was helping Thomas dig up the tomb, where were you?"

"In Edinburgh," came the reply from the bushes. "Dr Young was there. I went to convince him to help you excavate the tomb."

"But that's – How can that be? He was in Egypt with me… wasn't he?"

"Not yet," said Wilhelmina. "I should have thought that would be obvious."

"Not to me. Explain."

"It's simple. Time, as we know, operates independently in different frames of reference."

"As we know," Kit agreed.

"So I simply had to reach him before he left for Egypt on his expedition."

"But that would mean I was already with him, digging up the treasure *before* you even asked him," Kit pointed out.

"Right," said Wilhelmina. "Neat, eh?" She stepped out from behind the bush, wholly transformed. Gone was the girl in the camouflage jumpsuit and sky-blue scarf and desert boots; in her place stood a winsome lass in a long skirt, white blouse with puffy sleeves, and multicoloured shawl. She carried a cloth bag, which she handed to Kit.

"This way, chaps," she said, and soon they were moving through the long grass and down a gently sloping hillside.

Kit could see the gleam of a river at the bottom of the incline and, sure enough, a road.

"If we don't dilly-dally, we can have dinner tonight at one of the best restaurants in the city."

Kit stopped walking and stared at her, as if seeing her for the first time. "Gosh, Mina. You are amazing. How do you know so much about all this?"

"Practice," she said. "Lots and lots of practice. And mistakes."

CHAPTER 24

In Which a Destiny is Determined

The end, when it came, was swift and unexpected. Lord Gower had complained in the evening of feeling unwell. He had taken tea and a bit of dry toast and retired to his rooms. By morning he was no better, so a doctor was summoned to attend him. That same afternoon, in a feverish sweat and complaining of a headache, he had lapsed into a fitful sleep from which he was not to be roused. Archie was with him when he died two days later; standing by the earl's bed, he marked the toll of the nine o'clock bell from the tower of Saint Mary's Argent Square as his benefactor's spirit fled its mortal confines. Archie bent his head and shed a private tear for the man who had been his teacher, friend, and, as far as Archie was concerned, the only father he had ever known.

The next day was spent in the offices of Beachcroft and Lechward, Lord Gower's solicitors, who arranged for the funeral and burial according to the earl's will and special instructions. The funeral was held seven days later at Saint Mary's, with nearly two hundred in attendance. The mourners were provided tea and cakes at Lord Gower's London residence after the graveside service, and Archie received the condolences of his guests with a dignified decorum the earl would have approved and commended. The next two weeks were spent doing an inventory of the property in preparation for what Archie considered the inevitable invasion to come.

The calendar turned over another leaf, and one morning George Gower, the estranged cousin of the earl, came knocking on the door in the company of his wife, Branca; a Peckham bailiff; and a solicitor in a top hat and black frock coat. Archie received them in the earl's sitting room.

"The hand-over of property will not be delayed," intoned the lawyer imperiously. "We will be taking immediate possession. It would be most helpful if you were to collect your personal possessions and vacate the premises at your earliest convenience."

Archie, who had braced himself for this moment, was nevertheless stunned by the abruptness of the eviction and the coldness of the greed on display. When he found his voice, he said, "I have had an inventory prepared, if you would care to —"

"We will make our own inventory, thank you," the lawyer sniffed. "In any case, you will vacate the premises by three o'clock this afternoon. The bailiff here will be pleased to help you gather your things. He will accompany you now to ensure that you do not inadvertently remove any articles not belonging to you and to which you are not entitled."

"Your foresight is admirable." Archie offered a grim smile to the new tenants. "How you must have longed for this day and prayed for its coming."

"*Silencie a sua lingua!*" snarled the woman, her potent Portuguese temper quick and hot. "You are not family. You have nothing to say."

"Indeed," Archie agreed. "I assure you that I have no wish to remain in your odious presence a moment longer than necessary."

"Now, see here, you —" sputtered George Gower. "You bounder!"

But Archie was already moving towards the door and departed without another word. "Summon Beachcroft," he told the earl's valet. "Then pack your things and, if I were you, I might spare a thought to the days ahead — if you know what I mean."

The valet nodded. "It is in hand, sir."

"You may instruct the rest of the staff to do the same."

"Very good, sir."

While the new owners began totting up the silver, Archie went to his rooms and began to pack his things. He was joined a few minutes later by the bailiff – a suspicious oaf who insisted on examining everything Archie put into his cases until Archie suggested, "Perhaps it would be best if you packed for me; then you could give your keepers a precise inventory of what I have taken."

"Never you mind my job," muttered the man. "Get on with you."

Beachcroft, the earl's solicitor, arrived with a copy of Lord Gower's will just as Archie was placing his cases in the foyer. In the presence of the inheritors and their lawyer, he read out the relevant portion of the earl's last will and testament, which explicitly stated that Archibald Burley was given leave to choose any five objects from the earl's extensive collection of exotic artefacts.

"*Any* five objects he so desires," stressed Walter Beachcroft, "without let or hindrance."

When Archie took his leave a short while later it was, much to the relief of the new owners, with five small dusty antiques of negligible interest. Had George and Branca known the true value of the items Archie selected, fits of apoplexy would have ensued all around. As it was, their ignorance allowed them some measure of insulation from the stinging reality. Taken together, the objects Archie chose amounted to a very tidy sum that would allow him to set up in the antiquities trade.

Nor was that all.

In truth, the far greater portion of Archie's now-considerable fortune was already safely stashed in six large tea chests that had been safely deposited in the vaults of Lloyd's Bank, and another that had been delivered with his cases to King's Cross Station a week earlier. After his summary eviction from Lord Gower's London residence, Archie paid his mother a visit and bade her farewell, leaving her with a Lloyd's Bank book for an account containing five hundred pounds in her name. Then he kissed her goodbye and caught the evening boat-train to the Continent. Visits to Paris, Cologne, Vienna, and Rome were followed by more lengthy sojourns in Prague, Constantinople, Jerusalem, and Cairo. At each stop along the way he acquired *objets d'art* and exotica that would form the basis of a collection of almost legendary proportions to tantalize the jaded palates of London's elite collectors.

Archie's only contact with England during his sojourn abroad was in the form of a letter from Beachcroft, the solicitor, informing him that the earl's estate had been sold to a sugar magnate. George and Branca Gower had taken their fortune and returned to Lisbon, where, presumably, they would live out their days in comfort and ease at the expense of their late relation.

On the second anniversary of the Earl of Sutherland's death, an extremely dashing tycoon answering to the name Archelaeus Burleigh, Earl of Sutherland, arrived in London. The dark, distinguished young lord took an apartment in an expansive Kensington Garden mansion.

In the weeks and months to follow, the wealthier citizens of the metropolis would be buzzing about the rare and exquisite antiques this knowledgeable and well-spoken gentleman could produce from his seemingly inexhaustible store. Tales circulated about the earl's extensive connections with the aristocracy of Old Europe and the royal palaces of the Middle East, which were the principal sources for the wondrous items he traded. These objects did not come cheaply.

Certainly, the fine rings, bracelets, and necklaces; jewelled pendants, statuettes, daggers, and diadems; carved reliefs from attic friezes and pediments; intricately decorated red-and-black amphorae, bowls, lamps, beakers, and urns, and all the rest carried breathtaking price tags. But then where else could one obtain such superb specimens?

"Beauty is all too often fleeting in this world," Lord Burleigh was wont to remark. "I live only for one thing – and that is the pursuit of beauty that outlasts the ages."

This sentiment, and much else about the young aristocrat, mightily impressed his clientele, which now included a growing number of marriageable young women. As word of the eligible bachelor of Sutherland spread, his wealth grew – and grew in the telling – until he could not attend an evening performance at Covent Garden or the Proms without attracting a bevy of beautifully groomed and gowned young things. The situation did not go unnoticed. As one mildly envious onlooker was heard to opine, "I say, the Earl of Sutherland must love his gardening."

"How so, Mortimer?"

"Why, to be surrounded by such a profusion of ravishing flowers he must work those beds like a very slave."

"Quite."

The young earl himself appeared to enjoy the feminine attention, yet remained slightly aloof from it, maintaining an air of mild amusement at his own apparent availability. And, while he displayed no favouritism in his choice of companions, being seen in public with a different beauty every night, there was one who began to emerge from the pack: a willowy, blonde lovely named Phillipa Harvey-Jones, daughter and sole surviving heir of prominent industrialist Reginald Harvey-Jones, a man in the chase for a knighthood if ever there was one. Reggie, as he was known to friends and admirers, enjoyed his reputation as a bruisingly tough businessman whose only pleasure in life was doting on his daughter.

Naturally, when her name began to be linked with the dashing Burleigh's, it roused Reggie's considerable interest. Within minutes of their first meeting, he cut right to the point. "Your money, sir. Where did you get it?"

"Beg your pardon?" Archelaeus raised his eyebrows.

"We are men of the world," Reg told him. "Let's not be coy – especially where money is concerned. We both know it is nothing to do with character. At best it is only an arbitrary indicator of a man's place in the world." He fixed the young lord with a narrow, uncompromising gaze. "So, how much have you got, anyway?"

"Difficult to say," replied Burleigh, easily sliding into a tone of confidentiality, "what with the northern properties, the southern holdings, and the London house. Most of that belongs to the family, of course." Archie had long ago learned to play on Londoners' innate ignorance of Scotland generally and its gentry in particular.

"Just your private assets, then – your own private accounts – how much do you command personally?"

"Oh, I should say around ten thousand."

"Not bad."

"Annually," Burleigh added, almost apologetically.

"I am impressed." Harvey-Jones gave him a look of renewed respect. "That is twice as much as my income, and I work hard for what I get."

"I am certain that you do," agreed the young lord mildly. "My own work is more in the way of a leisure pursuit."

"A hobby, sir?"

"Something of the sort." The young gentleman allowed himself a sigh. "Still, one must fill the empty hours as best one can."

"If you were married," suggested the industrialist, "you would find other ways to fill those hours."

"I daresay."

"What is more, you would soon have fewer of them to fill!"

"Daddy," chirped a warm feminine voice, "you are completely monopolizing our host with your chatter." She affected a frown of disapproval. "You aren't talking about money again, are you? Tell me you're not."

"Furthest thing from my mind, Pippa dear." Reggie gave his golden-haired daughter a peck on the cheek. "We were just now speaking of hobbies and avocations. The earl here complains of too much time on his hands. I told him he wants a wife."

"Daddy!" Phillipa gasped, horrified, embarrassed, and excited all at once. She glanced at Burleigh to gauge his reaction to this bold affront to his dignity. "Oh, do please forgive my father. He can be such a rascal sometimes."

"Yes, forgive me," echoed Reggie. "I did not enjoy the benefit of the good upbringing my daughter had. But there it is. A man needs a wife. Well, sir, what do you say?"

"I say," answered Burleigh slowly, holding Phillipa in his gaze as he spoke, "that happiness, like wealth, means nothing unless there is someone to share it."

"Spoken like a true romantic," hooted Reggie.

"Oh, Daddy, do behave." Laying a hand on the impeccable black sleeve of Burleigh's dinner jacket, Phillipa said, "I assure you, my lord, it is a sentiment I share."

"Then perhaps you will do me the honour of sitting beside me at dinner tonight, so we can discuss it at the greater length it deserves." Burleigh took her hand from his sleeve, raised it to his lips, and kissed it. "That is," he said with a glance at Reggie, "if your father can be persuaded to let you out of his sight for the space of an hour."

"A calamity, sir, but I shall bear up somehow." He waved them away. "Run along! You young folk go and enjoy yourselves."

"Shall we?" Burleigh offered his arm, which the lady graciously accepted, and the two strolled off across the marble vestibule towards the great hall. Later they would be seen again and again in one another's company – so much so that people began to expect it. They became an item of interest in the elevated reaches of high society and were treated as a courting couple – which certainly appeared to be the case – though whenever anyone ventured to ask, the question was lightly brushed aside with a laugh and an assurance of mutual friendship.

If that response was intended to stop the tongues from wagging, it effected the opposite result. The gossipmongers of the aristocracy spoke with ever more certainty of an imminent announcement of betrothal.

Alas, those expecting an early invitation to a gala wedding were disappointed. Summer came and went, gave way to autumn, and though the courtship continued, no matrimonial announcement was made. Those close to the earl intimated that the young gentleman's travelling schedule made such arrangements difficult at present; his various business pursuits dictated a return to the Middle East and quite possibly the Orient. Be that as it may, speculation remained high for a wedding the following spring as soon as the earl arrived back in the city from his travels.

But the young gentleman did not return – not the following spring, or the next. Then, when the diligent flow of his letters to his darling Phillipa abruptly stopped, the fire of speculation flamed in new and unexpected directions. As time went on, opinion began to harden that some dire fate had befallen him. Though the manner of his demise remained unconfirmed, imagination supplied no end of likely disasters: Burleigh's ship had sunk on its return voyage; he had fallen among thieves; the earl had been abducted and was being held for ransom; he had been caught in the crossfire of some local strife and been rendered a casualty of war; he had gone native in Arabia; the young man languished in a foreign prison on false charges... or any other explanation that occurred to the toilers at the rumour mill.

In fact, it would be three years entire before Archelaeus Burleigh returned to England. The reason for his absence and what had happened to him during his travels was never disclosed; no word of explanation for his delay was ever breathed aloud. But the man who returned to London was not the same man who had left the city almost four years before.

In the belly of the young lord was a new and insatiable hunger. Knowledge, the more arcane the better, was now his consuming passion. He was not to be seen without a book in his hand, and when he wasn't reading, he was making notes in one of a growing succession of journals, which he kept under lock and key in his desk. The ballroom of his spacious mansion was gutted by an army of carpenters; they lined the walls with a double tier of shelves, which soon began filling with obscure and archaic tomes. That architectural transformation served to underscore the simple fact that the wealthy young man had become an indefatigable scholar.

And though he still maintained a nominal presence in the antiquities trade, the Earl of Sutherland was more likely now to be seen at a lecture of the Royal Society than on the auction floors of Sotheby's or Christie's. When at last Phillipa realized that anything she said or did could have no effect on her paramour's new obsession, the young woman – who was not accustomed to suffer any rival to her affection – slowly withdrew, and Archelaeus Burleigh was consigned to his solitude and bachelorhood.

CHAPTER 25

In Which the Past Catches Up

Putting their feet to the road, the three travellers began walking alongside the river that was lazily winding its way towards the city. The sun was warm on their backs, and their wet clothes soon dried as they walked. Kit, who had grown used to the sweltering heat of Egypt in high summer, luxuriated in the balmy breezes wafting off the water.

"Really," he said after a while, "how did you learn so much about ley travel? The last time I saw you –" He paused. "I mean, the time *before* the last time – when I lost you in the alley in London, remember?"

"Of course I remember," she told him. "The best thing that ever happened to me – how could I forget?"

"Explain."

"Just wait." She gave him a bright smile. "You'll see."

"Okay," agreed Kit, "then tell me how you knew where to find the leys we've been using."

"I discovered this line with my ley lamp."

"That little gismo you have hidden in your pocket?"

"That's what I call it." She dug it out and showed it to him. "It seems to be able to locate ley lines and indicate when they are most strongly active."

He stared at the brass oval filling the palm of her hand. "May I?"

"Be my guest." She passed it to him.

It was heavier than he expected and warm to the touch. The small holes formerly filled with blue light were dark now. "Ever seen anything like that before?" he asked, passing the mechanism to Giles for his perusal.

"Only in Miss Wilhelmina's possession." He handed it back.

"Where did it come from?" asked Kit.

"Long story," Mina replied. "But I'm hoping to get an upgrade on this one."

Giles sang out just then. "Wagon coming!"

They turned to see a farm vehicle pulled by two large horses trundling towards them. "We're in luck," observed Wilhelmina. "We can hitch a ride with them." She glanced at Kit. "How's your German?"

"*Mein Deutsch ist nicht so gut,*" he said. "And yours?"

"Better than that." She laughed. "Just smile and be agreeable. I'll do all the talking."

The wagon drew nearer, and Wilhelmina hastened to meet it. "*Guten Tag!*" she called.

"Amazing," breathed Kit, watching her converse with the farmer. "I can't believe she's the same person I've always known."

"People can change," Giles observed.

"Too right."

The ride into Prague was a slow-motion delight as the wagon jostled along the dirt road in the easy warmth of a lazy autumn afternoon. And then, as they came around a sweeping bend of the river, there it was: the old city with its grand iron gates and stout walls. Proud flags fluttered on crenellated battlements, and the tops of steeples and towers could be glimpsed above the walls, the old cobbled streets leading into the warren of timber houses with red tile roofs and windows of tiny diamond-shaped glass panes. At once cosy and ordered, it was a sharp contrast to the arid wilderness of the Egyptian desert.

As the wagon was waved through the wide-open city gate by the guardsmen dozing in the shadow of the archway, Kit glanced at Giles, whose expression remained fixed and inscrutable. "What do you make of this, then?" he asked.

Giles looked around thoughtfully. "It all seems as it should," was his only reply.

Once in the city square, they disembarked. Wilhelmina paid the farmer a few small coins and thanked him. Then, gathering her charges, she said, "This is known as the Old Square. It is the main market square of the city and, in my opinion, the best place in the city to live."

"You live here?" wondered Kit. There was no market in progress, but the wide paved expanse was full of people plying their trades from small carts and otherwise going about their business.

"I do," she said, leading them across the square. "In fact, I have a partner and a shop." She pointed to the bank of handsome buildings lining the northern side of the square. "There" – she indicated one of them – "the green one with the sign in gold lettering. That one is mine."

"Grand Imperial Kaffeehaus," said Kit, reading the sign. "Mina, are you telling me you have a coffee house?"

"Coffee house and bakery," she replied. "The best in the city – the best in Bohemia, actually. We're unique."

"Crikey," murmured Kit, shaking his head in disbelief. "So this is how you have survived all this time – as a baker in a coffee shop?"

"Kit, I *own* the shop."

"You said you had a partner?"

"A business partner, yes," she added by way of clarification. She pushed open the door and beckoned them in. "Come on, I'll introduce you to him."

They stepped over the threshold and into a convivial room filled with cloth-covered tables where customers were being served by white-aproned waitresses in green dresses and little green bonnets. The travellers passed among the tables, and some of the shop's patrons recognized their hostess and greeted her politely. A counter separated the dining area from the kitchen, from which emanated the mouthwatering smell of fresh roasted coffee and warm pastry.

"This way." She led them around the counter and back into the inner kitchen where the ovens were located. "*Etzel, ich bin zurlück!*" she called, and a large, soft bear of a man wearing a flour-dusted apron and floppy green hat turned red-faced from bending over the oven.

"*Oh! Mein Schatz!*" he said, holding out thick arms for a hug. He all but buried Wilhelmina in his embrace. "I thought you would be gone all day, no?"

"I guess the journey did not take as long as I expected," she said. "Come, I've brought some friends. I want you to meet them."

He glanced up and saw the visitors for the first time. "*Das würde mich freuen,*" he gasped, and swept off his hat. He ran a chubby hand through his pale blond hair in an effort to make himself presentable – a gesture of such affable humility that Kit liked him instantly.

"Kit, Giles, this is my friend and partner, Engelbert Stiffelbeam," she said, repeating it in German for the baker, then adding for his benefit, "the best man I know."

"Oh, you flatterer," said Etzel, blushing at the compliment. He patted her with obvious affection, and she bussed his doughy cheek. Then, turning back, the baker held out his hand to his guests, who shook it in turn. "Welcome, my friends," he said, offering a little bow. "I am honoured."

"Glad to meet you," said Kit, and Mina echoed, "*Es freut mich, Sie kennenzulernen.*"

"*Jawohl!*" replied Etzel. "I hope you have had a good journey?" Mina translated, but before either of them could reply, he said, "What am I thinking? You must be starving. Sit down, sit down. You must have some of my fresh apple strudel. It will revive you."

While Etzel busied himself with the strudel, Mina donned a crisp, clean apron and began preparing coffee. Kit watched the efficient operation with interest verging on admiration; he could not get over the transformation he saw in Wilhelmina as she directed her staff and took charge of the kitchen, displaying an easy authority he had never before seen in her. Nor was that all: her hair was longer, more luxuriant somehow; her long, lithe form had filled out a little, giving her a trim figure. The dark circles, a perennial part of her appearance, were gone; she radiated a vitality and energy Kit had never witnessed. She was, he decided, a woman who had come into her own, and he liked what he saw.

Shortly, Etzel called for one of his helpers to bring plates and directed his guests to sit down. "*Setzen Sie sich, bitte.*"

"Just find a table," Mina told them, "and I will bring the coffee."

Kit and Giles returned to the dining room; evening was drawing in, but there were still a few people in the house. They chose a table in a far corner so they could talk without disturbing the others. In a moment Etzel appeared, humming to himself as he placed thick slices of warm strudel on plates before them and daintily laid a small spoon beside each plate. Satisfied that all was in order, the big baker urged them on, saying, "*Mahlzeit! Guten Appetit!*"

Kit and Giles picked up their spoons and simultaneously took an exploratory bite. "*Sehr gut!*" Kit said, making a pantomime expression of pleasure.

"Very good," said Giles, descending to his plate. He began spooning up strudel like the hungry man he was.

Kit's polite restraint lasted another two bites, and then he too began scooping for all he was worth and murmuring heartfelt appreciation between mouthfuls. Etzel beamed at them and chuckled, his hands folded across his stomach.

Wilhelmina returned with a tray full of small pots of coffee and cups. "Well, that's going down a treat," she observed. To Etzel, she said, "Your strudel will be world famous."

"It is that spice you have brought us," he replied knowingly.

"The cinnamon," she said, pleased that he was using this unfamiliar spice. "Do you think so?"

"*Ja*, that makes the difference." Seeing that the men had all but finished their portions, he said, "I will bring some more."

"I didn't know I was so hungry," Kit remarked. Giles nodded in full-mouthed agreement.

"We'll have a nice dinner after we've closed the shop – if you two can hold out that long." Wilhelmina set down the tray and took up a pot. She was pouring the first cups when she glanced towards the shop's front door at some customers just entering. "It looks like closing time will have to wait a little while. I'll seat these last customers and put up the shutters."

"Don't mind us," said Kit, taking up his coffee. "We're happy as clams in clover," he said expansively, sipping the rich dark bitter liquid. "Well, Giles, old buddy, it looks like we landed on our feet this time. Who'd have thought it, eh?"

As the newcomers passed behind Kit, he saw Giles' eyes flick their way. The young man's features froze in an odd expression – something halfway between disbelief and horror.

"What?" asked Kit.

"What is *she* doing here?" hissed Giles.

"She?" wondered Kit, swivelling in his chair.

"Don't turn around!"

He sensed a presence behind him, and then the last voice he expected to hear spoke his name: "Kit? Giles? Upon my soul – it *is* you!"

And then she was at their table, standing over them.

Kit looked up into the face he thought never to see again – as lovely as ever, but now contorted in anguish and fear.

"Hello, Haven," said Kit, voice husky, his skin tingling with instant revulsion. "Fancy meeting you here."

"You must leave at once!" she urged. Eyes wide, she stole a swift glance towards the shop entrance where another party of customers was just entering. "Quick!" Her manner became frantic. She clutched at Kit's arm as if to pull him bodily from his chair. "Flee! You must not let him see you. He thinks you dead."

"Who?"

Across the table, Giles, watching the entrance, let out a low growl of contempt as he spat out the name. "Burleigh!"

CHAPTER 26

In Which the Question of What to Do is Asked and Answered – Twice

"Is there a problem here?" asked Wilhelmina. She put down the plates she was holding and turned to confront the russet-haired beauty standing over Kit.

"Mina," said Kit, "meet Haven Fayth. No time to explain. Burleigh's here."

"Bloody great," muttered Wilhelmina, glancing at the party just entering the shop.

"Is anyone with him?"

"Help them, I pray you," said Lady Fayth, appealing to Mina. "They are in danger. You must help them flee this place at once."

"Right." Wilhelmina fixed a smile on her face as she observed the newcomers just then trooping into the coffee house. "I see Bazalgette... and now... yes, Rosenkruez is here too."

"Who are they? Do you know them?"

"Alchemists at the emperor's court," explained Wilhelmina. "I know them."

"All haste, I urge you," said Haven.

"Is there another way out of this building?" asked Kit.

"Through the kitchen. My apartment is upstairs. Go up there and wait for me," replied Wilhelmina, already moving to greet the newcomers. "You come with me," she added to Lady Fayth.

"Wait!" Kit said, leaping up. He snatched Haven by the arm. "The green book." He stretched out his hand. "Sir Henry's book. I want it."

Lady Fayth hesitated. "Burleigh is here! You must flee at once."

"Not without the book," insisted Kit. "Hand it over."

"Oh, very well," relented Haven. "Take it." From a fold in her dress she brought out a small cloth-wrapped square and pressed it into Kit's hand. "Get you hence."

Wilhelmina returned and drew the young woman away, throwing a command over her shoulder as she went. "You two get upstairs and keep quiet. Now hurry!"

Giles and Kit slipped into the kitchen. They heard the other party clumping into the room behind them, the flow of German fast and thick. Etzel was bending over the stove, banking the oven for the night. He smiled when he saw them. Kit nodded and mimed laying his head on a pillow and then pointed towards the ceiling as he headed for the staircase leading to the upper rooms. "*Jahwol*," said Etzel. "*Schlaft gut*."

They found Wilhelmina's room across from the landing, went in, and closed the door. The room was Spartan spare: a high bed, a chair, a small round table, a large and ornately carved chest with a domed top, and in a corner, a tall standing wardrobe. "The bed or the chair," said Kit. "Which would you prefer?"

Before Giles could reply, a knock came on the door. They turned as a young woman in green livery entered with a shallow pan of coals. "*Ich habe die Glut*," she said, offering the pan.

"*Vielen Dank*," replied Kit, indicating the hearth.

The maid busied herself at the grated fireplace and soon had a cosy fire going. She rose and, with a pretty curtsey, left, closing the door behind her. Kit lit a candle on the mantel from the fire and set it on the table, then settled on the bed to wait. Giles took the chair. "Some deal, eh?" mused Kit. "The one guy we hope to avoid shows up here first thing. What are the odds?"

Giles regarded him with a puzzled expression. "Sir?"

"Burleigh shows up here just as we're getting settled in," said Kit. "Some coincidence."

"Sir Henry always said there is no such thing as coincidence."

"So I hear," said Kit, sinking back onto the bed. "I'm beginning to believe it."

They talked quietly for a while, lamenting the cruel demise of Cosimo and Sir Henry at Burleigh's hands and allowing themselves the luxury of imagining what they might do to settle the score. "Did you ever see Sir Henry's book?" asked Kit.

"No, sir. I was not privy to His Lordship's papers," replied Giles.

Kit pulled the book from where he had stashed it in his belt and began unwrapping it. "Well, he made a careful study of all this ley business and wrote it down in this little book." He passed the green-bound volume to Giles, who regarded it with interest, cracked open the cover, and thumbed a few pages. "What do you make of it?"

He closed the cover and returned the book to Kit. "Very interesting, sir."

"But?"

"I cannot read, sir."

"Oh."

There was a rustle at the door, and Wilhelmina swept in. "They're gone," she said. "I told them we were just closing. Burleigh and the others have gone back to the palace. Come on, we've got to get you out of here – out of Prague."

"We just got here," complained Kit. "Can't we stay?"

"No. It isn't safe." She spun on her heel and darted back through the doorway.

"It's a big city. We'll lie low."

"Look, Burleigh doesn't know that I know you. Anyway, he thinks you're dead. Let's keep it that way. Now, come on!"

"My lady is right," said Giles. "It is best to avoid trouble whenever possible."

Kit tucked the green book back into his sash and climbed reluctantly off the bed and went back downstairs.

They passed through the kitchen, now dark save for a faint glow from the ovens. Etzel was gone and the dining room was empty.

There was a bit of strudel on a plate on the counter, and Kit helped himself. "Where are we going?"

"I'm taking you to a place I know – not far from here. You can hide out there until Burleigh leaves. He never stays long."

The three padded through the darkened coffee house, threading among the tables to the front door. Wilhelmina opened it, glanced out, and then beckoned them to follow. She started off across the near-deserted square; Kit and Giles had to scurry to catch up. They crossed the square and headed down a narrow street towards the city gate.

"This place you're taking us," Kit said. "Where is it?"

"It's near the river outside the city," Mina said.

"How far?" Kit wanted to know.

As Wilhelmina turned to answer him she nearly collided with three men approaching from the opposite direction. "*Entschuldigung,*" she said.

The three stepped aside and she sailed on, Kit and Giles in her wake. They had gone but a few yards, however, when one of the men called out, "Oi! You there!"

Kit glanced back over his shoulder to see three Burley Men standing in the street, frozen in momentary indecision.

"Run!" shouted Kit.

"Dex! Con! Get after them," cried the one called Tav. "I'll fetch the boss. Go! Go!" But Kit and Giles were already streaking away.

Wilhelmina had disappeared.

Kit and Giles pounded down the cobbled street. As they passed the corner of a house, a hand snaked out and caught Kit by the sleeve. Mina pulled him into an alcove. "It's the Burley Men," Kit told her.

"You two go on," she said. "I'll keep them busy."

Kit hesitated. "Are you sure?"

"Positive. Here, take this." She fished the ley lamp from a pocket of her apron and shoved it at him.

Kit looked at the smoothly rounded gismo. "I don't know how to use it."

"It's simple. It picks up ley activity – anything in the vicinity, and the blue lights shine. The brighter they glow, the closer you are to a line of force." She dropped the object into his hand. "Head for the river, and follow the road east out of the city. A mile or so outside the walls there's a little lane running perpendicular to the road. That is a ley line. I've used it before. The lamp will light up when you're there. Whatever happens, stick together."

"What about you?"

"Don't worry about me. Just make the jump and stay put. I'll come find you."

Kit nodded, drew breath, and prepared to make a run for it. "Ready, Giles?"

"One more thing," said Mina quickly. "You'd better give me the map. It'll be safer with me."

Kit hesitated, but only for a moment, then yanked the slender package from under his shirt and passed it to her. "Be careful."

"Always." She squeezed his hand and pushed him out into the street. Giles gave her a nod and then darted after Kit.

"Good luck, you two," Mina whispered, stepping from the alcove to watch them go.

Kit streaked off, running down a street sinking into evening shadows. The next thing he heard was someone shouting in German: "*Halt! Diebe! Halten Sie die Diebe auf!*" It was Wilhelmina, calling on passers-by to stop the thieves escaping. Kit saw her snag one of the Burley Men and, with much waving and gesturing, begin organizing the pursuit in German.

Kit ran for all he was worth, his shoes slapping hard on the cobblestones, Giles keeping pace right behind. Down the narrow street they flew, running for the city gate, naked fear making them flee. A few dozen yards or so further on, they came in sight of the gate.

"It's still open!" shouted Kit. "We can make it."

"*Bleiben Sie stehen! Bleiben Sie stehen!*" came the shout behind them. Kit glanced back to see that a few idle townsfolk had joined the chase. Wilhelmina was nowhere to be seen.

The shouting reached the gate ahead of them. The bewildered gatekeeper, pike in hand, stepped into their path just as the two fugitives came pounding up. "*Aus dem Weg! Aus dem Weg!*" shouted Kit, motioning wildly for the guard to get out of the way. "*Schnell!*"

The guard remained planted in the road, throwing his pike sideways to bar their exit. Kit, breaking to the right, hit the shaft of the weapon, tilting it down and leaping over the pole in one smooth motion, even as Giles ducked under the rising end. The flummoxed gatekeeper gave out a startled cry, but they were already past.

Three running steps carried them under the arch, three more and they were through the gate and out of the city. The gate man was shouting at them to halt, adding his voice to the shouts of the pursuers who had now reached the gatehouse. Twilight was settling quickly on the land, but the sky was still light; Kit caught a glimmer of water.

"The river is this way!" shouted Kit. "We'll try to lose them as we go."

Even before the words were out of his mouth, he heard another sound: the rhythmic clatter of steel horseshoes on stone paving. He looked back to see a dark figure in the saddle of a pale grey horse. One glimpse of the rider and he knew that Burleigh was in the chase, hurtling down through the streets, scattering the crowd that was now pouring through the gate.

The road before them was a broad curve around a long bend in the river, city walls on one side and riverbank on the other; there was no one on the road, and no place they might hide from the pursuit gathering pace behind them. According to Mina, the ley was a mile distant. "He's got a horse," called Kit. "We'll never make it."

"Keep running!" shouted Giles. "If we can reach the bend, we might elude them yet."

Gritting his teeth, Kit raced on. The bend was further than they estimated, and though they succeeded in gaining some distance on the mob, by the time they rounded the curve Burleigh was closer still and coming fast. Kit pulled up, lungs heaving, heart pounding. "It's no good," he gasped between breaths. "We'll have to try to take him."

Giles looked back, gauging the distance between themselves and the oncoming rider. "We must remove him from that horse."

"Right," agreed Kit. "How do we do that?"

"I know horses." The sound of the hooves pounding towards them grew louder. "There are ways to throw a rider."

The shouts of the chase echoed over the water, coursing along the riverbanks. Kit suddenly understood what it was like to be the fox desperate to avoid the jaws of the baying hounds. "What about the mob?"

"Once we have taken the horse, we can use it to escape."

"Sounds like a plan," decided Kit. "What do we do?"

"There." Giles pointed to a clump of elder bushes. "Hide yourself there, but make yourself ready to jump out as soon as I have the rider on the ground."

"You sure you can handle it alone?"

Giles nodded.

With a last backwards glance, Kit darted into the brush as Giles snatched off a long leafy branch from the elder bush and took up a stance at the side of the road. Holding the branch down and slightly behind him, he stood easily, waiting as the horse thundered nearer.

Burleigh saw him and shouted something. Kit, watching from his hiding place, imagined he could feel the earth tremble as the pounding hooves swiftly narrowed the distance.

Giles, steady as a stone, remained firmly planted.

Heavy hooves churning, the horse thundered closer and closer still.

Kit's breath caught in his throat as Burleigh swerved to ride down the unresisting Giles. But just as the hurtling beast closed on him, Giles stepped lightly sideways, swinging up the branch and throwing the leafy end into the animal's face. Its vision obscured by a tree that seemed to appear from nowhere, the horse shied and tossed its head high to avoid the obstruction. Giles drove forward, keeping the branch in the frightened animal's eyes.

The horse reared, and reared again.

Burleigh, unprepared for the attack, was thrown over the rear of his mount. He landed hard on his back in the middle of the road.

Giles was on him in an instant.

Kit leapt from his hiding place and ran to help Giles subdue the struggling Burleigh. He saw Giles's fist rise and fall – once… twice… and the writhing man lay still.

"Get the horse!" shouted Giles.

Kit hurried after the riderless animal that was now cantering away. It took a moment, but he finally managed to snag the dangling reins and pull the horse's head around. "Gotcha!" Holding tight to the reins, he turned to see Giles running to join him.

Then, even as he watched, Giles seemed to levitate in the air, his feet lifting off the ground. In the same instant, the report of a distant explosion reached Kit like a slap in the face. Giles was carried headlong and thrown to the dirt by the force of the blow. The horse reared at the sound, jerking the reins free from his grasp.

Kit saw a flash behind the struggling Giles as the slap of another report reached him. The glint of steel in Burleigh's hand warned Kit that another blast was coming. "Stay down!" he cried. "He's got a gun!"

A third shot ripped the dirt at his feet, and Kit skidded to a halt.

"Run!" cried Giles, waving Kit away.

Burleigh was on his feet now and moving forward, arm raised, hand extended.

Kit, caught between helping Giles and fleeing, hesitated.

"Mina will see to me," shouted Giles. "Go!"

A fourth shot decided the issue. As the bullet whizzed past Kit's head and the report split the air, Kit spun and ducked, instinctively heading back into the brush at the side of the road. He ran blindly, his only thought to lose himself in the lightly wooded roadside margin. Behind him he heard Burleigh calling, but ran on, heedless of all but the need to escape.

When the first fury of desperation had passed, he paused to catch his breath and collect his wits. The river was to his back; before him lay a field of barley. He considered diving into it, but the prospect of escaping on hands and knees through the barley held little appeal. He held his breath to listen. Above the sound of his own rapid heartbeat he could hear voices on the road and assumed that the townsfolk had met up with Burleigh and the pursuit would now resume.

A hasty estimate determined that he was still a little less than halfway to the lane that marked the ley line described by Wilhelmina, which he reckoned was now his best chance of escape. Keeping the road and river to his right, he proceeded through the wood in the direction of the lane. Behind him, he could hear voices and the sound of men thrashing through the undergrowth, searching for his trail. Others remained on the road; he could hear them, too, soon overtaking him and moving on ahead.

Kit, grim and determined as death, worked steadily along, dodging the boles and branches of trees and shrubs, trying to remain silent and invisible in the dying light. All at once, a clear, loud voice sang out – urgent, confident, assured – it rang loud in the silence and was quickly joined by others. Kit knew his trail had been found.

Fighting down the urge to bolt blindly into the darkening wood, he doubled his pace. But despite his best efforts, the voices behind him grew louder by degrees. When next he paused to catch his breath, he glanced back to see pale globes of glimmering light wavering through the trees: someone had brought torches.

Realizing he only had scant minutes before he was seen and captured, he snaked a hand into his pocket and brought out the brass homing device that Wilhelmina had given him. The little curved row of holes on the top was dark. Still running towards the line, he held the thing before him, urging it mentally. *Work, you blasted thing! Work!*

To his amazement, the small oval object began to glow – a faint fitful flicker through the tiny holes. But as he waved the curious instrument before him, the gently wavering lights strengthened and took hold with an increasingly bright blue glow. Clutching the ley lamp, Kit drove on, flying through the brush, dodging branches as he went.

The chase was getting closer. His movement through the brush alerted the pursuit, and soon the surrounding wood was echoing with cries of the townsfolk. Among the shouts and sounds of crashing feet he thought he heard Burleigh's voice raised above the tumult, urging his search party to greater speed.

Every now and then, Kit glanced down at the homing device, and saw the little row of lights still lit and shining ever more brightly. *It's got to be here somewhere*, Kit told himself. *It's close.*

There came a loud crash behind him, and he looked back to see Burleigh, back in the saddle, burst through an opening in the trees a hundred or so paces away. The earl saw him in the same instant and with a swift, assured motion drew the pistol from his belt. Holding the reins in one hand, he extended his arm to fire. Kit did not wait for him to pull the trigger, but ducked low and dived into the thicket. A second later a shot shivered the branches and ripped through the leaves above Kit's head.

He scrambled fast on hands and knees. Wilhelmina's ley lamp grew warm in his palm – enough to let him know that he was not imagining it. He looked around and saw that he had plunged into a narrow game trail: a single rutted line that stretched away on either hand, straight as an arrow's flight.

Another small explosion sent a bullet tearing through the screening brush, shattering a nearby branch, and Kit, clutching the device, started running down the track. As a third gunshot sliced the air a mere step ahead of him, he stopped, turned, and started back the opposite way. But the surrounding wood had already faded into the shadowy deeps of an all-pervading darkness.

Kit managed another step and yet one more before he tumbled headlong out of one world and into another.

CHAPTER 27

In Which a Little Light
is Shed

"The language of the angels allows no earthly utterance," Friar Bacon explained. "Therefore, it cannot be spoken by mortal tongues." He emphasized this point with a solemn shake of his tonsured head. "That is not to say that it cannot be understood. With the proper application of intelligence and logic the meaning can be deduced. It can be made to speak to us."

"What does the book tell you?" asked Douglas. After waiting almost three days while Roger examined it, his endurance was at an end.

"Patience, my friend. All in God's good time." The renowned scholar returned to his perusal of the parchments on his worktable. "First we must prepare the soil so that our understanding can be correctly seeded."

"Of course," muttered Douglas. "Forgive me, brother, if I seem over-anxious."

The priest brushed away the apology with a sweep of his hand. "As I believe I have indicated on a previous occasion," he continued, "the script in question is derived from an alphabet of symbols – as are all languages, to be sure. For what is a written text but a collection of symbols that substitute for the elementary sounds of human speech? However, unlike the symbols strung together to form the sounds used in speech, the symbols in this book are abstracted and thus removed from the realm of vocal representation."

Roger Bacon glanced at his pupil and seemed to require some sign that he had been understood.

"Intriguing," commented Douglas. "Pray, continue."

"See here," Bacon said, picking up one of the scraps he had prepared for Douglas's edification. "Notice how the symbols curve – this one to the right, this one to the left, some up, some down – each particular curve contains meaning, as do the small lines which branch away from the main, as well as those that cross the main. Where the lines branch and cross aids in determining meaning." He tapped the parchment with a fingertip. "It is a most cunning and ingenious cypher."

"Indeed," replied Douglas, feeling slightly overwhelmed by the prospect of decoding what amounted to another whole language in order to decipher the book he had stolen from the British Library. "How many symbols are there in total?"

"Hundreds," replied Roger Bacon simply. "As there must be."

"To be sure," Douglas agreed philosophically, thinking the greater part of his work lay before him. Then he remembered something the scholar had told him. "When I first gave you the book, you said you were the one who devised the script. By that, do you mean you invented the symbols in which it is written?"

"Only in part," Bacon conceded. "For my purposes, I chose a script based on a symbolism that is far, far older than any other. I adapted it for my use, but did not create it."

Douglas puzzled over the precisely parsed meaning of the priest's words. "Am I to take it that you wrote this book?"

"You flatter me undeservedly, brother." He laid a reverent hand on the small volume Douglas had brought him.

"Again, forgive my ignorance, but your name is most prominently displayed in the text."

"A mere formality of acknowledgement," replied the learned priest with a curious half smile. "Brother Luciferus, whatever his true identity, is merely declaring his debt to the originator of the script in which his book finds its voice. Nothing more."

"How fortunate for me," observed Douglas, "to have found the one man in England who can read it."

"Yes, and in order that we might gain the benefit of it, I have applied myself to the task of rendering a transliteration of the text for future reference." He nodded with satisfaction. "I am happy to say that work is now complete."

"Three days," mused Douglas. "My abbot will certainly wish to reward your service. You must allow us to show our appreciation."

"Learning is its own reward," replied Friar Bacon.

"But you made a copy?"

"Of the more interesting portions, yes. The rest is fragmentary. Perhaps, when time allows, I shall finish."

"May I see it?"

"I would be delighted to show you," replied Bacon thoughtfully. "However, I must first receive certain assurances." Before Douglas could ask what these might be, the scholar rose and went to a large ironclad box in the corner of the room. "Naturally, it would not do to allow what I am about to show you to be heralded through the streets of the city. In these difficult times, men of learning must resort to a stringent secrecy while we await a more enlightened age to dawn." He cast an expectant glance behind him.

Suddenly the scholar's meaning became clear.

"I am happy to provide you with whatever assurances you deem appropriate – material or otherwise," offered Douglas. "I know how easily particular aspects of our work can be misconstrued by an uneducated and unappreciative public."

"Alas," mused Roger Bacon, "it is not only the public which so often fails to appreciate the nature of our more delicate investigations – many of our leading churchmen are particularly lacking in the finer faculties of discernment. Led by the twin banes of intolerance and ignorance, they too often condemn where they rightly should revere. They traduce what should be championed. They denounce what should be praised."

Douglas knew that the eminent scholar was speaking from painful personal experience, having endured ecclesiastical persecution for some of his more daring ideas. "Pray, receive my most solemn and sacred vow that the secrets shared in this room will remain secret hereafter."

The scientist smiled. "I knew you to be a fellow pilgrim." He bent his angular form to the iron box and, withdrawing a key from a fold in his robe, unlocked the hinge, raised the lid, and withdrew a sheaf of cut parchment tied with a red band. "Come, let us sit by the fire where the light is better. We will read it out together."

He led his guest to the wide hearth where a coal fire glowed.

"The most valuable piece of scientific equipment yet invented," declared Bacon, indicating his chair beside the fire. There were two of them, one on either side of the bright-burning hearth. "They are of my own design. Please," he said, directing Douglas to sit. "You will find it supremely conducive to mental activity of every kind."

Douglas settled himself into what amounted to a low, straight-backed throne with wide armrests and deep cushions covered with sheepskin; the chair was tilted at a slight angle and was, he was pleased to find, eminently comfortable – a definite necessity, as it turned out, for they would spend the better part of the next three hours steeped in erudite discursion of the contents of what Roger Bacon called the *Book of Forbidden Secrets*.

"The identity of the author is hidden beneath a veil of wilful obscurity – I think we can agree that the name Brother Luciferus, or Light Bearer, is an all-too-obvious pseudonym. Nevertheless, the brilliance of the man's intellect shines out with unmistakable clarity. The vision which produced this singular document is as unique as it is revolutionary."

"And therefore readily mistaken and censured by those of, shall we say, more prejudicial opinion," commented Douglas.

Bacon offered a sage nod. "Hence the coarse appellation, *Forbidden Secrets*, which, I suspect, is a flirting reference to another highly influential work, *The Secret of Secrets*. At all events, the author wished his work to remain uncensored and chose the script devised by myself to preserve his work." He laid a long-fingered hand on the bundled parchments. "Moving on, the breadth of topics addressed in this tome is somewhat narrow in consideration of a yet greater work of which this is seen as a mere distillation – hence the title *Opus Minus Alchemaie*."

The title put Douglas in mind of one of Bacon's own works: the *Opus Majus*. Was Brother Luciferus really Bacon himself, hiding behind an alias?

"In the main, the subject matter concerns the author's explorations in the science of alchemy," continued the professor, "but he indulges in brief excursions into topics of more esoteric interest."

"Such as?" wondered Douglas.

"Immortality," replied Bacon, "spirit travel, the uses of earth energy, the power of human will – queries and speculations of this nature. Digressions, as I say."

"And yet not without interest to a mind hungry for knowledge of every variety."

The scholar offered an indulgent smile.

"I myself feel drawn to the very things you describe. This spirit travel of which you speak – is there anything of use for practical application contained in the book?"

"Oh, indeed. Brother Luciferus was keenly interested in this mode of conveyance and its implications for discerning what he calls" – the philosopher paused to consult the pages in his hand, scanning them for the place he had marked – "yes, here it is, 'a most salubrious mechanism which reveals the impossible breadth of creation and the deeper expression of the Mind of God.' In this, he is not wrong – as I myself can attest."

"Indeed?" Douglas affected surprise. He knew from his researches the legend that Roger Bacon had been credited with the ability to appear and disappear at will, and even to be in two places at once – both of which would be easily accomplished through ley travel.

"Oh, yes. I have indulged in experiments which have proved beyond all doubt that it is a repeatable phenomenon which, however poor our understanding of it, nevertheless affords ready application of its properties to those who know how to manipulate the more subtle energies."

"The book tells how to do it?"

Bacon nodded. "And more. Brother Luciferus expounds practical principles as well as concomitant philosophical considerations – such as deriving the dynamism by which spirit travel operates, the mechanism, if you will, and its salutary effects on the physical body."

"How very interesting." Douglas's eye fell upon the sheaf of parchment scraps. "And you have translated this?"

"For purposes of further experimentation, I have." Bacon paused, then added, "I hope your abbot will not mind. Of course, the translation is mine and must never leave my possession."

They talked on through the evening hours and far into the night, pausing only to take a little bread and wine so that they might continue their discussion. When at last the renowned scholar confessed to growing weary and needing a little rest, Douglas rose and with a low bow of deference thanked his host for his unstinting diligence and service. "I shall speak to my abbot, and no doubt he will wish to reward you for your intellectual generosity and service to scholarship. You have been more than helpful."

"I hope you will give your abbot my best regards." Bacon took the red ribbon and carefully retied the bundle in his lap, then returned to the strongbox and locked away the deciphered script. "Will you come to me again, brother?" he asked, dropping the key back into place inside his robe. "We have much to discuss."

"Alas, my time in Oxford has come to an end," replied Douglas. "My duties at the abbey…" He smiled apologetically.

"I understand."

"But, God willing, I may be asked to return for further instruction. If so, I will welcome the opportunity. Indeed, I –" He paused, as if embarrassed.

"What is it, I pray you?" asked the professor. "Was there something else?"

"I have already taxed you enough," said Douglas. "But there is one final matter which may interest you as much as it has excited the curiosity of many of our brothers at the abbey – a matter I have been pursuing in my own researches." He reached into his robe and brought out the copy of the Skin Map he had obtained from Sir Henry's strongbox in the Christ Church crypt. "May I?"

"By all means," granted Bacon. He pressed the back of his hand to his mouth to stifle a yawn.

"I am led to believe that this is a map. I mention it now because of its uncanny similarity to the symbol language you have translated from the *Book of Forbidden Secrets*."

Friar Bacon held out his hand for the parchment. "If you would allow me." He unrolled it and held it to the light. "Yes, I see what you mean."

"Can you make any sense of it?"

"A map, you say?"

"So I believe."

"Yesss…" the scholar said slowly. "Fascinating."

Douglas bit his lip.

"Yes, I do see what you mean," confirmed Bacon. "But it is not a map."

Douglas felt his strength leaking away through his legs into the floor. He swayed on his feet as if the floor were tilting beneath the knowledge that his efforts had been for nothing. He fought down his disappointment.

"Not a map in the common sense of the word," Bacon continued, "though I understand why some may think it so." He held the parchment to his face to study it more closely. "Yes. These are numerical coordinates." He tapped a finger on one of the meticulously copied symbols. "Given a key, I believe I could decipher them for you."

"A key?" wondered Douglas.

"A key to unlock the mystery of the numbers," said the professor. "For unless we know to what the coordinates correspond, the information provided by the numerals will remain meaningless." He passed the scrap back to Douglas. "Do you possess such a key?"

"I confess that I do not. But might a sample be provided which I can take away with me for further study at the abbey? I know my brothers would be grateful for even that much."

"For a certainty," replied Master Bacon. He crossed to his worktable, took up a quill, dipped it into his inkhorn, and began scribbling quickly on the parchment. When he had finished, he handed the still-wet copy to Douglas. There were now rows of numbers beside a dozen or so of the small glyphs – numbers that Douglas recognized as longitude and latitude coordinates.

"I am in awe of your erudition," said Douglas with a bow. He thanked him and took his leave.

"My greetings to your abbot," called Roger Bacon from the door of his tower. "We will speak again when next you return to the city."

Once outside, Douglas paused to rouse the sleeping Snipe, who was curled in his cloak at the foot of the stairs. "Wake up," he whispered. "I have work for you."

The boy awoke, instantly alert.

"There is an iron box in the corner of the room…" He described the strongbox and where the key was kept. "Inside the box is a document tied with a red band."

Snipe gave a shrewd and silent nod.

"Steal it."

Part 5

A House Made All of Bone

CHAPTER 28

In Which Feeling Good and Strong is Not Enough

Kit landed with a jolt that rattled his bones from ankle to skull, then crashed headlong onto a path soft with alder leaves and pine needles. Heart racing, blood pounding in his temples, his breath coming in gulps and gasps, he braced himself for the wave of nausea that, when it came, was a mere ripple that passed through his gut and disappeared. *Not so bad*, he thought. *Maybe I'm getting used to this.*

He lay for a moment, listening. Bubbling up from somewhere below, he could hear running water – a stream peacefully slipping and sliding over smooth stones – a calm, agreeable sound. Mixed with intermittent birdcalls from the trees round about, it immediately put Kit at ease. There was neither sign nor sound of pursuit. He had succeeded in eluding Burleigh and his mob.

When his vision cleared, Kit lifted his head and looked around. A woodland path lay arrow straight before him, slanting down at a fairly steep angle. Rising in the distance, directly opposite, was a curtain of grey-white rock, mottled green with moss, shrubs, and small trees – the sheer wall of an enormous limestone gorge a few hundred yards away. It was, he decided with considerable relief, the very place Wilhelmina had told him about.

The air was crisp and cool, the sun directly overhead, but pale in a sky of silver haze. It felt like autumn to him – something about the scent of dry leaves and the tang in the breeze put him in mind of October, a month he had always ranked high among his favourites.

He climbed to his feet, thinking, *Now, to find a comfortable spot to wait for Mina to show up.* The way the girl played fast and loose with time, he reckoned he would not have to wait long.

Glancing around, he made a quick survey of the immediate vicinity and spotted a rock ledge jutting out from the sloping wall beside the trail; dry and flat, it seemed as good a place as any. He walked over, brushed off the fallen leaves, and sat down. The ley lamp, still warm in his hand, was dark now, and the animating warmth fading fast. An intriguing device made of burnished brass, with a row of little lights along one gently curved side, it was about the size and shape of the average potato, and it looked more than a little like an ocarina — one of those funny little musical instruments introduced in school music class. The smooth metal surface was incised with ornate swirly lines radiating out from a button-sized knob below a slightly larger circular hole covered by a crystal lens. Resisting the urge to twist the knob to see what would happen, he instead stuffed the device back into his pocket and settled himself on the stone bench, where his thoughts soon turned back to the harrowing chase he had just endured: Burleigh on his horse, the horse rearing, the gunshots, Giles suddenly on the ground urging him away, the mad dash through the dark wood along the river, stumbling onto the ley… it had all happened so fast he had reacted on instinct.

Now that he had time to think, what he thought was that he was probably extremely lucky to be alive, and he hoped Giles had survived too, and that the wound was not too bad. He wondered how Wilhelmina would deal with this kink in the plan. No doubt she had a remedy ready at hand and was already employing it.

The day had grown warm, and after cooling his heels for a while, listening to the drone of bees working the dog roses growing along the slope, Kit grew drowsy and decided to walk to the top of the path, have a little look around, keep himself awake, and see if he could tell where in the world he might be. Not that it mattered very much; he did not plan on remaining here long. It was more just something to do while he waited.

The path up to the top was steep, and he was sweating by the time he reached the trail's beginning, where a broad plain of low, gentle hills rising and falling in heavily wooded waves greeted him. There were no roads, no towns, no fields, not a hint of human habitation anywhere – only the fading green and gold of an autumn woodland in every direction as far as the eye could see.

A track through long grass joined the trail leading down into what Kit now realized was a very substantial canyon. He followed the grass path a few dozen yards to a place where it divided into several more trails – one to the left, one to the right, one leading into the wood directly ahead. He took this one and was soon strolling through a very pleasant grove of ash, larch, birch, and alder with a few beech and walnut scattered throughout. The air was heavy with the scent of leaves and moist soil, and a pungent animal smell. But if there were any creatures about, they kept themselves hidden.

When the path divided again, he took the right-hand way and continued through an unvarying landscape of trees interspersed now and again with small clearings or meadows. Although he kept his eyes peeled for the merest hint of human activity, he did not spot anything more substantial than a trail made by animal feet, much less a road. Realizing he might trek for hours this way, he abandoned his excursion and turned around, retracing his steps to the track leading down into the gorge.

Kit descended at a steady pace and, upon passing the place where he had landed, pulled out Mina's ley lamp. The little lights remained dark, the instrument cold in his hand. He shoved the gismo back into his pocket with the thought that, some leys being more time sensitive than others, the ley was obviously dormant for the moment. He would check it again later.

His walk had made him sweaty and thirsty, so he resumed his excursion and followed the old straight track down to the river at the bottom of the gorge. A few dozen yards from the ley, the trail widened, losing the arrow-straight line as it followed the natural undulating curves of the cliffs down and down into the valley. The walls were marked with striated bands of grey-and-white stone – limestone and shale laid down in ribbons and layers over countless millennia. As the surrounding rock walls rose ever higher around him, Kit had a sensation of riding an escalator down through successive ages of time, each layer another eon or so.

Eventually the path ended in a bowl formed by a wide, lazy bend in the small river that picked its way among boulders the size of cars and garden sheds littering the centre floor of the valley. On either side of the river lay a wide grassy verge; along the low banks were reed beds and scrub oak, and small bushes and trees. Here on the valley floor, the air was warmer and more humid.

Hopping from one large stone to the next, he worked his way along the river's edge until he found a small pool, as clear as glass. Kneeling, he scooped up cupped handfuls and drank his fill of sweet, fresh water. He sat down and let the pale sunlight drench him. In a little while, he was dozing...

Kit came awake with the sharp realization that he had fallen asleep in a place where Wilhelmina would not know to look for him. He rose quickly and made a hasty return to the place he had landed earlier, driven by a sense of exasperated urgency. Jogging along, worried about missing Wilhelmina, he at first failed to notice that the smell he had encountered up in the wooded hills had appeared again. The moment the scent registered, he stopped and looked around, sniffing the air. Stronger now, it was unmistakable: a rich, earthy pong redolent of fur and sweat, blood and musk – the scent of the bier and kennel, the sty and stable, den and warren. Despite these associations, the odour was not entirely disagreeable. In fact, there was a wildness about it that stirred him strangely; had he been a hound, he imagined his nose would be quivering and his hackles would be raised.

Out of the blue, the thought occurred to him that perhaps whatever he was smelling might be smelling him.

Kit moved on, more quickly this time, casting frequent glances behind him. Although he saw nothing, he grew increasingly certain that there was something behind him.

Calm down. You're letting your imagination run wild.

He forced himself to pause and take a deep breath.

There, that's better.

The thought was still winging through his mind when he heard the crackle of dry leaves. He shot a swift glance behind and glimpsed a grey shape fading into the deep-shadowed greenery along the curtain wall of the gorge – a mere flicker of movement, and then it was gone.

So silent, so quick. In a moment, he was not even sure he had seen it. Again he tried to shrug it off; he moved on, forcing himself to proceed more quietly. Even so, he could not easily shake the feeling that he was being followed.

Every few steps, at random intervals, he cast a backwards glance to see if he could catch sight of the shadow again. He saw nothing, but the silence of the gorge had begun to exert an uncanny pressure of its own – as if the entire valley were holding its breath in expectation of something dire.

Okay, that's just silly. There's nothing there.

And then, just as he resumed his progress, he heard the unmistakable snap of a dry branch beneath a heavy foot. Whirling towards the sound, he thought that once again he saw a shudder of movement – a shadow fading into shadow. Swift and silent, but... massive. And this time he was certain he had seen it.

Certainty sent a sick dread snaking through his gut: he was being stalked. Into his mind burst an image of himself running, exhausted, chased by a pack of howling wolves until he fell and was ripped to bloody ribbons.

Before his fevered imagination could throw up another gruesome image, Kit took off, skittering over the stone field along the river. Although it was rougher going, he decided to remain out in the open where he could see around him rather than take to the tree-lined marge where the thing stalking him had the camouflage advantage of shadows and timber. This decision sat well with him until he glimpsed, on the other side of the river, sloping through the trees, another shadowy shape keeping pace with him.

Kit was running flat out now, little caring that he was easily visible to the creatures stalking him. His feet flew over the uneven bed of water-smoothed stones of all sizes, clumsy in his haste, heedless of all but the driving need to distance himself from the pursuit.

In his flight, he blew past the turning that led up to the ley line trail. But he gradually became aware that he was no longer in territory he had seen before; the valley was the same – only different now. Glancing around desperately, he saw that the curtain walls of the gorge had opened out; the river was wider here, and more shallow, dancing across the rocky bed in ripples a few inches deep.

"Where's the bloody trail?" he muttered.

Unwilling to backtrack to find it, he felt impelled to move on. He began looking for a place to hide and was heartened to see that the trees were larger here, the surrounding wood thicker. When the river kinked around another sharp bend, Kit decided to abandon the waterway and take to the trees. Almost at once he struck a wide path of bare earth; it snaked through the wood, passing around the boles of the larger oaks and larches. It was easier to run here, and he determined to put some distance between himself and his pursuers. He leaned into his stride and flew like a mad thing for freedom.

His feet pounded a mantra with every step: *I feel good. I feel strong. I feel good. I feel strong.*

Indeed, he was feeling good and strong right up until the split second he tumbled into the trap.

In the space between one step and the next, the ground gave way beneath him and he plunged through empty air. Time seemed to expand, and everything became almost unbearably clear: the golden motes adrift in shafts of sunlight, the clean-etched fronds of a fern, a dragon fly hovering above a thistle head with slow beats of its delicate wings, a blackbird taking flight from a branch overhead… All the world seemed to pause on a long intake of breath.

His first fleeting thought was that he had somehow made a ley leap. And then the walls of the pit closed around him, and he landed in a heap in the half light of a deep, square hole with a mass of broken twigs and leaves showering over him.

The force of his rude landing drove the wind out of him. He lay gagging, trying to draw breath but unable to make his lungs work properly. His vision grew dim and hazy. Then, when it seemed he would implode for lack of oxygen, his breath returned with a whoosh and he lay spent and wheezing like a broken bellows.

On his back, looking up at a perfectly square patch of blue sky framed by the dirt walls of the hole in which he lay, Kit took a quick mental inventory of himself. Aside from the mighty thump of the deadfall jolt that had knocked the breath out of him, there was no pain. *A good sign*, he thought. He patted himself down; he still had Mina's ley lamp and Sir Henry's green book safely tucked away and, as far as he could tell, all his faculties. He raised one hand, then the other, and waved them both around. He shook out his legs. All seemed in working order. No broken bones, then.

The light in the pit dimmed as he was taking stock, and he looked skyward to see that a face had appeared in the square opening above him. At the first glimpse of that face, he froze – not in fear, but stark astonishment. For it was a face at once familiar, yet utterly foreign; Kit recognized it instantly, but knew he had never seen it in the flesh before. The face peering down at him was attached to a swarthy, rugged, square head covered with a heavy pelt of hair so thick and matted it looked like yak fur. And the features were those of a clumsily executed caricature. In fact, if those same features had been carved out of timber with an axe, the result would have been nearly identical – except for the eyes. And it was the eyes in that face that astonished him and held him fast: big dark eyes so quick and intelligent and expressive they could only belong to a creature of at least modest self-awareness.

The fact that the creature seemed to be as surprised to see Kit as Kit was to see it completed the circle of amazement. He lay gazing up at that rough-hewn face, and with a childlike fascination, the sense of wonder was so overpowering it drove out all fear. Kit simply forgot to be afraid.

Chapter 29

In Which a Most Peculiar Predicament Arises

Time slowed to a trickle. Lying on the floor of the pit, Kit fought his way back to a more reasoned frame of mind: he was in big trouble. He was in a killing pit, for heaven's sake! He was for the chop, and there was nothing he could do about it. Still, he did not *feel* at all distraught. Every instinct jangled noisily, insisting that he should be rigid with terror. Instead, more than anything – aside from the initial astonishment – he felt only relief.

There was a movement above him, and the face disappeared, replaced by a sturdy length of wood, smoothed and rounded, polished with use. The shaft of a spear? The implement hovered over him; when he made no move to touch it, the creature on the other end prodded him, first in the shoulder, then in the stomach. Kit brushed the thing away, but the blunt wooden pole continued to poke him, ever more insistently, until Kit realized that the creature on the other end of the stick wanted him to take hold of it. Tentatively grasping the smooth, rounded haft of the branch, he was pulled upright in a single, effortless jerk, and quickly scrambled to his feet.

The top of the hole was still two feet or so above his head, so the pole was offered again and, grasping it tightly with both hands, Kit was hauled bodily up out of the pit to stand before creatures whose existence was the stuff of myth and dusty museum dioramas. There were two of them. Large, shaggy, and extremely inquisitive creatures, they regarded him intently, bright curiosity burning in their dark eyes. One was larger than the other, older, but both were dressed in skins held together with strings and bands of woven rope and dried gut. Their flesh was a healthy nut-brown from the sun and weather; their hair long and dark, but sun-bleached at the tips; the older one was aggressively bearded, and the younger lacked any facial hair. Both were barefoot, with broad, splayed toes and thick calloused soles. Both held identical stout-shafted spears with stubby blades made of chipped flint.

Although no taller than Kit himself, they gave every impression of being giants – perhaps owing to their perfectly solid presence and heavy muscular build. They were magnificent specimens: broad of shoulder and deep of chest; with large, square heads on short corded necks and huge muscled forearms, legs, and thighs; short-waisted and thick about the middle, they appeared almost as broad as they were tall, yet there was not an ounce of fat on them, just pure, lean, hard muscle and lots of it.

They gaped at Kit, then at one another, then at Kit again – their wide, expressive faces registering unalloyed wonder at the sight of so strange a being hauled from their trap. Then, after a moment's consideration, the younger one reached out with a thick, grubby forefinger and poked Kit in the chest as if to test his corporeality. It was the most natural gesture in the world, yet it made Kit's knees buckle. He swayed and stepped back, whereupon the older one reached out and, taking his entire shoulder in one massive hand, steadied him with a grip so gentle and reassuring that Kit almost swooned at the touch. His heart skipped a beat or two, and his breath caught in his throat as the utter impossibility of this most peculiar predicament broke over him: he had been captured by cavemen.

Kit's heart thumped in his chest, and he felt faint and dizzy with the surge of adrenaline and high-octane emotion crashing through him. His thoughts skittered off in every direction, leaving him with an utterly useless question. *What now? What, under holy heaven, now?*

Without a sound or sign, the older of the two creatures turned abruptly and started walking away; after a few steps, the big hunter paused and with a curved hand gesture – the kind a child might make to a playmate – indicated that Kit was to follow. Kit, afraid to do otherwise, obeyed. The little hunter fell into step behind him, and the three moved off in single file together. For beings so stocky, they moved with the agile grace of wild things, as silent as shadows; the only sounds Kit heard were those of his own making – swishing through grass, breaking the odd twig beneath his shoes, the rustle of dry leaves.

Every now and then, Big Hunter would pause and sniff the air in an odd doglike fashion, his wide, flat nostrils flaring; he seemed to taste the air as much as smell it and, after each reassurance, moved on again with a little backwards glance at Kit as if to say, "All is well, we go on."

They walked a long time, and the day began to fade. They were deeper into the wood now, the trees larger, the shadows thicker and darker. Branches closed overhead to form a green canopy, and the river narrowed to a slow-running stream. Moss and lichen grew on the trees and rocks all around, and a scent like that of mushrooms filled the air. They stopped to drink from the stream, first Little Hunter, then Big Hunter – each keeping guard over the other – while Kit lapped water from his cupped hands. They resumed their trek, moving ever deeper into the wooded valley, pausing every now and then to sniff the air. Kit used these little rest stops to surreptitiously check the ley lamp on the off chance that he might find another ley. But there was never any sign of activity.

After the third or fourth pause, Big Hunter gave out a gruff snort and picked up his speed, moving through the forest with long, ground-eating strides. Little Hunter gave Kit a shove from behind that nearly knocked him off his feet, and Kit stepped up to double time. That was not fast enough, however, and soon he was having to trot just to keep pace.

This went on for a considerable time. When at last they slowed again, Kit was sweating and gasping and all but falling over. By his hazy estimate they were several miles from the ley line that had brought him to this world. If Wilhelmina were looking for him, she would not find him there. At the first opportunity, he told himself, he would escape and make his way back to the ley and wait there as instructed. Kit keenly regretted having wandered off, but who could have foreseen being kidnapped by cavemen?

By now Kit was getting thirsty again, and footsore. During the next pause to sniff the air, Kit ignored his captors and knelt to drink. Little Hunter grew agitated and jabbed Kit with the butt of his spear a few times until the older one grunted a command that made his companion desist. Kit drank his fill, and when he was done, rose; Big Hunter stooped down and drank too – just a few mouthfuls slurped out of the palm of his wide hand, as if to be polite.

They moved on again, keeping the river on the left as they threaded through the undulating valley. And then, just as the light began to fail, Kit caught a whiff of a pungent stink: a rich, musky ripe scent, as he imagined a den of wolves might smell after a long, hard winter.

The three passed under a low-hanging bough and through a screening wall of bushes, and suddenly Kit was standing in a clearing amidst a collection of crude rounded domes made from branches pulled full-leafed from the surrounding trees and shrubs. They were home. Four primitives rose to greet the returning hunters; Kit saw their eyes flick to him, and all at once there arose a tremendous yowling of excitement. Five more creatures, all female, materialized, some emerging from the rudimentary shelters, others from the nearby wood, and all jabbering at once in what sounded to Kit like an excited, guttural yap.

One or two of the boldest primitives thrust forward and began touching him with little pats and prods. They touched his skin and hair and clothes. Meanwhile, the females formed a muttering, murmuring circle around him. The poking and prodding continued for a time, the chatter coming in waves, until one of the younger primitives, baring his teeth in a ghastly smile, picked up a stick and, in imitation of his elders, jabbed Kit in the leg.

"Ow!" Kit announced, not so much from pain as from the unexpected attack.

That response encouraged the youngster, so he stabbed Kit again, harder, with a sound that Kit could only interpret as laughter.

This time Kit kept his mouth closed, which provoked a third attack and a rapid fourth. A slightly older creature joined in, giving Kit a firm punch in the ribs and then crying loudly for everyone to see what he had done – at which point Big Hunter, who seemed to be the leader of the group, loosed a low, rumbling growl that even Kit recognized as a command.

Instantly, all poking and prodding and chattering ceased. Silence claimed the clearing as the woodland swallowed the sound. Big Hunter pushed through the mob, taking charge of Kit with a proprietary gesture of control and possession: cupping a heavy hand to Kit's head, then thumping himself on the chest with a closed fist. The others appeared to understand this, and the nature of the interaction changed; the whole proceeding became immediately quieter and more respectful.

In this simple act, ground rules were established that even Kit could not fail to understand. One moment he was a strange new animal that had been hauled in for observation and comment, and the next moment Kit was a guest. A new status had been claimed for him and boundaries established. He was not to be poked and jabbed with sticks; he was not to be yapped at or buffeted about for their amusement. Still, the others stared and murmured.

Ignoring the behaviour of his fellow beings, Big Hunter touched him on the arm and beckoned Kit to follow him. Kit was led across the clearing to the biggest bower in the camp; a log lay lengthwise across the entrance and, before the log, a ring of large river stones encircled a heap of glowing charcoal embers. The setup was exactly the sort of bivouac Boy Scouts would have fashioned for a forest jamboree – a generous hearth with benches.

It was almost dark in the glade, though patches of sky glimpsed through holes in the leaf canopy still held a bit of pale pink. Kit was made to sit on the log while dry branches were broken up and tossed onto the smouldering embers of the previous fire. In no time, the glade was lit with a flame that continued to grow as more and more wood was thrown onto the pile. The older primitives busied themselves with some activity or other – huddled together as they were, Kit could not see what they were doing – but while

273

their elders worked, the younger ones gathered around to watch Kit watch the fire.

Presently, a long green reed was produced on which were threaded strings of meat. Kit did not see what kind of animal produced these gobbets, but it was red and fresh. More of these makeshift spits appeared and were put into the fire, and soon the entire group was sitting around the ring toasting meat on thin skewers. The scent of sizzling fat and meat juice brought the water to Kit's mouth, and though he was seated in what was surely a place of honour, everyone ignored him. Apparently, where important matters of life were concerned – such as cooking and eating – ceremony could wait.

When the first skewer was done, Big Hunter took it and bit off a healthy chunk. The others watched him as he chewed. He gave a lift of his chin and everyone else proceeded to pull their spits from the fire and commenced eating. Rising from his place at the fire, the chief came to Kit and held the reed out to him. Kit, nodding and smiling, reached to take it; he pulled a morsel of roasted meat from the charred reed and popped it into his mouth, much to the delight of the others.

Big Hunter made a rumbling noise and took up two more uncooked skewers; one he gave to Kit, keeping the other for himself. He sat down on the log beside his guest and then, with gestures and grunts, instructed Kit in the art of cooking meat on a reed. Kit proved himself to be a ready and able student – as if he required any schooling – and his evident ability to feed himself so expertly seemed to meet with the approval of the gathering. The others murmured among themselves and, with much nudging and many a sly glance, let Kit know they were discussing him.

As grateful as he was for the food and the chance to sit and rest a little, Kit could not help feeling that his next act must be to escape. There was little hope for that, he decided, while they were all still watching him. He would have to wait until the camp was asleep to make his move.

Kit planned to return to the ley line and find a place to wait for Wilhelmina to show up – if she was not there already. If he had done that in the first place he would not be in this improbable situation now. Just thinking about how Mina was no doubt searching high and low for him, muttering dark oaths against his name – deservedly so, he had to admit – made him that much more eager to be on his way.

Then another and altogether worse thought occurred to him: maybe he had already missed her. What if she had arrived as planned, seen that he was not there, and promptly left again to search somewhere else? What then?

It did not bear thinking about – so he tried not to, but the glum thought cast him into an apprehensive and fretful mood. The meal went on for a considerable time, and at a pace that could only be described as leisurely. Kit grew increasingly anxious to be on his way. When at last the younger primitives began to drowse and fall asleep, some of the older ones picked them up and carried them into the nearby bowers. Finally, as the food disappeared, the others drifted off – most to bed down in the shelter of their leafy hovels, but a few of the young males simply curled up in the root hollows of the larger trees or on the ground near the fire ring. Big Hunter crawled into his shelter behind the log and gestured for Kit to join him. With reluctance bordering on dread, Kit acquiesced, thinking that any refusal on his part would only delay the inevitable, or worse, rouse the suspicions of his host, who might then take steps to forestall any escape.

So Kit crawled into the bower to wait. The problem was that the interior of the rude, branch-constructed hut was much more comfortable than he imagined possible. The floor was carpeted with alternating layers of moss and leaves covered by dry grass; there were even pillows – animal pelts rolled into bags and stuffed with grass and, of all things, fragrant lavender. The excitement of the day – which had begun a long time ago and far, far away – combined with a good stint of healthy exercise, served to smother Kit's resolve. He drifted off to sleep on clouds of lavender and was soon dreaming of lambs frolicking in sun-dappled meadows.

He woke again with the sound of a nightjar singing in a nearby tree. Otherwise the camp was peaceful and quiet, and dawn, he guessed, still some way off. Big Hunter was sound asleep, his breathing deep and regular, so Kit gathered himself and, creeping as quietly as he could, backed from the hovel and, rather than cross the camp, slipped around the side and directly into the forest behind.

Once away from the camp, he paused; the moon was low, but there was still enough light to navigate his way without stumbling around. He listened for the river, then followed the sound until he reached the stony bank. The rounded stones appeared like humps of overgrown mushrooms, grey and white in the soft moonlight, the water gleaming all slithery and silver.

It was, Kit decided, merely a matter of retracing the route back through the valley until he reached the place where he had entered the gorge. He had a fair distance to travel, but time enough if he did not dally along the way.

He started out with a determined step and hope in his heart, his pace quick but measured. Fed and rested, his spirits high, he covered ground at a respectable rate, pausing now and again to listen for any sound of pursuit. Each time he continued with greater assurance that he had made good his escape and would reach the meeting place in reasonable time, counting on the fact that it would be morning by the time he approached the vicinity and he would recognize the turning when he saw it again in the daylight.

Assuming, that is, he lived long enough to see the light of another day.

CHAPTER 30

In Which Kit Embraces
the Stone Age

Ignorance may be bliss, but it is still ignorance, and Kit, hoofing through the night-dark valley, had not the slightest twinge or premonition of the danger into which he had blithely wandered. To give him a little credit, Kit saw the three black humps beside the river, but took them for stones – one large, two slightly smaller: boulders in a field of boulders strewn along the river path. It was not until an unseen fourth stone, off to his right, reared up on its hind legs that he realized his mistake.

By then he had already passed the point of no return.

It was a bear, as black as an ink stain, beady little eyes glinting in the wan light of a fading moon as it swung its head left and right to pick up the human scent that had aroused it from a midnight snack of crayfish and clams. There were, as Kit now understood, four of them – a mother and three half-grown cubs. And without knowing it, he had made the most elementary error – the one transgression every schoolkid on a field trip is warned against committing in the wild: never get between a mother and her young.

Scenting him, the bear gave out a half-strangled cry of alarm as it stood motionless. A scant few dozen paces across the field of stones, the mother bear's massive head came up sharply in response to her bawling infant. The great dark muzzle swung first one way and then the other as the creature homed in on him, nostrils twitching. Then, rising on its hind legs, it spread its massive arms, opened its toothy maw, and loosed with a roar to shake the stars from the heavens. The raw, feral snarl of an enraged meat-eater loosened Kit's bowels, instantly giving the animal a new and more pungent scent to follow.

The great beast shuffled forward on its hind legs – a move Kit missed because he was by then frantically searching for a tree to climb. Unfortunately, the only trees near enough to offer sufficient shelter were behind the bear that was even now gathering itself to charge. When the animal roared again, Kit was already back-pedalling, making for what he imagined was the safety of the wood behind him – *too far* behind him.

There was no better option. He turned around and within three steps was in full arm-flapping retreat.

Kit ran with the abandon of the truly desperate, scrambling over rocks large and small, stumbling, splashing, banging his knees and shins, picking himself up and floundering on over the lumpy, treacherous ground. The bear had no such difficulty. It surged ahead with the fluid momentum of a runaway freight train, gathering pace with every step. The smaller bears joined in the chase.

A stand of slender white birches stood shimmering in the moonlight a few hundred paces away. If he could make it to the grove, Kit imagined it just might slow the animals down long enough for him to find a tree big enough to climb. Gulping air, he drove himself to greater speed, willing strength to his legs and fleet to his feet. And for a moment it seemed as if he had actually gained some ground on the pursuing beasts.

Alas, whatever imagined advantage Kit might have enjoyed was instantly lost when, skittering over the uneven surface, his foot slipped on a moss-slick stone and he fell hard, whacking his chin on the river rocks. Mother Bear was on him before he could get his feet under him again. Squirming onto his back, he faced the beast, kicking and screaming as if that might drive the enraged animal away.

The bear, seeing its quarry helpless on the ground, reared for the final assault, jaws wide, claws extended. It made a mighty sweep with one great, death-dealing paw. Kit anticipated the blow and rolled to one side, narrowly avoiding having his entire stomach ripped open.

He shouted and kicked out blindly. The toe of his shoe struck a leg as solid as a tree trunk.

Astonishingly, that kick appeared to confuse the bear. It paused mid-lunge and shook its shaggy head. Emboldened by this unwarranted success, Kit kicked again. The blow was accompanied by a loud, meaty thunk. The bear reared back.

Before Kit could launch another kick, there was another thunk, and another. The bear swiped at the empty air, and fist-sized stones began to rain all around. Thick and fast they came. Striking, glancing, bouncing as they smacked mercilessly into the animal's bulky frame.

The bear staggered back in confusion, and Kit heard a sudden loud cry erupt behind him; he twisted his head around to see three primitives break from the birch grove, all with fist-sized river rocks in their hands, and all shouting and heaving stones as they ran, throwing with unerring accuracy; every missile struck home with a satisfying thump.

The great ferocious beast cowered under the attack. After being struck a few times on the head and chest, it turned, lowered itself to all fours, and beat a hasty retreat, crying for its cubs to follow. The young bears did not wait for the stones to begin falling on them. They scampered after their mother, mewling all the way.

Then hands were thrust beneath Kit's shoulders, and he was hauled to his feet by his armpits. While two other primitives continued to hurl stones at the fleeing bears, Big Hunter patted Kit around the body as if feeling for wounds.

"I'm okay," Kit told him, knowing full well he would not be understood. "I'm only a little grazed. It's okay." He gripped the heavy hand. "I'm all right."

This brought a response from Big Hunter, who ceased pawing at him. "*Gangor*," he said, plain as day, his voice coming from somewhere deep inside him. It was the first word, if word it was, that Kit understood. He said it again and pointed to the bears.

"Gan-gor," Kit said, trying to repeat the sound of the word as near as he was able.

Big Hunter's eyes went wide with amazed delight. He called to the other primitives, and when they had returned and gathered around, he said the word again, looking at Kit with an expression of anticipation. "Gangor," said Kit, eager to oblige.

The effect was electric. All three primitives began jabbering at once and patting him – stroking him like a dog that has just learned a new trick. Kit endured this enthusiastic buffeting. "No, really. It was nothing," he told them. Turning to Big Hunter, he pressed the primitive's hand. "Thank you." He gazed into the bearded faces around him and, with all the sincerity he could muster, said, "Thank you all for saving me."

The celebration finished and the primitives started back to the settlement. Through gestures and proddings they gave Kit to know that they expected him to accompany them. But Kit had a better idea.

"No, wait!" he insisted, planting his feet. Stepping quickly behind the nearest bush, he removed his soiled underwear and, with some regret, left it. He washed as best he could in the shallow stream, then emerged from the bush to rejoin the party. Pointing up the valley, he indicated one of the tiered ledges of the gorge and said, "I need to check on something." He knew full well that there was not the shred of a chance that any of them would understand him, but it was a relief to talk and he harboured the small hope that he might make them understand – in the manner of British tourists abroad who, not knowing the local language, just speak English – but loudly. "Up there. I have to go there. Won't take a minute." Kit spread his arms and then drew a circle that included them all. "You can come with me. In fact, I hope you will." He turned and made a show of starting off. "Come on!" He made a sweep of his arm as if calling the start to a marathon. "Let's go, chaps!"

He stepped off half a dozen paces and glanced back to see them still standing there watching him. On a sudden inspiration, Kit made the gesture Big Hunter had made with him earlier – the curved hand "come along" motion. Then, with a single grunt of command, Big Hunter started after him, and the rest fell into step. As they walked, the sky began to lighten, and Kit was glad to see that he remembered this region of the gorge. He walked with purpose, urging on his new friends at each turn.

The sun was rising by the time they reached the cutting Kit recognized as the ley trail leading down into the valley. "Here it is!" he cried, pointing like a wild man at the long, sloping incline. "This is the place!"

He made such a show of his excitement that the primitives stood bewildered by his odd behaviour, murmuring among themselves. "Wait here," he told them, holding up his hands. "Just wait right here."

With that, he turned and started up the trail. His entourage followed, so Kit had to repeat the "Stay put" gesture – as one would with a dog determined to follow its master to school – until they at last got the message. As soon as he turned away, he took the ley lamp from his pocket and made a quick survey of the site. The device was dead. No warmth. No little lights. Nothing at all to suggest the ley might be active.

Thinking that perhaps the instrument had been knocked around so much it had stopped working, he shoved it back in his pocket and instead took a few running steps down the centre of the ley. When he failed to raise so much as a tingle on his skin, he stopped, drew a deep breath, cleared his mind, and then with deliberate steps began walking swiftly up the inclined ley, fully confident that this time he would be transported.

Again his expectation was confounded. Kit closed his eyes and tried again. But upon opening his eyes he found he was still in the same place, same world, same time as before. If he had travelled at all it was only the few paces between where he had started and where he had he stopped. Growing frustrated and a little desperate now, he tried three more times in quick succession before finally admitting defeat. The ley was not open and not active.

He gave up and walked back down to the valley to join the waiting primitives, who were watching him with undeniable expressions of concern on their broad, hairy faces. "Sorry to keep you all waiting," he said. "I'll try again later."

In fact, over the next days he did try again – four times, twice more in the morning, and twice in the evening – each time making the arduous trek from the place he called River City Camp to the ley. Four times – with no better result than before. Though he resisted the idea that he was now trapped here, he had to admit that something had gone very wrong. To keep despair at bay, he immersed himself in observing his little community of primitives, all the while trying to remember what he knew about the Stone Age.

Like most people, what he had gained had come from jokes and B-movies. Were these the cavemen of cartoon fame? Were they heavy-handed dullards who hunted such things as mastodons and dire wolves and giant sloths? Were they subhuman ogres that eked out a nasty and brutish existence in a world of dinosaurs and spewing volcanoes? Were they hairy, monosyllabic troglodytes that lived in holes in the ground? Were they any of these things?

The first discovery to surprise Kit was that he could no longer think of them as primitives, much less call them *creatures*. Since the night they had risked themselves to save him from the bear, they were people – albeit of an alien race and species. Kit spent a considerable amount of time trying to determine the blood relationships and hierarchy among the members of the River City Clan. Big Hunter seemed to be the chief, though he was not the eldest; there were two females that Kit pegged as the oldest members of the group of sixteen individuals who ranged in age from three or four years to, well, whatever age the oldest ones were – sixty, seventy? That is how old they appeared; though, the privations of a hard-graft hunter-gatherer life being what they were, Kit doubted the aged ones were anywhere near that old.

The clan consisted of seven males and nine females. In appearance, aside from the primary sexual characteristics such as beards and breasts and such, the two sexes differed little: both were of stocky, muscular build, thick-framed and sturdy; both more or less the same height, with the males only a couple of inches taller on average and females slightly less bulky; both dressed in the same skins and furs – some of the women chose to cover their upper chests, but others did not; both possessed the same long, dark, coarse, wiry hair that they either plaited into thick ropelike braids or bound in leather bands into which they stuck interesting leaves, feathers, or other found objects.

As the days gave way to weeks, Kit gained a more rounded appreciation of their habits and means of survival. The world was their larder, and they ate whatever came to hand, bolting down many things Kit would not allow past his lips – insects, worms, and larvae included. For the most part, they ate with their fingers, but used sticks to sear raw meat in the fire. But the thing they seemed to relish most of all was marrow from the bigger bones of the larger animals they hunted.

One day the hunting party returned carrying an antelope or sheep – Kit could not tell because they had already gutted and skinned it, leaving the entrails far from camp so the scent would not draw predators. The carcass was roughly quartered with flint hand-axes and then cut up into smaller chunks, which were put onto the reed skewers. Later, when the meat was cooking, a special cracking stone was fetched and the larger bones expertly broken open to allow access to the dark jelly-like sweetmeat. Kit watched as the treat was doled out – Big Hunter first, and then the others in turn. Though one or two got bigger pieces than the others, no one appeared to complain. Kit, too, was offered a piece.

He lifted the broken shard of bone to his lips and sucked, imitating the clansmen. The congealed substance tasted of blood and meat, and though not altogether distasteful, and undoubtedly healthy in any number of ways, he could not work up the enthusiasm for it that the clansmen seemed to share. He ate some out of a sense of politeness, but did not ask for more.

The clan's mostly carnivorous diet was supplemented by roots, berries, and various greens, most of which he enjoyed, though he began to miss simple seasonings, especially salt. He made a mental note to remedy this situation at the first opportunity. But all in all, they ate well enough – some days better than others, as determined by the hunt – and Kit reckoned that if he did not grow fat on the primitive regimen, neither would he starve.

One of the more arresting features of their society was how very quiet they could be, and most often were. They could speak, but usually became talkative only when excited. Kit marked an entire day when no one spoke. From the moment he opened his eyes in the morning until he crawled into bed that night, not a single vocal utterance had been made. He wondered about this for a long time, until it occurred to him that perhaps it was a basic survival tactic, an inbred desire to keep from drawing unwanted attention to themselves from passing predators. Despite this innate reticence, they were extremely communicative in other ways, employing a full repertoire of facial expressions that would have done a professional mime proud. Added to that was a range of gestures that bordered on sign language. In combination, the gestures and expressions were often all that was necessary to get surprisingly complex messages across.

But that was not all. In the first few days, Kit observed that the entire clan appeared to possess an uncanny instinct for empathy within the group – a sixth sense that told them what the others were thinking. At first he imagined that perhaps it was due to the fact that they lived so closely and in such harmony with one another that they had simply developed a fundamental understanding that did not need words. But as time went on he saw that it was something far more subtle and specific than that: it was a sort of telepathy. As Kit got to know them better, he came to believe that the clan did not talk much because each just instinctively knew what everyone else was thinking.

The most potent demonstration of this came late one afternoon a few days after he had come to River City. An early dusk was settling on the camp, and some of the females were chopping a haunch of wild pig in preparation for cooking; a few of the males were chipping flint to make scrapers or axe blades. Everyone was busy, working away quietly, when all of a sudden one of the males dropped his flint stone and stood up. Instantly he was joined by the three females. Not a word was spoken – not even a grunt – but all four disappeared into the wood. Those who remained behind also stopped working and began preparing a bed of fresh reeds and rushes by the fire ring.

Intrigued, Kit watched as they heaped the reeds high and covered them with skins; they then built up the fire – clearly in anticipation of something that was about to take place. And only a few minutes later, the group that had gone into the wood returned carrying one of the younger males – scratched and bleeding and obviously injured. They laid him on the reed bed and nursed him through the night.

All this took place without so much as a single syllable breathed aloud. The more he thought about it, the more convinced Kit became that at the moment of the young one's injury, they all knew that he was in trouble and had gone to rescue him. They just knew.

Yet, as extraordinary as that was, the thing that impressed Kit most was how very gentle they were with each other. In those first days with them, he did not witness any angry or aggressive behaviour. Indeed, they seemed to tolerate one another very well, if not to enjoy being together. The older ones definitely doted on the younger – at least in camp, for the smallest of the clan were not allowed to wander very far into the surrounding woods unless an adult was in tow.

There was still much to learn about them, of course, but Kit was content to allow that learning to take place naturally. In the meantime, he tried to be a good guest and not bother his hosts or make a nuisance of his presence. Nevertheless, the clan appeared as fascinated by him as he was by them. For their part, they missed nothing he did, following his every move – from the way he washed his hands and face, to brushing his teeth with chewed hazel twigs, and taking off his shoes to sleep – which drew great excitement the first time he performed any of these activities.

The younger members of the clan tried to imitate him, the older ones merely watched from a polite distance. The thing that produced the greatest amusement for the clan was Kit's attempt to wash his clothes.

One morning, awakening to the fact that his shirt and trousers were filthy and that he had not had a proper wash for more days than he cared to think about, Kit decided that the time had come to take the plunge – literally. He took himself to the river and found what he imagined to be a secluded spot where the stream ran deep and slow, and then waded out. He dived in, swam around a bit, bobbing up and down to thoroughly soak his garments, and then waded back to the bank and disrobed.

All this splashing about drew a crowd, of course, and he was soon the object of intense observation. For although they understood that his clothing, while different from their own, served the same function, the younger ones reacted with the same mixture of fascination and disgust he might have felt upon seeing a businessman shedding his skin like a snake. They jabbered excitedly at the first glimpse of the extreme white hairlessness of his skin – at least that was what Kit assumed they were remarking on, and not on his inconsequential and wholly unimpressive physique.

Despite his initial qualms, he found he did not mind being naked in front of the clan – any more than a farmer might baulk at being caught naked in front of farmyard cattle. Not that he thought of them as cattle, but the sense of species separation was so great that once he had wriggled out of his sopping shirt and trousers and was slapping them against the smooth, flat river stones, he simply did not care any more.

In any event, the exercise proved mildly successful; after drying on a sun-facing bush, his garments did seem fresher, if not cleaner. But, lying in the sun on the riverbank, he felt the chill that was never far from the air even on the warmest days, and knew that he was enjoying the last gasp of a splendid autumn. The days were already drawing in, the nights growing steadily cooler. Often now the morning air held a frosty note, and days were overcast. He wondered what the River City Clan did for the winter – where did they go? He did not think they would stay camped by the river, and he was right.

CHAPTER 31

In Which a Sensible Course of Actionis Proposed

Why, oh why, can't everyone just for once do what they're told, for heaven's sake? Wilhelmina tapped her foot and gazed darkly down the empty trackway. No Kit. He should be here. Her instructions had been simple, specific, and clear: Stay put. Do not wander off. Wait for rescue.

Was that too much to ask?

Okay, Giles getting himself wounded had thrown a kink into the plan. *That* had taken a good deal of sorting out, admittedly – not to mention putting her carefully maintained cover at risk – and had delayed things considerably. But that was no excuse for Kit to go wandering off when she had told him not to move a muscle.

But could Kit manage even that much? Could he, heck!

She decided to give it another fifteen minutes, and if Kit didn't show up, she would have to abandon her present time location and try another. This particular ley leading into the valley was completely reliable. In all her experiments, learning the ropes of ley travel, practising her technique, mapping the destination, and basically just trying to get her head around the incredible facility to simply pop out of one world into another… in all those early training trials she had come to believe that the one she called the Big Valley ley was fairly uncomplicated. Its time window seemed to be limited, and there were not a lot of branches or forks, or whatever they were, leading off to other places in other universes –

just a simple, straightforward thoroughfare. In motorway terms, she thought of it as the M4.

So, if Kit had made it to the ley ahead of the chase, why the devil was he not here waiting for her?

The only explanation was that Kit had left the trail and gone off somewhere into the valley. Searching for him there would be a chore, and one she was not prepared at the moment to undertake. She glanced down at the smooth-tooled object filling her palm – the new ley lamp Rosenkreuz had made for her. Although roughly the same size and shape as before, it boasted a few improvements, most of which she looked forward to trying. The chief difference in the new model was a second row of little lights, which, she was told, glowed from yellow to red in the presence of the searched-for traveller. The young alchemist had offered to explain the mechanics of its operation, but with everything going on, there had been neither time nor inclination.

In any event, she had been able to get Giles bandaged, medicated, and tucked away without Burleigh tumbling to the fact that she was in cahoots with the two fugitives. Lady Fayth, a willing accomplice, had helped – unwittingly, true, but necessarily. If Haven had known the full extent of Wilhelmina's involvement she might not have been such a keen collaborator. If things had fallen out differently, Mina would have been forced to join Kit and Giles on the run. But the young lady had kept her head and, when it mattered, backed Wilhelmina's risky play to the hilt.

Now Mina cast yet another longing look down the trail and, with an exasperated sigh and a roll of her big brown eyes, trudged down the trail and into the valley. When she reached the bottom she paused and then shouted for Kit. She listened, then repeated the call. Satisfied that if he had been within the sound of her voice he would have answered, she moved on – eventually coming to the little half-abandoned village.

The settlement was one of several that seemed to have been settled and constructed by country folk in the region. The few who lived there maintained fields on the riverbanks and on the highlands above. The river provided water for a mill, duck ponds, and a little fishery. She had met some of the inhabitants, and they in turn were used to seeing her now and then; they were simple, peaceable folk who kept to themselves and avoided conflict and confrontation – which is why Mina had felt good about sending Kit and Giles here. They were unlikely to get into difficulties with the locals.

She walked along the valley floor, following the river and calling for Kit. There was never any reply. After walking a mile or more in one direction, she turned and repeated the procedure in the opposite direction. At the end of the exercise, with darkness falling, she returned to the ley and made a last call for Kit to hurry or miss his rescue. She waited. As before, there was no answer.

Turning on her heel, she took up the ley lamp and, in four quick strides, departed the valley for home.

By the time she returned to Prague, the sun had risen on another day. At the city gates she joined the trickle of farmers fresh from the fields, trundling produce to market in barrows and donkey carts. She walked through the old town as the day's traders were setting up their stalls in the square; she greeted those she knew and promised to return later to buy. Etzel was just opening the Grand Imperial Kaffeehaus, removing the shutters and pulling down the green awning she had designed and Herr Arnostovi had commissioned to be built and installed.

"Good morning, *mein Schatz*," she chirped, and gave him a quick peck on the cheek.

"*Ach!* Wilhelmina, you are here!" Relief pinwheeled over his round face. "I did not see you return last night – all the kerfuffle – I was worried something might have happened to you."

She smiled and patted his arm reassuringly. "Nothing is going to happen to me. Remember what I told you?"

"If I should turn around and find you gone," he said, repeating her words by rote, "I am not to worry. You will always come back."

"I will always come back," she echoed. Then, on impulse, she gave him another kiss. He stared at her, blinking in the early-morning light. "That is a sacred promise, Etzel. I will always come back."

"*Ja*, I believe you," he said, dropping his head shyly. "But sometimes I think it might be better if I helped you with this..."

He searched for a word. "This *work* that you do."

"I know, *Liebling*," she said, resting her hand on his arm and feeling the warmth there. "Maybe someday you will. But for now, there is too much I do not understand, too much I must learn –"

"I could help you learn these things, I think."

She smiled. "You *are* helping me. You help me more than you can possibly know just by being here when I come back."

"But maybe –"

"It is true, Etzel. I need you to be here, to be my rock and my anchor. One day I will tell you all about my other work. But for now it must be this way." She held his eyes with her own, willing him to understand. "All right?"

"Of course, *meine Liebste*." He gave her a small, contrite smile. "If that is what you want. You know I cannot refuse you anything."

She gave him a pat on the arm. "And I will try never to ask you for anything you would not willingly give." Mina moved to the door of the shop. "I am famished. I could eat a horse – nose to tail."

"There is fresh bread and good sausage," Engelbert told her, resuming his work of pulling down and spreading the heavy cloth awning. "I will join you when I have finished here."

Mina paused in the kitchen on her way through the coffee house. She greeted the staff and commended them to their labours, then went upstairs to change her clothes and to check on her injured guest. Thanks to her cunning intervention and Lady Fayth's help, Giles was not only alive, he was safe in Wilhelmina's care. Left to Burleigh, she had no doubt Giles would be pushing up daisies.

"Do you really want the city militia nosing around in your business?" she had asked.

"What is that to you?" Burleigh had asked, bristling with belligerence.

Knowing she skated on very thin ice, she had shrugged. "Nothing. I don't know the man. But I know the city bureaucracy. He's been seen, and questions will be asked. If you wanted him dead you should have killed him when you had the chance. It's too late now."

"She is right," Lady Fayth chimed in.

Turning to Wilhelmina, he had asked, "Could you take care of him?"

"Me?" She feigned surprise. "I have a peaceful life here. I don't want any part of this."

Burleigh stared at her so hard she thought he had worked out the ruse. But then he pulled her aside and said, "I want him gone. See to it."

"Why should I? This is nothing to do with me."

"You have friends in high places. I wonder what these friends of yours would say if they knew the truth about you." He gave her a sly, knowing look. "What would happen to your peaceful life then?"

"You wouldn't."

"Oh, I could think of all manner of things to tell them." His eyes narrowed dangerously. "Do you know what they do to witches here?"

Wilhelmina bit her lip.

Lady Fayth, who had been watching this exchange, said, "Giles was just my uncle's coachman. He knows nothing. Please, Archelaeus, let him go."

"Very well," the Black Earl relented. To Wilhelmina, he said, "I don't care how you do it, but I want him gone. Disappeared."

"I got it," Wilhelmina replied petulantly. "I don't like it, but I'll do it."

The two had left then, consigning the wounded man to Mina's care. The barely conscious Giles had been carried to an upstairs bedroom, and Wilhelmina joined him there to assess the damage. He had been shot through the upper shoulder, the pistol ball passing through the muscle back to front, nicking his collarbone and making a mess of his pectoral muscle, but high enough to miss his lung and any major arteries. The ball had exited the wound, so she did not think he would suffer lead poisoning. He might well die of septic infection, however, if she could not keep the wound clean. To aid in this, she fetched a generous portion of Engelbert's excellent schnapps, in which she soaked Giles's bandages. She also gave him a sip of laudanum to lull the pain and then, as the wounded man drifted off to sleep, she had gone out to bring Kit home.

Wilhelmina moved to stand beside the invalid's bed; she put a hand to his forehead and with some relief determined that there was as yet no fever. The patient stirred at her touch and surfaced from his groggy sleep. Momentarily confused, he started up. Pain instantly grabbed him. His face contorted, and he fell back once more with a groan.

"Easy there," Wilhelmina told him. "You're safe now. Take a deep breath." She waited while he pulled himself together. "You've had a pretty narrow escape. I gave you some laudanum, and you've been asleep. Do you remember what happened?"

He nodded on the pillow. "Mr Livingstone… did he escape?"

"Kit got away. Some of the townsfolk think they saw him jump into the river. Burleigh thinks Kit might have swum to the other side. They've been looking for him there."

Giles licked dry lips.

"You will be thirsty. I'll get you some water. Is there much pain?"

"No, my lady." He gave his head a feeble shake.

"Liar. I'll get you some more laudanum. It makes you groggy, but it will numb the pain." She put her palm to his forehead again. "Don't worry. You're going to get through this."

He bent his head to try to see his wound; when that did not work, he touched it gingerly with his fingertips. The touch made him wince.

"I'm no doctor," Mina said, "but I don't think there was very much internal damage. You've got a broken collarbone – that seems to be the worst of it. One of the better physicians in the city comes to the coffee house every day, and I'll have him look in on you when he arrives."

"Is Burleigh still here?"

"Don't you worry about him. He's out chasing Kit and won't be coming back here any time soon."

"And Mr Livingstone? Will he come here?"

"Soon," she told him. "No. I went to fetch him, but he was not where I told him to be. I don't know what happened. Probably he just wandered off. I'll go back and try again as soon as I can." She turned to go. "But now I'll bring you the laudanum and some water. You should rest."

He nodded. Then, as she left the room, he said, "Thank you, Miss Wilhelmina."

"You're not out of the woods, so don't thank me yet. You won't be completely safe until you're far away from here. We have to get you well enough to travel."

"Where am I going?"

"Home."

CHAPTER 32

In Which Confidences are Frankly Shared

"I never meant to betray them," insisted Lady Haven Fayth. "Believe me, I pray you."

Wilhelmina regarded her doubtfully. There was much about the young woman to admire – her startling beauty, her quick and ready mind, her formidable strength of will – but there was also much about the russet-haired lady that invited distrust.

When Mina did not respond to this confidence, Lady Fayth continued. "Our circumstances were desperate, and worse. Poor Cosimo and my dear Uncle Henry were already dead – there was nothing whatever to be done for them – and we were slowly dying of thirst. When the Black Earl condescended to see us, he arrived bearing an offer of survival. Gramercy, I seized the opportunity forthwith, lest it prove a chimera." She pressed Wilhelmina's hand earnestly, willing her to accept the truth of what she was saying. "There was no time to explain; I was compelled to act at once." She frowned, remembering that awful day. "Kit and Giles were no use – all full of affronted bravado and doomed honour – they were no use at all."

"That much I do believe," allowed Wilhelmina. "But why did Burleigh choose you? Why you and not Kit?"

"We had a glancing acquaintance," replied Haven, and then went on to explain how she had met the earl previously when he had come looking for Sir Henry at Clairvaux. "It fell out that my father invited him to supper, and I dined with them." She paused, her expression pleading. "In clearest hindsight, I see that he was seeking to draw my uncle into his nefarious schemes, but there was no hint of it then. Quite the contrary, indeed."

"So, Burleigh shows up in Egypt and makes you an offer you cannot refuse – is that it?"

"But you *do* see, do you not?" replied Lady Fayth, as if obstinacy alone could persuade. "There was simply no point in *all* of us dying in that tomb. By remaining alive, I perceived that I might return to rescue the others. That, I most heartily assure you, was my sole hope and most fervent intent."

"You meant to come back and free them?" said Wilhelmina dubiously. They were sitting in the Grand Imperial at a table in the rear of the house. It was the middle of the afternoon, the slow time of day; the serving staff were waiting on the few patrons, and Etzel was napping upstairs.

"It was my plan to return to the tomb as soon as I could slip away from the Black Earl's knavish clutches."

"Then why didn't you? Why did you wait so long?"

"Burleigh's men," answered Haven readily. "The day after we left the tomb, His Lordship's hired ruffians arrived in Karnak with the report that the two young gentlemen had died. The disease of the desert tomb had taken its dreadful toll, they said. I was devastated… inconsolable, of course."

"Of course."

"To be sure, I knew nothing else until I saw Kit sitting in this very coffee house not two evenings ago." She gazed across the table at Wilhelmina, suitably contrite and forthright. "What is more, I can vouchsafe that Lord Burleigh was ignorant of any other outcome until he was apprised of their presence by his hirelings."

Wilhelmina considered this. It was all plausible, and it fit with most of what she already knew. She was inclined to accept that, however self-serving, Lady Fayth was telling the truth – at least insofar as Kit and Giles were concerned. About her involvement with Burleigh, Mina still doubted the young woman's sincerity.

"The Black Earl was not best pleased with his minions," Haven continued. "They have been consigned to outer darkness with much weeping and gnashing of teeth – until such time as they can redeem themselves in His Lordship's sight."

"Then I suppose we all owe you a debt of gratitude, my lady," ventured Wilhelmina.

"Pray, not so!" she objected. "Kit lost and poor Giles wounded – that is hardly a result worthy of commendation or merit."

"It could have been much, much worse," Wilhelmina conceded. "Thanks to your timely warning, they were able to get away. As to that," she continued, "what was that package you gave Kit just before he fled the coffee house?"

"Package?"

"That little parcel…" Mina described a small square with her fingers. "What was that?"

"It was a book."

"A book? That's all?"

"Oh, not just any book, mind you," Haven said, then lowered her voice. "It was the *green book* – that is to say, Uncle Henry's private journal of his investigations into ley leaping."

"By ley leaping, you mean –"

Haven nodded. "I believe you know well enough what I mean."

"Do I?"

"Do you not?"

"I do."

"I knew it!"

Lady Fayth took a sip of coffee and resumed her confession. "The Black Earl knows about the green book. He has read it, in fact…" She allowed herself a sly smile. "That is to say, he has read the portions I permitted him to read. Certain pages of Sir Henry's book I thought best to keep to myself." She finished her coffee and pushed her cup aside. "Do you have any idea where Kit has gone?"

"Across the river," Mina hedged. "That's what they're saying. No doubt he'll turn up again once Burleigh has gone."

"Yes, well, we must hope and pray he remains out of sight. I do not expect the Black Earl will allow him to escape a third time."

"It must have been a sight. What will Burleigh do now?"

"Resume his search for the map," replied Haven. "What else can he do? It is clear that neither Cosimo nor Uncle Henry possessed the map; it was not passed on to Kit. So Cosimo's portion remains to be found."

The young woman stood and brushed her hands down the front of her dress. "I must go. His Lordship will be wondering what has become of me." She smiled nicely. "Thank you for the coffee, and for your confidence. The knowledge that I have a secret ally in this fight – and mark you it is a *most* desperate fight – renews my faith and courage." She took Wilhelmina's hand. "May I call you my friend?"

Wilhelmina was taken aback by the question. "Of course."

"Good. I like that. I have no other friend in which to confide," she said. Then, still gripping Wilhelmina's hand, added, "The burden of the quest is ours now. It falls to us to see it through – for better or worse."

Lady Fayth took her leave, and Wilhelmina saw her to the coffee-house door. "For better or worse," echoed Wilhelmina, watching as her new ally sailed into the great market square. "We're in it up to our eyeballs, girlfriend. Be true to me, and I will love you like a sister," she said under her breath. "Betray me, and you will wish you'd never been born."

CHAPTER 33

In Which Formal
Introductions are Made

The trees all along the river turned spectacular shades of red, orange, and yellow, and one morning Kit arose to the sight of the leaves falling all at once in a silent golden storm. The next day rain came to the valley. A chill north wind stripped the remaining leaves from the trees. The clan gathered all the weapons and tools – the stout spears and axes, the scrapers and pounders, the short, stone-bladed knives – and bundled up their skins and sleeping mats and coils of woven fibre rope, and moved out.

This happened, as so much else, without any discussion that Kit could detect. They simply understood that today was moving day, and everyone began packing. Kit pitched in by rolling the skins he used for sleeping, and shouldering the spears. He had learned that whatever he did by way of helping with the chores was always remarked on by the clan, who more and more seemed to regard him as an exotic and unexpectedly useful pet.

When everything had been gathered, Big Hunter led them back through the valley. They followed the river downstream and, owing to the mostly bare trees and shrubs, Kit could get a better sense of the size and shape of the great limestone gorge that was their home. In places the grey curtains of stone rose to tower hundreds of feet above them – now so close the sheer walls cast the narrow gap in perpetual shadow, now so far apart they were but a hazy backdrop rising above the forest. At the narrow parts, the river ran fast over a lumpy bed of well-tumbled stones; when the walls receded, the water widened and deepened to a dark, slow-moving river. But whether quick and shallow or deep and slow, the river wound and wiggled its way through mostly deciduous woodland.

As they passed the trail that marked the ley, Kit tested the ley lamp yet again, but received no response. He had not expected any, but nevertheless resumed the journey with a slightly heavier footstep than before.

They walked all morning and stopped to rest around midday in a grove on the edge of a spacious meadow of long grass, now dry. They picked and ate some late blackberries and lazed in the sun, which shed a thin warmth from a dead white sky. Kit found a flat rock, stretched himself out on it, and napped until it was time to move on again. They did not stop until the sun had dropped below the cliff tops, and then they found a hollow near the river where they made a simple camp.

No fire was lit that night, and Kit discovered just how inadequate his clothing had become. He wrapped himself in his sleeping skins, but nevertheless spent most of the long dark hours shivering and wakeful. He had known the day was coming when he would have to augment his wardrobe with furs such as the River City Clan wore, but he thought he would have a little more time to get himself properly outfitted.

They decamped early the next morning and trekked along the ever-deepening river. Pausing only to rest and drink, the clan reached their destination as the sun sank below the canyon rim. Their new home was a massive limestone ledge carved out of the great curtain wall of the gorge, perhaps fifty or sixty feet above the valley floor and overlooking a wide expanse of river. Kit could see why they had chosen it as a wintering place: the ledge was south facing to catch the sun and, owing to the generous overhang, away from the wind and very dry. Further back, the ledge gave way to two chambers, the smaller of which was a natural basin filled with water that seeped down through the stone from somewhere above. Aside from having to gather firewood and haul it up from the woods below, it was perfect.

In all, Kit estimated they had travelled at least twenty miles from the first camp, which meant they were fifteen or so miles from the ley that had brought him to the valley – too far to just nip round and check it from time to time, a fact he noted with some regret. But soon he was too busy to worry about it for, with their move to winter quarters, the clan also set about stockpiling food and supplies for the winter.

The hunters – both males and females, for Kit had long since noted that hunting was not strictly a guys-only pursuit – had gone out only every third or fourth day when they were back at River City. Now they went out every day, leaving before sunrise and coming home around midday. The hunt had taken on a sense of seriousness and purpose previously lacking.

The older, non-hunting females likewise busied themselves with gathering roots and berries, preparing furs and skins, weaving rope, and storing nuts and other odds and ends they would need for the long, cold season ahead. Gradually they transformed the bare rock ledge into something resembling a utopia as envisaged by a band of survivalist gypsies.

At first Kit stayed in camp and watched the little ones so their elders could hunt and gather. Kit had yet to figure out the parentage of the young ones, since none of the elders seemed to take any proprietary interest in any particular individual; all treated each and every one with alike deference and regard. By way of helping out, Kit was content to play babysitter, inasmuch as it allowed him to spend some time getting to grips with Sir Henry's book – as he had been in his idle moments ever since joining the clan. While he read, the youngsters played around his feet. The littlest of the lot accepted him as a natural part of their world and responded to him as they would to any other elder. The slightly older children seemed more aware of his otherness and were shy around him.

But that changed the day Kit began to learn their language.

The adults had trooped off, leaving him in charge as had become the custom. This time Kit noticed that some of the older tykes had begun vocalizing to the younger ones, repeating the same sounds over and over again, which the infants imitated. So Kit joined in the game and was soon enrolled in this rudimentary language class. The clan thought this a smashing good game and vied with each other to teach him sounds. When he had mastered the basics, one of the older children brought him a stone and put it in his hand.

Kit held it up. "What?" he said.

To his amazement the child paused and very clearly replied, "*Tok*."

"*Tok*," said Kit. He put down the stone and picked up another pebble and held it in the palm of his hand.

"*Tok*." The young one tapped the pebble, repeating the word.

Just to see if he understood correctly, Kit tossed the pebble away and then patted the smooth stone surface of the limestone ledge on which they sat. "What?"

Again, the same word was repeated: *tok*. And Kit had effectively doubled his Stone Age vocabulary. He now knew the word for stone to add to his mental dictionary beside the word for bear. Next they tried water, which turned out to be simply *nah*.

"*Nah?*" asked Kit, raising his eyebrows in imitation of their own inquisitive expressions. He poured water from the gourd back into the catchment pool, then put in his hand. "*Nah*." He shook off the water from his fingers.

"*Nah*," said his small teacher, pointing at the pool, then dipping his own hand and shaking it. Then, cupping his hand, he slurped up some water. "*E-na*."

The lesson continued until the elders began to return, by which time Kit had a dozen fresh words. He was polishing his new acquisition so that he could show it off to the elders when they gathered that evening, but he was not given the chance. As soon as the first adults appeared, his small teacher, in full view of everyone, picked up a stone and presented it to Kit with an expression of such keen anticipation, Kit could not help laughing. "*Tok*," he declared.

The effect was stunning – as if he had set off a roman candle or pulled a rabbit out of a hat. Everyone gathered around, and before he knew it they were all offering him rocks and pebbles just to hear him say the word. He moved on to demonstrate his mastery of the word for water and for drinking, and wood, and fire, hand, leg, arm, and the rest of the few he had learned. Then, as he had their rapt attention, he placed the flat of his hand on his chest and said, "Kit."

His gesture was met with baffled silence. He repeated the gesture and said his name once more. The clansmen regarded him with quizzical expressions, their heavy brows furrowed, their broad faces pinched. Kit began thumping his chest and saying his name, slowly, clearly, willing them to understand. His repeated attempts failed to gain any result until Big Hunter stepped forward and, in a fair imitation of Kit, put his own hand on his chest and in a voice that seemed to come from somewhere deep underground, said, "Dar-dok."

Kit repeated the word to himself, then pointed to Big Hunter and said, "Dar-dok." Then, with the same gesture, he indicated himself and said his own name once more.

Big Hunter drew himself up and with evident pride said, "Kit."

The fact that it came out more like *Ghidt* was easily overlooked in the moment as Dardok's success brought coos of amazed delight all around. The rest of the clan began chanting his name. Kit revelled in the fact that he had successfully crossed a communication divide; he could teach them, as well as learn.

To be sure, they were only getting started. A forthright young female shoved in, made the chest-pointing gesture, and repeated Kit's name. Then placing a hand to herself, she uttered with remarkable enunciation, "Ne-ek."

Kit swiftly mastered this name and was instantly inundated by the entire clan who pressed forward all together, each one speaking a name and demanding Kit's repeated reply. In the days that followed, alongside his study of the green book, some portion of each day was devoted to learning new words; and when Kit was not adding to his word store, he was practising the ones he had already learned. In this way, he gradually built up a working vocabulary and, with it, a sense of how the River City Clan saw the world.

Among themselves, they still did not speak all that much. But around him they became regular chatterboxes. The difference was stark, and Kit wondered about it – until the obvious explanation occurred to him: they needed very little speech because they had this strange telepathy, or whatever it was that allowed them to know what others were thinking. Among clan members, they communicated just fine without any speech at all. It was only Kit who was forced to vocalize to make himself understood.

Confirmation of this fact was conclusively demonstrated by the arrival of visitors a few days later.

The weather had been growing steadily colder and wetter, the days shorter. More often than not they awoke in the morning to frost on the ground. Nestled in their rock-ledge fortress, however, they remained dry and reasonably warm. Kit was sewing a handsome new suit of fur – deer and rabbit, mostly – which with patience and dogged perseverance he was patching together using the flint knife, bone needle, and hemp thread they had given him. He was putting the finishing touches on a feature of which he was inordinately proud: a roomy inner pocket designed to hold Mina's ley lamp and Sir Henry's book and keep them safe. The clan was lolling around the fire at the rim of the ledge, when suddenly Dardok stood up and gazed off into the foggy treetops along the river.

Instantly, four others joined his survey of the valley below. The rest of the clansmen dropped what they were doing and fell absolutely silent. An atmosphere of intense anxiety descended over the camp. Again, not a word or sign passed among them, but all were wary, the tension swirling around them like the sinewy coils of a serpent. Kit stood too and quietly crept to the rim of the ledge to see if he could discover what had alerted the others. A minute or two eked by, and then he heard a sound he had heard every day since coming to the winter quarters: heavy feet on the rocky trail leading to the ledge.

Someone was coming.

Kit waited, every sense prickling, bracing himself for a fight. Who was it? Were they under attack? He cast a hasty glance around for the nearest weapon.

Then, as one, the clan relaxed. Although Dardok still stood watching the path below, the palpable sense of imminent danger simply melted away. Something had changed. But what?

Before Kit could determine what had happened to alter the mood, he saw movement on the path leading up to the ledge, and a moment later their visitors arrived: a group of fifteen – seven females, five males, and the rest young ones of various ages and sizes. From the enthusiastic welcome that commenced, Kit reckoned the group was well known to the River City folk. In fact, seeing how naturally the newcomers were accepted and how easily they insinuated themselves into the life of the group, Kit began to think that perhaps they were not merely visitors but part of the same extended valley clan.

Then the newcomers saw Kit, and he was subjected to the inevitable examination with much murmuring, touching, and rubbing of his skin and scruffy beard. They appeared fascinated by the colour and texture of his pale skin and fine curly hair; and were amused by his thin frame, short arms, narrow shoulders, and curious upright posture.

The round of buffeting had no sooner concluded than a second group of visitors arrived – four sturdy males bearing a fifth on a litter made of birch poles and skins. This fifth male was the oldest Kit had seen so far, with wispy grey hair and a long white beard and a face so ancient and wrinkled that, wrapped chin to ankles in hides and furs, he looked positively mummified. The bearers carefully lowered the bier to the ground, and several of the nearer clan members helped him to his feet. As soon as he was upright, he waved off his aides and shuffled forward with unsteady steps to meet Kit.

At his approach, Kit became aware of a tingling sensation at the base of his skull. Time seemed to slow – the ordinary flow dwindled down to a mere trickle and pooled around them. Moreover, Kit was aware of a very strange and powerful emotion – one he had only ever felt once before in his life. As a youngster, Kit had been introduced to what was reputed to be the oldest tree in England – a massive, gnarled, tangle-rooted thing called the Marton Oak, which had survived almost 1,300 years of earthly life. Kit remembered standing there beneath the twilight canopy of its enormous spreading boughs among roots that were as big as he was, and feeling an almost supernatural force that gave him to know that he was in the presence of a living entity of such peace and gentleness and strength of spirit that it inhabited a whole other plane of existence, and beside which he was as small and notional as a clod of dirt.

In the presence of the old one, Kit felt that way again, dwarfed by a spirit not only far older and wiser but also far larger and more powerful than any he had ever encountered. And like that ancient oak, the old man was unutterably regal: a king of his kind. Once more Kit was that young boy standing in the shadow of a vastly superior entity and knowing to his very pith and core how extremely insignificant he was.

Yet he felt no fear. A boundless and placid acceptance seemed to emanate from the aged being before him, and Kit understood that despite the yawning abyss between them he had nothing to fear.

The Ancient One examined Kit slowly head to toe, and Kit saw that while one of the old one's eyes was bright and piercing keen, the other was clouded and almost opaque. Upon concluding his examination, the aged chieftain raised his head and fixed Kit with an ardent, determined look, and Kit was aware that this was an attempt at communication; he could feel it as a physical force of considerable intensity. Kit, beguiled by the power and directness of the approach, simply opened himself to it.

The result was staggering.

What kind of creature are you?

The question struck him like a closed fist, and Kit instinctively took a quick backwards step to recover his equilibrium. It took a second before Kit realized that the question had not been spoken aloud. Moreover, it had not, in fact, used words at all.

"I am a man," Kit blurted, even though he knew this would not be understood.

But he was wrong in this assumption.

Ma-an, echoed the disembodied voice in his head.

Clear as a bell and distinct from his own thought, with its own timbre and texture and cadence, the unspoken voice of the Ancient One took shape, and the unprecedented interview commenced.

Ma-an... Kit's word for himself was then combined with the idea of being, or existing... *is*... then Kit got a sense of growing things, action, breathing, change... *living*... life inextricably entwined with something tangible, yet amorphous, an animating fire, present yet hidden within... *living soul*.

The question, as it entered Kit's mind, was: *Are you, Man, a living soul?*

"Oh, yes! Yes, indeed. I am – I have a soul," Kit assured him, speaking aloud. He suspected it was probably unnecessary, but it was just easier to vocalize his thoughts.

Goodness… the feeling of fullness and rightness… *satisfaction,* flowed from the Ancient One, along with an awareness of a soul's unique value and place in the world. Kit's instant interpretation of these interconnected conceptual traces came out as: *That is good. Creatures with souls are rare.*

"Rare, yes."

The chief gave a grunt of satisfaction. The next thought that formed in Kit's consciousness was the recognition of a long and varied experience allied with surprise at a sudden and startling uniqueness. The sense Kit made of it was: *We have seen many things, but never one like you.*

"I have not seen any like you," Kit replied.

Next Kit received what he interpreted as a sort of formal introduction. Into his mind poured a complicated and much mingled concept, an association of metaphors: pure animal strength and courage allied with majestic dominance – a lion, perhaps? – and this was combined with a sense of longevity – like a yew tree or a mountain – and lastly, the concept of serenity as applied to a calm, deep, freshwater lake of immense size and limitless depths. All this, then, was somehow combined and united in an affirmation of individual personhood – the being standing right in front of him, in fact: the Ancient One.

Then, with a delicacy of gesture that Kit found endearing, the old chieftain placed a thick hand over his heart and said aloud, "En-Ul."

There was no question but that this was the Ancient One's name, and Kit repeated it at once, saying, "I am pleased to meet you, En-Ul." He lowered his head in a little bow – an automatic response, but one Kit felt appropriate to the situation – and received a grunt of satisfaction in reply. The next question flowed into Kit's mind already formed: *Where is your home?*

"My home is far from here," was how Kit chose to answer. To say more would have been unnecessary, and probably impossible anyway.

The next two questions followed so quickly in succession they formed a single inquiry: *Why are you alone? Are you cast out from your clan?*

"No, no – I am not an outcast," Kit hastened to assure him. "I am alone because I am… lost. I was travelling and became lost." He did not know if the concept of travelling would translate. "My clan – my people do not know I am here."

A feeling of sympathetic sorrow flowed in inundating waves to Kit – empathetic commiseration, mingled with a sense of the wrongness of such a state as Kit described: *That is bad. You…* possessive… *fellow beings – your people*, Kit decided… strong imperative… *must*… outpouring of grief and anxiety… *mourn*… an empty place… *absence*…

Your people must mourn your absence.

"Some of them do, I suppose," admitted Kit lamely.

The Ancient One gave another grunt of satisfaction, and then, peering deep into Kit's eyes, expressed a largess of generosity and inclusive fellowship Kit could only describe as a feeling of welcome to a long lost and much loved son; it felt as if he was being adopted into the clan. It felt as if he was coming home.

The intensity of the emotion so directly conveyed took his breath away. Kit could not speak for the sudden stirring of his own long-suppressed feelings. Tears welled in his eyes, and he began to weep. They were tears of grief for his own inadequacy, his frailty, his shrunken and limited intelligence, his woeful dependency.

He wept hot, miserable tears, and with the weeping came a kind of solace, a comfort like that of a friendly hand reached out to steady a tottering child. As if in response to his misery, he sensed an empathy and understanding. There was nothing superior in it, or condemning. Into his soul flowed, simply, acceptance.

When Kit found his voice again, all he could say was, "Thank you."

CHAPTER 34

In Which the Future is a Dream

The River City Clan remained encamped on the stone ledge as winter deepened across the valley. A few days after the arrival of the new clan members, Kit noticed that at daybreak each morning all the younger males left the warmth and shelter of the rock ledge and disappeared into the woods. They returned an hour or so before sunset, but try as he might, he received no answer to his admittedly clumsy attempts to find out what they were doing.

Very obviously, they were not hunting – Dardok and two of the women continued their hunting and scavenging forays on suitable days, as they had since coming to the winter shelter. Whatever they were up to, it was not about providing food for the tribe. Finally, when Kit had become absolutely eaten up with curiosity, he went to En-Ul, who since his arrival had settled himself in robes and furs at the far side of the ledge, where he spent his days overlooking the fog-bound river far below.

"I am sorry to bother you, En-Ul," Kit said, announcing his presence with a polite cough. He was learning, when speaking to clansmen, to try to make simple declarations while holding the images or concepts at issue forcefully in his mind.

The old one stirred and turned a bright eye on Kit. *Be welcome here, Ghidt*, came into Kit's consciousness.

The response surprised Kit; not because it was unusual in itself, but because he had not given his name to the clan elder, or heard anyone else speak it aloud in his presence. He must have picked it up from one of the others by way of the mental radio they all shared.

"I have come with a question," Kit said, settling in beside the old chieftain. "The young men," he continued, picturing the ones he meant as they had appeared that morning when he saw them leave the camp. "Where do they go? What do they do all day?"

Kit received back an image of the young males along with a sense of doing… of work… of dedicated labour – *they make with purpose* was how he interpreted the concept; along with this came the notion of bestowal… of presentation… of offering allied to the personal designation – *En-Ul.*

Linking all this together, Kit tried out this interpretation: "They are making a gift for you?"

This received the standard grunt Kit associated with satisfaction – a *yes.* The old one held Kit's gaze in his own, and with a slow, deliberate action, placed the flat of his palm on Kit's forehead. The touch was rough and heavy, but warm. Instantly, into Kit's mind came the image of a sort of house or shelter of extraordinary design – the most unusual dwelling Kit had ever seen: a house made all of bone.

"They are making a house of bones?" Kit said, half in surprise, half in question. "For you?" Again, the grunt of satisfaction as En-Ul removed his hand.

They sat for a moment in silence, then Kit received the sensation he had come to associate with the interrogative – a question – and with it the concept of sight, or seeing. "Do I want to see it?" he said aloud. "Yes," he said quickly. "I would like to see it."

"*E-li,*" the old one said, his voice as low as a rumble of thunder, and into Kit's mind came the image of sunlight flooding the horizon, allied with the concept of something unseen, yet present, along with expectation bordering on certainty… the future?

This kept him occupied for some little while. "Tomorrow?" Kit guessed, holding in his mind the image of a rising sun – the new day that would be.

"*Unh,*" grunted En-Ul. *The day that is soon becoming.*

"I will go with the young ones tomorrow," he confirmed, picturing himself leaving with the group as they went out the next morning.

"*Unh*," grumbled the old chief again.

The next morning, when the young males rose and made ready to depart – arraying themselves with skins worn like capes and wrapping their feet against the snow and cold – Kit did likewise, joining them in their preparations. There were four of them this morning, and they acknowledged his presence with sniffs and nods, and the leader – a large male Kit had begun calling Thag for no particular reason other than he bore an uncanny resemblance to a cartoon character Kit knew – patted him about the head and shoulders in a gesture Kit had come to understand as a sign of friendly greeting; adults often used the same behaviour with the children. As soon as Kit was ready, they picked up their stout, stone-bladed spears and set off.

The track they followed down into the valley was well trod now, the shin-deep snow crushed down by the passing of many feet over the last few days, and it squeaked as they walked. Once again Kit marvelled at the easy grace of the big creatures as they strode along. The trail led down to a bluff only a few dozen yards above the river; the ice at the edges caught the light of the rising sun and gleamed. A few more days of such cold and Kit would not be surprised to see it frozen over entirely.

They paused to rest a few moments and to listen and scent the air. At first Kit wondered about this, but it came to him that this behaviour was a simple defensive action: they were making certain they were not being stalked by one of the large predators that roamed the valley – a lion, say, or wolves. But this day they were not to be challenged, so they moved on.

In a little while the narrow track began to rise, and soon they were walking next to the sheer limestone curtain. Kit enjoyed the exertion. It felt good to stir the blood, feel the cold air in his lungs, and move about after lolling around camp. Silent as shadows, save for the squeak of their feet on the crisp snow, they moved, up and up, following the contours of the undulating wall.

The trail grew narrow and steep, and soon they had climbed out of the valley altogether and onto the thick-wooded plain above. Thag paused at the rim of the gorge to scent the cold air and listen. The forest stretched before them, draped in heavy blankets of snow, softening all sound to a muted hush. From somewhere in the dark wood's depths Kit heard the keening cry of a hunting hawk and the soft *plip-plop* of snow dropping from branches.

Assured that there was no danger, the group continued, following the deeply entrenched trail into the wood. Here and there Kit spied animal tracks crossing the trail: the small traces of mice and rabbits and the larger tracks of ferret, marmot, and some of the smaller antelope-like animals. Once he saw what must have been the tracks of one of the larger predators they were trying to avoid – either lion or wolf, he could not tell, but his companions would know, and they did not seem to pay them any mind.

If not for the ribbon of beaten-down snow, Kit would have quickly lost his way; the wood was dark and wreathed in hoar frost and frozen mist. Abruptly, they arrived at a crease in the land – a little canyon formed by a tributary that carried spring melt and summer rain into the larger valley. Here the canyon formed a cliff with a sheer drop of fifty or sixty feet. The group did not linger at the edge but continued along the rim for a way until they came to a defile leading down to the bottom of the dry streambed. They followed the defile as it curved around and back to the cliff.

And there, directly below the sheer drop, lay a fantastic heap of bones. Devoid of flesh, and partially covered with snow, they made a stark white-on-white mound at the bottom of the streambed. All at once, Kit understood what he was looking at: a crude but brutally efficient method of hunting that consisted of driving the fleeing prey over a cliff, where they would either be killed by the fall or injured and finished off by the hunters. Judging by the massive tangle of carcasses, the River City Clan had been using this kill zone for some considerable time.

There were bones of all kinds: some that looked big enough to be dinosaur bones – though Kit was fairly certain there were none of those around… mammoths, then?… or mastodons maybe; were

311

those the same? – all jumbled together with those of elk, deer, and antelope; and some that looked as if they might have come from giant oxen or buffalo – definitely bovine in nature – and even some from horses.

Without any discussion – there never was any, in fact – the clansmen began dragging the larger bones from the heap, disentangling them and reforming them into a smaller, more ordered heap. Why some bones were chosen and others discarded, Kit could not readily tell, but he joined in all the same. The work party soon sorted out a number of sizeable piles; then, using the ropes made of braided hemp they had brought with them, they bound the bones into bundles. These unwieldy collections were then heaved onto their shoulders and muscled up out of the defile.

When all the bones had been trundled up out of the graveyard, each clansman hefted a bundle or two onto his back and trudged off into the woods once more. Kit could only manage to lift the smaller bundle he himself had made, but picked that up and followed his companions walking single file into the dark, snow-clotted forest and to a clearing that was suspiciously circular in nature – an almost perfect circle, which Kit concluded had been made somehow by the clan. He could not determine how they could have achieved this, lacking anything but simple stone axes. Yet here it was: an almost perfect circle sixty feet or so in diameter, surrounded by tall pines and larches, but offering a clear and unobstructed view of the sky overhead.

And in the precise centre of the clearing: the Bone House.

Kit recognized it at once as the dwelling made of bone that En-Ul had pictured for him – a simple, mound-shaped hut formed of the interlocked skeletons of all manner of animals. There were no windows as such, and but a single low tunnel for a door, over which hung the entire skull of a giant elk with splayed antlers as big as palm branches. The lintels of this door were solid ivory in the form of two enormous curving mammoth tusks. More elephant tusks lined the foundation of the house, whose framework was made up of the most fantastical conglomeration of skeletal fragments: pelvises, spines, leg bones, vertebrae, and rib bones by the score; there were skulls from more than a dozen different creatures – deer of several kinds, as well as bison, aurochs, and horses, sheep and antelope, what looked like dog or wolf, and even that of a horned rhinoceros. These were the ones Kit thought he recognized, but there were as many more that he could not readily identify.

Taken as a whole, the bizarre structure possessed a distinctly eerie, alien air. The work party began untying their bundles and fitting the bones they had brought into chinks and gaps in the structure, and Kit imitated their example, finding places to work in what he had brought. They laboured with purpose and in silence. When one or the other got thirsty, he would go outside the clearing to eat handfuls of snow, then return to continue working. When the last bone from the bundles had been placed, it was back to the kill zone for another load.

Three more trips to the bone heap for materials brought them to the end of their labours. The short winter day was hastening on, and the workers were growing hungry – at least Kit was starving, and he imagined the clansmen, who appeared to require more than twice as much to keep them going, must have been ready to eat the trees.

Thag stood back, coiling his hemp rope and regarding the Bone House, his big shaggy head held to one side in the precise manner of a carpenter inspecting his handiwork. It was such a classic pose, Kit smiled to see it. Thag gave a grunt that signified satisfaction and turned away. Now that the official verdict had been received, the others grunted too, and the group departed, making their long way back through the forest. The returning labourers ate a hearty meal and, exhausted with the good fatigue of useful work, went to sleep. Kit drifted off too; but if he imagined a restful day to follow, he was mistaken.

For just before sunrise he was awakened by a touch on his shoulder. He opened his eyes to see En-Ul crouching beside him. Into his mind came a possessive urging he understood as: *Attend me.*

The old chief turned away and Kit followed, moving silently through the sleeping camp. The night's fire had burned to embers,

313

and the sky still held a sprinkling of stars as sharp as ice crystals in the cold, cold heavens. They picked their way carefully down from the ledge and found the well-marked trail leading up out of the valley. Within a few minutes of leaving the settlement, Kit realized their destination was the Bone House, and for one who had been carried into the camp, the aged En-Ul surprised Kit with his stamina. They paused only twice to rest and catch their breath – once halfway up the trail and once at the top of the gorge – and arrived in the forest clearing as the sun rose above the trees.

In the thin winter light the strange edifice glowed with a pale and alien pallor – a white mound set in a snow-white field – taking on a ghostly, almost ethereal aspect as if constructed not of bones but of the mammalian spirits of the creatures themselves. A profound apprehension crept like the stealthy cold into Kit's soul. This curious shelter had been erected for a purpose, and it was for that purpose they had come.

En-Ul turned to him and, gazing into Kit's eyes, willed him to understand. Kit received an impression of immense importance, of an unfathomable weight of consequence, a significance of unimaginable magnitude – as if whole worlds of significance converged in this place. There was no single word for it, but the force of the concept struck him with an urgency that was as powerful as hunger and thirst.

Kit, trying hard to understand, was overwhelmed by the thought that had been conveyed. "Why have we come here?" he asked aloud.

The old one tilted back his head and looked at the pale white sky for a moment. Then, returning his gaze to Kit, breathed into Kit's mind the image of living things of many kinds – the creatures of the forest, the entire forest itself, whole Stone Age tribes – combined with a feeling of swimming against the strong flow of the river, or struggling against a powerful grinding, uncompromising force bent on mindless destruction: *survival*.

Their presence at the Bone House had something to do with the survival of themselves and their world, was how Kit explained it to himself; and although he could not see how this was so, he did not doubt En-Ul's sincerity.

As soon as this thought had passed through Kit's mind, the ancient chieftain turned and walked to the entrance of the Bone House. He paused at the low doorway and stood for a moment, then raised his hand and placed the palm on the forehead of the skull of the giant elk, and bowed his own head in a gesture Kit had never seen one of them make before. Then, bending low, he entered the bone hut, beckoning Kit to follow.

Inside, the bones formed a dome-shaped room of weird, undulating design lit only by the watery winter daylight that found its way through the chinks and crevices of the interlocking bones. The floor was packed snow over which pine branches had been spread, and these piled with skins and furs. Kit saw that a small cache of food — dried meat and berries — and little heaps of snow for water had been set aside.

En-Ul crawled in and sat himself cross-legged in the centre of the room. He looked around and gave a grunt of satisfaction, as if approving of the finished product. Then, when Kit had sat down across from him, he addressed himself to conveying what was about to happen.

In imitation of the old one, Kit crossed his legs and pulled furs around him as into his mind came the image of himself asleep — as seen by one of the clan, perhaps — and then immediately, a sort of curious sensation of flying, of actually having wings and soaring high on the wind... *dreaming*?

This thought met with a satisfied grunt, and instantly Kit felt once again the immense, bottomless ocean of consequence — only this time it was an ocean, a vast tidal stream in endless flux... *time*?

"Dreaming time," Kit said aloud, although strictly speaking, this did not make any sense to him at all.

The mental contact faded, evaporating into the ether, and En-Ul closed his eyes. His breathing altered, his body relaxed, and soon Kit realized that the old one was asleep.

He waited.

When nothing more happened, Kit crept from the Bone House and went out to the perimeter of the circle to relieve himself. The day was growing blustery; a sharp wind, rising out of the north, was soughing through the tall pines all around. The pale sky was darker now with heavy, snow-laden clouds. There was a storm on the way; he could smell the metallic tang on the air. They would have to go back to the shelter of the rock ledge soon, but he was reluctant to disturb the Ancient One's sleep. Kit did not know what to do, but one thing was certain – he did not care to be out in the forest alone. It was not safe.

Kit returned to the Bone House. En-Ul was, if possible, even more deeply asleep than before. Kit settled down to wait, but after what seemed like an age of doing nothing more than listening to the old chieftain's deep and regular breathing, he grew too anxious to put off leaving any longer. He took the furs he had been using and wrapped those around En-Ul's body. Wishing his sleeping companion well, he departed.

Running, jogging, floundering through the snow, Kit scrambled back to the safety of the valley encampment, arriving as the last light faded into twilight mist. The River City Clan greeted his return with grunts of recognition and seemed to accept his absence as a matter of little interest. Kit sought out Dardok, thinking to gain an explanation of what had taken place that day. Holding an image of the Bone House firmly in mind, he said, "En-Ul sleeps there."

This appeared to be understood – as least as far as Kit could discern – for it met with a snort of gruff acknowledgement.

"He says he is dreaming time," Kit continued, pushing his luck. "Is that so?"

Dardok's expression grew opaque, and he grumbled low in his throat – a sign of dissatisfaction. And that was that. The discussion went no further. It confirmed what Kit already knew: whatever faculty En-Ul possessed that allowed him to communicate with Kit, the others did not have it, or at least not to the same degree.

Later Kit ate and, unaccountably tired from his exertions, crawled off to sleep in his customary place. But sleep eluded him. For a long time, he lay pondering the possible meaning of the concept *dreaming time*. What could it mean?

Wrapped in fur against the cold, Kit stared past the glowing red embers of the dying fire into the fathomless sea of darkness beyond as into a daunting future. His mind, filled with the strangeness and wonder of the Bone House, conjured a vision.

He saw a full moon rising over a high windswept plain, its silvery light illuminating a curving slice of river cradled in a shallow bowl of a valley. The great round moon poured down its light as it passed overhead, and the stars wheeled slowly in the sky until it sank again below the western horizon.

All was dark then… but only for a moment. Before Kit could blink, the moon rose again, faster this time, passing over the bend in the river once more. The moon soared and sank, only to repeat the process again and yet again. With every repetition the moon flew faster, its rising and setting merging into a single fluid tracery of light, a shining arc across the limitless star field. This bright arc widened, expanding into a luminous band encircling the wandering earth.

Out on the plain he saw a mountain rising in the distance, white and ghostly in the silver moonlight. The mountain rose higher, and Kit saw that it was moving, slowly, inexorably, following the course of the river, which now ran with chunks of ice. With the mountain came snow. Kit could see the drifts deepening over the landscape, spreading, merging, covering the land, covering the rocks and trees, filling the valley, covering everything. And still the snow fell – as if the inexhaustible vaults of winter had opened and poured out their unending store upon the world below.

And all the while the mountain lurched nearer, a glacier on the move, growing even as it came, driving all before it: trees, rocks, boulders, entire hills. On and on it came, tearing, grinding with the low rumble of constant thunder, annihilating everything that fell beneath the massive wall of its leading edge, gouging the land, carving deep into the soft soil of the river valley, its stupendous weight forming new hills on either side, shaping landscapes as it passed.

And still the ice mountain grew, spreading as it came; it stretched now from horizon to horizon, gathering cold, draining the rivers, lowering the seas, leaching moisture from all it touched, from the very atmosphere until the air became dry and brittle, and still it grew, shimmering with a terrible majesty beneath the brilliant band of light that was the ever-racing moon: a continent of ice on the move, pushing up mountains, slicing out canyons, tilting the earth with its passing.

More images wheeled before Kit's unblinking eyes: an endless line of enormous woolly mammoths staggering across a plain drifted high with wind-whipped snow... fire falling from the sky in burning chunks the size of boulders, setting the hills ablaze... an ocean locked tight, its waves thrashed into hard, motionless peaks... bony carcasses of starved creatures piled in a frozen bog... a bear on its hind legs gnawing at the bark of a tree... a man, woman, and two infant children dressed in wolf skin and forever huddled in a frozen embrace... a high mountain pass leading down to lands yet green, lands that had not felt the bitter sting of killing cold... and more, faster and faster until one image could not be distinguished from another.

Reeling from what he had seen, Kit closed his eyes, but the images persisted, flickering through his consciousness in a mist of motion and light: fusing, swirling, all detail muted and lost, merging into a dense, luminous fog that resolved into the Milky Way, the measureless star path of the galaxy. The shining mist slowly dissipated until at last it was swallowed in the end by the eternal darkness of empty space.

CHAPTER 35

In Which a Remedy is Pursued

Dazed and drained, Kit waited for the dawn to lighten the sky to return to the Bone House. If the remedy for his bewildered state could be found, he imagined it might be there. When the first faint traces of daylight gave texture to the winter landscape below the rock shelter, Kit rose, stepped carefully over the sleeping bodies around him, and stole down the narrow trail leading into the valley and, ultimately, up to the high woodland above.

Fresh snow had fallen in the night, and he ploughed through the drifts, moving with an urgency born of a dream-troubled night. He reached the woodland on the plateau above the valley and, alert to lurking predators, hurried through the frigid, winter-bound forest to the clearing. It was further than he remembered; impatience drove him to greater haste until he burst into the circle of standing trees to see the tangled mound of chalky, snow-covered bones standing in the centre of the clearing, pale and spectral in the dead winter light. The renewed sight of that singular structure, woven of ivory, horn, and bone, brought Kit up short. He halted, then approached more slowly, circling the Bone House to reach the low entrance, now almost hidden by snow.

Kit dropped to his knees and crawled inside. En-Ul was there, and in much the same position as Kit had left him the previous day: so still and silent he might have been dead. Kit held his breath until he heard the long, low sigh of the sleeper, then relaxed and settled into his place. In the thin light filtering through the latticework of interwoven bones, he saw that some of the food had been eaten and two of the little piles of snow were gone. En-Ul had taken nourishment at least once, then. Kit took comfort from that. Whatever the old chieftain was doing, it did not involve starving to death. Thinking of this, he wished he had brought along something for himself to eat; he considered helping himself to some of the sleeper's cache, but immediately decided against it, restrained by the potent feeling that doing so would violate some taboo.

He pulled some of the furs around him and made himself comfortable. Now that he was here, he wondered why he had rushed so; it had seemed important, but now he could not think why. He settled back to wait. Some while later – it might have been a few hours, it might have been only a moment – he could no longer be certain how to measure time's elapse. In the presence of En-Ul and his dreaming, time took on an elastic quality and seemed not to behave properly. Then again, since coming to the valley Kit's internal clock had ceased to function in the usual way. However long it was, Kit had the sensation of having sat in the Bone House for hours if not days, and was beginning to feel light-headed from hunger. He reached out for a handful of snow and filled his mouth, letting the frosty crystals melt and run down his throat. It felt good, and it was as he stretched for another handful that he felt a warmth begin to pulse near his heart.

Placing a hand to his chest, he traced the smooth bulk of the ley lamp, then dug into the inner pocket of his rough-made robe and brought out the brass device, immediately dropping it in the snow where it shone a bright incandescent blue.

Scooping it up, he brushed off the snow and gazed at the glowing instrument. The little row of lights on its face filled the dim interior of the Bone House with a brilliant indigo radiance brighter than ever before, and which pulsed slowly, rhythmically, steadily – like a long, slow heartbeat.

His skin tingled with the telltale sign of a nearby ley. The small hairs on the back of his neck stood up. The air inside the house of bone crackled with pent energy, as if building to a lightning strike. Holding the ley lamp before him, Kit rose.

He made to step over En-Ul in his dreaming trance, but as his raised foot touched down, he plunged through the floor of the Bone House. The snow-packed floor simply gave way, and Kit was suddenly tumbling through space. Down and down and down he plunged. Instinctively he curled himself into a ball and leaned sideways to take the force of the fall on his hip. But the expected impact did not come, and he continued to fall.

The shadowy light of the Bone House swiftly faded to a pale point far above, and darkness closed over and around him. The light of the ley lamp was all that he could see, and then that, too, slowly faded, leaving him in a darkness that was so close and pervasive it was more like a cloak or second skin than the emptiness of the void. The air condensed, becoming so thick and close it could be taken only in gulps. Oddly, Kit was not afraid. Or, if he had been, the fear shrivelled away so swiftly it left no impression. He did not seem to be falling any more, but flying.

Without any orienting markers, Kit could not tell where he was going, nor how fast, yet the sensation of moving at extreme speed over inexhaustible distances persisted. Again time shrank away to insignificance; Kit imagined he could actually feel it peeling away from him, layer by layer.

How long this lasted he could not say. A moment? The length of time it took for the thought to enter his consciousness and leave again? An entire lifetime? More? An age? An eon? An eternity?

Nothing seemed adequate to explain his current state. Past and future melted together, mingled, mixed, became one until there was only the unchanging present moment. So far as he could tell, he might exist like this forever, living in a timeless void – a never-ending now.

Kit perceived that though this void might be empty of time, it was nevertheless full of possibility. Anything could happen, might happen, might have already happened – anything he could think might suddenly take form, might gain existence from his thought alone. This insight, if that is what it was, brought a sobering realization that the merest whim might bring a whole world into existence, a world replete with living creatures whose lives were suddenly called into being by a single careless thought. Kit shrank from the horrific responsibility and instead turned his attention to his journey.

The sensation of travelling remained strong. Kit knew he was covering heroic distances, and while it seemed likely this could go on without end, he did have the feeling that a destination awaited. Again, the thought had no sooner formed than Kit sensed he was arriving. Between one heartbeat and the next, the all-pervading darkness began to thin, becoming ever more transparent. Spots appeared before his eyes, tiny pinpricks of light. Suddenly, they were everywhere – shimmering, glittering, winking in and out of existence like sparks from exploding fireworks. They rippled through the void in waves, all around him, some passing through him. Faster and faster they came.

Kit became aware of a sound – the rush and wash of the ocean surf crashing onto the shore. Suddenly, he was there. His arrival happened so fast, he had no time to brace himself. One moment he was sailing through space, and the next he was scrambling on hands and knees over an expanse of sand. There was water behind him and a bank of green rising before him. In fact, he comprehended now that his clothes were wet – had he emerged from the sea? If so, he could not remember. The sensation of swift downward movement was still so strong, it drove out all else; he closed his eyes and drew deep, calming breaths into his lungs until the unsettling sense of falling ceased.

He raised his head to look around. A vista of fine white sand stretched away on either side as far as he could see: a perfect beach washed by the cool waters of a turquoise ocean. The sun was warm on his back and the air balmy; a gentle seaward breeze wafted over him. Before him lay a land of shining green and gold – the deep, vivid emerald greens of the tropics and the bright yellows of exotic flowers in reckless profusion. Giant ferns and date palms poked above the verdure, spreading into a sky so blue it sent an ache through Kit to see it. *This is heaven*, he thought. Or, at least, someone's idea of paradise.

Gathering his feet under him, Kit stood and, without any particular aim, began to walk up the sloping strand towards the forest. As he stepped from the sandy verge onto soft grass, he saw that his feet were on a well-trod path. It felt good to move under his own power again, so Kit followed the trail as it wound its way into the jungle. The further he went, the more luxurious the foliage became – extravagant in the variety of colours and shapes, all different, all delightful to the eye. Trees with leaves shaped like pale lime-coloured stars, like rusty fans, like golden feathers; fronds like sawtooth blades, like delicate lace; flowers like drifts of jewels, like multicoloured clouds, like frieze works splashed with an exuberant painter's brush, and more. Many of the trees, shrubs, and plants bore fruit – in globes, in clusters, in clutches and bunches and bundles – all in riotous abundance. Everything he saw was so intensely real, so manifestly present, it seemed to vibrate, to palpitate with the animating force of life, a force so strong it leaked, shimmering into the very air he breathed. The entire forest resonated to a sound Kit could not hear, a sound just beyond the threshold of hearing, like the final triumphant chord of a symphony – only he had entered the concert hall too late to hear the music. Still, the majestic waves of what must have been a glorious sound lingered, trembling in the air.

The further he walked, the higher grew the trees. He passed through sun-dappled shade and cool shadow, content to follow the path wherever it led until the trees thinned abruptly and he found himself standing in a wide clearing before a lake of what looked like… glass? Crystal?

No, not glass – but not water either. Intrigued, Kit stepped closer and knelt down to examine it more closely. Translucent, glimmering, fluid, yet giving off a faint milky glow: a pool of liquid light. As impossible as that might have been anywhere else, here, in this place, it felt natural and right.

Kit reached out a hand to touch the gently gleaming substance and, just as his fingers were about to dip beneath the surface, he heard a rustling in the nearby leaves and branches. Pulling back his hand, he shrank away from the edge of the pool to watch. The foliage on the bank of the pond shuddered and thrashed; a moment later the fronds of the tree ferns parted and out stepped a man of middle height and compact frame, dark hair and eyes, the shadow of a beard on his jaw; he was dressed in a loose white shirt and dark trousers, boots and belt. All this Kit noticed as a sort of afterthought, because his attention was wholly absorbed in the burden the man carried: the limp and lifeless body of a young woman with long black hair and an oval face and almond eyes.

Kit's first thought was that the woman was asleep. She was dressed in a long gown of thin white stuff, crushed and rumpled, and stained at the neck and under the arms as if sweat had dried there over time. Then Kit observed the ghastly tinge of the woman's flesh: ashen and waxy, the sick pallor of the grave. No living human had flesh like that. At a glance, Kit knew that she was dead.

The man, his face set in a grimace of determination, tightened his grip on the body in his arms – as if gathering his strength for a superhuman effort – then, steadying himself, the man took a purposeful stride towards the pool of liquid light. His first step took him to the brink, his next step carried him into the pond and up to his shins; another stride and he was in to his knees. The opalescent liquid swirled around him, as thick and glutinous as honey, radiance scattering in waves across the surface disturbed by the man's measured plunge into the pool. The dark-haired fellow waded further, sinking deeper into the strange liquid now lapping around his shoulders, swallowing the corpse he clutched so tightly in his arms.

Another step, and the man and dead woman sank beneath the surface without a sound. Kit watched the place where they had disappeared; it was marked by rings of shimmering light. These rings spread in waves across the pool and were soon lapping at Kit's feet. But something else was happening: the place where the couple had sunk from view was now glowing with a rosy golden hue. This luminescence grew and spread until the entire pond was the colour of heated bronze glowing fresh from the crucible.

Kit watched, fascinated, as a dome of light appeared, a great bubble rising from the liquid light. In the centre of this dome emerged the head and shoulders of the man, rising once more. He still clutched the body of the woman close to his chest, but where before she had been a limp dead weight in his arms, now she clung to him, her arms clasped around his neck. Her face was buried in the hollow of his throat as he carried her alive from the pool; her skin, gleaming with the sheen of living light, no longer bore the taint of the grave.

Kit would have stayed to see the couple reunited, but the tenderness with which the man knelt to lay his lady down and cupped a hand to her face gave Kit to know that this moment was for the two of them alone. He backed away from the edge of the pool and, as he turned to leave, cast a last backwards glance across the pond to see that the man, standing once more, had removed his shirt to make a pillow for the young woman's head. The man's torso was tattooed with a spray of tiny blue symbols – dozens of them – symbols he had seen before.

"The Man Who Is Map," breathed Kit. "At the Well of Souls."

Epilogue

He waited until after dark and then, to be certain that he had not been followed, Charles Flinders-Petrie approached the Sacred Way by a torturously circuitous, wandering route, doubling back time and again until he could put his mind at rest. The last passage had been fraught, and he feared he had alerted his enemies. But it seemed that he had given them the slip, if only for a little while. That was all he would need. A few more crossings and it would be finished: the map would disappear forever.

Then let them do their worst. Nothing would make him talk. He would die first. The thought of taking his secrets to the grave made him smile.

Now to the business at hand – the reason he had come to Etruria. Although he had never met the king of Velathri, he had heard the name Turms since boyhood, and had longed to meet the royal sage and seer. It would not happen now, but Charles was glad to be here just the same. The funeral of the king lasted most of the day, and he had arrived in time to witness the procession, standing reverently among the grieving subjects. As a representative of his family, it was right to acknowledge the passing of a longtime friend of his father and grandfather. Charles congratulated himself on correctly navigating the ley and calibrating the time of his arrival. True, it would have been better if he had managed to reach his destination while Turms was still alive, but as things stood he considered it a singular victory. The tomb was unsealed and would remain so for another seven days in order to allow mourners to place their gifts and remembrances in the chamber. Having dressed in the style of a rural labourer of the day, Charles did not expect to be challenged by the soldiers guarding the tomb. As far as anyone was concerned, he was merely one more rural peasant come to pay his humble respects. His modest stature and unremarkable features, together with his wholly unassuming demeanour, often made it possible for him to move unseen through the various worlds he visited. Also, he had found that few in authority pay much attention to those they consider beneath them. So, to accentuate his lowly state, he had cut his hair short and allowed his beard to go unshaved a few days, giving himself a more grizzled, rustic guise.

If fortune favoured him tonight, he would pass unnoticed once more. Charles hoped he would not have to speak to the guards or, worse, bribe them to let him into the tomb.

Bearing a cluster of grapes in one hand and pressing the bundle containing his grave gift to his chest, Charles descended the long staircase leading to the sunken road cut deep into tufa stone beneath the surface of the surrounding landscape. He walked along, his way lit intermittently by torches, advancing from one pool of light to the next, until he arrived at the place where an iron brazier had been set up outside an elaborately carved doorway. The tomb had been whitewashed and painted red, green, and gold, designating a royal burial. The doorway was festooned with white flowers, and little red pennons had been strung from the top of the high banks of tufa at the top of the Sacred Way.

Two guards stood either side of the door – yawning and leaning on their long lances – and three more sat on camp-stools across the narrow roadway. A table had been erected, and the remains of the funeral meal, as well as gifts of food and wine, were piled high in baskets along the walls and steps leading to the tomb. The guards gripped cups and had obviously been helping themselves to the wine, bread, and sweetmeats. Why not? There was no danger of thieves or grave robbers. Turms the Immortal was a just and revered king, well loved by the people; exceedingly long-lived, he had survived plague and drought and war – the banes of rulers in every age, and in every age the same. He had lived long enough to enjoy that rarest of elixirs: the loving acclaim of devoted subjects. Even among his enemies, the bellicose Latins, Turms the Immortal was renowned as a sage and seer of extraordinary powers. Any thief foolish enough to risk stealing from this tomb would be torn apart by the mob, so high was the esteem in which the late king was held. The presence of guards was a mere formality.

Rounding his shoulders and lowering his head, Charles affected a stoop and, for good measure, a slight limp, smiling obsequiously as he approached. The guards at the door gave him a cursory glance as he hobbled into view. Nodding and smiling, he bowed once, twice, three times – as one would to his betters – and stepped to the tomb entrance. As he mounted the steps, he heard one of the guards behind him speak out – a single word of command. He did not know what had been said, but he halted nonetheless.

The soldier rose from his stool and moved unsteadily towards him. Charles turned as the guardsman confronted him; he raised a hand to his ear and touched it lightly with his finger as a deaf man might. The soldier spoke again and Charles, still smiling, shook his head. One of the standing guards spoke a word to his comrade and gestured with his lance for the visitor to enter. Charles stepped to the threshold, but the other soldier put a hand on his shoulder, turned him back around, and then, as if to assert his authority, took the bunch of grapes from his hand. Then, with a lift of his chin, he directed the old man to do what he had come to do.

Charles paused just inside the chamber as his eyes adjusted to the darkness. The little light that entered the tomb came from the torches outside, and that was not much. Although every instinct screamed at him to hurry, he forced himself to wait until he could make out the mound of gifts and tributes heaped on and around the stone sarcophagus of King Turms. The marble casing itself was fairly plain: a large box with a slightly domed lid, the sides decorated with the name and title of the resident within and an oval lozenge containing a relief depicting a figure on a throne attended by winged figures in flowing robes. That was all.

Garlands of flowers had been draped over the sarcophagus, creating the fragrant atmosphere of a garden. Grave goods filled the corners and were heaped round about: plates and bowls and chalices in decorated ceramic and hammered silver, sealed amphorae filled with wine and beer, elaborately fashioned loaves of bread, baskets of grain, an olive tree in a pot, cured meat, figs in sweet liquor, spiced honey in jars, and other delicacies a hungry soul might fancy.

Charles stepped to the great white stone coffin, removing the short iron bar from the bundle he carried. With an efficiency born of practice, he jammed the tapered end of the tool into the crack where the lid joined the base. He paused, listening to the half-drunk guards talking outside; when he was certain their attention was elsewhere, he leaned all his weight on the iron bar and succeeded in raising the heavy lid sufficiently to slip a second tool into the crack. Working quickly, he levered up the coffin top. The stone was heavy, and it took all his strength, but he managed to force a tiny gap – just enough to slide in the last item from his bundle: a thin scrap of parchment sealed between two flat pieces of olive wood.

He would have preferred better tools and more time to hide the item properly, but neither luxury was possible in the circumstances. He felt the placket drop into the coffin and, with a sigh of relief, gently lowered the lid back down and removed the tools, which he swiftly hid – one beneath a sack of barley, and the other in a basket of persimmons. Then, with a bow of respect to the dead occupant, the visitor exited the tomb.

As he emerged, one of the soldiers at the door insisted on giving him a perfunctory pat-down, although anyone could see well enough that he was not hiding anything stolen from the tomb in his thin tunic. The guard sent him on his way with a nod. He bowed again and hurried away, threading back along the sunken road.

"Three down," Charles said to himself as he flitted like a shadow along the Sacred Way. "Two more to go."

Just two more. He prayed for time – a little more time to complete his mission. Then let his enemies plot and rage. Come what may, Charles could face the future unafraid.

Quantum Physics and Me

Thomas Young (1773–1829), who has a significant role in this story, was one of the world's great polymaths. Born in the tiny village of Milverton in Somerset, England, he was an infant prodigy, having learned to read by the age of two. The firstborn son of a devout Quaker family, he worked his way through the entire Bible (twice!) at four, and soon topped this achievement by acquiring the basics of Latin grammar. He was able to converse and write letters in Latin to his no-doubt perplexed friends and family when he was six years old.

Young Thomas outgrew teachers faster than his family could find them – a few weeks of study and he would know as much as the master instructing the class. When he landed at Thompson's School in Dorset at the age of eight, he found a tutor who understood his genius, gave him free rein of the library, and assisted the voracious student in learning whatever he happened to fancy – which, apparently, was *everything*. By fourteen years of age he was fluent in not only ancient Greek and Latin – he amused himself by translating his textbooks into and out of classical languages – but had also acquired French, Italian, Hebrew, German, Chaldean, Syriac, Samaritan, Arabic, Persian, Turkish, and, of course, Amharic.

Medicine inevitably captured his interest, and that took him to London and Edinburgh, briefly, before moving on to Germany to delve into the toddling discipline of physics. His expertise and authority in various and wide-ranging fields were such that in a few short years it was being said of him that he knew everything there was to be known. As a practising physician he earned his daily crust, and devoted his spare time to experiments, which often led to revolutionary discoveries: it was Young who devised a means to demonstrate in simple and elegant experiments that light did indeed behave as a wave – not only as a particle, as Isaac Newton had theorized. He also established that the different colours we perceive are made by light at different wavelengths that correspond to variations in electromagnetic energy.

Never confined to any singular endeavour, Dr Young's insatiable curiosity stretched to other, even more exotic pursuits, including – conveniently for my story – archaeology: especially the deciphering of Egyptian hieroglyphics. No one at the time could read the ancient pictorial rebus script but, aided by the discovery of the Rosetta Stone in 1799, Young – not the Frenchman Champollion, as most history texts have it – cracked the code and defined the basic rules of translation that others (including Champollion, who grudgingly admitted as much) have followed and built on ever since.

A more recent genius, Albert Einstein (1879–1955), was a great admirer of Dr Young and ranked him next to Isaac Newton, mentioning Young's inestimable contributions to science when he was asked to provide a foreword for Newton's *Opticks*, when that seminal work was republished in 1931. Einstein knew a thing or three about physics himself. In addition to creating the powerhouse $E = mc^2$ equation, Einstein also had a knack for pithy sound bites. His observation that "the distinction between past, present, and future is only an illusion…" speaks directly to one of the central devices of *The Bone House*, as characters struggle with the diverse yet interconnecting realities of a universe unlimited by space or time.

Although the idea of a many-dimensioned universe had been knocking around for some time – the word *multiverse* itself was coined by the philosopher William James around 1895 – it was Einstein who laid the theoretical groundwork for the notion – a suggestion later picked up and given more definite shape by physicists and cosmologists such as Hugh Everett, Max Tegmark, and John Wheeler, among others. The idea gained momentum in the scientific community through the 1970s and 80s until it became such an accepted feature in the landscape of scientific thought that it is now a useful construct for theorizing about the apparent anomalies encountered when dealing with the universe in its largest, and very smallest, expressions.

It is also a highly useful construct for a writer of imaginative fiction. For the characters enmeshed in the *Bright Empires* quest are not time-travelling explorers, à la H.G. Wells's *The Time Machine* or Steven Spielberg's *Back to the Future* series – merely running backwards and forwards along chronological train tracks, confined to rails permanently fixed in a singular direction. Rather, Kit and company are bouncing around a multidimensional universe in the equivalent of a helicopter that can travel in any of a thousand different directions. And if that hypothetical helicopter is a vehicle that can also zoom off into hidden dimensions and lands in any possible alternate world – with a dose of time slippage thrown in for good measure – then we have the situation I am trying to describe in *Bright Empires*.

Over thirty years ago, a physicist friend who worked at Fermilab – the massive proton-antiproton collider in the suburbs of Chicago – took me on a tour of the facility. The lab itself was still fairly new at the time, and the physicists there had just identified a range of new subatomic particles: quarks. They were preparing to begin experiments in super-cold conditions with temperatures approaching absolute zero. As I look back, I think that the experience of getting up close and personal with that high-tech laboratory and coming under the spell of my friend's enthusiasm for high energy physics launched my own interest in a subject that continues to fascinate: which is why my reading table supports a tower of books on physics (both quantum and astro), as well as cosmology, philosophy, anthropology, theology, and, to be sure, history.

In the current climate, when new discoveries are announced nearly every day, it is difficult to recall that as the world marched towards the third millennium scientists were beginning to hint – not without a tinge of sadness or regret, I suspect – that science was very close to explaining everything. The sentiment was so widely expressed that by 2000 a *Time* magazine article was wondering, "Will there be anything left to discover?" Science, the louder voices decreed, had conquered the universe; all that was left was to write up the notes and fill in the few remaining blanks. Every major discovery had been made, and there was, sniff, nothing left.

Not only has that eventuality failed to materialize, but in the few short years since *Time* floated the question something very like the reverse has transpired instead. Discovery itself has exploded. Old and established certainties are being swept away by new theories driven by new discoveries.

Just now, scientific eyes are on the Large Hadron Collider in Switzerland, where physicists are sifting through the results of proton-proton smash-ups looking for dark matter, whatever undiscovered subatomic particles might exist, and perhaps those elusive extra dimensions of the universe. They are struggling to make sense of a universe none of them would have imagined even ten or fifteen years ago, a universe that constantly reveals new depths of wonder.

Theories, like eggs and promises, are made to be broken. Even the most perfunctory dabble in the history of science should be enough to remind us all that the closer science gets to describing something, the more it discovers how much there is to describe. Far from explaining everything, each new discovery or theory opens up whole new regions of exploration; each new advance uncovers more data that must in some way be accounted for, requiring the overhaul of old theories or the creation of new ones, and so on. In such a world, it would be useful to have a polymath like Thomas Young on the case.

In their book *Quantum Enigma*, Professors Rosenblum and Kuttner express their intention and hope that readers will be brought to the boundary where the particular expertise of physicists is no longer a sure guide. This is the realm of *Bright Empires* – a place where all the old ways of thinking about reality break down in the face of a new conception of the universe. "When experts disagree," they write, "you may choose your own expert. Since the quantum enigma arises in the simplest quantum experiment, its essence can be fully comprehended with little technical background. Non-experts can therefore come to their *own* conclusions."

That being the case, why shouldn't a novelist participate in the conversation?

Acknowledgements

In addition to thanks previously given to Wael El-Aidy, Danuta Kluz, Clare Backhouse, Suzannah Lipscomb, Drake Lawhead, and Ross Lawhead, the author now acknowledges the assistance of Michael and Martina Potts (German language). All errors and flights of fancy are my own.

Coming July 2013

A BRIGHT EMPIRES NOVEL
Quest the Third

THE SPIRIT WELL